LA CHINA POBLANA

Books by LOUISE A. STINETORF

CHILDREN OF NORTH AFRICA, 1942

CHILDREN OF SOUTH AFRICA, 1945

WHITE WITCH DOCTOR, 1950

BEYOND THE HUNGRY COUNTRY, 1954

ELEPHANT OUTLAW, 1956

MUSA THE SHOEMAKER, 1959

LA
CHINA POBLANA

by

Louise A. Stinetorf

THE **BOBBS-MERRILL** COMPANY, INC.
A SUBSIDIARY OF HOWARD W. SAMS & CO., INC.
Publishers · INDIANAPOLIS · NEW YORK

To my brother,

CHARLES W. ALLENDER,

in loving memory.

FOREWORD

I SPENT the summer of 1942 in Mexico. It was my first visit to that country and a memorable one because it was my introduction to a woman who has pre-empted a large portion of my life since: La China Poblana—or just "La China" as she is affectionately called by the present-day countrymen of her adopted land.

I was immediately aware of the fact that La China had been a remarkable woman, for although her earthly body had been laid to rest upward of three centuries ago, her spirit was a living and vital thing and one felt its presence everywhere. It was as though this woman, long dead, still walked the streets of Puebla and rode her white stallion over the surrounding fields and up the slopes of the twin volcanoes, Lord Popo and his Sleeping Lady, in plain sight of the city's present-day inhabitants.

I don't believe I ever spent even a quarter hour in the company of any Mexican without there being some mention of La China. Princess Royal, slave and concubine, poet and musician, scholar, friend of the friendless, and intimate of the mighty—her character was so many-faceted that the same person speaking of her on different days did not seem to be discussing one woman, but two—or several.

Naturally, I soon wanted to know more about this rare creature. Had such a one ever really lived? Or was she simply a myth, a creation of the folk mind? I began asking questions, and I have seldom met a Mexican who was not eager to talk about the beloved China. My curiosity was further whetted by the fact that the flood of information loosed upon me was contradictory in many ways, but only to the sublimation of the character of La China and the enhancement of her contribution to Mexican history.

In some minds she is confused with the Indian girl, Malinche, mistress of the Conquistador Hernando Cortés. Many people firmly believe that it was William Dampier, English nobleman, scientist, man

7

of letters and highly successful freebooter who transported La China from Manila to Acapulco at the behest of the Marquis de Gelves. Others swear that the liberation of the peons is due to her having led these unfortunates in massed, armed rebellion against their Spanish-born masters. A large number argue stubbornly that it was she who tumbled the French usurpers, Maximilian and Carlotta, from their thrones. However, recorded history disproves each of the above claims—and many others less grandiose. For example, Cortés was long dead and Sir William Dampier not yet born when La China stepped ashore at Acapulco.

But in spite of discrepancies in the stories told about her, one fact stood out clear and indisputable: La China really was a most remarkable woman—in some ways the spiritual Joan of Arc of Mexico.

Always eager to know more about her, I went to the library of the University of Puebla for books—and unwittingly embarked upon a period of research that did not end with the summer, but has covered a decade and a half and probably will never be completed to my entire satisfaction. It has taken me back to Mexico repeatedly, and sailing on the pages of many books, I have circumnavigated the globe several times in search of information. From Mexico to Portugal, to Spain, to Africa, to India, to Cochin China, to the Philippines, and back to Mexico—round and round I have gone, each bit of truth gleaned making me ever eager for more.

I have taken very few liberties with known facts in writing this account of La China Poblana, but a few were necessary to make a logical whole. Sometimes I have had to choose between two versions of seemingly equal authenticity. For instance, whether she was born in Delhi or on the banks of the Mekong. The known details of her kidnaping—or sale—made the latter seem more logical to me. Then, in order to paint adequate pictures of life in a Grand Mogul's harem, on a pirate ship, in an Oriental slave pen, and a small portion of seventeenth-century Mexico, I have had to borrow from books that did not always mention La China. Similarly, in order to develop growth of character and acceptance of radically different ways of life, I have had to put words on La China's lips and in the mouths of her companions which have seemed to me logical in the circumstances used. And I have tried occasionally to describe the thought processes of a woman who accepted "the slings and arrows of outrageous for-

8

tune" with the deepest and sincerest humility to the very end of a long lifetime—humility, by the way, out of which grew incredible strength and a sort of immortality which few mortals ever enjoy. Her fame does not lie in strife and conquest, as is the case with most heroes of history, but in being perpetually vanquished. Curiously, this fate resulted in a rare and indefinable spiritual victory over life.

It was often said following La China's death, that the memory of her lingered on in the cloisters of the Conceptionist Sisters like the fragrance of an ever blooming plant. That particular convent is no more, but the memory persists. Perhaps because, although denied the vocation of a nun, she was in the truest sense a Sister of Mercy. She would have liked to robe herself in black, but—ever obedient to the will of the Church—she did not. Instead she wore till her death the red, white and green dress she had patterned after the costume which her mother, The Pearl, had made famous in the harem and beloved among the fisherfolk on the banks of the Mekong. When asked in her old age why she continued to use these brilliant colors when Spanish matrons of uncertain years invariably chose black, she replied that the white of her costume was for the snow-capped volcanoes of her adopted land, the green for its many palm trees and the red for the spilled blood of its heroic sons, native and transplanted.

Years later, when New Spain became an independent nation, La China's colors were chosen for its flag for the same reasons she had given for wearing them—since no one could think of better. And her dress became the costume affected by the women of Mexico to this day when they relive the glorious history of their country in their fiestas.

La China's physical body is now dust, but her spirit is a living thing, shining, vibrant. Memory of her is a precious heritage nurtured in the hearts of a proud, remarkably resilient people who are completely worthy of the respect of their neighbors—to the North—to the South, throughout the rest of the world.

As one hears so often at a fiesta:

¡ VIVA LA CHINA !

LOUISE A. STINETORF
Celina, Ohio

ACKNOWLEDGMENTS

To THE PEOPLE of Mexico, great and humble, wherever I was privileged to meet them—in modern mansions and simple, one-roomed, abode houses, on the streets, in the markets, in the cathedrals and the luxury shops, and at their fiestas—my very grateful thanks for their fine courtesies and even finer patience with an inquisitive stranger whose Spanish was never more than halting and problematical at best.

To my former neighbors in the Hollywood and Topanga-La Costa-Malibu areas of California who, having come from the four corners of the earth themselves, were able to help me with any needed translations—and never failed to do so with the utmost graciousness—my warm gratitude.

But my deepest debt is to four hard-working professionals and their staffs: the librarian of the University of Mexico, Mexico City; the librarian of the University of Puebla, C. Puebla, E. Puebla, Mexico; the librarian of the City Library of Santa Monica, California; and Mrs. Fred Weitz, librarian, Celina, Ohio. Without their patient, painstaking, unstinted and selfless help, this book could never have been written.

PART ONE

CHAPTER ONE

THE Princess Myrrha lowered her eyelids so slowly that, as she veiled her eyes, the effect was much the same as when she drew a wisp of gauze across her face. The gossamer was merely a pretense at hiding her features, for Myrrha, daughter of a woman who was said never to have possessed a veil, did not observe strict purdah—when she made the pretense at all. The downcast glance was also only token humility. Although still barely nubile, she knew how to bait a man with a show of hesitancy and withdrawal.

There were few men in her life on whom she could practice the simple arts and graces of being a woman: the eunuch slaves in her father's harem were at best only half men; her father, now more child than adult because of his many years; and occasionally a soldier, a member of the palace guard, who dared not look at her directly although they met face to face. She knew, however, that these latter stared at her covertly and appraised her intrinsic value, even though, because of her birth, she was beyond the reach of even the highest officer.

She was also well aware that, highly placed or lowborn, these men responded to her beauty as spontaneously as a lark answers to the morning sun. When she stood beside her father as he listened to music or gambled with some lesser lord, she knew there were many guarded glances at the delicately carved features of her face and her exquisite figure. Out of the corners of her eyes she had often seen a soldier's knuckles go white about the haft of his sword when she walked past him, swinging her body just lightly enough for her draperies to brush against his leather armor.

These men were inferiors. But the one standing before her now was her equal in birth since he too had been sired by a Grand Mogul.

By virtue of being male he was her superior in every other way—with one single exception. It was upon her and her alone, the almost miraculous fruit of his old age, that the ruling Grand Mogul heaped his fierce if doddering affection. Consequently there were times when this man, her uncle, the Vizier—the richest, the proudest, the most envied, the most feared and certainly the most hated man in all Cochin China —must humble himself before her.

"Exalted lady," the Vizier was saying in a soft, obsequious voice as if he were only a minor eunuch addressing a first wife, "heart of my lord's heart, a jewel has lately come into my possession which is not worthy of you, I admit. But if you will accept this trifle, it will put me in your debt. Then, perhaps, I may have the occasional privilege of seeing two jewels of inestimable value, each adorning the other."

No one could be more gracious than the Vizier when he chose. Myrrha smiled at the flattery.

He flicked a finger almost imperceptibly. A slave leaped forward instantly and knelt before Myrrha, holding a pillow in his upstretched hands. On it rested a teakwood box inlaid with satinwood and rose-colored nacre. The child within the Princess was delighted with this beautiful trifle. But it was no more than a trifle and it was of no great value. Myrrha was becoming accustomed to small gifts from the Vizier —in return for small favors, of course—and she wondered what her uncle wanted to buy from her this time. One little word from Myrrha in her father's ear would get the Vizier what he wanted.

Still staring at the box, Myrrha smiled at the memory of another favor the Vizier had sought from her—the placing of one of his daughters in his brother's harem. The girl was younger than Myrrha but, even so, less childish than her proposed husband.

"Which brat will swaddle which?" the privileged First Wife shrilled when Myrrha spoke to her of the Vizier's desire. "You were hoped for when Our Lord married your mother, Myrrha—but scarcely expected! And that was well over a decade ago. Does the Peacock Money Changer imagine miracles will happen forever?"

Few people denied the Vizier anything, even the harem women— beings without souls presumably shut away from all contact with the outer world, protected by armed guards, stalwart eunuchs and the tall, thick, windowless walls of a seventeenth-century harem. Myrrha

16

had been instructed to ask her father for a playmate, and the Vizier's daughter had been admitted to the forbidden enclosure. Everyone knew that the marriage could come to nothing as a marriage; but a daughter in the royal harem on any terms was a keen and powerful weapon in the hands of the Vizier, someone to prattle to him of the secrets in her new home.

When Myrrha's cousin became a bride, the toyon bushes on the hillsides were frosted white with tiny blossoms, but the toyon fruits had not reddened enough to attract the birds before the child died. Her death had been caused by a fever, Myrrha was told, but she could not remember that the child had complained of any illness.

As these thoughts raced through her mind, Myrrha pulled the corners of her arched lips upward in a smile, hoping thereby to mask her thoughts, and lifted her eyes to her uncle's face. The movement surprised a look of warm admiration on her uncle's usually expressionless visage.

She lowered her gaze to the cushion and the teakwood box again, and slowly swung her eyes from side to side so that her long black lashes rippled like the antennae of a night moth. Then she glanced back quickly at her uncle and bit her lip to suppress laughter. "He looks like a hungry dog ready to leap for a scrap of meat," she whispered to herself. Then, in spite of herself, she shivered slightly, remembering that sometimes the fingers that tempt a cur too long feel the brute's teeth. It would not do for her to let her cruel, greedy uncle sense her uneasiness.

"I have many boxes," she said with an assumed air of petulance. "And this one is too large to carry well in the hand."

"Aaaah! But never a box with a heart like this one, exalted lady," the Vizier replied in a tone that, in spite of the exaggerated respect of his address, contrived to let her know she was still only a woman, and scarcely more than a child.

An upward sweep of his long-nailed finger brought another slave from behind him to open the box. Myrrha caught her breath at the sight of what lay within. She did not look up although it cost her effort not to do so, but she knew that her uncle was watching her as intently as a snake watches a bird it seeks to hypnotize and then swallow.

In the box on a bed of sea-green silk lay a black pearl as big as the knuckle of Myrrha's thumb. It was such a gem as her father himself would have worn in the days when adornment of his person had filled him with delight, as the Vizier might carry about with him. It was a jewel on which any man who loved the ethereal spirit of beauty would feast his soul as well as his eyes—that a miser would hide away from the sight of other men and gloat over in his darkest hidden hours. A Persian satrap or a Chinese khan from beyond the fabled Great Wall might be ransomed from the greediest captor by a jewel like this.

"There has probably never been another pearl like this one dredged up from the muck of the ocean's floor," the Vizier was saying when a new emotion surged through the girl, shaking her as from an unexpected physical blow.

Suspicion, then certainty and finally anger gripped her, so over-powering it choked the breath back in her throat. Slowly, slowly, as though that member of her body moved by itself and against her will, she put out her hand. But before her fingers reached the pillow on which the box rested, she sensed rather than saw that her uncle's robe was motionless. The gentle undulation caused by his breathing had stopped.

Was this, then, no petty bribe? But worse? What did this man, who never gave anything to another save for calculated personal profit, seek to gain by a gift which in itself was equal in value to many a small principality? Did her uncle by some devious chance seek to play upon her mother's name and humble antecedents? Was he watching now, as breathless as herself, to note if she were acute—and mature—enough to understand the implied insult? But why?

The overwhelming intensity of her anger did not permit at that time possibility of the thought that the Vizier, for all his cunning, could make a mistake in his manipulation of other people's lives. Her fury exploded like a Chinese firecracker. With no thought of what she did, or of the possible consequences of her act, she swept the teakwood box from its cushion with a blow of her hand. As she ran from the room she heard the priceless pearl clatter across the marble floor like a worthless pebble.

Even as she fled to the comfort of the First wife's arms, she knew what the old woman would say to her, and with perfect truth in every

18

word of it. "You were a fool not to take the pearl, child. Whatever the Vizier's purpose, he will have his way ultimately. And the next time it is you who will have to bargain with him." Then the old woman, in order to soothe and placate her, would play at gambling with her, letting her choose whatever game of chance she liked: dice, tricktrack, mah-jongg or cards. The purpose of the game would be to let her win a bauble or two from the other's lifetime horde of similar calculated gifts.

Myrrha knew, too, that along with the sympathy she craved and would receive, there would be words—gentle but at the same time stern words—of advice concerning the nature of men. Young as the Princess was, she understood and appreciated the truth with which the old First Wife's oft-tendered wisdom was freighted. Her dislike, her very fear, of her uncle was tempered with some pity. What doom is there for a man more cruel than to be highborn, able and ambitious, yet younger brother to a dullard, subservient to a doddering travesty of a man who, instead of going to his grave at a decorous age, takes a young wife and within weeks boasts to his fawning cronies that at well-nigh hopeless last he has surely fathered an heir?

"Mother-of-my-heart," Myrrha cried out as soon as she reached the women's quarters, using the pet name for the First Wife that never failed to secure small privileges for her. "The Vizier insulted me."

"Indeed? And who hasn't the Vizier insulted?"

"He heaped shame upon the memory of my mother."

"Your mother has been dead for so long, child, that only a few people remember her," the First Wife consoled by tone of voice rather than words. "Still, if she were to be remembered by any man, it would surely be the Vizier. What did your exalted uncle say? Or do, my little cuckoo?"

"He offered me—*me!*—a pearl. I could see for myself, without his assuring me, that it was priceless. And he laughed when he told me about its having been dredged up from the muck of the sea. He was very hateful, heart-mother."

Myrrha exaggerated, but when she spoke of her uncle she always felt that mere words were poor and ineffectual weapons against his guile.

"The sea is full of pearls," the First Wife murmured with a hint of boredom in her voice. "Let me see the Vizier's latest gift. What must you—and we too, I suppose—do for your uncle now?"

Her right hand, stripped of the silver guards which protected her long nails from breaking, rested in a dish of perfumed water so that when sufficiently soaked and softened, a slave might scrape and trim and polish these ornaments of her body which were a mark of her exalted caste. She held up the other hand for the pearl.

"I don't know what he wanted," the princess answered. "He didn't tell me because—perhaps because I didn't accept his gift."

"Are you mad, you sparrow!" the old woman cried out in a shrill blend of anger and surprise. "Have I not told you many times, Princess, that your sole source of wealth can never be anything but gifts? True, you are already rich as a result of these—these tokens of esteem —received from your uncle in the past; but no one—not even you!— is ever so rich that he can afford to offend those richer and more powerful than himself. The Vizier is cunning and tireless, and the next time he sends for you——"

"I—knocked the pearl off the pillow onto the floor," Myrrha interrupted.

But the old woman did not seem to hear. "Now we shall not know what was in his mind. And if we do not know what he wanted, how can we discover what he was up to?"

For a second Myrrha felt like laughing, for there was nothing the First Wife liked better than to circumvent some scheme of a eunuch, or particularly her uncle. It was a dangerous pastime, but the old woman's zest for intrigue was almost as intense as the Vizier's. She was as childish in her pursuit of excuse for plotting and counterplotting as the greediest most ruthless man. And in spite of her years her mind was as keen and she was as resourceful within her limited world as her equally aged lord was apathetic and indifferent to the struggles and conflicts around him.

But Myrrha did not laugh. She knew she had done a stupid thing. Her uncle might strike out at others with words or deed, whichever he chose and whenever he chose; but it was only the exceedingly fool-hardy or the hopelessly desperate who dared to strike back.

"I wonder what he will do to punish me?" Myrrha whispered, but the First Wife did not seem to hear her.

20

Instead the old woman had risen to her knees and was pointing a dripping finger at the Princess. The outstretched fingers curved toward the back of her hand as easily as work-hardened joints curve forward like the claws of a bird. They were another mark of the home of luxury in which she had been reared. When she was still very small and her joints were as yet mostly soft cartilage instead of hard bone, a slave had sat beside her day after day, month after month, and had forced her fingers backward against their knuckles until the tender joints were loosened and the muscles stretched; now she could bend her fingers in one direction almost as easily as in the other. Myrrha's fingers had not been deformed in this way because she had screamed at the pain and her father had forbidden the harem slaves to torture her against her will.

Myrrha had long since learned to watch the First Wife's forefinger in a moment of stress, for the backward arc it assumed was an accurate indication of the intensity of the old woman's emotions. Now it described almost a semi-circle and the girl knew that the other was deeply moved or greatly excited by some sudden thought.

"That pearl . . . the pearl he offered you, was it a black one? As big as the knuckle of your thumb?" she demanded.

Myrrha nodded and waited.

"Child, I bought your life with that pearl," the First Wife said softly. "I loved your mother. I envied her for her strength of mind and body and for the freedom of her behavior. When I saw the slave seize your naked, still blood-stained, tiny body, clasping one hand about your middle as though you were a puppy, I held out my arms for you. But he refused to give you up. I felt I must have you and I struggled with him, but he was much stronger than I. Then I demanded the name of whoever had sent him to abduct you, and the slave would not tell me. But when I asked him how much he had been paid so that I might double the price for your insignificant life and so keep you, he replied that there was no wealth great enough to tempt his master. I offered him many things, and finally my black pearl. It was the finest jewel I ever possessed. It was famous in those days, and men gossiped about it enviously; but it has been hidden away for so long now that I suppose they have forgotten about it—all save he who possesses it and I. In any case, the slave could not resist it, and his greed and treachery

21

to his master cost him dearly. It was said at the time that when he left the palace, he had an arrow in his back before he reached the first turning in the street. But I had you! And I have kept you ever since." She paused to stare at Myrrha with the unblinking gaze of the aged.

"And now the Vizier returns my pearl—or attempts to return it! He knows I will remember it was the price of your life," she went on finally. "What does he mean by such a move? Can it be a warning that he has been patient long enough?"

CHAPTER TWO

THE Vizier, the much younger brother of the Grand Mogul, had already assumed the airs and some of the prerogatives of suzerainty when his royal lord took a new wife and boasted to his cronies that he was again to become a father. Faint as was the hope engendered by the Royal Dullard's maudlin words, men seized upon that shred, for the character of the brother of the Grand Mogul of Cochin China was well known. The Peacock Money Changer, as the Vizier was called, and his ruthless greed had become a byword throughout the land. He was proud and ambitious, as a man of his birth would naturally be; but his bitter malice, the outgrowth of his frustrations, had been felt by many and was feared by all. Although it was ever present in men's minds, none dared put into words the dread which drenched their beings in a flood of despair at the thought of the Vizier's becoming their supreme lord.

Gossip always percolates through the lacy stone fretwork of a harem, no matter how straitly guarded. The court pressed hungry ears to all the cracks, avid for scraps of information from the royal enclosure. The more crudely direct of the courtiers bribed the eunuchs handsomely for details of their royal master's love life. The subtle sent messengers far and wide, even into foreign lands, for new and more potent aphrodisiacs—gifts for the Grand Mogul which were presented with a great but studiously titillating pretense of secrecy. It was the diplomats, however, who whispered to each other and finally into His Majesty's ear that love, like any other gourmet dish, can become common and lose its sipidity.

The best-flavored melon needs a dash of lime, they suggested. The most succulent vegetables are more pleasant to taste when properly sauced. The choicest cut of meat is dust on the tongue without salt.

Why, even when a king's palate tires of wine, that elixir of the gods is heated and spiced for him and he again drinks with gusto. At the banquet table a wise ruler feasts on what his years and experience tell him his body needs to maintain brawn and vigor. Health and strength! These common things are a duty which The Most Exalted owes his people because these feed another appetite—and on these hinge another duty: "An heir, Your Majesty!"

The diplomats had been clever with words. A thousand times a day, couched in a thousand subtly different phrases, one plea beat upon the Grand Mogul's ears, insistent, inescapable as the din of a tropic tempest on a tiled roof. "Give us that most precious of royal boons, Great Khan, a worthy heir of your own sacred seed."

These flattering words erased from the mind of the kingly dullard that there was already an heir to his throne. He forgot his blood brother, capable and ambitious. Forgot that as Vizier, this brother was experienced in power second only to that of the throne. Forgot that no princeling as yet unborn could attain the maturity necessary for the capable administration of power before death claimed the father.

But the court could not forget. When the Vizier walked among them his presence scintillated like a peacock's tail in the sun. Noblemen lowered their eyes as though dazzled by the sight, but more often than not the obsequious-seeming lids veiled resentment. It had been for himself that this one had bought the gold brocade of the robe the Vizier wore. But when envious gossip of the purchase had been bruited abroad, the Vizier had sent congratulations on the acquisition of such a treasure. From the description of the cloth, which had just come to his ears, he wrote, it must truly be of surpassing beauty, fit to garb only the noblest in the land. The note was not a demand. Certainly not! But in the court of the Grand Mogul of Cochin China at the beginning of the seventeenth century, a man was very foolish indeed if he did not know when and how to be magnificent with his gifts. Many courtiers practiced pulling jeweled rings and bracelets from their persons and presenting them to the Vizier as though the act were a spontaneous gesture of friendship, respect, even reverence. For the time came to all of them when gifts, although not actually impressed, had to be tendered with a show of lighthearted spontaneity. Moreover, more noblemen were fathers-in-law to the Vizier than had given daughters to the Grand Mogul himself. But no one presumed on that relationship, either with familiarities or petitions.

No one knew the extent of the Vizier's wealth, but his estates were said to be limitless, and his godowns were without number. It was presumed that the latter were crammed with "gifts" he had been pleased to accept from the rich, and taxes he had extorted from the humble. The insatiable greed of the Vizier had ravaged the land like an epidemic, crushing the backs of the poor and palling the spirits of the rich. On entering his presence an indefinable something oppressed one, like entering a room the ceiling of which is too low and so seems to rest upon one's head. The pitiless justice the Vizier administered in the name of his royal brother and his coldly calculated favors cost too dearly for any subject not to fear him as supreme ruler.

There was no way out of the dilemma except for the dullard on the throne to give them an heir. He was old and tired, however, and his love play had long ceased to be of a nature that sows a harvest of sons. Perhaps he needed a new and zestful plaything in his harem? But that was an old remedy, some scoffed. Many a virgin had oiled and perfumed her hair, shadowed her brows and lids with kohl, scraped and polished and depilated her body, bedecked her ankles and toes with tinkling bells and finally swathed herself in unconcealing gossamer. Thus prepared, she had danced before the Grand Mogul, equaling in grace the most enchanting houri in paradise.

Gold loosens the tongues of eunuchs as readily as it stirs the lips of the non-castrate, and so it became known that the Royal Dullard was as likely as not to fall asleep during the nuptial dance. So many a delectable virgin had spent her wedding night in tears, but they were tears of bewildered frustration rather than maidenly modesty.

With the coming of the morning sun, she would be compelled to submit as was the custom, to examination by the oldest wives in the harem, the despots of that hidden world of women. She would hear scornful accusations that she had not done her duty. "Are you a woman or a toad?" some would shriek, thus slandering her with the old belief that the toad does not procreate its kind after the usual fashion, but springs always a spontaneous creation, from the foulest slime. Others would liken her to a worm-infested fruit which, in spite of its outward-seeming perfection, when pressed close to the teeth

25

warns sensitive nostrils of the corruption within. On such occasions ears were always pressed so close to harem doors and windows that the desolate bride's own mother knew the heartbreaking truth before her daughter's message of shamed confession reached her ears.

Too many highborn maidens had thus failed, the diplomats whispered to each other. Perhaps an odalisque that herself supplied the brawn and vigor the Grand Mogul lacked, rather than the usual culture and breeding, would nettle the age-chilled remnants of his virility as a dash of fresh, raw pepper stings the dullest tongue. Other sovereigns in other ages and other realms had sired heirs upon peasant women; and these sons—properly schooled by royal advisors, of course—had become such robust and lusty monarchs in their turns that to remember their miscegenetic origins smacked of treason.

The newest candidate for the Grand Mogul's love would have to be beautiful, but that would not be difficult, for comeliness knows no caste. Costly draperies, unguents, jewels, everything for the adornment of her person could easily be supplied. Most difficult of all, perhaps, the creature would have to be taught to handle her body like a gazelle instead of a skittish heifer in the last cumbersome stages of a first pregnancy. The wench must be intelligent enough to understand her function as queenly broodmare and, equally important, recognize the wisdom of being docile, amenable, flexible and obedient to her real masters.

These men would never expect to look upon her face again once the doors of the royal harem closed behind her. Nevertheless, through the strictest purdah, instructions to her would be a simple matter of crossing the palm of the head eunuch with some, not too trifling bribe, and with extravagent frequency, as one indulges a greedy but loved child. Even so, it would cost less than perpetually rebuying favor— perhaps their very lives—from the Vizier. If the Grand Mogul left an heir in direct descent, the investment would pay off handsomely in the long run. And if this nostrum failed the courtiers, the clod could be forgotten, or restored to the muck from which she sprang, stripped of all wealth save for a silken cord drawn tight around her peasant's neck.

The search for the mother of an acceptable heir had been launched with all that heavy secrecy with which people of power seemingly love

26

to cloak their intrigues, but which really conceals very little if anything at all. On the surface life at court seemed unchanged and with the best of reasons, for underneath the surface nothing at all was changed. All the usual currents of intrigue and counterintrigue ebbed and flowed in their accustomed and well-worn channels. Men lied, schemed, plotted, employed character assassination and cold steel indiscriminately and imperturbably—and sometimes were even driven to acts of simple honesty when all other expedients failed to further carefully calculated self-interest.

Every scintillating stride of the Peacock Money Changer continued under merciless scrutiny; yet the most arctic glares unfailingly melted into the thoroughly deferential half smiles of perfect breeding when the Heir Apparent rested his perpetually appraising eyes upon a face. Many a one, bowing thus to the Vizier, stiffened the muscles of his shoulders to keep his body from shivering before the cold malignancy in those unblinking, cobra-like eyes.

No one spoke of the search for a virgin with the transcending beauty and charm imperative for a royal odalisque—and, in this case, the health, vitality and presumed potential carnal appetite enough for two. No one spoke of the search, that is, above a whisper, or elsewhere than in the concealing shadows of some deeply embrasured window or on a secluded garden path. No one spoke of the search, yet everyone knew of it: concubines, wives and eunuchs, lesser courtiers and sycophants, peasant slaves and the Vizier. Everyone except the Royal Dullard. All eyes were full of darting queries as to its progress.

When Myrrha's mother was found, the Vizier was aware of that fact as soon as the diplomats themselves. These latter continued to tuck their long-nailed fingers into the flowing sleeves of their rich robes and to bow in deepest reverence before the brother of the Grand Mogul. After all, the finding of the peasant-virgin was only a preliminary skirmish in their campaign, not the victory for which they fought.

There was still much work for them to do. They left little in the hands of the gods, these Oriental grandees of another day. All acknowledged the omnipotence of Allah, but taught their sons that a goal left to the vagaries of fate was nothing more than an idle dream. The girl, once found, must be trained, the clod polished until it shone

27

like a jewel in the palm of one's hand. That accomplished, there was still the question: Would she succeed in that ultimate duty where the highest-born maidens of the realm had failed? Or would the burden of years, the apathy of a tired and too greatly surfeited body again defeat youth and lusty animal spirits?

Only fools and the desperate burn bridges behind them even in triumph, the courtiers again counseled their sons. For triumph is a fickle wench whose pleasure is to lead men on with false and cunning promises so that she may gloat over the destruction of the unwary.

The most charming, seductive and lustiest woman in a harem is nothing if denied motherhood. And however greedy and malicious and vengeful a man may be, he is everything if fate encircles his brow with the symbol of supreme power. But however contained and decorous conduct may be, there is an aura, an indefinable effluvium about one who enjoys any measure of success that cannot be hidden from the basilisk eyes of a predator. Such an individual must outwit his prey or himself be destroyed.

The Vizier knew that all of Cochin China had been searched like a head raked with a fine-toothed comb in quest of a louse. A truly amazing quest, the Vizier snorted into his carefully curled and perfumed beard. A quest for a female louse that was, by the fruit of her body, to snatch a kingdom from his grasp. A louse!

On more than one occasion and even while smiling into the face of a courtier, the Vizier raised a heavily ringed hand and toyed with the jeweled chains that rested on his bosom in order to conceal a breath quickened with rage. How many times in the past had he paused before some window curtained on the other side with black cloth, and cocked his head this way and that pretending that his brother's diadem already crowned the splendid figure faintly mirrored in the darkened glass. And now these smirking diplomats would surreptitiously thrust a louse into his hair. A bit of vermin to crack between two careless thumbnails, yet mighty enough in its sheer nothingness to tumble a crown from an arrogant head.

Court intrigue was as easily conned by the Vizier as a vellum scroll, and the diplomats were well aware of this fact. They also knew that they themselves were safe as long as their agents could elude the Vizier's spies. True, many henchmen dreamed of the vast rewards that would be showered upon them in payment for a half dozen words in the right ear; but at the same time they had no illusions regarding the fate which sooner or later would surely overtake such a misguided vassal, and so they remained faithful to the trust laid upon them. Of what value to a man would all the treasures in all the Vizier's godowns be if one ultimately sprawled flat on his back in some ditch and stared with unblinking eyes at the sun until the scavangers had picked his traitor's bones clean? More than one man so muttered to himself as he virtuously put the temptation of untold wealth behind him.

So the Vizier for all his acumen and power and knowledge of the nature of the intrigue swirling about him, remained as ignorant of the specific details of the plot against himself as though he were as big a dullard as his brother. Rumors filled his ears, yes, for rumor is like a fecund seed in warm, wet muck. The more carefully hidden it is, the more vigorously it sprouts and flourishes with life.

It was whispered that the incomparable peasant-virgin was the daughter of a nomad hillman who herded cattle for the Vizier himself. Some men were certain that a village of tree-dwelling head-hunters of the deepest upland jungle had been ambushed and every soul within it slaughtered save only one girl whose beauty, dignity and grace had proved her an elfin changeling, more alluring than any mere mortal woman. Others could not leave the sea out of their wistful fancies. For although the jungles, the uplands and the hills gave them food and some wealth, was it not from the sea that the greatest treasures came? The great galleons that took shelter among the deltas of the Mekong River estuary during storms were always laden with jade from Cathay, diamonds, rubies and emeralds from Hindustan, brocades and damasks from Persia, yellow gold and towering black eunuchs from Africa. And did not the depths themselves give up that most beautiful of jewels, the pearl? Surely she who had been chosen to mother a khan must be a pearl among women.

That much settled, new suppositions arose. Had she been merchandise from some pirate's hold? Ebon flesh from Africa? A sungilded beauty from Persia? Or a treasure from one of those human studs hidden away in the Caucasus Mountains and producing a never-failing crop of turquoise-eyed, milk-skinned, male and female concubines for the lusty and lecherous?

29

Then there were those who pretended to know that the girl was the daughter of a simple fisherman of their own race. For some reason, tales of the fishing village origin multiplied, and the other rumors died away.

The Vizier, who already knew so much that was a torture to him, would have razed his godowns to their foundations for one whisper of incontrovertible truth. One breath of cold fact, and the swords of thousands of professional assassins would transmute this virgin-changeling, primitive savage, or treasure from the sea—whichever she might be—into a stinking clod. One little word and her bowels would crawl with maggots instead of twitching with embryo kings!

Either the virgin must have been clever and learned quickly, or those who kept hawk eyes on the chilling zest for life in the aged Mogul may have feared need for haste. In any case, the delectable peasant seemingly acquired in a few short moons graces that highborn women spend a lifetime mastering. The wedding date was announced; and although the bride's participation in the ceremony consisted solely of stepping through a briefly opened door, royal entertainment of high and low alike, and public feasting, had been inaugurated on an incredibly lavish, wide-spread scale. In no time at all simple folk, their bellies bulging painfully with the unaccustomed plenty, and their drudgery-dulled eyes dazzled by the myriad lights and brilliant streamers fluttering from every inch of wall surrounding the palace gardens, were certain that the new royal favorite must indeed be a pearl—perhaps a pearl miraculously stemmed from the seed of Mohammed himself.

On the day of the wedding, a golden palanquin, borne on the shoulders of a continually changing stream of courtiers threaded the streets of the capital city for hours. These great men, who appeared to fight among themselves for the honor of bearing this gem to their sovereign, were surrounded by hundreds of splendidly accoutered men-at-arms. The diplomats put on a magnificent show for the rabble, but they did not intend to soil their costly habiliments by too close physical contact with the filthy tatters of the poor. Moreover, this show of military strength had precluded the possibility of ambush by the Vizier's men—and consequent damage to or destruction of The Pearl.

No one among the peasantry knew when or where this procession had begun, or why it wound around and about among the hovels and on the docks of the fisherfolk. The humble ones were not given to asking questions. They merely accepted what fate and their earthly masters tossed their way. So they gorged on the unaccustomed food, feasted their eyes on the splendid spectacle, and wished that other odalisques entered harems with like pageantry and largess for themselves instead of being quietly whisked through garden gates without fanfare of any kind.

The curtains of the magnificent man-borne sedan never stirred once during the entire procession. But that, too, was to be expected. In Cochin China in the days of the Grand Moguls, even the most respectful and fleeting admiration of a pretty face was thought by many to defile and depreciate its worth. Peasant women who went about with uncovered faces were deemed little more than beasts of the field.

When the procession entered one of the gates in the wall surrounding the palace, the Vizier stood before the soldiers turning the windlass that raised the portcullis. He was not curious, although he gazed fixedly at the spectacle below him. His presence was token of respect for his brother, public proof that he shared in the general rejoicing at the good fortune of his khan. He stood thus a long time, for the procession was a long one, and sedately unhurried. But at last the teeth of the portcullis clattered down onto the stones of the roadway, and the palace was again secure from all intrusion save that of the highest-born.

The Vizier turned to a captain-at-arms standing at his shoulder, a man who, under his mail, wore the Vizier's livery instead of the Grand Mogul's. His lips parted slightly, and his teeth showed between his mustache and beard in a yellow crescent. It is possible that he intended a smile, but his eyes were cold and unblinking. His words, when they came, sibilated like the hissing of a half-roused, torpid snake.

"A splendid procession! A magnificent palanquin!" he exclaimed. "A sedan chair worthy the body of the Grand Mogul himself. It would be too bad if no one has enjoyed its sumptuous cushions this day!"

It was as though he spoke to himself, and the captain-at-arms lowered his gaze, embarrassed at this unwonted self-revelation. But the Vizier was not given to idle speech, and the soldier raised startled eyes to his master's face at his next words.

"On the other hand, to defile its damask pillows with muck from some rice paddy would be outrageous."

The captain-at-arms stared at his master until the latter's eyes narrowed, and he pointed imperiously in the direction of the palanquin.

The soldier hurried away and returned minutes later to report that the magnificent chair, its curtains still tightly drawn, stood deserted outside the garden gate of the royal harem. Nor could even the cleverest and most assiduous spies report to the Vizier that they had seen the incomparable virgin enter the royal sedan. Nor could they find anyone who had seen her step out of it and through the harem gate.

There was no dearth of reports from the palace kitchen, however. All day long golden dishes passed from noble hands to even nobler hands until finally ranking courtiers sank to their knees beside the couch of the Royal Dullard and presented cunningly tempting viands calculated to restore a waning lust for life. There were oysters, pink and tiny as cherries, from islands to the south. Yaks' milk sewed up in lambskin and packed in snow brought by runners from the mountains to the north. There was soup made of wild leeks gathered by pregnant women while the vegetable leaves were still wet with dew. Pickled tiger tongues from China. Unusual tidbits cut from living bulls, boars, and stallions seasoned with that reputedly most powerful of aphrodisiacs, a powder from Africa said to be made of dried rhinoceros horn. There was even that strange fruit discovered by the Spaniards growing on the slopes of the gold-veined mountains of the New World. The western savages called it *tomato*, but civilized men had renamed it more appropriately, the love apple.

With the sinking of the sun soft music welled over the harem walls and filled the palace and surrounding gardens. Lutes, timbrels, dulcimers and rebecs blended their tones with the sweet soprano voices of castrated boys. As night settled down over the city and humble folk crept into their hovels, inside the brilliantly lighted palace the Vizier sat on a couch in his apartment and henchmen brought and read to him records of fees and taxes due and collected from various

32

cities and provinces. Occasionally he asked a question or dictated a brief note to the secretary squatting cross-legged on the floor before him. His glittering eyes, however, were focused on something so far away that his minions squirmed uneasily as his cold glance seemed to pierce through and beyond their faces.

Elsewhere in the palace golden coins and gems of value passed from palm to palm until they touched and stuck to the fat fists of harem eunuchs. As a result, every door to the forbidden enclosure stood slightly ajar, and none of the curtains over the stone fretwork of the windows were pulled entirely together. The Vizier counted his wealth and gazed into space. The diplomats, their eyes glued to the purchased peepholes, waited in breathless silence the success or failure of their pawn.

There was a sharp intake of many breaths outside the not entirely closed doors, not completely curtained windows. Shoulders twitched and neighbor jostled neighbor aside. Diplomatic bottoms wiggled as courtiers dropped to their knees and crawled between legs to get a better view. Eager, prying fingers widened cracks and slits for avid eyes. No one seemed aware of the danger run. Many a man would have traded half his wealth for a more preferred position; but so much hinged upon the reaction of their lord to this newest odalisque that no man would sell his vantage place.

It is said that some women are born wiser in the ways of men than their sisters ever become after a lifetime of wifehood. Perhaps this was true of the incomparable virgin. The music of the lutes and timbrels and dulcimers and rebecs quickened, the castrated boys squealed in a higher octave, and the diplomats pressed their noses further into the cracks as the Grand Mogul, lolling on a bed of many cushions, waved negligent permission for the nuptial dance to begin. But his bride did not raise her arms, flutter her draperies or twist her hips in the prescribed ritual. Her eyes were as steady, direct and coolly appraising as the Vizier's. Perhaps wisdom as old and intangible as love itself warned her that lust in age is fickle and frail and dies a quick and easy death. She did not dance at all. Instead she ran across the room and threw her vibrant young body upon the reclining figure of her lord, tearing at his robes with both her hands like a kitten's paws with a clew of yarn.

To a man the diplomats gasped audibly. Nothing like this had ever been spied upon before. The girl was truly a gem among women, wiser by far than her erstwhile instructors, a good investment of the time, the effort and the money lavished on her!

A moment later, when she laughed as merrily as a carefree child, and aped the pleasure and exhaustion of her senile lord, the diplomats withdrew their noses from their peepholes. Slowly and decorously they hid their long-nailed fingers in their sleeves, bowed courteously to each other and slipped away to their own wives.

In his apartment the Vizier touched his secretary with an imperious toe, and his servants scurried from his presence. Alone, the Peacock Money Changer sat unmoving, giving no further sign of the turmoil within him. Yet by some strange omniscience he knew that another skirmish in the campaign against him had come off successfully for his enemies. The rape of the Royal Dullard had been accomplished.

CHAPTER THREE

FROM the very beginning of what was in fact his last marriage a change had been noted in the Grand Mogul. The palace poets likened him to a garden tree that puts out blossoms instead of dropping its leaves at the end of summer. He was flattered by the pretty figures of speech and lilting phrases, and he also composed a poem. Long before the old women of his harem were certain of the evidence, he pointed out in measured and grandiloquent phrases, that it is not at all uncommon for a fruit tree to blossom in the fall; but for it to blossom and fulfill this belated promise of fecundity is rare. He, the Grand Mogul asserted in rippling rhyme, was above the laws of nature.

If there were those who questioned their monarch's bombast, they kept such incredibly disloyal, not to say dangerous, opinions strictly to themselves.

There was another change which amazed the courtiers, scandalized the well-to-do but ignoble, and delighted the wives and daughters of the fishermen who lived in the hovels perched precariously on the steep, soft banks of the Mekong River. Seldom before, after the doors of a rich man's harem closed behind a maid, was she ever seen outside his gates. Oh, true, harem doors frequently opened and shapeless figures stepped outside; but they were always so heavily swathed in voluminous billows of thick cloth that a chance passerby merely inferred as a matter of habit that they were female. Moreover, while on their mysterious comings and goings, these scurrying bundles of cloth were always herded along like so many sheep being driven through an alley. There was one difference: their shepherd was not a hungry-looking man carrying a crook and wrapped in tatters; he was always an enormous enunch, dressed in silks and carrying a drawn sword like a staff of office.

But only one month after the Grand Mogul's marriage the gate to the harem garden opened one morning, and a young, unveiled girl stepped into the main courtyard. She carried a basket on her arm, like a fishwife on her way to market. Her dress was of gossamer embroidered with precious stones flashing red and green points of light as she moved. The coils of her long black hair were held tightly to her head by a snood of pearls. While the soldiers guarding the great gate of the palace outer wall stared at this apparition, she calmly pushed the harem gate half shut behind her and tripped up to the sergeant-at-arms.

"You will please open the gate for me, soldier," she said, looking straight into the man's eyes. There was no note of uncertainty in her words, although she was well aware—as all women in Cochin China were in that day—that a woman is a thing of no account, without even a soul. That the only way in which she might achieve an afterlife was to make herself so attractive to men on this earth that Allah might make her one of the houris whom men were to enjoy forever and without surfeit in paradise. That no inmate of the royal harem had ever before accosted a guard with such an incredible request as she now made.

It was said that a soldier tittered at her words, but that when the girl's great black eyes swept over him in a contemptuous glance, he clapped a hand over his mouth like an abashed child.

"By whose command do I open the gate, lady?" the sergeant-at-arms asked.

"By mine, soldier."

She stood tall and very straight, but the morning breeze shook her draperies and made her look as though she were gently swaying in the beginning movements of a dance of seduction. The sergeant-at-arms dropped his eyes as a wise retainer does when accident or fate reveals a glimpse of one of his master's harem treasures. He had never seen her face before, but the soldier did not need the girl's next words to tell him who she was. "Open the gate to the street, man. I have permission from the Grand Mogul, your master as well as mine, to visit my people."

The sergeant raised his head and again met the girl's eyes in a long and estimating look. It was evident that she, nothing more than a mere female creature without a soul, expected to be obeyed.

"Before I open the gate to the public street, I must have the command from the Grand Mogul, or someone I know can rightfully speak for my master," he said.

The girl rushed back into the palace.

There was an insucking of breath from the common soldiery, and the sergeant whirled on his men, half drawing his huge, two-edged scimitar as he did so. The girl was as beautiful as the houris that people one's dreams, and displayed her face as immodestly as an old peasant woman who no longer has charms to hide; but she was another man's possession. The sergeant had sworn to protect that man's person and all his possessions from the very demons of the nether world should that be required of him. If he discovered so much as the ghost of a lascivious leer on a single face, he would lop that man's head from his shoulders without an instant's hesitation.

But the cruel, curved blade was scarcely out of its leather scabbard when the hinges of the harem gate creaked. Again the sergeant spun around; and then, as though it were all one movement, twirled his scimitar before his face in flashing salute. A man with a face as black as a starless night, and so huge that his sleeves brushed both sides of the gateway, was approaching—the Grand Mogul's head eunuch.

"Whenever my lady, the most treasured jewel my master wears upon his heart, wishes to pass into the street, you will open the palace gate to her," he said in the thin, warbling, high-pitched notes of the professionally unsexed man. The piping voice sounded absurd coming from the head eunuch's immense bulk, but there was no questioning his authority.

The sergeant lowered his scimitar until the tip rested in the dust and laid his bare left arm across his breast in token of respectful obedience. The head eunuch stepped to one side; and the sergeant found it difficult to keep his jaws from dropping in boorish wonder as the mountain of a man bowed low to the wisp of a girl until now hidden behind him. The soldier pressed his lips together in a grim straight line as he shot the bolt of the gate and pushed the ponderous slab of solid teakwood ajar.

Almost as though he were not aware of the gesture until it was completed, the sergeant again twirled his scimitar above his head in a flashing arc and brought it to rest upright with its meticulously honed inner edge less than an inch from his nose as the girl tripped past him,

37

seemingly completely unaware of the honor each man had done her.

The sergeant grasped the leather latchstring, but did not pull the gate to immediately. Steadily his eyes followed the girl as with both hands she lifted her skirts above her ankles and sidestepped the puddled dung and urine cast from the second stories of rich men's homes that morning.

Then the sergeant turned to see the head eunuch also watching the girl, staring after her as intently as a hungry leopard crouching on a limb above a game trail in the jungle watches the approach of a buffalo calf ambling along not too close behind its mother.

"My lord eunuch," the sergeant said, "would it not be well for me to send a man . . . or myself follow behind . . . our master's . . . treasure, guarding her . . ."

His words faltered into silence, for the eunuch was grinning, his eyes submerged in billows of fat.

There was no humor in his words, however, as he answered, "Worthy and Most Estimable Sergeant, I do not believe the lady needs your sword. There is a light glows within this Pearl that . . . There is a force in her . . . She carries a protection . . ." He paused and threw up his pudgy hands in a gesture of helplessness. Then: "Sergeant, I do not know how to say this, nor do I understand why I think so, but there is an indefinable strength about her which will stand her in better stead than the best blade ever forged in Damascus."

That night everyone in the city knew that the Grand Mogul's newest favorite was indeed a pearl snatched from the sea. Only the head eunuch and the sergeant of the guard had watched The Pearl—as she was soon called by everyone—wend her way through the streets until she stepped into a side lane and was lost from their sight. It would have been an indiscretion meriting a summary and degrading execution for anyone to have spied upon their supreme master's favorite. Yet any foolhardy person could have traced her steps through the narrow winding alleys until she reached the village of the fisherfolk perched on the banks of the Mekong River. No one spied, of course, but many eyes saw a fishwife run from her hovel and clasp The Pearl to her bosom, soiling the gossamer draperies with the filth of her own tattered garments.

These fisherfolk had always been an independent lot; and their customs, where their women were concerned, many said, mocked simple decency. Others called these people temporarily land-stranded pirates. In any case they rendered no more than half allegiance to any man, including the Grand Mogul. The hardships of their lives they laughed at and in ages past when oppression bore down too hard upon them, whole settlements had deserted their hovels and disappeared into the sea under the protection of some dark night.

Many of those who had been most careful *not* to see The Pearl come or go through the city laughed in malicious although hapless glee at the thought of the Peacock Money Changer. For the fisherfolk was the only group of laborers who had not built him a godown and crammed it with the fruit of their toil. The Vizier had never excused them from any of his many *corvées;* but when he sent his tax collectors among them, the wretches who crept back to their master carried what they had acquired in a most unusual manner—alive, scaly and wriggling, stuffed down their gullets and well up into their anuses.

No punitive expedition availed against the fishermen, for these denizens of the riverbanks were like fish themselves, in the water more often than out of it. The ease with which they eluded the keelless, tublike, bullock-skin rafts of the soldiers, put the latter to ridiculous, pathetic shame.

"Aaaah! The diplomats have been clever to find a favorite from among the fisherfolk," was whispered behind the backs of many hands. "Now, if only The Pearl should bear an heir, what good fortune!"

The diplomats themselves continued to bow to the Vizier, but they began to smile more or less openly to each other. "Yes indeed, we have been clever!" one read in their sly eyes. Such a girl should bear them a princely paragon—one who even while being molded as a child into the pattern of their desires, would at the same time stand between their own greed and the might of a greedier.

Thereafter The Pearl visited her people almost daily, and there were few occasions when she did not carry a basket on her arm. There was food in the basket—crumbs from the harem's extravagant abundance. There was good stout cloth which for years had lain unused in treasure houses. Moreover, the fisherfolk began to spend gold and silver coins in the market place instead of bartering only fish for their necessities.

Also, The Pearl must have carried something to her people in her

39

heart and head as well as in her hands, for slowly the hovels were made wind and rainproof until they could almost be called houses and homes. The women began to bathe in the Mekong, scrubbing their bodies with ashes and handfuls of coarse cocoanut fiber. They stripped off their garments daily, dipped them into the water and beat them across rocks or pounded them with small paddles until the cloth was as clean and odorless as when first taken from the loom.

Then time revealed that wherever The Pearl went she carried still another burden with her. When the Royal Dullard had begun his senile boasting about an expected heir, many answered him with due and sincere reverence that: "A kingdom is truly fortunate whose queen knows when *to eat a grape*." Covertly they watched and saw "the grape" swell into a plum, then into an apple, even into a melon. Finally—Praise be to Allah!—as the time neared when The Pearl must deliver the fruit of her body to her lord and his people, she was quite openly called the Grand Mogul's golden pumpkin.

Her steps grew slow in those days, and her carriage as sedate as the most jealous husband could have wished. But there was no longer any need for her to side-step the city's night soil and other filth, for minor eunuchs with besoms and shovels ran before her cleaning a pathway. Nor did her body bend crookedly under the weight of a basket on her arm. Old women walked behind her carrying her gifts to her people. In those last few days that she was seen in the streets, The Pearl bore only her love for her kind in her heart—and the hope of a kingdom beneath it.

Then one afternoon, The Pearl and her retinue of eunuchs and old women left the fishermen's settlement earlier than usual and seemed trying to hurry. But the Grand Mogul's Golden Pumpkin, who now bulged in the middle until she could no longer see where she placed her feet, stumbled many times. Finally she leaned against a wall and either could not or would not try to go further. The old women, screeching at the eunuchs all the while, pressed about her, some trying to pull her along willy-nilly. Others propped her upright with their own bodies. The eunuchs dashed out of sight and returned panting and breathless with a palanquin. The Golden Pumpkin was tumbled into the chair almost as unceremoniously as the garden variety is heaved onto a farmer's cart.

That night the windows of many homes as well as the palace blazed

40

with light. Many a game of tricktrack that began with the falling of
dusk was unfinished when the pheasants flew over the rice paddies and
greeted the rising sun with their soft whistling. Men's minds were in
one of the small alcoves of the forbidden enclosure and not upon their
games. In the city the bits of carved wood with which the game was
played were gathered up and laid away when, with the first light of
dawn, the time came for men to work instead of play while they
waited.

In the palace the Grand Mogul and his brother made a show of
whiling away the tedious hours with no more energy or imagination
than their subjects, but with infinitely more luxury. Except for a row
of silken cushions on which the players and a privileged group of
sycophants lolled, the tricktrack board was the entire floor of a room,
the design piercing the marble pavement in mosaic traceries of sard
and lapis lazuli. Their draughtsmen were young boys, naked except
for enormous, befeathered turbans that made them look like top-
heavy birds and indicated their value as pawns. The Grand Mogul's
"men" were painted with gold gilt; the Vizier's were silvered. Even
the soles of the boys' feet were gilded, for these sometimes showed
when one of the animated pieces leaped from one position to another
in obedience to a player's command. And the soles were completely
revealed when a boy, his skin clogged by the paint and his body accordingly poisoned, fell into a stupor from which some never regained
consciousness.

As the hours wore on and the desultory game continued between
the snoring interludes of the Royal Dullard, more than one young
draughtsman was unable to prevent his body from swaying with weariness—and was haled off into a courtyard and lashed for having been
guilty of showing human weakness before his lord, interrupting the
great one's pastime as well as giving offense by unseemly behavior.

Finally, when a cloudless day forced enough of its light through the
heavily shuttered and draped windows to put even numberless tapers
to shame, the gilded draughtsmen were excused, and the Grand
Mogul breakfasted with his brother. Each tossed an occasional tidbit
to this or that friend among the attendants who knelt about them—
jerking along awkwardly on their knees when some service was required. Those favored with a morsel caught the fruit or comfit in
cupped hands, rolled forward onto their elbows and gobbled up the

41

dainty food with only their fingers between it and the floor. The Grand Mogul and his brother were served from trays on knee-high stools. No man of lesser rank could devour the succulent largess on a higher level than his masters dined.

The meal ended and one courtier ran for a golden ewer from which a stream of water was poured first over the Grand Mogul's hands, and then the Vizier's. Each man then carefully picked his teeth with quill picktooths set in handles of jeweled gold. Each hawked loudly and spat on the floor—or the garments of a courtier if he carelessly happened to be in the way. In the meantime, other men had brought two bowls, again gold for the Grand Mogul and silver for his brother, and held them in the proper positions as each indicated that he wished to relieve himself. Sprigs of lightly bruised mint and other herbs were waved under the nose of each during this service. A lighted brazier was carried into the room and a handful of rock sugar was scorched on the coals to mask any lingering stench.

These elementary necessities of life over, various entertainments were proposed by numerous men, but the Royal Dullard was frankly impatient. He would no longer be bound by an etiquette which maintained that the bringing forth of young was exclusively the business of women. After all, he excused himself, this was not an ordinary child being born, a mere wriggling, screaming brat which any man might have sired. This was a princeling, an heir which the entire world—meaning Cochin China and bordering subject states— awaited in breathless wonder. A messenger was dispatched to the harem, and returned shortly followed by the head eunuch.

That worthy prostrated himself before the Grand Mogul and humbly begged his master's forgiveness that affairs in the forbidden area had taxed His Majesty's indulgence. Then with a sly smirk he reminded his lord that it was not unusual for a pullet to become egg-bound and experience difficulty expelling the first fruit of its body. A breathless hush followed these words. Would the Grand Mogul consider the man impertinent? Or would he——

But a slow grin began deepening the creases in his withered skin; and when the head eunuch, emboldened by the grimace, began to cluck like an old hen, the Grand Mogul laughed openly and his courtiers hastened to share but not quite equal his merriment. Then the head eunuch implied rather than openly advised, that it would be

42

well to consider this merely another day, since the princeling seemed in no hurry to assume his waiting state of mortal grandeur. So the Grand Mogul prepared for a morning nap after complaining that it had been a strenuous night and dismissing his attendants to their other duties with a negligent wave of his hand.

In the hours that followed, the obeisances of the courtiers were noticeably deeper whenever they encountered the Vizier. As usual their faces revealed no emotion, but the very air of the palace and all its environs was charged, tense and expectant. Had a flaw developed in The Pearl, a gem which wishful thinking had hitherto deemed flawless?

Outside the palace walls the riffraff in the streets began to make coarse jokes about their betters. The fact that men covered their bodies with silks, rested on the softest cushions, and dined as delicately as a moth on a flowering plum tree, did not protect them from the pranks of evil genii, was being said. Many a lord had been so blinded by desire that he became childlike and might call a pretty pebble a gem. A pearl, for instance! And in extremity one could even bewitch himself into pretending his bauble had turned pumpkin. In any case, what man in his right mind, they queried among themselves, was capable of imagining that the brightest jewel in the Grand Mogul's crown was to be found in the inner slime of a lowly garden vegetable?

CHAPTER FOUR

N O ONE could say just when the crowd began to gather outside the palace walls except that it was after night had again fallen. That much is known because those who stood in the dust of the street and awaited news of The Pearl were those who had come to love the peasant queen for what she herself was, not for the public need the fruit of her body might fill. Those folk of necessity must spend the daylit hours wresting their sustenance from the sea or the soil or by selling the brawn of their backs and arms to their betters. When the pheasants once again flew over the rice paddies to feed, the street before the palace was packed with men in coarse garments and women with unveiled faces. There was some restive stirring and more babbling from the close-packed throng as it grew light enough for familiar faces to be recognized. A few fought their way out of the crowd and hurried off to accustomed chores. More would certainly have left, had not others, without revealing the source of their information, kept declaring positively that an announcement would be made at any minute.

But it was a long minute before word from the harem came. A minute during which the shade between the palace wall on the one side and the buildings lining the street on the other shortened and finally shrank into nothing. Men donned the straw hats which had been rolled into narrow cones and stuck through their belts, and the women who could not steal a little protection from the blazing sun under one of these head parasols hauled up the skirts of their dresses and draped them over their braided hair.

But at last that clanking was heard which always precedes the movement of armed men, and a company of guardsmen appeared on the wall above the gate. At the sharp command of a sergeant, they jerked into a stiff line behind the parapet, standing like so many jointed, wooden dolls. Not a one moved a muscle except as his eyes swept the throng below. There was no hint in their stern faces that they searched for—and some found—fathers and mothers, brothers and sisters staring back at them.

There was no mistaking the surprise on the face of the peasantry when the soldiers appeared. Then a soughing sound swept through the street, a sound which deepened until it might have been mistaken for a resigned, hopeless wail, although it was never more than the sum of wordless sighs from countless throats. For, instead of wearing the imperial livery, the soldiers were unmistakably members of the Vizier's personal guard.

Silence had barely settled down upon the humble folk again when two soldiers in the middle of the row stepped aside, making way for the Peacock Money Changer who seemed more resplendent than ever in his silks and jewels. As the Vizier leaned slightly against the parapet, he put out a hand as though seeking some support; but before it could come to rest on the bare stone, a lackey leaped forward and pushed a tiny pillow under the great man's knuckles. As the Vizier scanned the upturned faces below him, his eyes seemed more unblinking, more cobra-like than ever before. Behind him, but without the trained precision of the guardsmen, the noblest men of Cochin China, also resplendent in incredibly costly dress, gradually appeared and gazed down at the serfs with carefuly impassive eyes.

Then the Vizier lifted his other hand and drew a web of linen across his face as though he sweated like a common man and swabbed at the moisture. Again an audible gust of sighs swept over the canaille, for the Vizier's handkerchief, and the handkerchiefs which all the diplomats and courtiers behind him showed instantly, were white—the color reserved for mourning. But the inarticulate burst of woe from those waiting before the wall died as quickly as it had been born, for the Vizier was speaking.

"This day in the royal natal oda, a child was born."

The Vizier, emissary of his brother, delivered the Grand Mogul's message to the waiting people so slowly, watching them unblinkingly the while, that many a man was reminded of the tales told of chance encounters with hamadryads. These enormous, incredibly malignant and venomous kings of the jungle paths, sometimes longer of body than twice a tall man's height, were said to rear above a man's head,

45

and to sway back and forth, distracting and hypnotizing him while inching the rest of their bodies closer and closer. Nothing about them was ever hurried except the lunge at the end which dealt swift but agonizing death.

"The child . . . will be known . . . among you . . . as the Princess Myrrha."

The Vizier paused and pulled the corners of his mouth upward as though smiling at some whimsy. *Myrrha?* That meant the Sweet Smelling One. Meant that the infant's father already loved her and had probably already forgotten his disappointment in her sex. Probably was already imagining that The Pearl's next child . . .

As though he read the minds behind the faces below him, the Vizier put an end to their dreaming with his next words: "The slave who presented our Supreme Lord with this newest . . . slave . . . is dead."

Not a single *ai-i-i-i-yuh, ai-i-i-i-yuh* of grief at the death of a loved friend burst from a woman's throat. Nor did a solitary man drop his chin onto his chest and voice the traditional *E-e-e-e-e-e-yuh! E-e-e-e-e-yuh! E-e e-e-e-yuh!* with which loyal subjects notify their lord that they share his disappointment when an ungrateful woman has erred in her duty so grievously as to produce a-thing-of-no-account instead of a son.

There was no mistaking the undercurrent of triumph in the Vizier's emotionless voice. The best that had been thrown against him in the struggle for power had failed.

The humble folk stood motionless, wordless, and watched the diplomats and courtiers bow low to the now undisputed Heir Apparent. Watched the almost Celestial One brush past the great men as though they were no more than serfs themselves. They, too, these great ones, acknowledged defeat openly—and thanked Allah within their hearts that their rebellion against the Heir Presumptive had not been overt in a manner that could be traced to them individually.

The Royal Dullard continued his indecorous grasp on life into a senility scarcely more animate than death itself. In the streets of the city, in the market places, on the farms, and on the banks of the Mekong River, men forgot him. None had known him personally. Few had ever even seen him. Yet, when The Pearl had walked among

46

them, many had come to think of him as a friend because of his kindnesses to that extraordinary woman who, in her turn, passed what
portion of those kindnesses she could along to the people she had
never ceased to love. For a little while a few villagers wondered what
would be the fate of her child. None dreamed that it would be good
or pleasant. But since their own lives were so full of hardships and
miseries, they quickly put concern for the orphan out of their minds
as one burden they did not actually have to bear.

Within the palace, whenever the Grand Mogul appeared in any of
the state chambers, he was accorded that obsequiousness one man
shows another of whom he stands in mortal fear, or whom he worships
as a god. But at the same time the diplomats and the courtiers hum-
bled themselves even more profoundly before the Vizier. For day by
day the Vizier assumed more authority in matters of government,
more of the prerogatives of a monarch, and the power of life and
death over his brother's subjects. The number of his godowns multiplied like rabbits in an unhunted area. The gifts he impressed became
so numerous and costly that the time came when wealthy men hesitated to adorn their persons with their choicest jewels—and at the
same time were afraid not to wear them, for it was certain to give
offense if note was taken of such caution.

As for the Vizier, he knew men and was well aware of the fact that
the hatred many bore him was born of their envy.

In spite of his greed, the Peacock Money Changer was an able
ruler. He restored order where disorder had flourished during the
slack reign of the Grand Mogul. The market places, the winding back
streets of the city, the dikes separating the rice paddies were all
policed by armed stalwarts who brooked no license against their
authority. Consequently bands of men armed with knives no longer
swept through a bazaar demanding each merchant's small horde of
thin coppers and even thinner silver bits, and slicing through a man's
jugular vein when he was suspected of withholding a secret cache. No
longer were peasant families waylaid on their homeward treks from
the fields and robbed of the harvests they had so laboriously gleaned.
The streets and the fields became safe under the Vizier, but some men
complained that less had been lost to brigands in the old days than
now was extracted legally by the tax collectors.

But the Vizier was impervious to criticism if, indeed, anyone dared pass it along to him. After his soldiers had enforced order in and about the city, they pushed further afield into areas whose inhabitants had hitherto paid allegiance to no Mogul. Those tree-dwelling jungle creatures, believed to be half man, half beast, who raided isolated villages for *long pig*—as they called the captives they devoured at their savage orgies—were driven back into their impenetrable swamps and thickets and kept there by regular patrols. Bands of the wild men of the hills, the Tuans, the Karens, the Cochins, and the Chins, who were incredibly fierce and were said to be so virile that they could sire only males, were wiped out completely when they ravaged the homes of their more peaceful neighbors for the women they could not normally supply themselves and their sons. Finally the Grand Mogul's ships, whose sails had long since dropped in rotten tatters on the sun-warped decks while the hulls rotted in the delta mud, were made seaworthy, furbished, armed and manned; and the Portuguese pirates soon were avoiding this coast, which for many years past they had raided for slaves for the infamous Philippine market.

Apparently there was only one stew into which the Vizier did not publicly dip his imperious fingers—the royal harem. But it was whispered that on more than one occasion the most delicate flower in a courtier's harem was apt to be plucked by the Vizier before the rightful lord of that forbidden garden had sniffed her fragrance.

As the Grand Mogul grew older—and still unbelievably older— the ladies of his harem enjoyed an increasing degree of freedom. Like The Pearl, the older ones among them began to appear in the bazaars, shopping unaccompanied by eunuchs, and with their veils not too carefully secured against sudden gusts of wind. If the Vizier saw them, he turned a bored face away from their eagerly curious, wrinkle-framed eyes. Other men stared covertly, and went home to impress upon their own slaves, with silken cat-o'-nine-tails when necessary, that the license of the royal ladies was not to be considered social precedent.

As the years went by, the Grand Mogul spent more and more of his time in his harem with the daughter The Pearl had given him. One babe playing wth another! On the increasingly infrequent occasions when he appeared in public, she usually crouched beside him in the royal palanquin, or perched in front of him on his horse. Even as a very young child, her beauty became known and was so great as to

48

provoke wondering comment. Perhaps no one was more impressed than her own father. He seemed to hunger and to thirst for her companionship as other men do for food and drink. Contrary to all previous custom, he exhibited her to other men as though she were a jeweled, inanimate ornament. He pointed out her grace and beauty that others might also marvel at her perfections.

Her golden skin glowed like slanting sunlight through the crest of a wave. Her hair was as sleek and black as the wet skin of a leaping dolphin under a storm-darkened sky. Her tiny nose was as gently and smoothly rounded as a windless swell at the break of a new day. When she spoke, her lips were like two rose petals touching on a ripple of water. Her teeth were pearls the color of whale's milk. Her eyes were big, round and solemn, and as utterly black as the depths of the sea itself.

"She is one of us—born of the sea!" the fisherfolk boasted to each other proudly.

As the little Princess grew in body and grace, it was noted that her uncle glanced at her often. Men watched his face intently at such moments, hoping to capture a fleeting expression that would betray some inkling of what went on behind those basilisk eyes. But it was as hopeless as trying to judge what had gone on in the hearts of the sculptors who carved the thousands of Buddhas which decorated the walls of the ruined and long-forgotten temples one sometimes stumbled across in the jungle.

If Myrrha had not been a child of the harem, she would have become willful beyond conduct permitted women of her era, race and religion. The little Princess was as greatly beloved within the royal forbidden enclosure as out of it. Although she was indulged there, too, it was within very straight limitations. One of the duties of any man's first wife in Cochin China was to superintend the rearing of all of his children, whether born of lesser wives or concubines. Myrrha was trained to unquestioning, instant obedience, and in all the arts and graces which might please a man.

"To whom will her father give her in marriage when her time comes?" the harem women asked each other, but seldom before the First Wife.

"Who is highborn enough for her?" that old woman had stormed when she first heard the question.

No one answered, for there was only one man in all the kingdom to whom she could rightfully be given whose birth equaled her own. It was clear that the First Wife was a bit senile, too, her companion wives gossiped. But she was still the First Wife and almost as powerful within the harem as her senile husband was in the outer world. So no one reminded the First Wife that those of Myrrha's sisters who had lived to adolescence had of very necessity been given to lesser men. The Head Wife seemed to assume, in her training of the last of her master's children, that the Princess was reserved for one of the supreme lords of the earth.

As Myrrha grew to maturity she could almost be said to have lived two lives. She expected to be given to some man, for that is the only lot of Moslem women. She hoped for the rank and privileges of a first wife. But whatever her standing, she knew what would be expected of her; and she was prepared to fulfill those duties, pleasant or otherwise.

At the same time she came to understand something of the world of men—and of the character and quality of the rapaciousness of the men who peopled that world. She became so adept at reading in ordinary men's eyes what they sought to conceal by control of their facial muscles that men began to shake their heads and wonder vaguely if one so acute—and even astute at times—might not be as capable as a man in other ways. Then they would shake their heads in troubled, even more doubtful wonder. No, it could not be. It was not Allah's will that a woman should order the lives of men.

"Let a man win from you at tricktrack when you wish to ask a favor from him. Let him win in proper proportion to the value of what you are going to ask. Let your Supreme Lord win a prince's ransom when you seek of him the governorship of a principality," was a law of diplomacy at the Grand Mogul's court.

These things the little Princess seemed to understand untaught and quite by instinct. Demure as any other slave in the harem, she could be imperious as a prince among men. "What is it you wish to ask of my father?" she would sometimes demand abruptly of a fawning sycophant, thus cutting short a flood of fulsome bombast. "Give my father the gifts you have brought for him, and do not force him to a show of labor over the tricktrack board for what he really has no need of. Then make your request and go. Can you not see he is tired and wishes to rest?"

Another time she stormed at a group of courtiers who sought to direct the Grand Mogul's participation in a public ceremony. "My lords, who do you think my father is? A peasant to be told he must labor in this field today and another one on the morrow? A gilded peasant, perhaps! But still, only a slave if he has no more freedom of conduct than you would allow him."

Yet she listened, with a great deal more attention than the Royal Dullard was capable of giving to any problem, to the representatives of two neighboring, subject states as they placed before him rival claims to the fish that spawned in the river dividing their lands. Each managed to insinuate more by innuendo than forthright statement that a decision in his favor would add to the wealth of the Grand Mogul also.

"So now my father is a fisherman who must cast his net on which-ever side of the boat he is told the largest school of fish is running," Myrrha had twittered in tones of birdlike sweetness. Then, although her voice shrilled, it was also resonant with anger as she commanded, "Go home, you fools, and each fish from his own side of the river. And let there be no arrows flying from either bank toward the other."

The foreign diplomats, scorched and wilted by her scorn, had scurried out of the Grand Mogul's presence before either realized that it was only a female—scarcely more than a child at that—who had routed them. She had made no threats in dismissing them, but each man felt that disobedience would not go unpunished.

Many men envied her the ease and seeming impunity with which she sometimes baited her uncle, although Myrrha would have denied that she had ever been guilty of such. The seat of honor when the Grand Mogul held courtly audience was at his right. It was a position which had always been occupied by the Vizier—until Myrrha pre-empted it. The reason she gave—begging her uncle's indulgence sweetly and with the most becoming humility—was that her father had expressed the wish to rest his head and shoulders against her rather than a slave.

It did not seem possible that her slender body was strong enough to bear the burden of his weight, and fatigue did often tighten the

51

muscles of her face into a somber mask. But it had to be admitted that the Grand Mogul had never sighed so contentedly or looked so serenely peaceful when resting against the shoulder of a slave, or even his brother.

The Vizier had stared at the face of the girl sitting cross-legged in his accustomed place, and then without a word had seated himself on the Grand Mogul's left—tumbling all the courtiers lined up on that side downward a notch. No one imagined that the Vizier acknowledged Myrrha his superior or even his equal, but he did submit to the semblance of each with poise and outward equanimity.

No one heard what it was that the Vizier whispered in his brother's ear that day, but everyone saw the Princess pull her father's head around and pillow it on her shoulder. She covered his cheek with the flowing draperies of her sleeve and said in a calm but accusing voice clearly heard by all, "My lord uncle, you have dined on garlic today. As you know, garlic is a food for strong men and for those who seek to bolster waning vigor. It is not pap for children, or for one who is as delicate as a child."

The Vizier had drawn back; and in spite of his lifelong habit of dissembling and concealing his emotions, his swarthy skin had turned the color of an old campfire leached by a season's rains. But instead of uncovering her father's face, Myrrha had held the veiling cloth firmly in place with one hand and had held up the other requesting a fan.

Some wondered if the Vizier thought to shame her into acknewledgment of her rightful position as a female when, like the lowliest among them, he rolled forward onto his elbows before his sovereign, but unquestionably addressed his niece. "Forgive me, exalted lady. Your nostrils are keen, for three days have passed since I dined on garlic. But still, I offend! Therefore, have I your Celestial permission to retire?"

Myrrha gave no sign that she conned the mockery in the title reserved for supreme rulers—or their heirs to supreme power. Again she smiled as prettily and demurely at her uncle as any child eager to please. "Oh, my lord uncle, it is not for me to say who may leave my Celestial Father's presence," she exclaimed. She smiled at him with an air of consummate innocence possible only in the very stupid, or the very young or the very clever, as she murmured in pleading tones, "But neither can I let you stay. That I dare not do. You stink!"

She was never again referred to as the *Little* Princess. As with her mother when The Pearl's body had first been burdened with the germ of a new life, from that day onward, Myrrha's footsteps grew noticeably more sedate.

Men waited for time to reveal the true nature of this new and disturbing spirit within their Princess. Some remembered strange legends of other lands which had on occasion been ruled by women who had actually been skilled in statecraft, some of whom had even been capable soldiers. These tales were hard to believe, but the professional storytellers swore by the Beard of the Prophet that they were true.

The First Wife clucked about Myrrha like a setting hen that has seen hawk and weasel carry off all her brood but one—and then is compelled to watch that remaining chick take to water like a duckling.

"It is a dangerous game! A dangerous game you play," she warned the Princess more than once.

"I am not playing any game," Myrrha protested. "I am merely returning my father's love with loving care."

But the old woman had only moaned further warnings: "Dangerous! Dangerous! Foolhardy! A game for men who have little to risk but their heads! You do not know what you are doing! Who can point out the consequences to you, since no woman in Cochin China has ever before interfered in the councils of men?"

"But I do not interfere." Myrrha would protest. "My father is old enough so that when he wants—and needs—to rest, he should have the comfort of sleep. Even the tatter-clad beggars in alleyways and hiding in country thickets have that privilege. He deserves as much consideration as they. Does he not?"

The First Wife was not interested in human derelicts or their rags. But she was stunned and then titillated with the implications of a new thought. "All men of ambition must climb a ladder with few rungs and rotten uprights," she murmured to herself. "How much weaker the wood will be in your case, dear heart! How much farther apart anything on which you can rest your feet will be. Allah be merciful

53

to you always, child, for only God's especial care can guard you now."

If Myrrha was fully aware of the nature of the forces with which she played or the possible consequences of those forces to herself, she did not betray that knowledge. She tended her father with the solicitous care of a woman whose sole ambition at that moment is the fulfillment of her filial duty. Still her heart leaped and she had to discipline her eyes and her breathing to hide the exhilaration that surged through her whenever her father, fired by some unexpected spark of memory, called his courtiers into audience for reasons which were usually forgotten before they could bow before him.

The next time the Grand Mogul summoned his court following the skirmish in which "the Vizier had been routed by a whiff of garlic," as many men described the incident, that worthy—who was really no longer young himself—behaved with surprising petulance for anyone so normally astute. Every official except the Vizier had assembled and was in the place prescribed for him by protocol, and the Royal Dullard had begun to gape and yawn, when Myrrha called out angrily asking why the Grand Mogul must be kept waiting. Every man bent forward on his knees as though the shame of such conduct bore down upon his body as heavily as upon his spirit.

Myrrha closed her fan with a snap of the carved ivory blades and slapped a courtier seated next to her across the knee with it.

"Run and fetch my uncle," she commanded.

The moment the words had left her lips she realized that she had behaved discourteously to one great man and had spoken impertinently of a still greater. The Head Wife would surely have slapped her for similar conduct in the harem. No light flicking blow to remind her of the virtues of decorum, but a sharp rap that would have bruised her lips against her teeth.

She stared at the courtier, wide-eyed, waiting. Apparently he misinterpreted apprehension for authority, for after only the slightest delay he rose and scurried away. His heavy rolling gait as he tripped along backward reminded the Princess of a Chinese woman whose feet had been bound from birth. He returned almost immediately with a slave in the Vizier's livery behind him.

"Exalted lady——" the courtier began and wrung his hands in anguish.

54

"Let the slave speak. Since he comes from our Lord Vizier, he surely brings a message," Myrrha interrupted.

The slave did not kneel, which deplorable lack of decorum surely must have been by his master's express orders. However, he was visibly frightened and he shivered and had to make an effort to steady his voice. "My lord desires to know if whatever his niece wishes of him cannot be accomplished through the usual channels open to the harem by way of her father's eunuchs and his own?" he said. He spoke slowly and woodenly as though he had rehearsed the lines.

Myrrha sat rigidly staring at the man. She had been slapped, but the weapon employed was crueler than any fist. She realized that if her uncle did not appear in audience immediately, the covert respect which had just begun to warm the hearts of these men toward her would die as quickly and easily as plants sprouting out of season are nipped by frost.

She wished she could ask the Head Wife what to do, but that was impossible, for she could not leave her father. In her desperation she tightened her grip about her father's shoulders. The old man whimpered. She turned to him, fiercely protective. The look in her eyes must have shocked some semblance of reason into the Grand Mogul's befuddled mind. He raised his head from her shoulder, looked about him and cried out in a plaintive, reedy voice, "What is going on here? Why are all these people——"

"It is the Vizier, father. Instead of attending your audience he has sent a slave."

"A slave! By Allah and His Prophet——" But the momentary flare of anger exhausted the old man and he leaned back against the comfort of Myrrha's shoulder, turning his head so that he could gaze into the beloved face. Questingly, like a fledgling bird not yet sure of the course of its flight, he raised a hand as though to stroke his daughter's cheek.

A flash of light caught the Princess's eye. Her father's ring! Of course, the ring of state which her father wore constantly unless he sent it with a messenger to add weight to his words. In her free hand Myrrha caught her father's fingers, now almost as delicate as her own. Then she called out loudly, partly so that all present might hear and partly because of her desperate need to recall her father to one more spark of authority: "It is your wish, is it not, Celestial Sire, that your brother attend your audience?"

He grinned vacuously at her and spittle from his slack lips moistened the bosom of her dress above her breasts. He nestled his head against her like a squirming infant seeking the greatest comfort for its body. He had already forgotten everything but the warmth of the love she bore him.

But she must rouse him again, and she thrust her shoulder forward so that it pushed against the soft flesh of his neck under his ear and his eyes cleared briefly because of the discomfort. Gently she slid the ring of state from his finger, exclaiming as she did so, "It is your wish, is it not, that I send your ring to command your brother's presence?"

"Yes! Yes! Whatever the most fragrant flower of my garden desires——" he whimpered, but loudly enough for those nearby to hear clearly.

The slave held out his hand within three fingers' length of Myrrha's face, but she ignored it. Instead she turned to the courtier whose knee must still be stinging from the blow of her fan and asked him in the set phrases of courtesy if he would do one more errand for her: carry the Grand Mogul's ring and message to the Vizier.

The courtier felt himself honored by the request, or so he said. Again he tripped backward with that gait which was so strangely pretty, although so awkwardly unnatural. Again he returned almost immediately, this time behind the person of the Vizier.

No other course was possible for her uncle, for whoever, regardless of birth or position, ignored the summons of the ring of state, courted summary execution. On his knees before his brother, the Vizier restored the ring to the Grand Mogul's finger. Then he seated himself in his accustomed place and waited for his Celestial Lord to speak. The assembled court waited also.

Myrrha wished she knew what to do now. She felt that something was expected of her, although she was only a woman. Felt her uncle's eyes upon her. Knew that others were watching both him and her, perhaps weighing and estimating them as antagonists. That thought pleased her, but at the same time disturbed her and left her uneasy.

Her father smacked his lips as though swallowing, and groaned as the very old do in excess of comfort. His stomach rumbled and she wondered if he needed the attention one must constantly give an

56

infant—a need which was becoming increasingly frequent for him of late. But that was a chore for his women and his slaves, not for his courtiers.

"My lords, as you can see my father sleeps," she called to the courtiers. Then, remembering the embarrassment she had suffered at the hands of the Vizier she added, "Is your business with the court of such a nature that it will not keep until another day and another audience, my lord uncle? My father's rest is always fitful and I hesitate to disturb it—except at your express command."

The Vizier, who had not asked for the audience, was clearly taken by surprise. There was a certain admiration in his eyes as he answered this female whose very life had always been a vexation to him. "My business . . . can wait . . . suitable time . . . and place, Celestial Lady."

With the others he backed slowly away until he reached the potted yews. There, once again he bowed, bowed so low that the silk of his full sleeves touched the floor. Before he turned he swept her person with a long and very careful look. Myrrha did not turn her head away or drop her eyes, but watched him. Thought and emotion played over his face, and he permitted her to read them as freely and easily as one gleans the thoughts and emotions of an untrained child.

"He thinks me beautiful—and he wants me to know that," Myrrha whispered under her breath. But beauty is so common and so cheap a thing that it could not have awakened the warm admiration he was making no attempt to hide. Homage from the Vizier, however honest, was something to study and weigh carefully. It frightened her.

CHAPTER FIVE

Myrrha's likeness to her mother was further emphasized by her dress. The Pearl had clothed herself in the finest cloth embroidered with the costliest gems the doting generosity of her royal master made possible, but patterned after the comfortable, full, swinging garb of her unsophisticated mother. The Princess wore a white gossamer blouse that barely covered her shoulders and molded itself to her swelling breasts because of the weight of the pearls embroidered upon it. She loved color too; and her skirt, ankle-length and voluminous as harem trousers, was heavy with red and green embroidery of pure silk, hand-rolled thread. She was never veiled. Not even when with the passing years her limbs lengthened and outgrew their infant pudginess and her whole body became lissome as a willow sapling, poised on the brink of a stream.

Fear of the wrath of the Grand Mogul had prevented many a wanton man from calling insults to The Pearl as she first walked unveiled through the city streets. It was something else much stronger than fear that stilled the tongues of their lecherous sons when her child, a brief generation later, followed in her footsteps. That something was not easy to express, and it made men vaguely uncomfortable; but when the Princess turned her face full upon a man and he gazed directly into her unfathomable black eyes, he suddenly wondered if there might not, after all, be treasures slumbering in the heart of a woman which could infinitely outweigh the fleeting ecstasy of ravishing her body.

Like her mother, Myrrha shared the Grand Mogul's bounty with her mother's people. As it had been with The Pearl, she walked through the streets without molestation as she carried her gifts to the fisherfolk. Nevertheless, Myrrha for all her unwonted freedom, had been bred in a harem. She accepted without question that being female she was a creature without a soul, that her primary duties in life were three-fold: to please whatever man possessed her and in whatever manner his fancy dictated, to bear him as many children as Allah willed, and to labor uncomplainingly according to his whims or the necessities of whatever stations in life variously befell her.

So, as the realm of the Grand Mogul prospered under the firm, purposeful hands of the Vizier, the Princess Myrrha blossomed into breathtaking, voluptuous womanhood. The beauty and grace of her body were equaled only by the perfection of her spirit. The reverent love she bore her senile sire was returned to her, full measure, by the concubines and lesser wives who shared her harem home, who, had she been a creature of lesser perfections, would have hated her implacably.

Although the youngest of these was her senior by at least a half generation, and many were decades older, the first dutiful care given the infant Myrrha quickly became honest, unselfish love of the winsome child. Then, as the passing years revealed the caliber and stature of her spirit, young and old did her the reverence usually accorded only a white-haired first wife, or the mother of an heir apparent.

It may have been this very reverence which bred in the minds of populace and courtiers alike, a train of strange thoughts. That remarkable woman, The Pearl, had been found and groomed for the marriage bed of the Royal Dullard so that an heir of his seed might rule over the khanate following his death. Now cautious men began to walk with lid-veiled eyes lest the wrong persons read therein a thought which frightened by its audacity as it quickened into life.

At first these thoughts were no more than the germ of an idea; but it was a sturdy, virile germ which continued to grow regardless of how one tried to smother its robust life. It was a dangerous idea, the mere thinking of which could cost a man his head if suspected in the wrong quarter. It was an idea which men discussed with one another by the flashing of eyes, restrained gestures of their long-nailed fingers, and slight shrugs of their shoulders. Was there anything in the laws of Cochin China, written or traditional, which forbade a man's making obeisance, and ultimately paying fealty to a woman? The query ran through many a man's mind, and he looked to others equally hopeful in a sort of timorous befuddlement for the answer.

59

"The Vizier is no longer a young man," many thought. "Surely he cannot live many years longer than the Royal Dullard."

Then it was remembered that the Vizier had many sons; but that among his progeny, as had been the case with his royal brother's offspring, there was not a man to command love or inspire respect. A white-haired fool may occupy a throne to at least some satisfaction of his subjects, providing that enough men remember his unfoolish youth; but brash ignorance and arrogant stupidity inevitably plunge men and nations into ruin. Would a realm be in a more perilous situation if governed by the already remarkable daughter of a remarkable mother, who would surely grow in discretion and wisdom, and would nurture these admirable characteristics on the advice of the long-experienced?

These questions had hardly taken form in the minds of the courtiers and diplomats when it was noted that the Vizier had begun to scan the face and form of the Princess as though suddenly surprised by her female perfections. She was his niece, yes, and ordinarily it was taken for granted that no closer blood kinship than a cousin should be taken to wife; but the great prophet, Mohammed himself, had allowed matrimony between his most beloved daughter and an uncle. That was an extraordinary situation, one the prophet disapproved for ordinary men. But who could call the Vizier ordinary? Or deny that the need of the realm was great? Might it not be possible that instead of The Pearl, it would be The Pearl's daughter who produced an acceptable heir?

No one was more quickly aware of the tangled threads of these thoughts than the old First Wife. With cunning equal to that of the courtiers of a decade and a half gone by, she began grooming the daughter for the role in life of which death had cheated the mother. But with a great deal more subtlety since in this case time, although important, was no longer critically so.

It was also proof of simple intelligence on the part of the young Princess that although she understood the covert glances and the whispered innuendoes of the courtiers and readily grasped the import of the First Wife's quickened interest in her future, she accepted each, not as something due her, but as kismet. Her fate! Love made her an apt pupil of the old woman, her mistress in the harem.

And true to her Oriental inheritance, no female slave could have

60

been more obedient to the shifting gusts of male arrogance. She remained a loving daughter, playing very sweetly upon the rebec, the zither and the dulcimer for the Grand Mogul, or playing games with him as his mood dictated. Although expert at tricktrack, she always lost to her father. When she seemed just on the joint of winning, she would guide his pawns to more advantageous positions with sly gestures at the least lapse of his attention. With a maturity of mind and deportment that contrasted oddly with her youth, she listened to and carefully weighed all the advice that came to her, whether it was blunt statements from the old women of the harem, or oblique whispers into other ears but intentionally loud enough to catch her own.

She knew of it instantly the first time the Vizier swept her body with a speculative glance; and although her years were such that her breasts as yet were mere plums and not pomegranates under her silken blouse, she wondered what manner of man her uncle was with his female slaves. She knew that he allowed them no privileges. They never appeared on the streets unveiled or unaccompanied by a eunuch. In fact, they were seldom seen outside their harem walls at all. Perhaps it was because of this knowledge that her fate was pressing in upon her that the Princess, as she walked in the rose gardens or on the palace walls with her father, cast her great black eyes in roving glances from bush to tree to sky.

It was at this point in her life that strength completely deserted the tottering legs of the Grand Mogul, and he now spent all of his days as well as his nights on the cushions of his couch. Although a thousand hands were ready and eager to perform the lowliest tasks for the old man, no one could please him like The Pearl's daughter. Even when the necessities of her own body separated them briefly, he called for her plaintively like a sick child.

"My daughter! My daughter! Why does she not come when I call for her? What is keeping her from me?" were the words most frequently on his lips.

When she sat beside him he was usually content to gaze into her face wordless, since the least effort exhausted him. So old and so frail was he that it was no longer possible to care for his body without inflicting pain, and some said that dissolution of the flesh had set in before he relinquished his grasp on life.

Sometimes when he did speak, it was with surprising lucidity. Once

61

he sat up on his cushions and called in a piping but shrill voice for the First Wife. She came running so fast and fell on her knees beside him so quickly that when he asked her bluntly if Myrrha's body was ripe for marriage, she could scarcely gasp, "Yes, my Lord, these two years past."

It would have been impossible for the aged man to have wrinkled his lined face further; but his brows, nose and chin seemed to shrink into a mere handful of bumps and ridges with the effort thought cost him. Then, "Have I provided a suitable husband for her?" he called out, pointing at Myrrha.

Before the First Wife could answer, a hand pulled her to her feet, and the silken-clad arm above it brushed her aside. The Vizier, who was never far from the royal bedchamber these days, answered in her stead. "My Lord, let me, your brother, perform that service for you. I will see to it that the Princess is provided with a spouse suitable to one of her lineage."

"He must mean himself!" courtiers and harem slaves alike twittered. "Who else but a grand mogul's son should pair with a grand mogul's daughter?"

No one remembered who had mothered the Vizier, princess or slave, wife or concubine. Myrrha's mother could not be forgotten, for as her father's tenuous hold on life slackened, he confused the person of his last child with the memory of her mother. She was his Gem-of-the-Sea more often than his Sweet-Smelling-One.

There was no jealousy of Myrrha in the minds and hearts of the old women of the harem. Some of them wondered if the Vizier would provide suitably for the comfort of his brother's widows. Royal etiquette demanded that he should, but entrenched greed is a formidable rival of custom, and life-long frustration can work more destruction than a band of looting savages. Since there was always a smile on the lips of the Vizier now whenever he looked at Myrrha, the well being and the favor of the young Princess gradually became the most important business of the women of the royal harem and courtiers alike.

So for a period the affairs of the khanate seemingly stood still, and there were no more court audiences. Power passed into the hands of the Vizier as naturally as a slave might pluck a bunch of grapes from a wayside vine. The gates to the gardens surrounding the Grand

Mogul's harem remained locked. The artisans and merchants in the bazaars of the city missed Myrrha's smiles—and the fat profits from her purchases, for she had never haggled with them over a price. The fisherfolk ceased bawling back and forth to each other, quieted their children, and hopefully searched the strand with their eyes at the hour when she had been wont to visit them. Then, like all the other humble folk of the realm, some of them after the day's work was done, trudged along country paths and through city streets to stand outside the palace and gaze at the red and yellow stones of its massive walls wondering, without daring to lift their voices in question, if the lips of The Pearl's daughter were still smiling.

Myrrha, grief-stricken at the approaching death of her father and wearied to exhaustion by his constant care, was ignorant of the silent reverence done her. It was her uncle who informed her.

When the Vizier craved an audience with the Princess, it meant that she must visit his quarters since it was not decorous for the Vizier to step inside the confines of his brother's harem while the Grand Mogul still held death at bay with his shallow, labored breathing. He did not state the nature of his business with the Princess, and the old women of the harem did not permit her to go to him immediately. They knew of only one reason why a man should command the presence of a woman. The Vizier was not a patient man, and they assumed that he saw no reason for waiting until her father's death before taking her to wife. That seemed natural enough to these women who were worldly wise in their own limited ways. They had never experienced either patience or diplomacy from the few men in their lives: fathers, brothers, husbands. But they understood fully that up to a certain point, the impatience of a sybarite is titillating when he awaits a woman.

Harem chatter was voluble as the young Princess was groomed for the occasion. She was bathed in perfumed water, her body smoothed with pumice, the palms of her hands and the soles of her feet tinted with henna, and her eyelids and eyebrows darkened with kohl. She had long known that, by virtue of her sex, her mother had failed the courtiers and diplomats. Now it was dinned into the daughter's ears that perhaps it had been the will of Allah that she, rather than her mother, should give a prince to the kingdom. As she was being prepared for the Vizier, she was made to memorize an incantation that was supposed to be effective in determining the sex of any child she might conceive. Certain words in such and such a tone repeated nine times—thus completing a mystical cycle in numbers—would ensure a son!

Even the head eunuch, who had supervised the preparation of many a luscious young morsel for her scant nuptials, nodded approval after he had picked up a brush of tiger's whiskers, dipped it into a bowl of powdered antimony, and joined her brows in one heavy, continuous line across her forehead. When she had donned her richest robes heavily embroidered with pearls and other precious stones, he adjusted a wisp of gossamer over her hair, drew a corner across her mouth and the tip of her nose, and beckoned for her to follow him.

At the door of the Vizier's harem, the Vizier's head eunuch stared at this vision of masculine delight but denied her admittance. His brother emasculate caught his breath in amazement when the Vizier's eunuch pointed a massive black arm and pudgy finger in the direction of the state chamber in which her father had always held audience.

At first Myrrha's legs trembled beneath her as she again followed her father's eunuch. Her entire training had been that women are chattels, that their services to their lords and masters are three-fold: to give intimate delight, to bear children and to labor. The dikes bounding her husband's paddies often furnished all the privacy a peasant woman could hope for when conceiving or bringing forth young. At all other times, she was one with his donkeys and oxen. But highborn women were not summoned to state chambers when masculine pique demanded pleasure or their flogging, or when fancied wrong could be assuaged with nothing less than a slave's death.

When her father's eunuch paused at the door of the state chamber to beg admittance of the guard stationed there, Myrrha drew a slow deep breath and held her slender body as erect as a young pine tree in the sun. She had been instructed that on coming into the Vizier's presence she should drop her eyes, let her head droop and then turn it ever so slowly and slightly to one side, so that the curves of her neck, both throat and nape would show. For, said the old women, the curves of the neck are very seductive when they melt flawlessly into a still unblemished body. Every wife knows, they told her, that masculine anger frequently melts before such loveliness, and a male fist falls to caress instead of chastise.

But that was a technique for the harem, and not for the state chamber. If she had not been summoned to lie with a man, why then? Even if her uncle wished to destroy her, he would scarcely do it so publicly —or dare the deed while her father still lived.

As the Princess stepped across the threshold, she dropped the corner of the veil she clutched, threw her shoulders back and swung her chin so high in the air that she literally looked down the clean, chiseled lines of her nose at her uncle. She did not miss an involuntary flicker of surprise and frank admiration in his eyes. Then he swept her body with a look which no woman misunderstands, the cool appraisal of a connoisseur of nubile charm. When his eyes paused upon her breasts, it was as though he had laid a hand upon her to test and measure their virgin quality and contours, as eunuchs purchasing slaves in the market for their masters were wont to do. Stubbornly she held her body rigid, but her nostrils flared into what would have been a contemptuous sneer had she relaxed the firm lines of her lips ever so slightly. It would have been impossible for the Vizier to miss the expression, but he gave no sign.

"Princess," he greeted her, and turned his face sidewise with a twisting motion of the neck, as a cobra, which has its attention distracted by a movement in the grass, might do; but his eyes never left her face. "Princess," he repeated slowly as though relishing the taste of the word on his tongue. "It has been called to my attention that of late many of the fisherfolk who dwell on the banks of the Mekong stand long hours before the gates of the palace. They are humble folk and give no offense other than—" he paused to wave a filigreed pomander before his nose —"the odor of their profession. May I presume to suggest that the indulgent master does not deny a begging dog a pat on the head? Since it seems that you have accustomed these . . . dogs . . . to unwonted largess——" There followed a carefully measured diatribe on noblesse oblige.

"Or do you neglect this duty of your exalted station, child, because you have nothing to share with our people? If the weight and sufferings of his years have erased from my royal brother's mind or heart the generosity which you once enjoyed in abundance, my coffers are ever open to gratify your slightest whims."

The Vizier's smile was as calculated and deliberate as his words had been. Myrrha understood perfectly that she was being commanded to renew her visits to the fisherfolk. But, yet again, why? And by this

65

least generous of men! She knew her uncle felt no honest concern for her mother's people, that he had never been moved by simple human need. As she waited, her uncle's smile widened and the slender lock of mustache that drooped at each corner of his mouth hung limply askew from the sharp lines of his chin. "Like the barbels of a mudfish," the princess thought. His lips parted showing the gaps where his front teeth were missing. The two canine teeth at the sides were unusually long and sharp.

The Vizier's eyes were again cold and glittering. It was the cobra man, not an inert creature of slime that leered at her. She dropped her eyes as anger churned through her mind, paralyzing memory that struggled for the required formal words of thanks. Then she felt the eunuch's hand behind her, turning her body about and shoving her toward the door. She could feel the sweat of his fat fingers through her blouse and she shrugged irritably, but she thought only of the cruel eyes in the face of the malicious man who had just dismissed two slaves from his presence.

But her uncle was not through with her yet. As she stepped across the threshold he called to her again. She turned to see him smiling benignly, caressing her with his eyes, as a father might beam upon a beloved child. He let her wait while he enjoyed her discomfiture. She tried to hold her face and body steady; but she knew that behind her uncle's smiling mask he was enjoying the certainty that she was afraid of him.

"My dear child," he said at last, "may an old man tell his niece that she is very beautiful? You could pass for a bride, garbed and groomed as you are. You need not fear that I have forgotten my promise to my royal brother to find you a suitable husband. I shall spare no effort to pair you—according to your just deserts."

CHAPTER SIX

THE harem of the Grand Mogul buzzed with excitement, for Myrrha's return had not been expected. The First Wife, almost as old as the Grand Mogul himself, a sibylline creature who shared complete authority over the harem inmates with the head eunuch, demanded accounting from The Pearl's daughter. Versed as the old woman was in intrigue, she still could not believe that a man who might gobble up so delectable a morsel as the Princess, would of his own free will refrain from doing so.

"Were these his exact words?" she asked insistently time after time as Myrrha recounted the details of her audience with the Vizier. The girl's answers, repeated again and again, were not enough to satisfy her or help her interpret the interview. "Did the lids of his eyes droop as he gazed at you?" she would interrupt. "Did the Vizier's fingers twitch? Did he shrug his shoulders? Did the old rooster shift his body on his cushions as though seeking greater ease?"

She persisted in ignoring Myrrha's insistence that her uncle had remained standing throughout the audience. That there had been no informality save at the end when he had enigmatically complimented her.

It would have been impossible for Myrrha to hold anything back from the old woman had she been of a mind to do so. But such never occurred to her, for the harem is also a school in which the daughters of both Mother Lilith and Mother Eve are taught obedience as well as preparation for their function in life. Only once did the First Wife smile—when Myrrha likened the Vizier's dangling mustaches to the barbels of a mudfish. In terse words, the old woman recounted a tale as old as the wisdom of the East.

"You should never forget, child, that when the world was new, there were no living creatures in it; but then, as now, the slime of

67

the riverbanks was fecund. In no time at all, myriads of creatures were wriggling about within it. Those in the shallows came to love the sun; some of them crawled out on the banks to enjoy its warmth more fully. Some of these flopped back into the slime whenever their skins dried off; others grew arms and legs and remained on dry land. Those which today walk on their arms and legs we call cattle. Those which swing through the trees supporting their weight on their arms are the monkey people. Only the ones who stood up on their tails and walked erect became men. Those among the latter whose strength remained in their arms are still today condemned to delve in the slime. For a few, however, the strength left their arms and took root between their ears; they are the khans, the princes, the courtiers and the diplomats of the world.

"But strength in the head has nothing at all to do with love between the sexes, my child, and even less to do with love between brothers. Some men become hungry for the flesh of other men, and Allah cast them back into the depth beyond the slime as sharks. Then other greeds awakened in the souls of men and grew so strong that God wearied of punishing the creatures and deserted them for eons of time. Many a woman believes he never returned, for there are sharks in palaces as well as in the ocean. So, Myrrha, never let a man see anything in your face but tremulous delight. And unbounded respect. And on occasion, abysmal fear. Each flatters a man—the last, perhaps the most of all. Each emotion will work for you according to his mood at the moment.

"Never show contempt lest the creature who should be walking on his hands as well as his feet treat you also like a companion beast. The highest-born men may be well deserving of the ocean slime, but such as you and I do not make mudfish of them."

With one hand she dismissed Myrrha, and with the other beckoned to the head eunch. The two were deep in whispered conversation as The Pearl's daughter stepped through the circular doorway and let the fly screen of strands of beads drop behind her.

In her own oda, lunch was spread for the Grand Mogul's favorite daughter: sweets of honey-encrusted grains and flower petals dried in sugar, fruits and mounds of snowy rice sprinkled with shredded meat, tiny fishes dried whole, chopped herbs, dried berries and pine nuts. The meal was served on a low teakwood table scarcely as high as her knees as she sat cross-legged on a floor cushion before it. In quantity the food would have fed a large family of hard-working peasants. But Myrrha, by the miracle of beauty and one generation of high position, was spared the torturing hunger of those condemned to drudgery. Moreover, she knew herself to be a gem of price, and that she must not allow her body, while still virgin, to become gross. The pleasure of unrestrained feeding was for those who had already savored the other joys of this life: the old, the wrinkled, those whose spirits were as gnarled as their bodies and who were no longer able to contain their boredom with the lecherous foibles with which a man amused himself until age chilled his blood. Until wed, the Princess must remain slender as a perfect seedling that has not yet been topped and forced to put out fruit-bearing side branches.

But along with precocious knowledge, the necessary restraints had been bred into the Princess with merciless rigor. In spite of the demands of her body, there was no evidence of eagerness or desire when, after toying with her bracelets and necklaces, she swept the table with an incurious glance. Finally she held out her right hand and three slaves quickly stepped forward. One held a golden ewer above her fingers and tilted it until a thin stream of perfumed water trickled from the long slender spout. The second held a golden basin far enough below her hand so that none of the water already defiled should splash up and touch her again. The third folded her hand between two pompons of wool, soft with unguents, so that the water would not dry out and chap her skin. It was a ceremonial cleansing. The left hand was not washed, for the hand on the offside of the body would not be used during the meal. It performed the unavoidable, filthy functions, and so must never touch food.

Finally the Princess picked up a grain of rice with thumb and forefinger and laid it on the tip of her tongue. The kneeling slave with the woolen pompons bent forward, doubling her body as though hinged at the hips, and dabbed at her mistress's hand. Myrrha did not close her mouth, in fact she scarcely drew in her tongue, for hunger can be appeased temporarily at least almost as completely by savor as by satiety. Perfectly steamed under a lid weighted with wet sand, the kernel melted between her lips, and she drank it in the saliva which flooded her mouth so uncontrollably she had to suck inward repeatedly to avoid fouling her chin with spittle.

Delicately, a kernel at a time, she ate as much rice as a peasant woman would have rolled into a sticky ball and bolted at a mouthful. Occasionally she took a shred of meat and held it between her teeth as she swallowed several times to empty her mouth of saliva. She laughed when she picked up a little fish, for it had dried crookedly and was now cross-eyed. She poked it into the mouth of the slave who held the wool. Then her right hand had to be washed again before she could go on with her meal, for it had been defiled by touching an inferior.

When the slave who held the ewer touched her shoulder, she turned away from the rice. That cereal, although sweet past all others on the tongue, seldom goes further in the body than the belly. And the delight of a moment for the lips is far outweighed by the shame and agony of a paunch which must be borne throughout life. She regarded the fruits and the comfits thoughtfully, for she could have a bit of one but not the other, and finally selected a peach. With equal deliberation she sniffed its fragrance and admired the rosy hue of that side which had hung in the sun, and the the subdued tint, neither green nor yellow, which colored the side that had hung in the shade. The sun-kissed half, she knew, would be a trifle softer, sweeter, riper; and it was there that she sank her teeth, sucking quickly at the juice which splashed her cheeks and chin with liquid amber.

She did not finish the peach, for the slave girl had no more than cleansed her chin when the head eunuch entered and summoned her again to the First Wife's chamber. Once more that *grande dame* questioned her as straitly as she had done before, making no attempt to repress a new and strange excitement.

"Repeat to me, Myrrha, what the Lord Vizier said when he told you to come to him for gifts," she commanded. "His own words, mind you. Do not change a syllable. And if you do not remember a phrase exactly, do not pretend and make up a statement which would certainly be false!"

But the Princess remembered her uncle's words and repeated them as spoken.

"Hmmmmm," and again, "Hmmmmm," the old woman crooned to herself tunelessly, rocking her skinny bottom back and forth on a plump cushion like an egg that has just been laid on a platter. She did not turn her head or lift her eyes, but merely jabbed the air with a long-nailed finger indicating that she spoke to the head eunuch. "Strange! Strange! The Vizier is not a generous man. What is he purchasing with his gifts? Not this child! No one knows better than he that she is his for the taking. No one understands more fully than he what he would be appropriating to himself through the possession of her body and the fruit of her womb. And yet he sent her back to us—with his wealth at her command. Or so he promised!"

The First Wife whirled with surprising agility for one of her age. It took quick eyes to see her uncross her legs and slide onto her knees with her rump resting on her heels. "Is there gossip abroad, lord eunuch, that the Vizier is no longer a man, and you have not told me?" she demanded in a strident voice.

"I have heard no such gossip, my lady," he assured her. "Nor do I believe such is the case."

This time the long-nailed finger stabbed the air in Myrrha's direction, but again she spoke to the head eunuch. "Then look at her well, man, and tell me: Is she not delectable? Or are my eyes dimmed by affection, and my wits so wandering from age that I do not know a jewel when one lies in the palm of my hand?"

As though to humor the old woman, the eunuch glanced at Myrrha briefly. The Princess did not turn away from his half-bored, incurious eyes. She could not have numbered the times he had supervised her bath and grooming. Less than two hours back he had tested the texture of her skin on the most intimate parts of her body and had commanded the slaves: "A little more pumice here; the roots of the hair show. She must glow like alabaster, and who ever saw alabaster sprouting a hairy pelt! Gently, slave! The Vizier desires his partridge plucked, not skinned! Now the unguent. Pat it lightly, slave. Must I always remind you that you are polishing a gem, not grooming a horse! And you, Myrrha, stand the way you have been taught to stand—revealing without seeming to do so. Remember, modesty in a woman is the greatest of virtues—providing it does not stupidly conceal her charms. A bit of a tremor is all that is needed. Now, let me see your belly muscles quiver, beginning here, a hand's breadth below your rib cage," and he had smacked her across the navel. That gesture was standard horseplay with the head eunuch. He always managed to make it sound like an angry blow, but it never really stung, for that would have left an ugly red stain on the skin, a temporary flaw.

71

"She is indeed a gem of price," the eunuch answered soothingly. "And we have trained her well for her role in life."

"What does any man desire more greatly than such a gem of a woman?" the First Wife asked softly as though merely thinking aloud.

"That we shall know only if we permit the Vizier to purchase it," the eunuch replied.

Suddenly Myrrha's eyes darted from the old woman to the half man, and she saw no questioning on the face of either, only an eager curiosity. Then it occurred to her that perhaps their words dropped from their lips too glibly, without the pauses and corrections of one whose thoughts are quickening as his words give them wings. Nor were the two peering into each other's faces as folk do who, consciously or otherwise, realize that words are but poor vessels, too small and shallow to carry the entire burden of great or deep thought. Instead they were watching her, studying her as intently as a kitten studies the antics of an upturned beetle. Secure in the love of her senile father, Myrrha had never had to defend herself from the scheming women about her, but at the same time she was no stranger to harem intrigue. She dropped her head as though in shame at her failure as a woman and searched her mind for words to express whatever was expected of her.

But the words would not come because she, too, was asking herself: Why had she been rejected as a woman? She knew she was beautiful, seductively garbed and well trained in the wiles which titillate man's desires. She remembered the transitory but nevertheless very real gleam of admiration in the eyes of the Vizier when she appeared before him. Why had her uncle offered her largess? Why had he, of all men, expressed concern for her humble kinfolk? Did the First Wife and the head eunuch know something she did not? She raised her head and gazed at the other two, and for the first time in her life sensed the panic inherent in helplessness.

Never in her short life had her father's generosity failed her, and it had not occurred to her to take advantage of her uncle's proffered aid. Yet she dared not question the First Wife who was saying, "I am told that my Lord Vizier wears on the first finger of his right hand an incomparable carbuncle. As a child I saw it often on my father's hand. I remember the day—you were not yet born, Myrrha—when my mother had permission to visit me here. She told me that My Lord's

72

brother had admired the stone, and that my father had sent it to him immediately—as a gift, of course!—although his father had worn it before him, and his father's father."

The old woman smiled at the Princess, but there was no more mirth in her eyes than there had been in the Vizier's when he dismissed his niece. Rather, there was the same cold gleaming light that slumbers in the eyes of all predatory animals.

The same expression was mirrored on the head eunuch's fat face as he murmured, "Our Royal Master once gave me a heavy gold chain of some value in itself; but I treasured it beyond all his gifts for the star sapphire which hung from it."

Myrrha's eyes widened, for she remembered that as her uncle spoke to her such a short time ago, his fingers caressed a star sapphire at the end of a heavy gold chain.

"Have you given any thought, my child, to what you would like from the Vizier?" the First Wife asked softly. "Jewels? Brocades? He has said that you have only to ask. Women cannot afford the rudeness of rejecting generosity, especially from high places. And to ask for a trifle offends, since it implies that the donor is a poor man."

"He has a turquoise carved like a Persian rose. A blue rose! There is nothing like it in all nature," the eunuch suggested temptingly.

The First Wife turned her head on one side and studied Myrrha as intently as a bird searching wet grass for a worm. "The Vizier has always had his choice—as taxes for the realm, of course—of all the pearls . . ."

"Except one!" the head eunuch interrupted with a short laugh.

The First Wife ignored him. ". . . and it is said there is no equal to the magnificence of his horde. But pearls you have in plenty; your blouses are heavy with their embroidery. Now with your golden skin, a topaz brooch——"

"*A-a-a-a-ah!*" the head eunuch broke in with a sigh as long and greedy as the desire of an undisciplined male child before a tray of sweetmeats. "My Lord Vizier has a string of beads of golden amber which is exceedingly rare, for only the uncouth barbaric merchants who come out of the Far West seeking our silks and spices have amber for sale. Each bead has a tiny insect imprisoned in its heart; and between every five beads there is a flawless emerald. When the Vizier wears his amber beads, he loops the strand about his neck these many

73

times—" he held up his hand with the fingers and thumb rigidly extended— "and still it reaches his sash. But he does not feel the burden of this treasure on his neck, for amber is a magic jewel without weight." The eunuch rubbed his palms together at the thought.

The First Wife laughed again, and this time in honest glee. Perhaps the eunuch's gesture prompted her to exclaim, "Jade! Do not forget his jade . . . which is as delightful to the touch as it is to the eye . . ."

"I had thought, my lady, that my uncle, the Vizier—that he opened his coffers to me—in order that my kinsmen by my mother's blood——" Myrrha stammered, searching for words as she spoke.

The First Wife stood bolt upright on her knees. The head eunuch gulped like a scavenging cur that has seized and attempted to bolt a morsel too big for its throat. Because he had difficulty closing his mouth, the First Wife recovered her poise before him.

"Of course, my child! What other thought could he have had? And we— we, too— we think——"

The sidelong glance she gave the head eunuch might have been an appeal for help. In any case he took up her refrain in gentle, soothing words. "Who would dare to question your uncle's motives? Not I of all men! But you should never forget, my child, that generosity is like a wild flower in a jungle glade. For all its exquisite beauty, its life is brief, and its memory fleeting. Now hunger, on the other hand, is like the jungle tiger. No traveler knows in what thicket it hides, or when it will pounce upon him. He must always be on his guard lest he fall prey to its fangs. Who can say when or how disaster will strike your— your fisherfolk? There are always killer whales in the deeps, and storm gales in the heavens. At such a time you—your friends will need most help. Then you would need wealth on which to lay your hands quickly, without having to wait on anyone's whim as you beg for it."

"My father has never denied me anything," Myrrha said.

"And he never will," the First Wife hastened to assure her.

"But only the very foolish look to the dead for continued generosity," the head eunuch added brutally. Then at her low cry, he went on in a gentler voice, "Our Royal Master still lives, but his blood is cold and no more than seeps through his veins."

"Let me go—go to him," Myrrha cried out. She turned quickly, eager to escape these two, as greedy in their own limited ways as her uncle. She stopped in midstep at the First Wife's command.

74

The very old and the very young woman stared into each other's eyes. The lines in the First Wife's face deepened as though the water clock in the corner were dripping out years instead of seconds. When she finally spoke, her voice was shrill and brittle, but not unkind.

"All a woman ever has is a gift from some man, Myrrha. Even the child she carries, and bears with weariness and pain. Then it is never she but the man who decides whether her child shall live or be cast over the harem wall to the dogs in the street outside. Yet life is as sweet to us as it is to any man. The thoughts of paradise are just as tantalizing to us creatures who were denied souls by Allah as they are to our masters. We—you and I—Myrrha, are as much slaves as any peasant woman who pulls her master's plow through his rice paddies, yoked beside one of his oxen. If you cannot, or will not obey the supreme lord in your life—in your case your uncle, now, and not your father—you will not be the first rebellious woman. Nor would you be the first foolish creature to disappear forever from the sight of her sisters. This may well happen to you! If it does, no one, regardless of the love she bears you, will dare question your fate. Not even I!"

That was only the beginning of the old woman's tongue lashing. The Princess listened respectfully and in silence to the end of the tirade. She had heard women rant like this before; but she had never until now understood the raging helplessness behind the words of admonition. She sensed, too, that stark rebellion shot through the words of wisdom, but rebellion without overt disobedience, through sheer helplessness incapable of violence.

"My lady, will you ask of my uncle, the Vizier, whatsoever of kind and quantity——" she began.

The eunuch interrupted her. "In whose name, Princess?"

"Please ask in my name, lord eunuch, since the offer of largess was to me."

The First Wife smiled, and the head eunuch relaxed like a sack of wet clams tossed out of a boat. The Princess knew without being told that at last she was free to seek her own quarters. But she had not reached the door before the First Wife again called to her and beckoned.

"Myrrha, beloved child, come here to me. I have often urged our lord, your father, to find a worthy husband for you, partly because I loved your mother, and partly because—well, because beauty as great as yours can wreak havoc in a woman's life. There is no safety for women like you, Myrrha, save through the protection of a husband.

"But your father cannot bear to part with you, and I cannot blame him for it. He has loved you more than any other child, more deeply than any wife or concubine. His love for you has seemed to me as nearly perfect as any human emotion can ever be. I suppose that kind of love is the most perfect thing in life; but perfection can be a cruel thing, dear child. Your father's love has robbed you of the husband you should have had two years ago. A lesser love one can enjoy—and forget when it dies. Love is a woman's whole life, but it can destroy her. When it is too great, it is like a disease that ravishes and devours."

She paused, and although Myrrha waited for her to continue, she remained silent until the Princess asked, "Do you think, my lady, that my father's love may destroy me?"

The First Wife roused herself from her thoughts slowly, as though recalling her spirit from a great distance. At first she looked annoyed by the Princess' question, but her expression softened as she answered. Still there was, perhaps, a shade too much protest as she exclaimed, "I think? What has one like myself to do with thoughts which are critical of man's behavior? Who cares what I think! And put dangerous thoughts out of your mind, too, child.

"Here! Here! I called you back to give you this. Take it before my generosity withers like a wild flower," she added with a sly look at the head eunuch.

As she spoke she slipped a ring from her finger—a garnet cut in the shape of a star and half framed in a crescent moon of gold encrusted with seed pearls. The star and the crescent of Islam. Myrrha had often played with the ring as a child. She knew that long long ago her father had given the ornament to his First Wife as a mark of his love. It had become a symbol of his continued respect when age had streaked her hair with gray and shriveled her skin like the rind of a dried plum. Myrrha dropped to her knees and tried to clasp the First Wife's hand between both of hers in thanks.

The old woman pushed her away, but not unkindly. "Do not thank me," she said. "Instead, let me go with you tomorrow when you visit the fisherfolk. You must go to them, you know. Your uncle's permission offered when unsought is really a command.

"I was born and passed my childhood in one harem; and although all of my womanhood has been spent within these walls, that does not mean I have never been curious of what lies beyond. I envied The Pearl many things. I have hated some of the women who supplanted me in My Lord's affections as my youth faded, but who could hate the Golden Pumpkin! Your mother was a creature of another world, Myrrha. I envied her that other world, but because I loved her so greatly I never once asked Our Lord to restrain her amazing freedom. I often helped her prepare the baskets of food and clothing she carried through the gates with her. I sometimes gave her money, too. I gave permission for other women—women sufficiently old, of course, so that decorum might be preserved—to go with her into the street and down to the riverside. But as First Wife in this harem, I never felt it befitting my dignity to do the same. But I shall soon be dead, and what will all the dignity in the world avail me then? Her freedom never harmed The Pearl, nor has it seemed to harm you. I have long yearned to know what a world is like where women traipse through the streets unveiled and yet remain eminently desirable as women!"

CHAPTER SEVEN

THE following day, after the physical needs of the Royal Dullard had been cared for with all loving solicitude, and while he lay on his cushions torpid as a lizard in the dew-chilled, early morning grass, the Princess Myrrha with a retinue of older women and lesser eunuchs once again walked through the streets of the city. Myrrha could not have told why, but the minute she stepped through the gate in the palace wall, a strange uneasiness seized her. She tried to put the feeling out of mind and to think of the happiness she carried in her baskets for the folk on the banks of the Mekong, but the feeling within her deepened into such dread that she glanced about and over her shoulder like a peasant lad threading his way through a strange jungle. At that moment the First Wife seized her arm and clung to her like a terrified child.

"You must not be frightened of this world out here," Myrrha chided gently, surprised at the apprehensive note in her own voice.

"No man can escape kismet," the old woman answered with a shrug of her shoulders as she was in the habit of doing when she was unable to explain any circumstance or happening in her life.

"You are making up things in your mind, now, to be afraid of because outside the gates you didn't know what to expect except that it would be different. People here are just the same as . . ."

Myrrha had begun in a soothing tone, hoping to comfort the old woman, but she was unable to finish. As she looked about her, she could not tell what was wrong or different. There was a subtle change that weighed upon her like hot, humid air before a thunderstorm. She opened her lips, but before she could shape her thoughts to words, the First Wife laughed shrilly.

"Is it possible that we creatures without souls, to whom so much is denied and from whom so much is demanded, also are burdened with predetermined doom?" she asked, suddenly impish as a child.

No one replied to her, but the eunuchs, who also seemed vaguely uneasy and without knowledge of cause, herded the women more closely together and flexed the wrists of their sword arms.

Myrrha's eyes caught the movement and she smiled. These eunuchs had all at some time received token training in the use of the scimitar, but none in her memory had ever been called upon to use that training. For all his ponderous scimitar, a eunuch in his effeminate harem silks was as vulnerable as a peasant lad armed only with a stout club. Perhaps more so.

Myrrha wondered that she had never before noticed this contradiction in the presumed duty of the eunuchs and their lack of preparation for its performance. Like the First Wife, however, she shrugged off matters too ludicrous for women to understand and tried to step along confidently.

It was a beautiful day with little birds twittering in willow and rattan cages suspended from balconies. There were bulbuls prized for the sweetness of their song; myna birds, treasured because they could be taught human speech and were natural clowns in any case; cockatoos and parakeets and lories whose gay plumage delighted the eye. Sometimes the scent of flowers from hidden gardens almost overcame the stench of decaying offal in the street. These were things she knew well and understood, and that calmed her. She had almost forgotten her first sense of unreasoning fear when the group entered the street of bazaars.

There Myrrha and the eunuchs and the old women who had accompanied her outside the walls before, stopped stock still in amazement. Although it was almost midday, the merchants were only just now unbarring their stalls and laying out a display of their wares. All of them seemed hurried, as though they had only within the last few minutes been apprised of the unexpected appearance of the Princess and the other harem women.

"Is there pestilence in the city?" one eunuch exclaimed. "Why have these money grubbers not been busy hawking their wares?"

"Has some merchantman tied up at the docks with plague aboard?" another queried.

"Has a band of brigands swept down out of the hills and through the bazaars?" a third wondered.

But it had been a long time since men of prey had dared raid the city. The Vizier's spies were everywhere—in the far-flung corners of the realm as well as behind the curtains of the palace and the shrubbery of every garden path. Myrrha could not remember when any band or marauders had earned more by their fiercest attacks on the city than crippling wounds or abrupt entrance into paradise.

The merchants did not reply to the eunuchs, but turned to the Princess. She had always been a good customer, if a somewhat foolish one in that she did not haggle over prices. This one held up a breadth of damask as beautiful as a carpet of brilliantly hued flowers. Another carried a bolt of muslin under his arm—cloth woven on hand looms by peasant women, and so fine and delicate that a length of it floated in the air like a down-winged seed. But there was no gleam at the thought of a good sale in a single man's eye. Every face seemed striving for the accustomed expression of servile pleading, and at the same time was furtively apprehensive. It was as though each merchant begged of her: Buy and be gone, Princess! In the name of Allah, make your choice quickly, so that we may once again bar our doors and cower behind them.

Myrrha bought the damask and muslin and other treasures held before her with a brief, "Take them to the palace and my father's head eunuch will pay you for them."

Then, since no one had replied to the eunuchs' wondering exclamations, she herself questioned a man pointedly. His answer to every query was the same, a hurried denial of any knowledge of danger; always obsequious, but so brief as to seem abrupt. "No, Most Exalted Lady, no disease, no plague, no sickness—except, of course, those puny ones which clutter every household and enjoy a dirge of moans and groans as a healthy man does the music of laughter. No! No blackguards. No footpads. No cutthroats, either.

"There has been none of these raiding our shops since the soldiers of Our Lord Vizier . . ."

Myrrha passed on to the next merchant, and the next, and the next. Their replies were like a refrain, for each tradesman answered in the same way and broke off in confusion at the same point in his denials.

80

Not one ventured a reason for the late opening of his shop even when it meant almost discourteous avoidance of a direct question.

Myrrha was used to all the innuendoes of servile flattery, the nuances of every word, the world of meaning conveyed by the half gesture of a wrist, a lowered glance sweeping sidewise before the lids closed. Half consciously she noted a new and subtle, although scarcely discernible, inflection at the mention of her uncle. It was somewhat like the tone of a man, miserable by reason of his own misdeeds, who prays Allah to spare him the consequences of his folly. Anger surged through her and she glanced at the First Wife, sharp, frightened query in her eyes.

The old woman nodded assent. "Yes. The city knows that your father lies dying, and already pays allegiance to the next khan. That is the way of men, Princess. It has always been so."

Myrrah turned to the eunuchs, but they met her gaze with looks of embarrassed ignorance. She plucked at the sleeve of the one in command, "What is the matter with them, Idrisi?" she asked.

"They are fools," the man snorted. "Cowards where they have nothing to fear."

"But there must be something. The streets are deserted. Even the sweepers are not combing the offal for anything of value cast out accidentally with the night soil, to carry away with them," she persisted.

"But they have said they know of nothing amiss, so their own tongues convict them of cowardice," Idrisi answered stubbornly, but without that peculiar quality which is born of conviction.

Myrrha hesitated as though undecided which man to question further, the eunuch or the merchant. Neither man would meet her eyes with his own. While she hesitated, the First Wife seized her arm and clung to her. The silver guards on her long nails dug into the Princess' skin like the claws of a kitten.

"Let us return to the harem, Myrrha. I—I do not like it here. I do not like these unfriendly streets." She began whimpering like a frightened, bewildered child.

Myrrha put an arm around the old woman's shoulders and soothed her as she herself had been soothed by the First Wife many a time in childhood. Then the Princess demanded an explanation in tones she had never used before to anyone, and which she hoped would not permit evasion.

The merchant cringed and replied in halting words as though quoting a half-forgotten adage. "When fish are running in big schools and yet the fisherfolk do not man their proas, the sea is not to be trusted, even when it is tranquil as a flooded rice paddy, Princess, and no storm clouds are rolling up over the horizon."

Myrrha stared at the man. Was he trying to tell her something? Yet he was obviously frightened that the meaning of his words might be too clear. Then, mindful of the tales she had heard of the fisherfolk's way of escaping the Vizier's taxes, she asked: "Have my mother's people disappeared into the sea once again? It was only yesterday that my uncle, the Vizier, told me they stood outside the palace gates and shared my grief over the failing health of my father."

"How can one visit a people who are not there?" the First Wife shrilled suddenly. The relief in her voice was laughable. But when she tugged at Myrrha's arm and the Princess did not turn, she fell to whimpering again. "Myrrha, dear child, let us return to the harem. Perhaps Our Lord has awakened and calls for you. It is not seemly that you should keep him waiting."

When Myrrha still did not turn, she cried out sharply as though an untenable, painful thought had just occurred to her. "Perhaps—perhaps even you would be safer there today."

But Myrrha's big black eyes never swerved from the merchant's face. They were no longer soft as sloes with the unmarred bloom of perfect ripeness upon them, but were as cold and glittering as her uncle's. Perhaps the merchant saw the likeness. In any case he hastened to speak:

"Princess, they say that the fisherfolk have not disappeared into the sea. But if they have not, then they must be cowering in their hovels; for their proas are hauled up on the banks, and their nets are strung out to dry. I understand desperation against taxes which snatches food from the lips of those who have harvested it from their fields and from the sea. But I do not know why hitherto boldly defiant men should cower in corners like wounded animals."

He seemed on the point of saying more, but the eunuch Idrisi stilled him with a wave of his hand. Idrisi bent over and peered closely into

82

the First Wife's eyes. "My lady, did you say that Our Lord, the Vizier
. . ."

"He did not command this visit," the old woman cried out. "He
merely suggested it." Then she pulled her shoulders erect and tried
to speak with the authority befitting a first wife in a harem. "We will
now return to the palace, Myrrha, since there is evil abroad in the
city."

But Idrisi shook his head. "The wishes of our Lord Vizier are not to
be flouted regardless of the language in which he clothes them. You
know that, My Lady."

The First Wife shrank back, again the obedient woman. Once more
Myrrha put her arm around the old woman and drew her close. She
noticed that she stood almost a head taller than the First Wife; and
for the first time she felt that inner glow which comes to one who pro-
tects a weaker. She liked the feeling because it carried with it a
strange sense of personal exaltation. It was a curious sort of strength,
a primordial one that did not depend on either noble birth or knotted
muscles, could not be intimidated by flashing scimitars, nor destroyed
by silken cords.

Idrisi motioned for his brother eunuchs to herd the women into a
knot too close for comfort, since the bulky baskets they carried
bumped awkwardly against their legs. They had not yet passed through
half the length of the bazaar when Myrrha noticed that the merchants
ahead of them merely stood in their doorways and no longer made a
pretense of setting out their wares. She glanced back over her shoulder
and saw the shops behind her being hastily barred again.

She tightened her arm about the First Wife's shoulders and bent
her head to whisper, "Step proudly. We can do nothing but go on. If
there is danger, my uncle knew of it since he knows everything that
transpires. Do you think . . ."

"Who knows what goes on in the mind of a cobra?" the old woman
answered in patient resignation, but in surprisingly clear and even
tones that carried to the ears of Idrisi.

The eunuch shook his head in warning, "Remember, My Lady, that
even the stones in windowless walls have ears for the Vizier," he said.

"I am old. What can he do to me?"

"If he staked you out over a bamboo sprout, the pain, as the living spear grew slowly piercing your body through, would be as great as if—" he glanced at Myrrha meaningfully—"as if you were only her age."

His answer had the subduing effect of a whiplash. No one spoke again, neither woman nor half-man, until the city had been left behind and the strand between it and the near bank of the Mekong had been half crossed.

The Princess walked with her shoulders erect and her head held high; but she always knew when the First Wife stumbled and was quick to steady her steps or give her a reassuring smile or pat on the shoulder.

It was Myrrha, daughter of a fisherwoman, who first saw the gay-diang. It was riding at anchor only half concealed by the brush which had taken root on one of the closer delta islands. Myrrha had seen gay-diangs before, and had laughed because they had always reminded her of a nide of pheasants.

Usually when one of the long, swift vessels hove into view, its curved decks were littered with the tiny, flat-bottomed gayyous its crew fished from. But until the fishermen put out from the mother vessel the gaydiang looked like a pheasant hen sunning herself in a pool of warm dust with her chicks sleeping on her back.

The men from Annam who sailed the gaydiangs were not above piracy; but because they, too, were fishermen, they were not feared by the folk on the banks of the Mekong. In fact, gossip had it that when Myrrha's people disappeared to escape the tax collector, they fled to Annam, and that the two peoples were of the same mixed blood. Whatever the case, they shared a common language, strange to the rest of the Grand Mogul's people.

Myrrha's eyes swept the broad expanse of river in vain as she searched for the tiny gayyous. In the distance, perhaps three miles out to sea, was a three-masted ship. Myrrha squinted through her lashes at the vessel in some perplexity, for although it carried its full complement of sail, and the sails even bellied slightly in the small wind, it seemed unmoving. The boat was riding at sea anchor. But if anchored, why were the sails unfurled?

As Myrrha's eyes again swept the Mekong, she remembered the merchant's words. The ocean was almost as placid as the sluggish river, and droves of sea gulls circled about overhead, constantly diving,

84

seemingly scratching the surface of the water with their claws indicating there was fish inshore, but not a single gayyou or proa rode the waters. Neither the strangers nor her own people were fishing.

"How beautiful! Like an immense bird in mid-flight," the First Wife exclaimed. "What is it, Myrrha?" The old woman was pointing at the distant vessel.

Myrrha was filled with amazement and then with wondering pity that one should live so many years and so near to both a great river and the sea and still never have seen an ocean-going boat. However, the old woman knew about boats, for much of the luxury to which she was accustomed had been brought to Cochin China in these strange, beautiful, water-borne, wooden birds. As the Princess answered the First Wife's questions the rest of the group stopped, for Idrisi was also staring at the gaydiang.

Myrrha laid a hand on the eunuch's arm and, with her head still held proudly high, asked in a carefully light tone, "What do you think of these two boats, Idrisi? Is it not strange that a fishing vessel carries no fishermen? And that an ocean-going vessel should be riding at anchor with all sails set? And why should fisherfolk not be fishing when the gulls scream over the plenitude of fish? I see the proas drawn up on the riverbank, but where are their owners? Do you see them? I myself do not like it, Idrisi. Do you?"

Myrrha would never know what made her laugh at the man. It was as though she were asking: For all your sex, your size, and your sword, are you stronger and braver than I before the unknown?

"Since we are here at the behest of the Vizier, Exalted Lady, dare we turn back?"

As the man spoke his eyes shifted from her face and fixed themselves, wide with terror, on something behind her. Myrrha glanced over her shoulder and screamed, for between the women and the city stood a band of armed men. All the bravado which had exhilarated her, the scornful twitting of the eunuch which had piqued her vanity, left her. Her body felt as weak and unreliable as a fruit comfit that has been taken from the fire too soon. First Wife and virgin Princess clung to each other in helpless panic. At a shrill command from one of the soldiers the eunuchs drew their scimitars and dropped them on the ground. Idrisi last of all. The sight angered Myrrha and gave her some courage.

"Take up your sword, coward! You are sworn to protect us," she shouted.

If the man heard her over the bedlam of now screaming women, he gave no sign. If she had been free, Myrrha would have beaten him with her fists, but she could not. Her arms were full of the First Wife who clung to her, scratching her with her long nail guards like a frightened cat.

"Pirates! Pirates! Save me! Ah God, what agony to have been born a woman!"

The Princess glanced at the scimitars on the ground, struggled free of the First Wife and seized one of them. It took the strength of both of her arms to lift it. Suddenly she laughed as she looked at her guard. The eunuchs, unnaturally large and strong men because of their emasculation, had never done more than rattle their blades in their scabbards or twirl them above their heads and pose them before their noses in flashing salute to her father. That was all harem life had ever required of them. Now, before men whose lives depended on courage and the strength and skill of their sword arms, they were nothing but quivering hulks of obscene fat.

After the first involuntary cry, Myrrha did not scream again. Harem-bred, child of a peasant woman who had failed in her paramount duty, she had always known that her life and death depended entirely on male caprice—her father's love, her uncle's ambition. Now, when at any second a scimitar might shear her slender neck in two, she felt more alive, more aware of life about her, than she had ever felt before.

Myrrha raised the scimitar upright before her face. The First Wife clasped her arms about the girl's waist and then slowly sank to the ground, sliding her clasped arms the length of the Princess' body. Myrrha dropped the huge sword and knelt to pick the old woman up. Because her feet were fettered in the old woman's arms, Myrrha's body swayed off balance. She threw out a hand to keep from tumbling full length on the ground. It came to rest on a stone the size of a small orange. She freed herself from the First Wife's frantic, grasping hands, stood erect, took careful aim at a soldier's broad chest and hurled the rock.

It struck the man on the one mortal spot exposed by his armor, the throat, and crushed his windpipe. A thin stream of blood trickled down over the man's leather breastplate from the skin ripped by the rock. A look of childish surprise softened the harsh lines of his features. He dropped his sword and clasped his throat with both hands. For a moment he struggled for the breath he was no longer able to draw, his leather armor creaking as his great chest labored. Then his body sagged to his knees, swayed sidewise and toppled over onto the ground.

Myrrha could not move a muscle of her body, save only her eyes. She no longer heard the women screaming about her, or felt them senselessly clawing her body in their frantic terror. She tore her eyes away from the dead soldier and swept the world about her. The blue of the sky was bluer than she had remembered it. The sea greener. The gulls more graceful. The shrubbery on the delta islands was clothed in a thousand shades of green to which she had been insensitive before.

She caught her breath sharply. The gaydiang had sailed out from behind its sheltering island and was making for the riverbank. Quickly she glanced seaward and was not surprised that the vessel there had hoisted anchor, came about and was tacking landward. The Vizier's assassins had swept in from the sea and it was only natural that, their mission accomplished, they should return to it, for a boat leaves no trail for a hunter to follow.

Idrisi had seized her arm and was shaking her so hard that she felt her head sway like a bird clinging to a bent reed in a windstorm.

"You fool! Do you imagine you can save me?" she screamed. "You will break my neck yourself."

Then for the second time she screamed. This time in terror, for Idrisi's features were twisted into a mask of rage and abject fear.

"You—you have destroyed all of us!" he shrieked. "You—you miserable spawn of a peasant slut! You———"

There was a blinding flash of sunlight reflected from the blade before the scimitar struck. For a moment Idrisi looked amazingly like the soldier she had killed. His eyes opened wide. He seemed astonished, like a child that picks a bee out of the heart of a flower and discovers that the bit of down bites cruelly. His fat lips twiched as though they were still shaping curses. Then his head slid sideways, bumped against his shoulder like a ripe peach striking a limb as it falls, and tumbled to the ground. A brawny arm encircled Myrrha and pulled

87

her to one side away from the fountain of blood that spurted upward between Idrisi's shoulders.

A foot pushed the First Wife away from her. Myrrha, staring at the headless trunk of the eunuch, saw it sway and then plunge forward, knocking the frail body of the First Wife before it. Then she felt herself being lifted into the air and swung over a shoulder like a bag of threshed rice.

The soldier carrying Myrrha broke into a run, heading toward the riverbank. The leather armor over his shoulder ground into the soft flesh under her rib cage, but she scarcely felt the pain. All she could see of the First Wife was one leg protruding from under the huge body of the eunuch. If she were not already dead, she would soon be smothered in the fat above and the dust below.

"God is great! God is good!" Myrrha heard herself whispering the formal prayer for the-creature-without-a-soul being left behind. "Allah is merciful——" But she could not finish that prayer; for God is a male creature and thus capricious—and caprice is too seldom merciful.

As the Princess stared behind her, numb with pain and terror, she saw a soldier stop at Idrisi's body and search it for whatever of value it bore. But the man had been only a lesser eunuch and his body yielded little more than a ring or two and a short chain of gold. Then the soldier turned Idrisi's body over and uncovered the First Wife. So quickly that his fingers seemed trained for the macabre chore, he stripped the fragile old woman of her costly garments. His hands were still fumbling among the delicate fabrics when he gave a bellow of triumph and held a small jeweled bag in the air for his companions to see. It was the sort of purse every harem woman wore, for in it she carried her most precious jewels. It was one of the scant bits of protection allowed against male caprice. For, should a woman so anger a man that he shouted at her, "I divorce you!" she must immediately leave his home and go to that of her nearest living male relative, bearing with her only that which she wore on her body at the time of the dread pronouncement. So a harem wife lived through her days and slept through her nights wearing all of her jewels, some displayed and the rest hidden in her bodice.

As the soldier poured the contents of the First Wife's jewel bag into the palm of one hand, Myrrha saw a loop of heavy gold chain slip through his fingers and dangle there like a snake over a limb. Something was fastened to the chain, something which might have been a star sapphire pendant. And she thought she caught a glint of blue, like a lump of turquoise carved into a Persian rose. If her eyes did not deceive her, the First Wife and the head eunuch had lost no time in petitioning the Vizier in her name.

A buckle on the shoulder of the man carrying her bit into her flesh. She doubled up her fists and beat his back with them. She merely bruised the flesh of her hands, and the brute did not even seem to notice what she was doing. She twisted her body until she could see his head—and his unprotected neck. Suddenly she threw an arm over his head, and pulling with the other hand for greater strength, tightened her elbow like a vise on his windpipe. Without slackening his stride, he pulled her from his shoulder, ripping her hands apart. Then he wound an arm about her middle and carried her with her head, arms and feet dangling like a puppy in a bitch's mouth. In her rage, she tried to bite his thigh; but his pumping knee bumped her chin and she bit her own tongue instead.

Then there was water just barely below Myrrha's face, for the soldier who bore her was wading out through the shallows to the approaching gaydiang.

CHAPTER EIGHT

THE gaydiang was a flat-bottomed boat of shallow draft and therefore able to come close enough inshore so that a score of long splashing strides brought the pirate carrying Myrrha to its side. He was a big man, as big as any of the eunuchs she had known, but all bone and muscle instead of fat, and he hoisted her above his head on his hands with ease. Men who were not negroid but whose faces and arms were burned almost black by wind and sun, leaned over the rail, seized her by her wrists and ankles, and hauled her aboard.

The prow of the boat had been spread with a piece of sailcloth and the Princess was deposited on this. There was nothing unkindly in the act, but no more consideration was shown her than inanimate but breakable cargo would have received. The other women were tumbled down beside her, and they crouched there shrinking close and tight together on the narrow deck.

Myrrha remembered Idrisi's last furious denunciation and recognized the truth of the eunuch's terror stricken words. She threw her arms about as many of the old women as she could, and they clung to her like frightened children. Then she saw one of the pirates dragging a woman along by her arm as a child drags a doll, with the unresisting body bumping along behind him over coils of rope.

"Stop! Stop that! She can walk. Do you want to rip her arm from her body?" Myrrha screamed.

Surprised by the unexpected command and the note of authority in the girl's voice the cutthroat paused. The foolish grin of a half-grown boy caught in some misdemeanor spread over his face until he realized that he obeyed not only a girl, but a girl who was a captive. Then his face flushed with anger, erasing its momentary humanity. He dropped the arm, inserted a blunt finger in the coil of hair on the old woman's neck, and with a jerk ripped it free of the confining pins. With a bellow of savage laughter he tangled the fingers of one hand in the thin gray tresses and lifted his victim until her feet dangled a third the length of her body above the deck. The age-loosened skin on the old woman's face stretched upward until her visage was distorted into a grotesque mask like an image glimpsed under rippling water.

Without thought of her own helplessness or the possible consequences of her act, Myrrha shook herself free of the old women clinging to her and dashed at the pirate, beating at him with her fists. He looked down at her as a bull might look at a sparrow that disputed a path with him. He leered at the raging girl as though he enjoyed the ineffectual punishment. Then a careless backward fling of his free arm swept her across the deck until her back and shoulder struck the mast. Such pain as she had never known before shot through her, but she did not lose consciousness. "I must not!" she raged inwardly, and held her breath with the intensity of her effort. All of her short life these old women had loved and cared for her. Now, because of her, they were the captives of men who were beasts of prey—more merciless than the four-footed denizens of the jungle who killed from hunger and not for the sheer pleasure they felt in the act of inflicting torture.

Myrrha had made no sound at her own pain, but now a shriek of despairing helplessness burst from her lips. For the same arm that had thrust her aside so easily, swept back in a curving arc. It was not a fist that landed in the dangling woman's stomach, but the palm of the pirate's hand in a smacking blow. The Grand Mogul's head eunuch could strike a woman thus, making a loud report and give little or no pain, but this was not such a blow. The old woman's knees and elbows jerked spasmodically like a marionette in the hands of an unskillful pupeteer. The pirate, who had not taken his eyes off Myrrha, again bellowed with laughter.

She clenched her teeth against the pain in her back and shoulders and started back again. Perhaps, she thought, he will seize me and let Lannice go. But she stopped abruptly at the second step. Another pirate, taller than the first and slighter of build and better dressed, had leaped from the boom of the mainsail. Almost before his feet touched the deck, he landed a smashing blow in the first man's face. The pirate crumpled to the deck and, fully conscious, lay there eying his opponent

91

as he spat out a tooth and wiped blood from his lips and chin with the back of his hand.

The second pirate stamped on the hand that still clasped the old woman's hair until the fingers sprang apart, then picked the old woman up and cradled her in his arms as though she were a child. With a sweep of his head he motioned Myrrha to follow him as he carried his burden aft and deposited her beside her companion wives. He gestured to Myrrha to seat herself beside the others. He was turning away even as she obeyed, but he stopped and swept her from head to toe with an all-encompassing glance. Nothing escaped those eyes, from the gilded clogs which had protected the satin foot-mittens, her jewel-encrusted dress and the budding form beneath it, the perfection of her skin and features, the size and depth of her unfathomable black eyes.

Myrrha did not turn her face away from the pirate's eyes, black as her own but set as straight in his face as those of any golden-haired Circassian beauty from the shores of the Black Sea. At first there was only curiosity in the man's face and no lust. Nor did lust flame in his eyes as he stared at her, but something nearer simple pity. This compassionate emotion he apparently did not welcome, for he shook his head as though to dispel the weakness, then hurled himself upon the fallen pirate, kicked him savagely, and apparently commanded him to get to his feet and be about his work of trimming sails. This man, Myrrha realized, must be the captain.

She stared after the captain, who kept his face turned from her—she could not say whether from accident or intent—while he shouted to the men still in the water and on shore.

Myrrha saw that the eunuchs were not assisted either through the water or over the side of the boat; consequently, their lower garments were muddied and their outer shifts were snagged and torn.

Although the pirates sailed an Annamese boat, and Myrrha would have understood at least in part if they had used the Annamese tongue, their words were utterly strange to her. From his harsh tone and the savage expression on his face she knew that the captain was cursing the remaining four half-men. Her father's head eunuch would have had them whipped for such destruction of costly raiment; and she wondered if the pirates would also beat the eunuchs.

92

Myrrha cradled the head of the injured old wife in her lap, crooned to her and smoothed her hair back with gentle hands—and wondered if these marauders would be more exacting, more difficult for a woman to please than the arrogant, sybaritic lords of harems.

When the captives were all on board, a dozen sweeps of poles thrust over the side into the mud sent the gaydiang out into the current of the Mekong. As the sail caught the wind it pulled the prow of the boat upward like the crest of a wave and for a few seconds Myrrha looked directly into the open doors of the fishing village. She scrambled to her feet.

The pirate captain was at her side instantly. He laid a restraining hand on her shoulder as though fearful that she might attempt to leap overboard. When she made no further movement, he removed his hand but continued to stand beside her, as she gazed at the homes of her mother's kinfolk.

One by one, like shamed children, the people of the riverbank crept out of their huts and stared after the gaydiang. Myrrha wanted to fling out her arms, to call to them, to shout a goodbye, to somehow let them know she did not blame them for her misfortune. Their only protection from the Vizier had been to disappear into the sea. Doubtless many among them would have helped her if they could have done so. But how could that be if the Vizier now also commanded the evil forces of the ocean?

How cunning her uncle was! She wondered how long he had planned this coup. Cunning as the hamadryad, the cobra king of the jungle! With what malicious delight he must have savored his scheme that the sea should swallow the daughter of The Pearl. Would he now avenge himself on her mother's people? She wanted to shout a warning, but she made no move or sound until there was a loud, harsh rattling behind her. The square mainsail of the gaydiang collapsed on the deck. Only a short distance away was the vessel which had ridden offshore at anchor yet with all sails set.

The larger vessel was two-masted and carried cannon lashed to its deck. Myrrha had never been close to a boat like this one before, but she had heard the fisherfolk describe such and she knew immediately that this was a Portuguese ship. She had no knowledge of Portugal as a country. The Portuguese were to her merely a race of fierce men who sailed up over the horizon in their fast brigantines, traded with whoever desired any portion of the varied merchandise they carried, and disappeared by sinking back into the horizon again.

Tales of the sources of the Portuguese cargoes commanded breathless listening, for the lands they visited were reportedly peopled with monsters both human and animal. And it was said that the Portuguese sailors—brigands, pirates, whatever one wanted to call them—found their only pleasure in plunder, maiming and slaughter. All this was strange in some ways, for although their prices for what they had to sell were high, they did not haggle with a customer. Moreover, none of the new slave girls and concubines that always appeared in wealthy men's harems, following the visit of a Portuguese boat, were ever maimed by man or misshapen by nature.

The deck of the brigantine was above Myrrha's head as she stood on the deck of the gaydiang. The sailors from above shoved a broad plank across their railing and lashed it there. The other end was laid across the railing of the fishing boat. Rope had been wound around the plank so that although it rested at a steep angle between the two vessels, it offered fairly sure footing for the bare feet of the men who came trotting across.

Myrrha's first glance at these strangers was merely cursory. Then she was certain she had seen some of them before. In any case, their eyes were set in their heads with the same suggestion of slant as her own. Their cheeks were broad, too, and their noses were thin in the bridge and flat at the tip. These were the breed of men who sailed gaydiangs and not pirate ships.

They stared at her with curiosity to equal her own. Evidently they had feared being recognized by the fisherfolk and the merchants of Cochin China and had stayed on the pirate's ship while the pirates had used their boat to approach land. One of the new set of strangers spoke to the pirate captain and Myrrha understood his words for they were Annamese. She had seen such men in the fishing village often— possibly some of those who were now staring at her. There might even be a distant blood tie between her and these strangers.

The one who spoke was saying, "Only four eunuchs, Captain? There should have been more! That is small pay for the risk we run!"

"What kind of risk have you run?" the pirate captain snorted. "If you keep your word and sail to the West the equal of three good days

94

in front of a strong wind before you sell these gelts, who will know you had any hand in this rape?"

But the Annamese pointed to the eunuch's bedraggled clothing and complained that his profit was halved.

The pirate laughed scornfully. "Put them on the slave block naked. Someone may want to examine their bodies. They are already too old and big and fat and ugly for concubinage, so their only value is as harem guards. Take your share of the prize and make sail before the wind dies. If you are becalmed here, you will be found out without fail. You know what your profit in this venture will be if that happens, man."

He tilted his head, drew a meaningful finger swiftly across his throat and made a sucking, gurgling noise. The pirate crew roared with laughter, but the sun- and wind-burned face of the man from Annam darkened further in anger.

"Your sailors say the most valuable of the eunuchs was murdered," the Annamese shouted. "He was ours! Do you pay for him?"

"The fool had to be killed lest he harm my merchandise," the captain bellowed. He drew his sword and waved it threateningly, and the fishermen from Annam drew back, still muttering but no longer truculent.

The eunuchs were pushed to one side and Myrrha and the five old women were picked up and tossed onto the gangplank. The one old woman who had been struck by the first pirate could not even stand, much less walk. Myrrha tried to lift her and was pushed aside by the pirate captain who again picked up the tiny, frail creature in his arms. It seemed to Myrrha that his face was sad as he looked at the helpless creature. The rest, with one exception, were herded across into the brigantine.

The exception was old Ayentili, who had often of late suffered from dizzy spells and sometimes stumbled as she walked along. She now fell to her knées on the steeply slanting, rope-bound plank. At her scream of fright, Myrrha hurried to her and saw her gripping the hempen cleats with fingers as delicate as those of a child, and with no more strength than an infant. As the Princess bent over to help her, a hand seized her by her girdle and jerked her backward.

"There! There is payment for the dead eunuch," a voice shouted and pointed at the terrified old woman.

At that moment the plank slipped off the railing of the gaydiang and Ayentili slid into the sea. Numb with horror, the Princess saw the old woman thresh the water between the two vessels with her arms and legs for a brief moment. Then, weighed down as her garments became wet and heavy and wrapped themselves about her legs fettering her movements, she began to sink.

Myrrha screamed, and turned to the captain. He was staring directly at her over the old woman still in his arms. He answered the frantic appeal in her voice and face with a gentle, "It is quickly over and therefore not an unkind death. Do not pity her."

The Annamese sailors watched the woman struggle in the water with unconcerned curiosity until a pirate shouted at them.

"Do you not want her jewels? She was the wife of a very rich man."

At the words a half dozen Annamese sprang into the water and hauled Ayentili to the surface. Supporting her there and brushing her hands aside as she clutched at them frantically, they stripped her fingers of rings and her arms of bracelets.

"Her legs! Her legs, too, you fools!" a pirate bellowed. "Do you not know, you stinking squid, that harem women wear anklets?"

"Search her girdle for her jewel bag," another roared instruction.

Huge hands used to hauling loaded nets from the water ripped the clothes from Ayentili's body. The jewel bag dropped out from between the folds of her sash and began to sink. A fisherman dived for the treasure, his legs threshing the water as skillfully as the flukes of a big fish. A few seconds later he broke surface and waved the jewel bag triumphantly over his head, as he clambered back into the boat. In the meantime his companions had upended the old woman in the water and stripped her legs as they might have stripped berries from a wild bush, then clambered back into their boat.

When the pirates had seized upon Ayentili's body to despoil it, the Princess had rushed to the captain pleading, "Save her! How can you be so cruel? She is only a woman, but— she is human! I beg of you, save her."

But again the captain had only looked at the frantic girl and in a voice she could barely hear had murmured, "Pity yourself, child. Hers is the kindly fate."

96

Myrrha's legs trembled under her. Her heart seemed gripped in a vise of pain as she stared helplessly at Ayentili's body. The corpse bobbed on the surface of the water face downward for a short while, arms and legs outflung at grotesque angles like a much-abused doll. Then as the old woman slid below the waves, her long black hair undulated slowly and gently as though waving a kindly goodbye to the callously indifferent men who had despoiled her.

The other old women stood clinging to each other, sobbing. Beneia covered her face with one hand. Irini hung her head so low that she seemed to grope blindly with her hands for the bodies of the others. Leahli extended one arm behind her, the palm upflung and the fingers of her hand rigidly outspread like a dancer who pantomimes the warding off of evil. The captain had carried Lannice across the gangplank. Lannice, the tinest of them all, seemed trying to squeeze into the center of the group like a child seeking to hide behind its mother's garments.

Lannice was an elfin creature and had often entertained the harem with her impish pranks. Myrrha had sometimes seen the old woman punished for this same impudence. Always, at such times, she had tried to hide behind others; and her harem companions had usually tried to protect her, even when they ran the risk of punishment themselves. Now, by long habit, the bodies of the other three women swayed momentarily and Lannice disappeared behind their draperies like a puppy under the edge of a cushion.

Standing on the deck of the pirate brigantine, Myrrha wondered that these old women, whose entire lives had been ruled by the caprice of men whose code of justice and honor and even simple courtesy had not included them but had been reserved for other men only, should now be so fearful of the caprice of new masters. She remembered the many words of advice each of these old women had dinned into her own ears in training her for her place in life as a woman. Did they not recall their own words? Was it she, now, who must take each one of them in her arms and comfort and advise her?

She took one step toward the old women but stopped when again a hand was laid on her shoulder. A hand as big as the head eunch's but without any padding of fat. It was a strong hand and it turned her around as easily as a slave shifts an ornament on a shelf. She looked up

97

at the pirate captain and saw pity and admiration struggling for supremacy in his face, and through it all that softness one feels for a helpless, beloved child.

The pirate was speaking. Although his words and tone were harsh, they were not unkind. "Come! Forget the old women—if you can. Is it not a saying of yours that no one escapes his fate, Princess? No matter how high the state or how great the love that has hitherto sheltered him?"

His words dispelled any doubt that this pirate slaver might not know whom he had captured. Myrrha sighed heavily and turned her head to look back at Cochin China. The pirate removed his hand from her shoulder, and she flung her palms upward in a little gesture—the farewell of the harem when a slave passes from the company of her sisters to the walled garden of a new master.

The next words of the pirate were as though he read her unvoiced thoughts. "Look well, Princess. Store up within your heart the sight of whatever lies there that is dear to you. I have contracted to take you so far away from Cochin China that you will never again see your native land."

The boat of the Annamese fishermen was already so far away that it was only a speck on the waves, and the village on the banks of the Mekong was hidden by the trees growing on the delta islands. The city beyond the river stood on higher ground. She could see a little of it, but the buildings looked so small and gray that they seemed no more than dovecotes. The palace of her father stood on still higher ground, but only the golden cupolas on the roofs of the many wings showed above the encircling wall. The light reflected by the gilt in the mid-afternoon sunshine was as glittering and hard to look into as her uncle's gaze had ever been. A pennant fluttered from a pole atop the highest cupola, but because of the distance and the reflected sunlight, she could not tell whether it was her father's or her uncle's standard.

She turned to the captain. "The pennant—can you see the figures on the silk?" she asked.

The captain hesitated for a moment and then, without glancing landward, shook his head from side to side. "It is too far away," he said.

His eyes fell before hers, and she knew that he lied. Knew that her father was dead.

"I am glad," she said simply. Then added, "Without those who love him to care for him . . ."

"He will suffer no neglect now, Princess."

"Strange, is it not, that what we have always feared most—death—should in the end be the greatest kindness of fate?" she said slowly.

A half smile played about the captain's lips. When he spoke, his words were as slow as her own had been. "Try not to forget that fact, little lady. God gives every creature a measure of strength, and those He has endowed with hardy spirits are the favored ones."

The words did not make sense to Myrrha, and she waited for this lord of creation to go on. He merely laughed abruptly, briefly and humorlessly at the blank expression on her face. "You do not understand, do you?" he asked. "You will! You will!"

He looked back at the land. Myrrha's gaze followed his. Beyond the palace the land was an intricate patchwork of paddies, the blue-gray of their stagnant water splotched with green where the young rice plants had taken root and were growing vigorously. Peasants were working in some of the paddies, but their forms were so small because of the distance that they looked more like flies crawling about on a silken screen beyond the reach of a slave's cow-tail, fly whip than men and women. Suddenly Myrrha wondered what they were like, these men and women who delved constantly in the mud. If she had ever known them, would she have come to love them as she loved the fisherfolk? She turned to the pirate captain as though to ask him.

But this time his words did not follow her train of thought as he sought to answer the query in her eyes. "I am like you in that there is no place for me either in my own country, Princess. But I remember it, and I still call it home."

Then with his hand behind her shoulder, he pushed and guided her down a steep flight of steps. As she passed the old women huddling together, she paused; but the hand behind her shoved her onward and away from them. She was guided through a narrow passageway and into a room as small as an ugly or aging concubine's oda. But where a concubine, or any other slave's niche, was bare except for a pallet and perhaps a pile of cushions, this room was so crowded with furnishings

99

that not only were they wedged side by side, but gear and trappings were fastened to the wall and hung from the ceiling. Myrrha stepped across the threshold and waited, having been well taught what a woman must do when a man's hands close upon her flesh.

But the captain made no move to touch her. Instead, "Are you hungry?" he asked. She shook her head. He pointed to a pottery jar hanging from the ceiling by a chain. "There is water in that for when you are thirsty." Then, without another word he turned and went out, closing the door behind him.

When she heard the key grate in the lock she smiled. She knew it did not matter whether a woman liked the looks and behavior of the man who possessed her; still she was glad that she was the captain's prize and apparently was not to be shared by his crew.

She could not have told how long she stood looking about the cabin, touching nothing, for women were often whipped for handling men's possessions. Above her head she could hear footsteps hurrying about, ropes creaking against their pullies and the captain bellowing orders. There was no sound from the old women and she knew that they like herself now awaited the whims of their captors. She sighed and wished she could care for and comfort the one who had been held by her hair and slapped in the stomach. She did not pray because she knew of no prayer which had been composed to still dread in a woman's heart or ease the pain and difficulties of woman's duty to man. She merely waited, as she was certain the old women above her waited. She wondered where they were. She hoped they were together, for fear and pain are easier to bear when shared.

After a while she lay down on the floor and in spite of her anxiety, slept. She wished at first for the comfort of a pillow; but although there were many cushions on the benches against the walls, she did not take one because the man who now owned her had not given his permission.

Myrrha was awakened by piercing screams that could have come only from women's throats. The terror in the shrieks cut through her like an executioner's blade in her flesh. It could be no one but her erstwhile, elderly companions, and again, as though her mind could grasp nothing else, she wondered that women who were so well versed in the cruelties of men should find a mere change of masters so difficult an experience. Then she remembered that harem-bred women are taught not to scream at torture of the spirit, for such uncouth sounds only further displease an already angered male. She heard a few splashes, and after that all was quiet again except for footsteps on the deck and the perpetual creaking of the rigging on the masts.

Then Myrrha realized that the low roof of the cabin was closer overhead than when she had fallen asleep. She was lying on one of the little benches along the side of the wall with a cushion under her head. She sprang to her feet with a cry of fear at having lain in the helplessness of sleep so dangerously far above the floor. If she had turned in her sleep, she thought, she would surely have fallen and at least bruised her delicate body—and it is a prime duty of a harem woman to guard her flesh against blemish.

Myrrha looked down at the bench and at the impression of her head on the cushion. Quickly she shook the cushion into smooth plumpness and dropped it back on the bench. Then noticing that all the other cushions were propped against the wall, she set the one she had used at the same angle and stood back to compare it with the others. The eyes of harem eunuchs were trained to detect any tampering with a man's possessions, and she studied the benches carefully.

While she wondered how she could have been so foolish as to touch either bench or cushion, a pair of footsteps sounded more loudly than the others. She glanced at the door, and then backed away from it until she stood against the wall. The breeze from the open porthole felt good on her neck, and she turned to look out of the tiny square opening. The daughter of The Pearl had always loved the ocean, and when she visited her mother's people on the banks of the Mekong she had never failed to pay the homage of silent wonder to its vastness and somber beauty. Sometimes it had seemed as though she carried a small fragment of its vast strength back with her into the harem.

Now, however, she failed to respond to either its beauty or the awe of its limitless reaches, for as she stared through the porthole she was conscious only of seeing the bodies of three of her father's wives. Each corpse was completely naked. Each bobbed grotesquely on the gentle waves more than half submerged. One fragile hand seemed for a few seconds to be beckoning her to join them.

At that moment two strange things happened to the daughter of the Grand Mogul. Ephemeral, fugitive things, born of emotion which sprang spontaneously into being within her since no seed of rebellion had ever been planted within her soul. Nevertheless, she would re-member this instant of rebellion at unexpected moments during the rest of her life. She prayed for the death of a human being—the fourth old wife, Lannice, the gentle, the childish, the elfin. Lannice had not been formed by nature for ordinary punishment, let alone torture. Myrrha wondered as she prayed if her father's executioner, when he lopped off the head of a condemned man, felt toward his victim as she did now—that he did a luckless creature a kindness.

Myrrha shrugged her shoulders. The pirate captain said strange things. Perhaps they fertilized the dormant seeds of rebellion in her own mind. In any case, the first prayer merged into a second of pas-sionate intensity that Allah would sometime grant women souls; for it seemed to her then that of all the cruelties of an unpredictable, often implacable God, none was so vindictive as the fate of woman who must serve and suffer all indignity without redress, without reward in this world or hope of earning peace in a world and life to come.

CHAPTER NINE

THE door of the cabin opened and Myrrha faced the pirate captain as he stepped into the room. The old women's clothing was draped across one arm. In the other hand he clutched their jewel purses. He threw the garments on one of the benches.

"Take what you need, or want of these," he said pointing. "The rest we will sell in Manila."

Then the captain looked at the porthole behind Myrrha and frowned. "How long have you been standing there?" he asked.

"I saw only three women—there," the girl gasped, pointing behind her with an inclination of her head. "Where is Lannice?"

"Lannice?"

Myrrha realized that he had never heard the old women's names, but as she started to explain, he seemed to understand her unspoken thoughts.

"Ah! You mean the poor soul I carried aboard?"

Myrrha nodded her head.

"She is with her companions," the pirate said very slowly. "It is better so. She would not have lived long in the sort of life left to her."

Myrrha smiled sadly, and the corners of the captain's grim lips curved upward slightly, not in humor, but sensitive companionship.

"Strange, is it not," she began, speaking slowly as the thought took shape in her mind, "in my father's harem we were taught that death is the supreme punishment. Yet you call it a kindness."

He looked at her quizzically. "Do you believe in God?"

"Of course!" she answered with some indignation. Did this barbarian think the people of Cochin China were savages?

Again replying to more than her spoken words, the man went on. "Then you must believe in Heaven; and if you can honestly believe in

Heaven, it is surely to be preferred to—to all this." He flung out his arms in a gesture that seemed to embrace the universe.

"Heaven?" Myrrha questioned. To her the word meant the sky, lighted and warmed by the daytime sun, adorned by the moon and stars at night.

"I forgot," the captain answered. "You say paradise."

"But paradise is for men!"

"Why should it not be for women, too?"

"Because the Prophet Mohammed has said so," she replied in shocked wonder.

"Was it God—or Allah, call Him what you like—speaking through Mohammed's lips? Or was it just another man who could force his will upon women, and did so? Mohammed was only a man—a very ordinary man—before he set himself up as a prophet. Did he ever cease being a man? A man who enjoyed dominating—particularly women? Up until Mohammed's lifetime, women were not locked away behind walls or . . ."

Myrrha gasped in surprise so loudly that the captain paused as though he expected her to speak. She had never known there was a time in the history of the world when highborn women had not observed purdah.

"Yes," the captain went on. "Women went about as freely as men—as freely as their strength and their household duties and their children would let them."

"You are sacrilegious!" Myrrha cried out, momentarily shocked into unawareness of the temerity of any woman accusing a man of misconduct.

"And you are afraid to be, aren't you?" the pirate challenged. "Tell me, Princess, do you believe that all the women in the world up until Mohammed's lifetime were bad women? Because they didn't cover their faces? Or were they just like women in the world now—good and bad? Then, quite suddenly when Mohammed was an old man, what made it bad for a woman to show her face?"

In her dumb horror, Myrrha shook her head that she could not answer this man's incredible questions.

"You know nothing of the history of your own religion, do you?" he pressed. "That half of the human beings in this world were made slaves to men so that man's lust might have the sanction of religion."

104

The captain paused and studied Myrrha reflectively before going on. "And you have been made to believe that for you to question the conditions of your slavery is sacrilegious. Can you explain to me, Princess, how it can be that if you are a creature without a soul, you can lose that soul? Something you have been taught to believe you never had? That is Allah's punishment for sacrilege, isn't it?"

Myrrha' shrank backward before the man's impassioned words until her body pressed against the wall. She was frightened, shocked, horrified, but she could not answer the questions put to her, and she dropped her eyes in perplexity. Woman could not possibly be the equal of man; and yet . . .

"There are as many people in the world who believe a woman has a soul as there are those who do not place her much above the animals."

"Then," she asked suddenly, "if women do have souls, how can men dare treat them, and use them as they do?"

The captain laughed humorlessly. "Princess, how do men dare treat and use other men—their brothers, even—as they do?"

Again Myrrha lowered her eyes. It was easier to think staring at this strange man's feet than at his face. Every question he asked, every answer he gave to her or his own queries, disturbed her. She searched her mind for words, then suddenly realized that the doubts this man aroused in her mind, the challenge of ideas new and strange to her, ideas which shocked but at the same time were not unacceptable that all this was pleasure of a sort she had never known before. "If only they might be true," she was thinking.

She lifted her head, meeting the man's eyes steadily, and searched his face as intently as one of her father's scribes studied an ancient, faded scroll. Perhaps it was the willfulness of the favored child of a supreme ruler to speak as she did, perhaps it was no more than long-fettered native intelligence breaking the first and weakest of its bonds and sensing the joy of dawning freedom at long last. Whatever the reason, she heard herself saying: "I like to hear the things you say. I do not understand why, for your words shock and even frighten me; but they make me feel different than I have ever felt before. And I like it. I do not believe you are speaking untruths, although those who have taught me would call you a liar."

She had not meant to say so much, but her wakening thoughts had carried her along as a cluster of leaves torn from a tree are borne along on a mountain stream. She could not depend now upon instruction from her father's wives, for none of them had ever been placed in such a situation as this. Her face crinkled into a smile. The surprise, the bewilderment on the man's face amused her. It was the captain now who was nonplused.

Then, since the bonds of habit born of lifelong training are not broken in a moment or a day, Myrrha remembered another harem precept: that until a man's indulgence has been proven, it is not seemly, or even wise, to meet him too steadily eye to eye. Although the Princess' mother had been The Pearl, and had broken every tradition of the harem, her daughter had been sired by the Royal Dullard. Submissively Myrrha dropped her head until she was staring straight downward at her toes, and waited until she was forced to look up again. There was a frown on the captain's face. The frown changed to a look of scorn, and the girl shivered before it.

"Sometimes I think people are slaves because they want to be slaves," he said.

"The man is a fool," flashed through Myrrha's mind, and anger surged up in her. "Can a woman help being born a woman?" she demanded.

"No," the pirate replied. "But no matter what her station in life, she can respect herself, and others will respect her accordingly."

Myrrha wanted to tell the man that he was wrong, that sometimes it was an offense for a man to stand tall and straight before his master. How then, dare a woman do anything but bow her head submissively? She felt that although he might hear the words with his ears, his heart would reject them.

Finally she heard herself saying: "My father's wives—they are all dead? Am I the only prize left? Too valuable for my uncle, the Vizier—or you—to murder?" Again she was angry, but this time with herself and because her voice trembled.

The captain nodded his head.

"And what do you intend to do with me? Sell me? Or compel me to your will, like any other woman?"

The man's eyes fell before hers.

"Will not submission stand me in better stead than all the self-respect in the world if my fate is either the slave block, or your bed?"

Myrrha watched curiously as the man's neck and face crimsoned. He

106

clenched his right hand into a hard fist and half raised it, then slowly, a finger at a time, unclenched it. For the second time in her life, Myrrha saw respect in the eyes of a man staring at her. But the captain's word, when he replied, were enigmatical.

"You dispute cleverly, Princess, as though you were a man, and the product of a great university. You turn a man's best words against him with ease." Then this unpredictable creature bowed and murmured, "With your permission, Princess," turned, walked through the door, closed it softly and again locked it behind him.

Myrrha stared at the heavy, iron-bound door as though it could answer the questions racing through her mind: If a woman approached equality with men, how else could it be save through her mind? It could not be physically, for even the stupidest could see that she was slighter of build and lighter muscled. Then Myrrha laughed with almost childish delight at a sudden, pixie thought: If women were physically stronger than men, they would not be hitched alongside oxen and made to pull a plow through the muck of a paddy. They would surely use their superior strength to force men to that task— just as men now compelled them to the cruelest labor.

The old women's clothing lay where the captain had dropped it. Since he had told her she might have what she wanted of it, Myrrha picked up a veil. It was then she discovered that the captain had dropped the jewel bags on the clothing. She seized them and hugged them to her bosom with both hands. Four women's lifetime hordes. The value her father had put on their love. The price that, in subtle ways, they had set for submission to his will! Myrrha's mind clung stubbornly to the word *submission,* as though she were still arguing the point with the captain. In their own ways these women had bargained with her father, and it had taken cunning to acquire each jewel. And what was required of any man in the way of innate ability, Myrrha wondered, to lay a whip across a woman's back? She remembered the tales of the professional storytellers about lands ruled by women—remembered the many, if furtive, speculative glances cast in her direction by courtiers and diplomats.

Then she shrugged her shoulders as though irritated by the audacity of her thoughts. Her uncle, the Vizier, had also heard the storytellers and noted the glances. Consequently, she would never rule in Cochin China, not even as a puppet in the hands of the courtiers and diplomats. Nor would hers be the honor of bearing a future ruler of her native land.

She was certain that the pirate captain—who looked upon death with as much callous indifference as her uncle and, at the same time, talked as strange nonsense as any unwashed, unshaven, half-naked religious fakir roosting in the shade of a mango tree against a temple wall—would let her keep any jewel she chose. But Myrrha did not loosen the drawstring of a single bag; instead she laid the purses in a neat row on one of the benches. Then she started straightening and folding the old women's robes. As she did so, she began whispering the ritual prayer for the dead that harem women always chanted as they prepared the corpse of a companion for burial.

"O Allah, the Great!
Allah, the Good!
Thou alone art God!
Hear us, O Allah,
This insignificant one was virtuous.
She was humble, obedient, submissive.
She was beautiful, Allah.
Now we return her body to thee,
Smooth as alabaster,
Fragrant with myrrh,
Robed in precious silk and spotless muslin.

"O Allah, be Merciful
We beseech thee.
Make her one of thy houris——"

Myrrha's voice had risen to a strident wailing singsong, but she now broke off abruptly. She could not—she would not!—go on with the rest of the prayer. Was it a divine mercy to reward a slave's best efforts on this earth with a continuation of like slavery for all eternity to come? In that case, the bad slave, the unvirtuous woman was the more fortunate, for through oblivion her drudgery ended with the grave. Even the most ingeniously cruel man could not heap pain upon a clod. Then Myrrha wondered suddenly: These women who have souls, how do their sisters pray for them?

It was the captain himself who brought the Princess her supper that evening. There was only fish and rice heaped together in the rounded half of a gourd. He waited while she ate, urged her to eat more and shook his head as though troubled by the minute quantity she consumed.

Myrrha did not call the pirate's attention to the robes and the jewel purses. When he saw them, she knew she had pleased him even before he turned to thank her. She did not know what to reply, for the men she had known had carefully refrained from courtesy to a slave lest the unfortunate one forget his station in life. She laid a hand lightly on her stomach, signifying that her hunger had been blunted—which is as much as a woman should eat while her chief value is the perfection of her body.

Her palm rested directly on top of her own jewel bag. She pulled it from her belt and held it out to him. He hesitated for a second, but only a second.

As he accepted her treasure, he apologized in a deliberately gruff tone, "If I did not take it, someone else would. You would not be allowed to keep it."

There was truth in his words, providing, of course, that he sold her. But if he should keep her for himself . . . Myrrha's eyes grew big and round with pleasure at the thought. If truth lay deep within this man, if his curious respect for women was sincere, it would be a light duty to be his wife—or slave. Myrrha turned her head and bent her neck so that he might see and be attracted by the curve of her body from shoulder to ear. In order to watch him she had to look upward out of the corners of her eyes.

"In God's name, don't coquette at me!" he burst out.

"Coquette?" she asked, having never heard the word before.

"Flirt!" That, too, was foreign. "Try to arouse the devils in a man's flesh," he ended savagely.

These words she understood, but not that a man should wish to control passion. Perhaps, she thought, he was one of those men who preferred a male concubine to a female. And then, of course, there were others who were afraid of—even appalled at the thought of love.

"Have you ever loved a woman?" she asked. It was a simple question and she was not conscious when she asked it of the double meaning.

"Yes," he answered. "Two women. My mother and—one other."

"Your mother? Oh, no!" she cried out in horror.

He swore in his own tongue, and she knew she had angered him now as greatly as she had pleased him before. But when he addressed her in Annamese again his voice was kind and his words pitying. "You think of only one relationship between men and women, don't you? But you are not to blame, for that is all you have ever seen or been taught to expect. In my country, all tender emotion that stirs the heart deeply we call love."

"Did you love the second woman as you loved your mother?" Myrrha pressed, and knew the answer even as she spoke.

"No," he said, and then added in a low voice, "But I never possessed her."

"Aaaah! A caged bird in a neighbor's garden!" Myrrha suggested archly. Poor men, disinherited sons of the great, loved in this fashion and storytellers chanted poems about them.

Sometimes it was as difficult for the captain to understand her phraseology as for her to understand him. For a moment he was confused and then, as her meaning became clear, the lines in his face sagged in a mixture of bitterness and grief.

"The other woman . . ." he began and broke off in perplexity. How could he describe to this girl something based so completely on the mores of another civilization that there was no parallel to it in her own experience? Then he smiled as he asked, "Did you know that there are countries where some women devote their lives to the service of God and——"

Oh yes, Myrrha knew of the temple girls who were in reality concubines of the priests in the Buddhist monasteries in Hindustan. "You desired one of these? And could not have her because her father had given her to the holy men?"

"She was never given to any man," he answered. "She gave herself to God."

"Of course," Myrrha agreed, not having caught the distinction he drew. Such a girl in Hindustan belonged to the god of the temple and served the men who served the god. These women were pitiful creatures because they aged so quickly and no one ever knew what became of them when their brief youth had been spent.

"No! No!" the captain exclaimed. Such a woman as he had loved, he explained, wore special clothing, all black; and she went about

110

into the homes of the destitute, carrying food and medicine with her and comforting the helpless unfortunates.

Myrrha thought of her mother, The Pearl, and murmured softly as though speaking to herself, "And such women are greatly loved by many and respected by all?"

Pleased surprise at the girl's ready comprehension spread over the captain's face. He repeated her words as though the mere thought comforted him also, "Such a one is greatly loved and greatly respected."

As though he sought privacy for a precious memory, he stooped so that his face was hidden from her and pulled a chest out from under one of the benches. In it he laid the folded clothing and tossed the jewel bags, then kicked the chest back into its hiding place. Finally he picked up her supper tray, and carrying it as though he were the slave instead of the master, left the room.

It was dark when he came back, but the time had not seemed long to the waiting girl. Thoughts new and wonderful raced through her mind. She wanted to know more of lands where women were respected, where even those who were committed to a religious life were not degraded. She promised herself that she would please this strange man who was her master, no matter what it cost her in patience, humility and submission. She was surprised, too, that although she sat on a bench and so did not exert herself while she waited, the bewilderment within her skull exhausted her.

When the captain entered again, he carried a lantern in his hand and apologized for having left her in the dark. "I thought you would surely be asleep," he said. "Aren't you tired?"

"Yes." But it was a new and different tiredness she could not explain.

After asking her if she needed anything—food, water or other necessity—he blew out his lantern and lay down on the bench on the opposite side of the room. Tiptoeing so as not to disturb him, she crossed over and lay down on the floor at his feet. It was thus that a slave, male or female, must always lie when sleeping in the same room with the master. Near at hand so that any service which might be required could be rendered without delay, and with the inferior status in life clearly indicated even in the darkness.

There was enough light from the moon and stars outside the porthole so that Myrrha saw the captain's feet swing out over her head and come to rest a handsbreadth from her face. She shivered and then clenched her fists in an effort at self-control. When the captain picked her up in his arms, she was able to smile.

But this man was full of surprises. "What are you doing there?" he exclaimed rather than questioned, and strode across the room with her. Before laying her upon her own bench he held her tight against him for a moment.

"How old are you?" he asked.

"I have been a woman for two years." She knew it was forbidden that a man should take a child, and that it was her duty to inform her master that her body was ripe for the role in life for which it had been created.

"No! Precocious, yes. But not a woman," her captor burst out. Then as though reassuring himself on a decision which had been difficult for him to make, he added, "There is something fresh about you. You will always be a child—and innocent—no matter how many men have you, or how much or in what ways they abuse you."

At that he laid her down on the bench under the porthole where she might enjoy whatever breeze found its way into the tiny cabin. He stood looking down at her and shaking his head. "I doubt that even the worse of monsters could destroy the soul which you are not yet certain that you have."

She came to know this pirate captain as no other captive ever knew him. It could not be said that she ever loved him, for his companionship was too confusing. It seemed to her that he had awakened her sleeping soul. Whenever she seemed in danger of slipping back into the submissive spiritual lethargy of the harem, he scoffed at her, sneered at her, needled her into alert awareness of herself as an individual. Then with consummate gentleness, he guided her mind into appreciation of herself as a creature worthy of the respect of mankind, high and low, male and female alike.

After entering the captain's cabin she was never out of it again until the day, several weeks later, when the brigantine crossed the bar at the entrance to the Bay of Manila and dropped anchor. From her porthole, Myrrha saw the walls of the old city, gray and dirty in the sunlight, not greatly unlike the walls of her father's palace. She wondered what manner of khan lived within these walls, and if she had been spared the fate of the old women because her uncle intended her as a gift to the ruler of this land. Her lips twisted in a wry smile at the thought, for she knew that never again could she be as completely and humbly submissive as in those days before she had tasted of self-respect.

CHAPTER TEN

YRRHA stood by the open porthole for a long time gazing sometimes at the old city of Manila but more often at the life on the dock immediately before her. She had known the banks of the Mekong well, but almost everything here was strange and new. Most of the people she saw looked gaunt and hungry; their few garments hung in tatters held together by thorns, but their voices were loud and shrill and clamorous like those of her mother's people. The Mekong had boasted neither wharf nor pier. Ocean-going vessels anchored far out in the estuary of the river, and merchandise of whatever nature was brought ashore in rowboats. Here the land seemed to have been paved with planks, and men leaped from the deck of a ship to them with as much ease as when stepping from a doorway into a street. There were more people running back and forth on shore than the Princess had ever seen together in one group before.

After the many days during which she had seen nothing from the porthole but an empty expanse of water, she stared fascinated by the shouting, turbulent mob before her. She inched closer to the small square window until at last she pushed her head through the porthole. The bulging side of the brigantine cut off her vision in one direction; but what she saw from the other amazed her still further. The Bay of Manila seemed as full of vessels as an unguarded cherry tree of blackbirds when the fruit is ripening.

Myrrha wondered who owned these vessels and suddenly was struck with an amazing thought. Whoever that man might be, he surely was as wealthy as her uncle, the Vizier. The thought had never occurred to her before that there could be another man in the world as wealthy as, or perhaps even wealthier than, her uncle. If wealthier, then it seemed quite logical that he would be more powerful. She wondered if her uncle knew of this vast wealth in the world, and how he appeased the greed and envy which must seethe within him if he did. The thought was also amusing, and she laughed aloud.

She broke off abruptly, however, for a woman on the dock screamed at her. Myrrha drew her head back through the porthole but could not tear her eyes away from the woman. The creature's rags only partially covered her body. A huge basket loaded with melons was strapped to her back and steadied by a tumpline across her forehead. A child, a filth-encrusted, scabrous, scarecrow child whose bones seemed ready to burst through its skin, was perched on top of the melons; the rinds of the fruit glistened from its urine.

Quick pity flooded the Princess' heart, but died before she could even part her lips in an exclamation of compassion. The woman, her head turned sidewise, saw Myrrha watching her. She straightened her back as much as the burden on her shoulders would allow, and spat toward the porthole. As the Princess drew the folds of one of her sleeves across her face, the woman shook a grimy, gnarled fist at her. Myrrha could not understand the torrent of her words, but there was no mistaking the tone of abuse and accent of anger.

Then she heard a whistling noise. It was only a soft breath of sound before the lash of a bull whip wound around the woman's knees and her abuse ended in a shriek of pain. The creature fell forward until she was balancing herself on the knuckles of her hands. Thus, like an animal on four legs, she scurried on, tripping over the tatters of her skirt, crow-hopping like a bad-tempered horse as the bull whip bit again and again into her buttocks. Through it all she hunched her shoulders at an seemingly impossible angle, and spilled neither child nor melons from the basket.

Involuntarily the Princess looked at her own delicate fingers and then smoothed the folds of silken cloth about her hips, wondering if the human draft animal which had so briefly and unpleasantly touched her life had once been beautiful. As she turned away so that her back was to the porthole, she wondered what manner of man had fathered a child upon a woman no longer quite a woman. She wondered, too, if that spark of divinity, which lifts man above the beast—a human soul —could live within a body so degraded, a mind so brutalized.

Then the cabin darkened as though someone had drawn a curtain over a window, and a hand seized her by the arm and jerked her backward. She looked over her shoulder directly into a face as dirty and dehumanized as the woman's had been. The mouth of the face opened with a grunting noise like an infidel's pig when swill is poured into its trough. The old women of her father's harem had never told Myrrha of such men as this one, but there was no mistaking the gleam in the fellow's eyes, and she tried to pull away. The two-legged beast clutched her arm still tighter and she screamed with pain and fright.

"Let go of me. You will mar my flesh!" she shrieked.

The brute laughed. His breath was foul, like air from the city streets before the mongrel dogs and scavenging birds had devoured the night soil splattered onto the cobbles and into the mud from the second story windows. Myrrha wanted to turn her head away, but she was helpless before the bestiality in the leering face at the porthole. She saw the shoulders of the man lurch backward, felt his gnarled fingers tighten on her flesh, and heard a bellow of rage. Then, so quickly her eyes caught little more than a glint of reflected light, she saw a blade flash downward, saw it cut through flesh, heard it strike bone. A shriek of anguish pierced her ears before she saw the blade jerked away and a stream of blood spurting upward where a hand had been. Then the darkness of deepest night engulfed her like the sack of the executioner who is to drown his victim.

When Myrrha emerged once again into the world of light, the pirate captain was cradling her in his arms as a mother cradles the infant she suckles. She must have been sobbing in that strange world between consciousness and the psuedo-death into which man escapes from the horrors of this world for brief interludes, for her face was wet. So strong was habit, however, that she bit her lip and tried to hold her breath in an attempt to stifle her terror, for woman must not annoy her lord with tears.

The captain bent his head over her face so close that his curling earlocks brushed her cheek as he murmured, "Weep, little one, if the tears ease you. Weep! Weep and know that your grief is my anguish also."

With this permission from one of God's preferred creatures to give voice to the pain within her, that pain ceased to wrack her. Her gasps for breath were still labored and shook her body, but her emotions were no longer turbulent. For the first time in her life she knew the ineffable sweetness and peace of a man's strong, comforting arms about her in a love untinged by lust.

She held her body as motionless as possible, wishing she might prolong this moment of ecstasy. What fools the old women had been! she thought. To all of them love had always been a duty, even though it might have been for a few of them—and by the merest, unimportant chance—also a pleasure. But none of them had valued a kiss above a jewel, or rated the stroke of a man's hand equal to a link in the slenderest golden chain. Maybe the old women who had reared her had forgotten their youth. Or perhaps they had never loved her father as she was suddenly sure The Pearl had loved him. Or as she, The Pearl's daughter, loved this man of two voices: one loud and harsh for the crew of fierce men he commanded; one compassionate and tender. That surely must be the voice of love, she told herself.

The old women had often told Myrrha to keep her eyes ever downcast before a man, for a woman may weaken an already incredibly weak position in life if she permits her lord to study the emotions which surge through her. But just as her mother had ignored the carefully prescribed ritual of her nuptial night, Myrrha now tried to smile into the captain's eyes. It was he who now turned his face away and would not look at her.

As she gazed at him she again noted, as she had done many times before, that his skin was as olive-tinged as her own. But she had always been carefully protected from the coarsening effects of wind and sun and toil, and she knew she glowed like a jewel. His muscles bulged, hard as metal, and the skin covering them was russet-hued like wellworn leather. He made her think of a tool—a sturdy, serviceable tool that awkward, brute strength might damage but could not break. He was like metal himself, she thought, substance for either a workaday implement or the setting for a fine gem.

With his eyes still averted, the captain set her on her feet. Then he fumbled in his belt and drew out what was his sole toilet tool, a tiny jeweled dagger. He used the little knife to part his hair and, like a onetoothed comb, to force the worst snarls from his curling, shoulderlength locks. He sawed off handfuls of beard with it occasionally. He also dug wax from his ears with the point, cleaned his fingernails and trimmed the rough tops and curling edges of dried scabs with it. But most often, he used it to pick his teeth.

He held the dagger out to Myrrha saying, "Cut away the pearls with which your blouse is embroidered."

When he finally turned his eyes back to her, she felt it was not only her face but all of her—from her hair, smooth, black and gleaming as a crow's wing, to the hennaed soles of her feet—that he saw. Yet at the same time he did not seem to notice her hands partially extended as though reaching out to him in timid pleading. She wished that her outstretched fingers, like those of so many Oriental women, curved upward and backward. Regretted that she had escaped the long hours of painful strain and exercise that would have forced her knuckles to a suppleness beyond their nature. She wondered if the captain, like so many people, did not believe the rigidly straight line beautiful. If the fingers curved inward, it was said, they resembled the talons of a bird or the claws of a beast of prey. And a woman must never seem to seize! If the fingers curved away from the palm, opposite to the clutching gesture, whether a man consciously thought on the matter or not, he would feel that a woman surrendered all because she was unable to hold anything back from him.

But Myrrha's quick, fluttering, upward glances at the captain's face told her nothing of what went on in the man's mind, and for a moment she did not grasp the full meaning of his next words.

"The pearls with which you have embroidered your blouse are not worth much. Seed pearls, we call them because of their size. Believe me, I would like to give them to you. But do not think, Princess, that your new master will permit you to keep them for as long as one day."

Myrrha was stunned. She knew she was a very beautiful woman. She had been well trained in all the arts of pleasing a man. She had been told she was naturally and innately seductive. What other kind of daughter could The Pearl have mothered? This conviction had grown during her confinement in the captain's cabin, for almost daily she had been conscious of the growth of not only her master's respect, but a deeper, more intimate regard. This she understood and valued, for it was through such regard that many a man's life—and a few kingdoms—were ruled from the harem.

Myrrha drew in a great breath and then half gasped, half sobbed: "My Lord, I am of royal blood, the daughter of a Grand Mogul. And although I am thy—thy thing . . ." She could not go on, for even a princess, once she passed from the royal enclosure of her childhood, enjoyed only those privileges granted her by her master. In her dismay

Myrrha forgot the studied wiles of the harem and stared the captain in the face with unfeminine, angry boldness. The pity and grief in his eyes were unmistakable.

He replied slowly, but firmly. "I am a pirate. A professional thief, if you please, Princess. But I still retain some sense of honor. I have been paid well to sell you to the other side of the world. Although I gave my word to a greater thief than myself, I gave it under oath."

"You respect women. Or so you have said, many times. Yet your honor does not include us."

Myrrha shrank from the violence in her own words; cowered before the anger and at the same time, shame in the captain's face. She stared at her companion, speechless now. Fugitive, half formed words of pleading skittered about in her mind. When words finally became possible for her, she still did not give them voice, for she had heard too many women beg abjectly and had seen that the craven behavior of the helpless only intensifies caprice in a man.

"It is not God's will . . ." The captain broke off suddenly, his neck and cheeks purpling under their leathery tan.

Myrrha wondered half contemptuously that he, a man, should attempt to excuse himself to a mere woman. She had no way of knowing that it had been many years since he had pledged his honor before God—that the emotion surging through him now had broken the bonds of long suppression. That she, whose life he had contracted to degrade, had been the cause of this painful, unwelcome resurgence of long-forgotten morality.

"In any case, I could not keep you with me, Myrrha, because men such as I do not establish homes. Or even take women in a holy union," he went on in a lower, still slower voice.

But the girl would not be placated by his pleading. "So I am to go on the slave block!" She clenched her teeth and balled her small hands into fists to control the fury within her.

"Not that! Not the slave block for you, Princess. . . ."

"Slave!" she corrected him.

She expected him to strike her for having interrupted him. She wanted to feel the pain of his hands on her body in anger.

He waited until sure she had no more words. Then he did not raise his voice as he iterated stubbornly. "Princess, on the other side of the world, in a colony called New Spain, is a Viceroy to whom you will go. He is a man of illustrious lineage, of immense wealth and unlimited power. Power as great . . ."

Sensing envy of another's good fortune in the pirate's voice, Myrrha finished the thought for him in as coldly contemptuous words as she could manage, "—power as great as my uncle usurped from my father."

Again the captain flinched before the scorn on her face. "I know of no reason, Princess," he said, deliberately emphasizing the title, "why you should not be as—as content in this great man's household as you were in your father's palace."

He turned back to her, searching her big black eyes for some hint of understanding of his problem.

She returned his gaze steadily, and fell to wondering about his eyes as she had done many times before. When he was casually happy, they were as blue as the eyes of the harem slaves imported from the Caucasus Mountains. In the throes of passion the blue darkened and softened until it was as deep as the petals of dew-beaded morning glories. In anger there was no depth, only surface lights, like the jewelry peasant women made of dried fish scales. At such times they appeared black as her own. Now, strangely, his eyes were gray as the sea under scudding storm clouds.

"You do not want to give me up," she half whispered under her breath, and took an impulsive, gliding step forward.

Then she knew he had held other slaves in his arms before her, for although his eyes never left hers and did not change color, he turned his body sideways. The pointed tips of her breasts did not stir the matted hair on his chest but brushed against the spike-spined leather armlet he wore between his elbow and the bulge of his bicep. She shivered lightly at the small pain.

"Cut away the pearls which embroider your blouse," he commanded in an even voice. "You would not be permitted to keep them anyway."

"I gave you my jewel bag, although what I carry on my person is mine. That is the law of the Prophet! I will not cut the jewels from my dress."

"The law you quote is for Moslems, but you now pass into the hands of Christians."

"And these Christians steal from women?"

120

He did not reply immediately, but when he did it was to say apologetically, "Christianity is a religion which does not take the nature of man or the world in which he lives into account. A true follower must speak only the truth, although the laws framed by Christian men punish him cruelly for doing so. One must not covet any possession of another, although those with no covetousness in their hearts are spat upon by the frankly greedy as they die of starvation in the gutters. The Christian must be chaste . . ." He paused as though wondering if the word had meaning for a harem inmate. When he went on, it was as though he forced the words past his lips with physical effort, and his eyes were grayer and stormier than ever. "The Christian's prime virtues are truth and compassion; but—remember this well, Princess—they will burn you at the stake if you do not say that you believe as they do—as they tell you that you must believe!"

Again he held out the small dagger with which he pared his nails and cleaned his teeth. Then he cupped the palm of one hand and held it out, too. Slowly and carefully so as not to puncture the cloth, she cut the pearls from her blouse and dropped them into his hand. When she had finished he poured them into a jewel bag.

Then he drew a bundle of black cloth out of a chest, shook it out, and handed it to her. It was a *haik,* a garment designed to shield the wearer from blazing sun and burning eyes alike. The veil he threw over her head was also thick and black and shut out all air and almost all light. When he grasped her hand through haik and veil all the former intimacy of physical contact was gone, smothered by the folds of cloth as completely as the cushion of a harem executioner snuffs recalcitrance from the body of a slave.

It was a long walk he led her over rough paths that bruised her feet through her thin silken slippers. Up the ship stairs first, through a narrow passageway that bumped her elbows cruelly if she did not follow his guiding hand with the utmost care, across the deck and over the gangplank. Then the dust and stones of streets which were only paths. Several times the captain lifted her across some sort of barrier. Several times he carried her a few paces, for such precious merchandise as she must not be fouled in some pig's wallow or the human sewage dumped into the streets. It was a long uphill walk, and the black cloth swathing Myrrha caught and held all the heat of the noonday sun. Her body was wet with sweat and she was breathing heavily when the captain stopped and hammered on an iron-studded door of heavy planks.

The city of Manila was deep in its midday siesta and the pirate captain was forced to hammer again and again on the iron-bound door with the hilt of his cutlass, and to shout many times, before Myrrha heard shuffling steps and a key grating in a lock. The huge door creaked on its hinges and Myrrha was lifted across a threshold that stood almost as high as her knees. The captain and the doorman spoke to each other briefly in a language the Princess had never heard before. From the stone flagging under her feet she knew she was in a courtyard. Then after a few steps sudden shade blotted out the merciless heat of the sun and she was in a house. It was an immense structure, perhaps a palace she thought; for still guided by the captain's hand, she glided along half beside, half behind him through several large rooms.

Then they stopped and she heard the captain speaking, again in the same soft lisping tongue he had used to the doorman. But it was not the servant who replied. Evidently someone who was not used to having his sleep disturbed was distinctly annoyed and making no secret of that fact.

The captain stripped the veil and haik from Myrrha's head and body. She blinked at the sudden light, but only for a moment, for the room had been closely shuttered against the sun and her eyes quickly adjusted to the subdued light.

She saw a man big and fat as her father's head eunuch, but his skin was only swarthy, not black. He had been lying on a heap of cushions and had raised himself on one elbow to point a stubby, indignant finger at the captain. His teeth were blackened and jagged and he had slobbered out of the lower corner of his mouth. Under his untrimmed face hair his pursy lips were as shapeless as a sick ape's.

Myrrha stared at the repulsive creature and trembled. Once, in the days of her childhood, it seemed so long ago now, she had watched a snake devour a field mouse. The mouse also had trembled but seemed helpless to make any other movement. She had wondered then why the mouse had not fled. She understood why now, for she, too, felt the paralysis of overwhelming fear.

This new lord—*El Diablo Grosso*, or The Fat Devil, as she later learned to call him—was affected as greatly at the sight of Myrrha as she had been at the sight of him. His torrent of words died with a few spluttering gurgles, as though drowned in the blubber swathing his bull's neck. His outstretched arm and jabbing finger wilted like a succulent herb plunged into hot water. Myrrha could see his tongue jerk convulsively in his gaping mouth like a mute struggling helplessly to voice the thoughts that wracked him.

While El Diablo Grosso stared at her with his insatiable, ravening eyes, and licked his slobbering lips, the pirate captain walked away. Myrrha wanted to turn and run after him, or at least call out to him, praying him to take her away. But all she could do was stand and tremble and stare back at this monster—like the field mouse before the snake in her father's garden. She heard the courtyard gate screech open and clang shut; and still she stood and stared and trembled.

The Fat Devil sat up on his cushions and crooked a commanding finger at her. As helpless as the mouse, and with tiny steps, each one no longer than half the length of her feet, she obeyed. When at last she reached the edge of the heap of cushions she sank to her knees, veiled her face with her outspread fingers, and laid her forehead on the floor—and sobbed like an untrained peasant virgin.

CHAPTER ELEVEN

THE home of The Fat Devil was neither den nor palace, but a stockaded combination of both. He surrounded himself with luxuries equaling those Myrrha had known in her childhood, but never once in the months that she lived with his women was she ever called to help him bathe or to assist in his grooming following a bath. Aside from an occasional soaking in a shower of rain when on a journey, she doubted that his body had ever been completely wet in his adult lifetime.

With time, irrational terror left her when summoned to share his cushions; but her repugnance when he pressed his greasy, filth-encrusted flesh upon her body was more difficult to control than simple fright. She performed her duties to her new lord, striving for control as she had never striven for anything before. Gradually she realized, as she fought this inward battle, that the fear and repugnance of his victims delighted the brute far beyond the simple sensuality of the love act itself, and that she would be tortured in other ways if she did not cower before him. As she had learned decorous behavior in her father's harem, she now learned to whimper and grovel.

Nor were the current favorites of The Fat Devil, even the very young and beautiful, treated to any special consideration within his stockade other than that dictated by their value as trade goods. He dealt in both male and female flesh and, with only two exceptions, penned the sexes together for the obvious reason that a man who bought a strapping wench advanced in pregnancy was securing two slaves for the price of one—and the incontrovertible evidence that the human brood mare was still fertile. More than once, when showing prospective buyers his wares, Myrrha heard The Fat Devil claim paternity of the unborn slaves as assurance of their probable size and strength and consequent ability to labor.

The slaves lived in a palisaded pen behind The Fat Devil's quarters. The ground was unpaved and ungrassed, and when it rained, those who strolled about sank in the mud to their ankles or above their calves accoring to the length of the latest tropical downpour. They slept at night, and for the better part of each day, crowded together and crouching under the meager shelter of carelessly thrown together bamboo lean-tos sagging against the outer walls. The only sanitary conveniences were gourds. These were exceptionally long-handled so that their contents could be tossed over the walls.

One of the chief entertainments of the slave pen was for a man who had just relieved himself to listen carefully to the sounds outside before casting the contents of his gourd over the wall. Bets were always placed as to whether or not the dung would land on a passer-by. The screams of dismay and anger from outside were usually drowned out by the howls of joy from within when the attempt was successful.

The wagers were of necessity small: a strip of ragged cloth tied around the shoulders for a shirt, or a man might even risk the sandals he had plaited of bamboo fronds stripped from the roof of his lean-to. Sometimes one of the stronger men might offer as his pledge the privilege of a night with some female slave he had temporarily taken as his own by virtue of his superior strength. If his opponent lost, he might demand one of two things in payment; the loser's food for the next meal, or the privilege of the loser's body for that night, for every perversion was rife in the slave pen.

Myrrha and a dozen or more of the very young girls were given some physical protection. They were fed better than the herd, for a roundness of limb was one of the assets to their sale value. The soft texture of their skins was another. Consequently, they were housed under the rain- and sun-tight shelter of a tile-roofed porch. This tile was not baked clay but the curved dried bark stripped from segments of tree trunks. No privacy, however, was accorded them, for the outer wall of their shelter was a lattice of green saplings which left every private act of their lives open to the surveillance of the guards perched on shelves fastened to the stockaded walls. A male slave might press his face to the lattice and leer at the girls, or shout uncouth remarks or whisper lecherous entreaties to one of the inmates—all with impunity. The girls' only recourse was to keep well back from the lattice, turn their backs and press their hands over their ears—another source of entertainment to the less fortunate ones outside.

In the first difficult and confusing days in the slave pen, Myrrha's ears were assaulted by a babel of tongues. During the early seventeenth century the city of Manila was the central slave mart of the Orient. To fill the ever pressing need for two-legged draft animals and to pique the appetites of sated sybarites, the purveyors of human flesh collected their wares by violence, cunning and honest barter from every corner of the earth. Men of great wealth in far-distant parts of the world placed standing orders for merchandise to fill special needs or designed to titillate the strange vagaries of erotic tastes. Italian, Portuguese and Spanish were the commonest languages of trade, and to be a successful slaver—whether land-bound or sailor—a man had to be something of a linguist. Moreover, every slave pen stocked a few old women who were relatively fluent in these languages, as well as Chinese, Hindi and some of the Polynesian dialects. When prospective buyers visited a slave pen, these old women were never offered for sale but served as interpreters if such were needed.

Between buyers these old women made desultory attempts to teach new tongues to the choice wares protectingly cooped behind the lattice of The Fat Devil's slave pen. They were neither particularly gifted nor even conscientious teachers. For the most part, they were simply tired old women. But according to their natures and strength they lisped or shouted a sort of jargon at the girls, for the grasp of only a few phrases in a language always meant a higher price and a quicker sale. The old women's names had long been forgotten and each was simply called Ayah—nurse.

Myrrha's ayah taught her only one language, Spanish, and the old woman's gossip verified what the pirate captain had said: that the Princess from Cochin China had been reserved for a very important customer on the other side of the world. She was never paraded before a buyer, or stripped of her clothing and twirled about before one so that her limbs might be examined with minute care. However, many men pointed at her and argued in loud, stridently quarrelsome voices. But The Fat Devil always shook his head from side to side, sometimes so vigorously that he squeezed greasy sweat from between the creases of his bull-like neck.

Myrrha neither liked nor disliked her ayah. However, as the days went by and she became accustomed to the misery of her life, pity for the poor old creature grew in her heart. Also, she soon realized that the old women who had any art or skill to pass on to others as teachers were the fortunate ones among the aged. Those no longer desirable as women became beasts of burden. And when a draft animal—male or female—became incapable of due drudgery, it was no longer considered worth the daily food ration of plantain and rice. Such were thrust out of their owner's gate into the street where they fought with the dogs for scraps of offal until too weak to do more than crouch in some corner and there await death.

Myrrha learned quickly and easily and would have enjoyed the simple, limpid music of the new language had it not been that Spanish was the native tongue of The Fat Devil. The fact that she must now try to converse with him as well as appease his brutish lusts, intensified her misery; for the man's mind was as crude and gross as his body.

"Por favor, amo, no le entiendo," was on her lips oftener than any other answer.

The words—Please master, I do not understand you—were often spoken falsely. They earned her many a blow, and spared her worse than the physical pain.

The Princess also learned much more than a new language in the slave pen of The Fat Devil. There was a second latticed porch adjoining the enclosure of the so-called virgins. At first she thought this second group of protected inmates were female like herself. They were similar in that they were beautiful, young and delectable harem tidbits, created and groomed for special customers with exotic appetites.

Their male bodies were swathed in folds of swinging cloth like women. Most of them wore corselets of leather which were seldom removed from their bodies. The boys, none of them more than children in their early teens, screamed with pain when the corselets were laced upon them, whether it was for the first time, or new ones adjusted to size as they grew. The corselets were made of wet, green hide, and the lacings were pulled so tight that the children gasped for breath. As the leather dried, it shrank, and the corselets became even tighter and molded the bodies they encased into exaggerated imitations of the female form.

The Fat Devil kept an even greater and more carefully zealous watch over the boys than over the virgins, clothed them better, fed them on finer food, although the quantity of food was so strictly limited that Myrrha often heard a younger child weep from hunger and between sobs beg for more. None of these boys was ever punished by the lash; but if The Fat Devil could not encircle a lad's waist with a short length of rope he carried tied to his belt, the corselet was laced tighter and all food and liquid were withheld for a day. The boys' legs were hobbled so that they learned to walk with mincing steps and they spent long hours in strictly supervised practice of swaying their hips, twisting their shoulders and fluttering their eyelashes in pseudo-modesty.

Their voices, regardless of their ages, were childish trebbles, lacking all resonance—a mark of the male castrated in youth. Myrrha had left her father's harem virgin, but not ignorant in the ways of her father's world. Still, theoretical knowledge scarcely prepared her for what happened fairly often within her sight if she did not turn her eyes away— the castration of each scarcely pubescent boy selected for his incredible role in life as a pseudo-woman. There was no closing her ears, however, to the shrieks of the victims of this brutal operation performed without anaesthetic of any kind.

A child was spread-eagled and held flat on his back on the floor. The brute who acted as surgeon sat on the boy's chest and inserted a splinter of bamboo in the urinal tract, then up into the body, jabbing and twisting the crude instrument the while, hoping thereby to sever the seminal duct or effectively block it with scar tissue. Then the boy's legs were bound tightly together and kept bound until the wound was completely healed—or the child was dead.

Such a boy, successfully castrated, and his masculine frame tortured into some semblance of the female figure, brought a much higher price than the most beautiful young girl. This was because girls were plentiful and supplied by nature without trouble to men. On the other hand, so many of the male victims died from shock and infection that there were seldom enough to supply the demand.

Each boy who lived through the operation was given a small ebony or sandalwood box beautifully carved or chased with silver wire, or inlaid with nacre. He was taught to use the cosmetics therein: henna

128

for the palms of his hands and the soles of his feet; kohl to encircle his eyes and to darken, lengthen and broaden his eyebrows; unguents to soften his skin; oils of various herbs and flowers with which to perfume his hands and shoulders and knees.

If a boy began to sprout a beard or mustache, he was sold as quickly as possible with little or no haggling over price. Failing a buyer with perverted tastes, the child was stripped of his woman's garb, his corselet and his cosmetics and turned into the common slave pen. When this happened, Myrrha learned that the poorest slave is made of the same stuff as the richest master; for the fate of such a boy was a cruel one indeed. Few lived beyond the first night. Even the old ayahs, brutalized by life as they had been forced to live it, shuddered with horror at the fate of these boys.

Curiously enough, The Fat Devil considered himself a religious man—or his pretense may have added to the prices he received for some of his merchandise. In any case, he lined his purse generously by rendering unto Caesar that which belonged to the Caesars of his day and age. And while he did not go into all lands to preach the Gospel, by his command the Gospel was hurled at the creatures gathered from the obscure corners of the earth and herded together in his slave pen.

At The Fat Devil's invitation a strange man periodically visited the slaves. He was garbed not unlike a Moslem peasant, except that his robes were always black, and instead of a fez he wore a hat something like a shallow, dented platter. This man had two names. When he was absent he was called *El Pietro*—The Priest. In his presence Myrrha was taught to say, *Padre*—Father.

As time went on, Myrrha and her companions behind the lattice gradually learned a type of rote behavior before this spiritual parent. Ordinarily the Padre spoke to them in Spanish; and as Myrrha learned more of that language, it seemed to her that he talked of Allah, the God she had always known. Allah, Supreme Being, even more powerful that her uncle. A Being who once used His power to create this world, and man to possess it, and woman for the delectation of man.

It was probably because of her imperfect grasp of the language that Myrrha silently questioned El Padre's concept of God on two points: first, he seemed obsessed with the life of a prophet whom Myrrha remembered as being of very little importance to Moslems. El Padre sometimes called this prophet something that sounded like Yehsu: other times he said Jesus. Secondly, El Padre said that women did not gain entry into Paradise by virtue of physical beauty and the skill and artistry with which they submitted to and pleased men.

Like the Portuguese pirate captain, he believed they had souls, the same as men. He said that they earned Paradise by the practice of the same virtues mandatory to men. Myrrha wondered how this could be since El Padre also stressed that unquestioning obedience to their earthly masters was an added virtue laid upon women. If he, like the pirate captain, held women worthy of respect, he never mentioned that fact. Nor did his admonitions to The Fat Devil's chattels do anything to arouse or foster self-esteem.

The first of the new prayers which were taught Myrrha by rote were to a woman—the mother, not of a khan or grand mogul, but of the god Jesús. She noticed that it was taught to man and woman, boy and girl alike.

"Ayah," Myrrha asked her nurse one day, "if women are creatures inferior to men, what do men hope to gain by prayers to a woman? What can a woman, even the mother of a prophet or a god do for those so far above her?"

The old woman did not know the answer, but she would not admit ignorance.

"Foolish questions! Always foolish questions! Why do you not listen to El Padre, then you will not have to ask foolish questions," she shouted. But for the rest of that day she watched Myrrha with a frown on her face.

The ayah's oblique pretense did not fool Myrrha, but it did suggest that if anyone could answer her questions, it would be El Pietro.

"Padre—Illustrious Señor," Myrrha murmured to the priest on his next visit to the slave pen. "Why do men pray to a woman?"

The priest turned startled eyes upon her. "So," he cried out. "Teach a woman a little, and then she asks a lot!" Then he turned to The Fat Devil with a sneer on his face, demanding, "Do you offer her for sale as a scholar? Or a woman?"

The Fat Devil made a noise with his mouth like a child striving to catch the juice from an overripe peach with which its face is splattered. Then he rolled his eyes about and hugged his fat chest with his ham-like arms. "Aaaaah! A woman! And what a woman!"

130

Both men bellowed with laughter, and Myrrha's ayah joined in with a shrill cackle. The Fat Devil turned to her with a snarl. "You!" he shouted. "Is this the way you teach my property obedience? You are damaging my merchandise, you—you hag." He lifted his arm as though to strike her; then, remembering that she would be difficult to replace, gave her only a shove that sent the frail old creature against a wall with sufficient force to knock the breath out of her. She sank to her knees, covered her face with one arm and whimpered.

Regardless of the inexplicable nature of the prayers, Myrrha liked the sound of the cadenced words; and although at first they were nothing but sibilant breath on her lips, prayer became a quiet power within her which gave her the strength and the courage to live through each day. In spite of the fact that it seemed irrational to her to pray to a woman, when one gave the matter sober thought, it was also a comfort to do so. One's heart could be opened to a woman as it never could be to any male creature, human or divine. Could a male god, who in the beginning had doomed woman to an existence of soulless serfdom, really be concerned with their individual miseries and insignificant desires? Myrrha asked herself many times. She could not arrive at a satisfying answer without help, but gradually the great and deep meaning of the words of that first prayer sank into her soul and permeated her being. After that, on those occasions when all peace was shattered by the shrieks of mortal agony from the boys' enclosure, or sleep was murdered by horrors perpetrated in the slave pen at night, she whispered over and over in an exquisite agony of relief that she had not been born male:

"Holy Mary, Mother of God,
Pray for us sinners now . . ."

Truly a woman who had been privileged to bear a god was blessed above all other women, as the prayer said. Possibly she could alleviate the agony of another female creature.

El Padre often talked to the girls in a language even none of the old ayahs understood. When he did this, sometimes he faced the girls and made signs over them with his hands. Other times he turned his back and bowed and waved his hands about. Myrrha and the "virgins" squatted on their heels since no cushions were supplied them to sit on except when they served their master in his bedchamber. Then at certain intervals El Padre nodded to the ayahs, and the old women commanded the girls to rise to their feet or to stand on their knees according to what Myrrha decided was whim, since no purpose seemed to be served by the activity other than to awaken them from the daydreaming into which they were lulled by the monotony of El Padre's low-toned, unending chant.

Then came a day when the girls were all swathed in lengths of white muslin. Their usual head cloths were taken away and wisps of the same white stuff were tied over their hair. They stood on their knees before El Padre and he threw a spray of water on the face of each, touched their cheeks with a thumb he had greased from a little phial, gave each a crumb of bread to eat and a drop of wine to drink—but not enough to appease a small bird's hunger or thirst—and rested a hand on the head of each while he prayed in the strange language.

Then he told them they were the same as newly born infants, that nothing they had ever done before in their lives was held against them as a fault by God. He also told them that if they repeated many times each day the beautifully sonorous prayers they had been taught by rote, and if they never lied, stole or lay with a man to whom they had not been joined in marriage by another spiritual parent like himself, they would enter Heaven, as he, too, called Paradise. And there, no man would—or could—demand anything from them. He ended this strange discourse by stressing that unquestioning obedience to those placed in authority over them was required of a good Christian, slave or otherwise.

All during this ceremony The Fat Devil leaned against the lattice and leered at his "virgins." He walked away with El Padre, promising as he went that the spiritual welfare of the now Christian "virgins" would always be uppermost in his thoughts—but not before whispering to an ayah and jabbing a finger in Myrrha's direction. Myrrha never saw El Pietro again.

She decided that El Padre was either a fool himself, or believed that women were incapable of reason. Harem-born, there was little she did not know of procreative processes. She knew that neither bird nor animal—including man—was ever full grown at birth. And it was obvious that neither she nor any other girl behind the lattice had been shrunk to infancy by the grease and the few drops of water dashed in

132

their faces. Nor could a slave obey a lecherous master and remain chaste. Very little that El Padre had said made sense. Myrrha tossed her head in a gesture of contempt, and followed her ayah to The Fat Devil's bedchamber.

By signs and with her first few words of Spanish, Myrrha tried to tell her ayah that she was with child. The old woman either ignored her, or deliberately misunderstood. During her master's infrequent moments of small kindnesses, she tried to tell him too of her condition. The Fat Devil seemed to look upon her gestures and stammered protestations as a sort of modesty designed to further heighten his lust. In any case, he was not Moslem and the injunctions of Allah demanding continence for a woman during her periods of uncleanliness or gestation meant even less to him than the commandments of his own God.

But one or the other understood her finally, for one day her ayah stripped her completely before the Fat Devil. Her body had not yet begun to swell, but both of them prodded her belly with insistent fingers as though searching out the size of the child within her. Still unsure in the language, Myrrha could not be certain that she understood all that The Fat Devil and her ayah said. It seemed, however, that they spoke of a land called New Spain, a country so far away that even with fair winds and no foul weather, it took a good ship at least a long season to cover the miles between it and the city of Manila.

"I can have her for another month," The Fat Devil gloated.

"Another month," the ayah agreed. Then she added, "But we dare no more than a month, before we make her a virgin again."

The Fat Devil roared with laughter and kicked the ayah until she cackled like a pullet that has just laid its first egg. There was no meaning in the words for Myrrha, and no humor, but she was afraid not to curve the corners of her lips upward in an obedient smile. At the expression her master bellowed with mirth so loudly that he was compelled to fall backward on his cushions and gasp for breath. Still cackling in a shrill falsetto, the ayah went away and left Myrrha alone with the monster.

Myrrha reached for her robe, but her master whirled about with surprising agility for one so obese and snatched it out of her fingers.

There was no question about it now—The Fat Devil knew of her condition. When he tried to seize her arm she drew back. He caught her ankle instead, and she had no choice but to come to him or fall on the stone floor. But even as she lay in his arms, she pleaded her right to continence and he laughed at her. Then in a confused hysteria, she beat his head and shoulders with her fists as he had his will of her.

His passion sated, he did not send her away with a careless wave of his hand as always before. Instead Myrrha was whipped. Not beaten like a common slave, but punished like a refractory concubine whose beauty—and therefore value—is still too great to risk marring. Her arms were spread wide and she was tied by her wrists to a rod held by a slave just high enough above her head so that she was compelled to bear her weight on her toes or the aching muscles of her arms. The whip was a long, flexible black rod of a strange substance called india rubber. She did not believe that the usual bamboo cane could have hurt more, but The Fat Devil told her, as her ayah laid stroke after stroke across her back and buttocks under his direction, that india rubber would not break her skin as bamboo would have done. However, to make assurance doubly sure, a heavy scarf of silk had been wound about her body first.

Myrrha knew that slaves were sometimes beaten to death; and although she knew she was too valuable to be killed, something within her died under the lash—that inexplicable feeling that royal blood sets a woman aside and makes her different from all other human beings except those also of royal blood. The Princess ceased to exist. It was only another trembling slave who was untied from the whipping bar. It was a fearful, abjectly subservient slave who answered The Fat Devil's summons for one more month.

At the end of that period Myrrha was given very little food or water for more than a week, and was drenched repeatedly with cathartics and infusions of herbs that puckered her lips and stung her mouth and throat unmercifully. After a few days she was so weak from hunger and the loss of body fluids that it was difficult for her to stand upon her feet, but her ayah was always at hand and would permit her very little rest, even at night.

"The life is stubborn within you," she said finally. "We must try other measures."

134

"No! No! I will lose the child if you do not let me rest," Myrrha pleaded, weeping and trying to pull away.

"Lose the child?" her ayah burst out. "You fool! What do you think we have been trying to do to you, all along?"

Myrrha drew back and turned, but there was nowhere to flee, no way she could escape the ayah and The Fat Devil. She was compelled to lie on her back while the old woman, at first resting a part of her weight on a table, kneeded her charge's stomach with the heels of her feet. But when hour followed hour, and even day followed day, and the life within the slave remained obdurate, the ayah finally trod with her full weight upon the girl. Myrrha wept from the pain in her abused body, but the old woman grimly ignored her pleas for rest— only a moment of rest! With the first pang that was like a red hot knife cutting her in two between navel and groin, her face twisted grotesquely and a shriek of mortal agony tore through her lips. The old woman stepped off her body immediately.

But the girl's torture did not end with that small relief. The ayah called to a huge male slave who had been loitering near the lattice, waiting. He seized Myrrha by her wrists and lifted her until she dangled from his raised fists, limp and helpless, without even her toes touching the floor. Vaguely, because her body was a sodden mass of misery, she wondered if there was greater pain in the world than that she suffered. Wondered until the ayah grasped her ankles, flexed her knees and then jerked downward with all her strength. Mercifully Myrrha fainted—and unmercifully revived without help some time later. And the torture continued and she fainted again.

When she regained consciousness the second time it was night. She was lying on a mat in a corner of the virgins' pen. The searing pain was gone, but she could not move her body which was so stiff and sore that it did not feel as though it belonged to her from the waist down. The ayah was squatting beside her, her head swaying loosely on her thin neck as though asleep. But when the girl stirred, the old woman peered at her nearsightedly in the gloom, rose to her feet and pattered away to return immediately with a bowl of hot rice water. The liquid sickened Myrrha, but the old woman made her swallow every drop. Then she told the girl that what had been life within her body now scampered through the streets of Manila in the stomach of some

135

mongrel cur outside the walls of the slave pen. There was no mistaking the triumph in the old woman's voice. It was as though she expected her victim to share in her satisfaction at a hideous job well done.

For the next few weeks Myrrha was fed almost as well as she had been in her father's home. But there was no control of her appetite now. Instead food was forced upon her at each meal long after she felt sated, for her emaciated body must round out again. She had just begun to believe that the torture of her body was ended when the ayah performed one more operation. The edges of her vulva were scarified and the raw flesh sewn tightly together, leaving only the smallest of necessary apertures. When, a couple of months later, Myrrha again changed masters, the festering had ceased and healing was complete. Even under the most brutal examination, she appeared a virgin, her chastity seemingly having been safeguarded by the oldest device known to the peddlers of human flesh of that day.

This time, as before, there was no bargaining over Myrrha—within her sight and hearing, at least. She was simply bathed, wrapped in clean clothing, and turned over to another man, a man who was to take her halfway around the earth to a place sometimes called the New World, sometimes New Spain.

136

CHAPTER TWELVE

So far as Myrrha was concerned, men were divided into two groups. Those whom Allah favored were born of rich and titled or otherwise privileged parents. Then there were the countless hordes born to serve. Perhaps it was a heritage from her mother, perhaps it was because of the lax harem discipline of her doting, senile father, in any event Myrrha differed from the usual harem offspring in her pity of those born outside the love of Allah.

Neither the pirate captain nor the Manila trader had changed her estimate of mankind. She had not been affected emotionally or spiritually by the equally superficial ministrations of the trader's ayahs or his Christian priest. Nor had she grown able to stifle or blunt within herself the quick pain which often left her weak and trembling when she had to witness the agonies inflicted on the unfortunates of her world. It was as though the whip fell on her back, too, when she saw another slave lashed. And although the infant torn from her body had as yet been only half formed, she shared the agony of women from whose arms living, breathing children were wrenched.

There was dread of the unknown in Myrrha's heart as she followed at the heels of her new master, but there was actually more concern in her mind that she should successfully avoid the heaps of human and animal excreta in her path. Whatever fate lay before her either of misery or privilege was unimportant because she herself, being a woman, was insignificant in the world that Allah had created for men. Allah was the only god that seemed at all plausible to her.

What was important at the moment was that she should not foul her sandals or the hem of the dress she wore. Both sandals and dress were evidence of the generosity of man—God's preferred creature. She was well aware that occasionally a slave passed from a penurious master to a new owner mother-naked—if the new master was not disposed to pay a good price for rags to cover her shame. Myrrha was honestly grateful that her body was adequately covered as she once again crossed the high threshhold of The Fat Devil's stronghold.

She feared the unknown, but she knew that in spite of her fear, whatever service was required of her by her master, she would perform it. She did not give that unknown service conscious thought, for in all her experience so far, the men of her world had required but one thing of highborn women—the gratification of carnal desire.

As they strode along the strip of land that served both as city street and public sewer she gazed in frank curiosity at the back of her new master. About her, jostling her shoulders and treading on her heels was a bevy of more female slaves, a few of whom had shared the latticed porch with her. These were followed by a much larger group of male slaves each with an iron collar around his neck and at least three chains radiating from it to similar collars on the necks of fellow slaves. It was an ingenious device whereby any slave making a break for freedom would be jerked in at least three directions by the comparatively inert bodies of his fellows. Less than a half dozen armed men were needed to guard any number of male slaves thus fettered.

Seemingly the guards paid no attention to the girls, anyone of whom could have darted down an alleyway and possibly have escaped. None, however, made such a move. Each knew that the world offered no more than the very briefest hiding place to a female slave. And if that slave were young and beautiful, her flight would quickly accumulate a tail of pursuing males until she was captured and shared by them even as she lay dying from the brutality of their lust.

Myrrha's eyes saw and grasped the situation, but she gave it scant thought because she was intrigued by the appearance of the man in front of her. She had never seen anyone so tall, not even the Negro eunuchs in her father's harem. From his waist down he seemed as slender as a young woman, but she could see that his bones were not small like her own or other Asiatics'. Not like the bones of the Portuguese pirate to whom she had come so close to giving her heart. This man's knob-kneed legs seemed clumsy to her, like the huge spiked war clubs carried into battle by the foot soldiers of Cochin China. Above the slender legs and hips the shoulders were massive. But the man's body was as lean as a hungry peasant's. The shoulders stood out

138

square from the neck with no hint of womanish slope; and the neck was as broad as the head it supported.

She remembered that his eyes were a cold, hard blue. One did not read his thoughts behind his glance.

His hair was neither straight like her own, nor kinky like the top-knots of the African eunuchs. It was caught at the back of his head, clubbed there, and tied with a ribbon. But the wisps which escaped and caressed his cheeks and neck, curved as delicately as the petals of a full-blown chrysanthemum. She guessed that the man was *Anglais,* English, and therefore a pirate like the Portuguese captain. The top of her head reached no higher than the middle of his back.

She wondered idly as she stepped along behind the frosty-eyed, golden-haired giant if the tales she had heard about the Anglais were true. That they had been bred on a cold, foggy, godforsaken little is-land at the barbaric end of the world. A desolate land whose frost had chilled their blood and so, where women were concerned at least, they were not quite men. And where men were concerned, they relied solely on the strength of their brutish bodies and had little skill in the use of their immense weapons and no understanding at all of the refinements of intrigue.

The Englishman's ship was also a brigantine, but bigger and in-finitely cleaner than the Portuguese captain's vessel. She was not com-pelled, as had happened before, to draw her breath in short, shallow gasps to overcome nausea. The sailors on this ship were always busy. When they were not aloft they did not loll about the deck drinking and gambling at cards or dice. Nor did the Englishman himself spend the bulk of his days in his cabin whiling away the long tedious hours with a woman. The fair-haired giant stood on deck, his legs wide apart against the rolling of his vessel, and apparently saw every move a member of his crew made, whether his head was turned toward that man or not. He would glance at the sails overhead and if one were only a little slack in the breeze, would bellow at the helmsman: "Steady as she goes, Mr. 'Awkins." Then the helmsman would put his wheel over a spoke or two and parrot his captain's command: "Steady as she goes, Sir William."

There was almost always a book in this captain's hand, and he seemed able to read while he watched his crew, for he frequently flipped a page even while shouting at a sailor. When he sat in his cabin, Myrrha learned, he filled many blank pages with writing.

The ever busy men worked at varied chores. Some sat cross-legged on deck and patched sails. Others inspected coils of rope and when a worn spot was discovered, cut it out, unwound the twisted ends and spliced them together again until the rope was once more strong as when new. That done, they shredded the discarded fragments until they looked like a tangled mat of the finest grass and stored it away in bags. When a crack appeared in the deck or the siding of the ship, this shredded rope was pounded into the seam and covered with hot pitch.

Hour after hour, day after day men hammered rust from the links of the huge anchor chain. And when at last the end was reached, they started back at the beginning, for the ocean air and the salt spray produced rust almost as fast as it was scaled off by the hammer. Because of the work these men did, their hair, their skin and the clothing they wore was as red as cinnabar—the ore of mercury from which jewelsmiths carved beads and rings and bracelets for women, and vases and other *ojets d'art* for men of wealth.

Although Myrrha's life in general on the Englishman's ship was radically different from her days with the Portuguese pirate, her hours on deck were strictly limited. She knew she was the most beautiful, the most delectable of the young morsels purchased and brought aboard, but she was never taken to her new master's cabin. Nor were any of the other girls called for often by this strange man whose blood must surely have been as cold as his frosty eyes. Instead, Myrrha and her companions were herded into a large room below the poop deck. There they were as carefully guarded and their days more carefully supervised than in a harem.

They shared the cabin with a black task mistress, less cruel but more exacting than any eunuch. Her first command was that the girls should call her Mother Mora. "Ai-i-i-i, ai-i-i-i, who can number the little daughters I have trained," she would exclaim sometimes in a voice that was a strange mixture of sadness and pride. But it was pure pride and nothing else whenever she added, "When I have finished with a girl, she is fit to grace the best home in New Spain."

"Have you ever borne a child? Of your own, I mean?" Myrrha asked her one day.

The woman hooded her eyes with her thick lids and looked away and would not answer other than to say, "You are my daughter for the moment. Let us each make as much of that as we can—for it is all we have!"

Mother Mora was not quite so tall as the English captain, but from her shoulders to the hem of her voluminous skirt she was twice as broad as any other human being Myrrha had ever seen. Myrrha could not help staring at her incredibly fat legs. They reminded the Princess from Cochin China of the legs of her father's elephants; and the splayed, down-curved, horn-nailed ends of her bare feet protruding from under the last billow of fat were like an elephant's toes. The woman's breadth made her seem as misshapen as a dwarf.

The Negress wore two garments only. She wound a red and yellow scarf about her head which she shaved almost daily with a fragment of broken glass. It fascinated her charges to watch her shave the back of her head, pressing the glass forward with one hand, but guiding it with a finger which rested half on, half before the cutting edge, and never once marking her skin with the tiniest scratch. The second garment was a voluminous dress caught in at the waist by a length of bast rope from which dangled a foot-long, heavy iron key. Presumably it was the only key to the cabin door, for on the infrequent occasions when the English captain entered the girls' quarters, he knocked and Mother Mora unbolted the lock to him. And except for the two men, always the same two, who brought and removed their bath water, carried them their food, and emptied their chamber pot, the captain was the only man to cross that threshold during the long voyage from Manila to Acapulco.

Myrrha noted on first sight of the huge Negress that there was no whip, silken, india rubber or otherwise, dangling from the woman's belt. A quick glance around the barren room revealed no other instrument of punishment or torture. Myrrha, naturally obedient to begin with and having learned caution in The Fat Devil's slave pen, resolved silently to study her mistress's whims carefully, for she shuddered at the thought of a blow from the heavy iron key. All the slaves learned very quickly, however, that Mother Mora usually controlled her charges by taking a frightened and therefore sobbing or defiant girl into her arms and pressing such a one's face deep into her soft bosom until peace and the will to obedience once again filled the slave's heart. But when it was not fear but simple recalcitrance that

141

made a slave unruly, it was surprising how swiftly and easily the Negress could hoist one knee into the air and flip a girl across it, stomach downward. She never bruised the flesh, but the smacking administered on bare skin stung for hours and was not forgotten for days.

Mother Mora's first act of authority was to assign each girl to a bunk, speaking to each in Spanish first; then if that was not understood, using various dialects of Chinese with seeming fluency. She did not ask the girls for their names, but quickly nicknamed each with what appeared to be willful caprice: Karen, Cochin, Twanin, even Yalu Doll, Pekin Pest, Szechwan Doe, and Thai-ee Kitten. One girl with a black dot tatooed between her eyebrows became Hindy.

When Mother Mora faced Myrrha, she swept the Princess with a swift look the length of her body and then stared into her face a longer moment than she had wasted on any of the others. Myrrha stood waiting, straight and slender as a yet unbranched poplar seedling, neither arrogant nor obsequious, until the Negress murmured, "Aquí, Chinita, tu tienes la cama." [Here, little Chinese lady, is your bed.]

To Myrrha, and Myrrha alone, she seemed to pay unconscious but fleeting respect, but a respect that Myrrha sensed it would be unwise to presume upon. Never, in the months that followed did the Negress show the Princess from Cochin China any favoritism, or coddle her with an laxity of discipline. Nor did she ever refer to the girl in other terms than *La China*—The Chinese Lady.

It seemed to Myrrha—or La China as she quickly came to think of herself—that Mother Mora was possessed by an irritating devil of busy-ness. Certainly, whether it was from personal conviction or a sense of duty, she did not believe in idle hands or empty minds; and she did not leave the girls much leisure time in which to be bored. Consequently, there was little quarreling among them, and some among them learned, for the first time in their lives, that it is a pleasant thing to help another freely and gladly.

No filth or vermin was tolerated by Mother Mora. Each girl bathed every day in a huge wooden tun filled with hot water, soaking and soaping her body until her skin glowed rosy as the last rays of sunset on a high cloud. Each rinsed herself in a second tun. The bath was water from the sea and the corrosive effect of the salt was counteracted by warm oil rubbed well into the skin. Each day each girl must rake

142

some other girl's head with a comb so fine-toothed that it took real effort to force the hair between the teeth. At first it was painful; but within a few days heads stopped itching and scalp sores, no longer irritated by nibbling insects or scratching nails, healed themselves.

Every day following their baths each girl washed the garments she had just shed and donned those washed the previous day. What seemed strongest of all to La China was that when night fell, she did not lie down upon her bunk in her garments of the day but must strip everything from her body and cover herself from neck to ankles with a shapeless, one-piece robe. This, too, had to be washed daily. And after all garments were clean, each girl must wash the floor under her bed, and the wall back of it and the ceiling above it.

"A stranger would not know that people lived in this enclosure," La China said to Mother Mora one day upon returning to the room from the deck. "There is no odor of human beings here."

"Do you enjoy the stink of dirty women?" the Negress snapped.

La China had never given the matter thought before, but admitted now that the stench of dirty flesh is one of the less pleasant experiences of life.

At first La China, as well as the other girls, thought their task mistress a fool, and were resentful of the servant's labor imposed upon them. However, while some among them continued to resent the effort it required, others admitted it was pleasant to sleep through a night untroubled by vermin in their hair or on their bodies.

When the daily cleansing had been finished, Mother Mora led her charges up on deck, each girl carrying her wet laundry heaped in her arms. Here, on deck, the passion for cleanliness was as great as below, La China discovered; for the male slaves, still chained neck to neck, were always scrubbing something about the ship. The deck was always damp, and white as new wood from its constant polishing with sand, cocoanut fiber and sea water.

The girls held their wet dresses and night robes over their heads and flapped them vigorously if there was not enough breeze to do that for them, until they were dry. Then Mother Mora compelled them to trot back and forth the length of the ship until their breath came in quick little gasps and their hearts fluttered.

The first few times on deck La China expected the blond captain's gaze. True, it did rest on her oftener and longer than upon her companions. But no matter how many sly glances she stole in his direction, there was never warmth in the cold blue eyes. Rather, he seemed always to be appraising her and her fellow slaves, as a merchant who knows he has exceptional art treasures at his disposal, and estimates their value carefully before naming a price. So gradually that she was not aware of its happening, she stopped watching him furtively, ceased wondering what artifices would lessen the pain and humiliation of submitting to him.

She wondered if this man who looked upon women coldly was passionless in all other masculine respects as well. That question was answered on the one day Mother Mora forgot to lock the cabin behind her when she herded her girls on deck. As usual, she did not walk before, beside or behind them; but with amazing agility for one of her bulk, was always between them and whatever man or group of men they passed. If those they encountered did not make way for her, she pushed them aside as easily as the ship below them parted the waves. If any man snarled at this treatment, Mother Mora brought her huge iron key down on his skull with a blow that could be heard from end to end of the ship and made the fellow draw back and blink at her in genuine if resentful respect.

When the girls returned to their cabin that day, the first to enter shrieked with fright. The Negress leaped forward and was the second person over the threshold. When La China first peered into the room all she could see was Mother Mora's broad back. A shift in her guardian's position disclosed a slave crumpled up in a corner where she had fallen and a sailor with his arms flung out before him, one fist clenched and the other holding a long-bladed knife. The Princess had seen women fight one with the other; she had even watched as some female struggled in the arms of a punishing eunuch. But she had never seen a man and a woman face each other in combat like equals—a man with a knife against a woman armed only with a key. Myrrha wished there was something she could do to help Mother Mora. She lifted one foot slowly, fearfully.

But she did not step into the cabin, for a hand grasped her shoulder. A hand which exerted no pressure and yet was heavy. A big-boned hand with repulsive tufts of rufous hair between the knuckles. She stood motionless beside her English master and waited for him to draw

144

his cutlass. He was as still as she, however, and merely watched his black Amazon.

Slowly the two in the cabin circled about facing each other at little more than arm's length. Repeatedly the sailor feinted, sometimes with his clenched fist, other times with the knife. La China could not see that Mother Mora so much as flinched. The woman's eyes were so wide open that the iris of each was white-ringed. They stared at the foolhardy man unblinking, fixed, like painted eyes in the face of a doll, yet they seemed to see everything before them.

Suddenly the sailor lunged, striking out at the woman's belly with his knife. Quick as he was, the Negress was quicker. There was only a flick of her wrist, but the heavy, foot-long iron key clubbed against the sailor's arm. His knife flew through the air, clanged against the ceiling, then clattered to the floor. The man howled once, then stared at his arm which dangled at a grotesque angle, both bones broken.

Mother Mora picked up the knife and handed it to her lord. Then as casually as though such struggles were an everyday occurrence, she placed a hand on the sailor's back and shoved him toward the door. The Englishman did not touch the man but motioned down the passageway with the point of the fool's own knife. The girls huddled against the walls until the two men were gone and then tumbled into the cabin awkwardly, like vegetables spilling from a basket.

"Pues, bien!" hissed the Negress, her face smug with satisfaction in a job well done. "Ahora, señoritas, hablamous Español." And she calmly proceeded with the daily language lesson because, as she assured them many times, they must all be proficient in the Spanish tongue before reaching Mexico. Unlike the ayahs in Manila, Mother Mora was a good teacher. She was fluent in the language she taught, and she demanded and got the respectful, sustained attention of her pupils.

The lesson this day, however, was interrupted by a howl of terror and a splash. Mother Mora leaped to the square-paned window overlooking the wake of the ship, the girls close behind her. The Negress spread her arms like wings and La China pressed her forehead against the woman's armpit. Behind the ship, towed like a log, was the sailor who had stolen into their cabin. A rope had been passed about his chest, and his arms tied behind his back. La China shrank

145

from the pain she knew the man suffered from the contorted broken limb but there was no indignation at the barbarism. Whoever offends those in power must expect to suffer excruciating pain; and though she shrank from the horror of the punishment, she did not question the justice of it.

From her position, only a few feet above the water, La China saw nothing but the struggling man in the ship's wake. Suddenly those on the poop deck above her head began hauling in on the rope. The sailor's body did not leave the water until it was less than twenty feet away from her. Then twice she saw triangular fins to the side of the wake. The man's screams pierced her ears until she pressed her palms over them to shut out the stabbing pain. She could not tear her eyes away from the spectacle, however, and she saw the sailor—scarcely more than half a body now—hoisted out of the water and disappear from sight above her. She did not have time to turn away from the window before the remnant of a man, now freed from the tow rope, came hurtling downward so close that she felt she might have stretched an arm out between the bars and touched him. She drew back and turned away, sick and trembling.

"Ai-i-i-i-i! Ai-i-i-i-i!" Mother Mora moaned, but in a tone devoid of grief. "Sir William only meant to cool his hot blood with cold brine. Ah well, he was a fool!" And she resumed her language instruction as calmly as though her lord had merely swatted a fly.

Three times more during the voyage La China lived through days of violence. Each of those times the Negress shuttered the stern window with heavy planking held in place by a massive wooden beam that swung down from the ceiling. All light was shut out, all ventilation stopped. The heavy, quickly fouled air, the darkness, and the feeling of loneliness which swept over her made La China wonder if this was what the grave would be like.

Mother Mora, however, did not allow her girls opportunity to give way to despondency or fright. Theretofore she had given no evidence of any religious knowledge. Now, there in the dark, she had her charges kneel, clasp their hands over their hearts and repeat after her verses in yet another strange language until they knew them by heart— cadenced lines which the Manila slaver's priest had told them they should memorize but had been too lazy to teach them himself.

With time their eyes gradually became accustomed to the gloom,

146

and periodically Mother Mora commanded them to rise, stamp their feet and rub their numbed knees. But as long as the stern window remained shuttered, the girls must keep on kneeling and with clasped hands repeat the newly learned verses endlessly.

The first time the endless *Glorias, Aves* and *Pater Nosters* were impressed upon the slaves occurred when the English captain sighted a caravel. The caravel was an old-fashioned tub, unseaworthy and certainly not much of a prize. Nevertheless, Sir William pursued and easily overtook it. After pillaging it, he rammed it and sank it with all hands on board.

The second time, the brigantine lay becalmed from early morning until mid-afternoon. It was hard to breathe, for the air was heavy and hot, and the sky, even at noon, glowed red as at sunset. As the sun began to sink toward the horizon, the world turned gray and cold. Then a wind sprang up. It was only a gentle breeze at first, but before the Englishman could furl all sails and throw out a sea anchor, it had become a roaring gale. It was a small typhoon—only a breath of a blow, Mother Mora called it later—but she kept her charges out of their bunks and on their knees until all immediate need for divine assistance was past.

The third and last time the girls prayed during the voyage, the brigantine fled before two frigates flying black pennants. On that day Sir William made two of his rare visits to the slaves' cabin. He did not enter the first time. He rapped at the door and, when Mother Mora opened to him, he laid a dirk in her palm saying, "There are two black hounds baying us this time, and we shall be hard-pressed. You now what to do if it becomes necessary. Do it!"

The Negress stared at the keen-edged, pointed blade, and then raised her eyes to her master's face. Her lips parted slightly, but she did not speak.

"It will be the easiest way for them—and for you, too," he said shortly, and strode away.

The sound of his footsteps had scarcely died before grappling hooks thudded on the deck above. The timbers of the brigantine strained and creaked as the two frigates pressed against it on either side. From then on, for what seemed like an eternity, the praying girls' ears were filled with the clamor of stamping feet, clashing swords, the rattle of sporadic pistol fire and the screams of wounded and dying men.

Then suddenly the din overhead died away and the brigantine began to roll with the waves again instead of jerking awkwardly. Still the girls prayed—and Mother Mora, too—with the dirk lying on the floor before her. When she heard the captain's footsteps in the passageway outside, she sprang to her feet, unshuttered the window and had the key in the lock before her master knocked. This time he stepped inside and looked about at his merchandise, a half-smile on his face.

La China was shocked at his appearance. His hair had come unbound and straggled across his shoulders in tangled strands like the unkempt locks of a professional beggar. His face was begrimed, his hands were bloody and his shirt was in tatters. Still he grinned, and his eyes were no longer cold. It was as though at last he lusted for life like other men.

Mother Mora held out the dirk, and the captain tucked it into his belt, remarking lightly, as he glanced at the still kneeling girls, "So you prayed, did you! For your own skins? Or mine?"

"It did you no harm," the Negress replied.

If the captain noticed that she answered his question obliquely, he made nothing of it. Instead: "Mora, that is an excuse for the weak," he said. "For cowards and women!"

"Had you not noticed, Your Lordship, that we are women?" she quipped, and shrugged her immense shoulders.

The captain threw back his head and laughed, filling the cabin, not so much with mirth, as with exultation. It flashed through La China's mind that in such a mood this normally harsh, cold-eyed man might be as easy to love as the Portuguese captain had been. But it would be a different kind of love. This man would not be satisfied with servile submission. He was as yet an untamed creature; and his mate would have to be feral with him, like a jungle animal. She was mortally certain that once this man loved, he would never surrender the object of his affection so long as he wore a sword and had an arm to wield it. To such a man a woman would be something more than a convenience —to be replaced by a similar convenience on a mere whim. The Englishman's voice broke into her thoughts.

"Mora, you are more than a mere woman," he was saying. "You are my most valuable possession, my right hand. Sailors and—" he paused to run his eyes over the young girls—"slaves I can always replace. You, *never!*"

As he walked away, La China glanced at the Negress, and then dropped her eyes quickly, embarrassed, uneasy and amazed at what she saw there. Was it possible, she asked herself silently, that this mountain of a woman loved her master? And now being too old and grotesque of body to arouse lust in him, manifested her devotion by service? But what delight, what satisfaction that?

Then she scanned the older woman's face with a sudden and untaught understanding of what may go on in another's heart. That one could so sublimate love was a new thought to La China; but once in mind it hung there, recurring and vexing her when least expected— foreign to all her previous experience of mankind, disturbing, even painful like a deeply imbedded splinter in her flesh.

That night the slaves did not sup on maggoted cheese, brine-toughened beef and chunks of unleavened biscuit so rock-hard it had been crushed by a hammer and then soaked in water so that the teeth could mash it into mouthfuls. Instead the captain sent down a tray of dried fruit and raisins and nuts and sweetmeats. Most of the girls seized the delicacies with both hands and crammed them into their mouths as fast as they could swallow.

La China ate delicately, savoring each delicious morsel as she had been taught to eat when a child. The tray was swept bare before she had swallowed more than a small palmful of fruit. Mother Mora watched her, and held out a bunch of raisins to her from the heap she had swept into her own lap. La China looked at the fruit, her eyes bright with desire, and then refused it. Instead, she ran a hand over her middle, wondering if her pregnancy and the poor food of the past year had coarsened her body. But youth was on her side, and the strict regimen of the Negress had kept her still lissome. She knew that in spite of her advancing maturity—she was at least sixteen, and possibly all of seventeen years old—she was still potentially a seductive plaything; and since all of her thinking was shaped by her harem background, she was sincerely glad.

PART TWO

CHAPTER THIRTEEN

YOUNG as the colony of Mexico was, there were other important cities in New Spain almost as large as the capital, almost as wealthy and certainly as proud. One of these was Puebla, capital of the state of Puebla, which took great pride in its culture. At the beginning of the 1620's there lived in Mexico City and in Puebla two men as different from each other as two men can very well be. Each respected the other but for reasons that were as different as the individuals themselves.

The first man was Don Diego Carillo Mendoza y Pimental, the Marquis de Gelves, whom the Spanish monarch Philip IV on his accession to the throne had appointed Viceroy, or *Virrey,* of New Spain. Upon his arrival in Mexico City, Don Diego assumed all the prerogatives of royalty, patterning his court after Philip's, and very quickly outdoing his royal master in extravagence and voluptuous immorality.

The Moor as a religious infidel had been expelled from Spain only a short century before the Marquis de Gelves' day, but there was much that Spanish gentlemen liked in the culture of the Moors which lingered on after the infidel was gone. Harems, in fact though not in name, were commonplace, without the approval yet with the full knowledge of the church. Christian women did not go heavily veiled, but they lived behind locked doors and iron-barred windows and their social conduct was straitly governed by their fathers and husbands. There were many men who still looked upon women as playthings at best and chattels in any case. The Marquis de Gelves was one of these.

It is remarkable that a man could have, in only a little more than three years, milked a vast land of so much money and acquired so bad a reputation as the Virrey. Among his other excesses was the stable of singing and dancing concubines, both male and female, with which he

153

amused himself and the members of his court. Daughters of local grandees were offered him—as men of varying religions and throughout the ages have sought to buy personal preferment and advantage with the bodies of their women.

The Virrey, however, preferred slaves from the Orient because of their delicate beauty and their inherent exotic charm, and because these women had been trained from birth in all the arts of pleasing men. Moreover, they were completely submissive, even under torture. One of de Gelves' first acts upon assuming the Virreyship was to place a standing order with the Governor of Manila for the most beautiful merchandise of that city's slave pens. The slaves he did not want for himself, and those of whom he tired he passed on to his favorites like a true monarch bestowing a gem upon a deserving courtier.

The Marquis de Gelves, fresh from Philip's court, assumed that all men were like himself and his royal master; that is, avaricious, amoral and untrustworthy. There was one man, and one only in all of New Spain, in whose code of honor as a gentleman he had sufficient faith so that he trusted him to transport him newly imported Oriental virgins from Acapulco to Mexico City. That man was Señor Miguel de Sosa, a wealthy merchant living in the city of Puebla.

The Virrey's trust was well placed. Señor de Sosa—a very able businessman, a cultured gentleman and a devout Christian—had never questioned the divine right of Philip IV or his forebears to the throne of Spain. Similarly it had never occurred to him to disobey an order of his king's representatives, however distasteful the task might be to him personally.

Consequently, when Indian relay runners—faster than horses since horses had to travel circuitous routes and became winded more easily than the specially trained Indians who were kept drugged on small daily portions of *peyote*—brought news to de Gelves that an English privateer had put in to Acapulco and had brought merchandise for the Virrey from the Governor of Manila, Miguel de Sosa was sent for.

As he had done many times before, Señor de Sosa, the Christian, presumed upon the good will of his lord and tried to dissuade him from the immoral excesses of his dissolute life. This time his words should have borne great weight, for he reminded the Virrey that His Eminence, Don Juan Pérez de la Serna, Archbishop of Mexico, had threatened him with excommunication if he continued the worst of

154

his sybaritic practices—a fate worse than death in his day and world. In addition to the religious consequences of excommunication, it would also mean the loss of the Virreyship, and the unbounded wealth and privilege which went with the office.

But de Gelves was used to threats and thought he knew how to deal with them, even those coming from the most highly placed. Perhaps he relied upon the protection of the distance between Mexico City and Madrid. And perhaps he had become drunk on power and forgot that he was not king but only a vice-king, a substitute for the real thing, subject to the laws of Holy Church and not above them as Philip thought himself to be.

In any case, the Virrey laughed at de Sosa's admonitions with the air of a sophisticate who is lightly amused by the naïveté of a child. He made broad and at the same time barbed jokes about virtue, calling it the wealth of serfs and peasants. He implied that grandees and courtiers should scorn a way of life which any slave might practice without cost or power. He declared haughtily and loudly, so that even hidden ears might hear, that if the Archbishop aroused him to sufficient anger, His Eminence might find himself paying a tax like lesser men. He summarily commanded de Sosa to be on his way to Acapulco. Señor de Sosa, the loyal subject, obeyed as he had always done in the past.

The merchant from Puebla did not travel rapidly or alone. The way to Acapulco was only a trail, often tortuous and difficult, which crossed steep, rugged mountains as well as broad, fertile plains. No one could predict if, or when, or where *bandidos*—for the most part Spanish gentry and their descendants who had failed to amass a fortune in the golden New World—might attack a caravan. Indians, even half-breeds, were never members of these roving bands, for the rigid caste system of the day excluded the indigene of the New World from even this doubtful profession.

The Virrey appointed a captain of his own guard and a band of soldiers to accompany and protect de Sosa. The captain was a professional adventurer who had bought his post from the Virrey because of the opportunities it offered for rapine and plunder. Differences between his background and way of life and methods of operation, and that of the bandidos were largely theoretical.

The soldiers under the Virrey's captain were all landless and un-

155

successful adventurers who had been impressed into service. They were underpaid, when they were paid at all, and to a man they were usually hungry and so had become savage creatures. It was not uncommon for such mercenaries to desert, singly and in wholesale lots, to their brothers, the bandidos. Their lot was practically the same in either camp, and most of them seemed to think it a matter of simple common sense to trade honor for their lives when the going got too rough.

Consequently Señor de Sosa was compelled, as had been the case many times before, to choose with great care and arm a group of men to accompany him and protect him and, on the return trip, the Virrey's merchandise from the Virrey's own guard. A partial payment of wages was made in advance to the families of these men, and a substantial bonus promised upon the successful completion of the trip. Señor de Sosa had never broken such a promise in the past, a statement which could not be made of many of his compatriots. His reputation was as secure with the peasantry as with the elite. When traveling with his own guard, he was as sure of safe conduct as any man in the colony.

The combined forces of the two groups of guards made a large company, too large a group to be fed by the Indian villagers encountered enroute. Runners were sent ahead to warn *hacenderos*—white rural estate masters and managers—to have needed supplies in readiness. This was a custom of the times which amounted to a tax laid on the vast estates which, although they had been crown grants, were held only by the good will of the reigning Virrey.

Señor de Sosa, a true Christian, was so tender of his soul's welfare that he never traveled over dangerous terrain or very far from home without Father Enrique, his own personal confessor. Father Enrique had been a member of the de Sosa household for many years. He had always been so saintly in his personal life and so compassionate of others that even in youth he had shrunk from the fires of ambition. He had a good life as a priest and scholar and he was wise enough to be satisfied with that abundance.

Father Enrique was also warmly, lovably human. Although he was sworn to poverty and possessed nothing of material value save his jeweled rosary—a gift from Señora de Sosa—he had become accustomed to luxury and liked it. His patron, whose business ventures sometimes carried him as far away from home as Paraguay, Bolivia and even Peru, could rough it with the sturdiest of his hirelings; but Father Enrique was silver-haired now, and his comfort must be assured. Delicacies were provided for his table. Smooth-gaited mules of known gentle temper were secured for him to ride since his strength was not equal to rugged travel on foot. Fur-lined cloaks and boots protected his spare body from sleet and snow and biting winds in the mountains. An Indian servant fanned away the mosquitoes and the small black flies, which bit as viciously as mosquitoes, when the party camped at night.

Then, since the merchant de Sosa would naturally expect to find other ships in Acapulco with cargoes for sale, some of which would be of interest to him, a drove of pack mules was taken along to transport whatever might be purchased on the coast. Any of these animals that were not needed ultimately could always be sold at a good profit to other merchants gathered in Acapulco. When preparations were completed for the journey, more than a hundred men and an equal number of animals camped the last night in the great plaza of Mexico City before the already famous cathedral. This was the usual custom of such caravans, so that lone travelers and small defenseless groups could join the stronger for protection. Also messages and gifts could be sent with the travelers to be delivered to estates and hacenderos enroute.

It was mid-February, 1624, when Señor de Sosa, his father confessor, his two bands of protectors and his riding and pack animals left the plaza, skirted the Hill of Grasshoppers, passed the floating gardens and began the rugged descent from the central highlands to the western coast. It was more than a journey of miles. It was a trek from one season into another, from the frost and ice and snow flurries of winter to the warm days and soft nights of a semi-tropical spring. It was a trip through a land of awesome grandeur, breath-taking beauty and incredible fertility.

The Indian peon had only to gouge a few holes in the earth with a pointed stick, drop a few grains of maize therein, and press the hole shut with his heel to grow food enough for his master, his family and himself. Countless herds of cattle grazed in lush valleys where grass grew the year round faster than it could be eaten. Silt and sand bars in the streams glittered with gold dust, and every rock slide in the

157

hills revealed veins of precious ores in the newly carved escarpments. It was truly a land to fill the coffers of Philip IV to overflowing in spite of heavy losses to English pirates and his own equally voracious, corrupt colonial administrators.

There is little wonder that Miguel de Sosa and unnumbered others like him were glad to call this new land home for themselves and their children, although by doing so they gave up the rights and privileges of citizens of Old Spain. Señor de Sosa had made the trip to Acapulco many times, and though it was a rigorous journey and full of danger, his delight in the marvelous and varied beauty of his adopted land erased all memory of hardships as soon as they were passed.

Acapulco itself he did not like. The countryside was barren and rockstrewn, and as yet no men of sufficient wealth and leisure had settled there to build gracious homes and plant gardens. There was an air of impermanence about the town that made a man of settled habits uneasy if he had to remain in it for an extended period. The streets were of sand and dirt, and in dry weather one's feet stirred low-flying dust storms with every step. After a rain one sank to the ankles in the mud, and sometimes floundered knee-deep where a herd of peccaries, after foraging during the night for garbage, had wallowed. There were a few shops of undressed, unmortared stone; but for the most part a merchant transacted business and corralled his family and other livestock in a makeshift hut of grass and bamboo.

Even the food sold to strangers repulsed a fastidious man. The tortilla women were as gray and unwashed-looking as the wild pigs, and the tops of their braziers and *metates*—on which they ground their lye-softened maize to a smooth pulp—were so low that the dust from a galloping horse's hooves smothered and darkened their cooking fires and overlaid their wares with a gray patina of gritty filth. A tortilla vendor was often obliged to take her hands out of her dough and balance herself on her knuckles in the dust or muck while she blew at her fire until the charcoal once more glowed red as a sun ripened cactus apple. Some then wiped their hands on their skirts before they went back to slapping tortillas again; others were not so careful.

It sometimes seemed to Señor de Sosa that in Acapulco there was at

158

least one dog for every human inhabitant, and that most of the human beings—sailors and derelicts from the four corners of the earth—were as fawning, cringing, vicious when opportunity offered, and uncertain of ancestry as the dogs. He never lingered in this town, but transacted what business he had there as quickly as possible and hurried back to the clean lakes, fragrant valleys and bracing mountains of the interior.

The Englishman's ship had ridden at anchor in the Bay of Acapulco for three weeks before Miguel de Sosa arrived. There was no one of sufficient responsibility in the town with whom a virgin intended for the Virrey could be left. It didn't matter, for the Virrey with the illimitable wealth of New Spain at his fingertips could afford to pay a ship's captain for any amount of lost time. So the Englishman waited for the Virrey's agent, and as he waited he transacted other business from his ship like a land-bound merchant in a stone-walled, tile-roofed shop.

From time to time as the days passed La China saw small boats approach the brigantine; and when some of them returned to land they carried slaves as well as other merchandise. Almost daily her companions were herded out of the cabin by Mother Mora for the inspection of potential buyers. One by one they were rowed ashore until finally there was no one left in the cabin under the poop deck but the huge Negress and the Princess from Cochin China. In their goodbyes, each girl prayed to her god that she and all the others would pass into the hands of kind and generous masters and that these same gods would not curse any of them with a long life.

Hindy of the caste-marked forehead was the first to go. It was Mother Mora who commanded each girl to clasp the little Brahmin in her arms and to whisper in her ear, "God grant you an early death, sister."

"Now that is a sensible prayer for such as us," La China remarked one day to Mother Mora.

The Negress did not reply for a moment. When she did, it was as though she voiced a long familiar thought, and for her own ears. "It would be interesting to know whether God created man for His own entertainment, as the folk tales all claim He did, or whether man created God out of his extremity. Certainly most heartfelt prayers are in that spirit."

"The professional storytellers sometimes told us of a poet who claimed that the gift of life was a divine impertinence," La China said. "Do you think it is?"

"I think it is unwise to voice certain doubts," she said finally very slowly. "Life is simpler and perhaps easier without doubts. Stifle these questions within your heart, little lady, and perhaps they will die, and the part of you that can be hurt most easily may die with them."

Just as La China had been surprised, and a little piqued, by the Englishman's indifference to her as a seductive woman, she wondered at his conduct while his ship lay in harbor. Never once did she see him rowed ashore or hear him return to ship cursing, stumbling drunkenly and roaring obscene songs as did the masters of ships lying nearby.

"He is a strange man—if he is a man," she said to Mother Mora one day.

The Negress looked at the girl sharply before replying. "The English love the Spaniards' gold more than they love the Spaniards—or the Spaniards' God."

The words did not have much meaning for La China, but she did not know how to question them. "When shall I, too, leave this ship?" she asked instead.

"How should I know?" the Negress snapped. "When you are sent for, you will go."

It had been several days since anyone had visited the brigantine when Miguel de Sosa's boat put off from shore. La China watched it idly for a moment and then, without knowing why she did so, turned to the Negress and said, "My new master is coming for me."

"Ptsch! How do you know?" Mother Mora replied. Then, after peering out of the window over La China's shoulder agreed, "Perhaps you are right. The visitor is obviously a wealthy man."

By habit La China had always stood as tall and straight as her delicate body allowed. She drew a deep breath and stiffened her neck and shoulders as she gazed at the man who commanded the approaching boat. She noticed the white plume in the broad-brimmed black hat; the cloak lined with scarlet silk and held together at the throat

160

by a massive jeweled pin; his boots of soft leather that came halfway up his legs like hose. When he was close enough she saw that except for dust on his feet and legs, he was immaculately clean. She let the air out of her lungs in a long sigh of relief. Men could be difficult enough at best, but a filthy man—she thought of the Manila slaver and shuddered briefly. It had been like tumbling in the gutter with a beast.

As the boat neared the brigantine, she saw a figure behind the first man and again shuddered. This second man was dressed in the black robe and shovel hat of a priest, and the only priest she had ever known was the coarse, brutal henchman of the Manila slaver. She continued to stare at the boat. When it was less than twenty feet from the port-hole, both men lifted their faces and looked directly into her eyes.

The face under the plumed hat was olive-skinned like her own, and handsome, but she paid it little attention. Her glance swept past it and searched the face under the shovel brim anxiously. Her eyes widened in surprise, for there were no marks of cruelty and bestiality here. The hazel eyes were the kindest she had ever seen. Kinder, even, than her father's. She could see that the priest's hair was silvery white, yet his eyes, which held her in spite of herself, were bright and keen and not dimmed by age as her father's had been. They looked as though they would weep at another's pain of soul or body. The skin at their outer corners was crinkled into many wrinkles as though he also laughed easily and often.

Suddenly something within her stirred, as her heart always seemed to move whenever she thought of her father and of her mother, The Pearl, whom she knew so well but had never seen. She knew with complete certainty that this black-clad, silver-haired, kind-eyed man understood the heart of a woman perhaps better than a woman understood herself. She smiled in simple happiness and as the boat passed from her view, she thought she saw the thin lips widen and part and the maze of wrinkles deepen in the thin cheeks. It was a simple smile of honest unstudied friendship on the face of a guileless man.

Then Mother Mora was turning her round and around, inspecting her from head to toe, and nodding satisfaction at her appearance. The Negress smoothed a lock of her charge's hair, rubbed her hands with a drop of oil and smeared a bit of perfume on the collar of her dress with a careful finger. Then she opened the door and bade the girl follow her down the passageway. La China walked with tiny steps that scarcely stirred the cloth about her knees. She moved as in a dream, as though the gentle, friendly hazel eyes beckoned her on and she had no will but to obey. As she stepped across the high threshold into the captain's cabin, she was still smiling.

Then she felt Mother Mora's hand on her shoulder and she remembered that she was merely a female slave and that her prime duty in life was prompt, unquestioning subservience. Quickly she crossed her hands over her breasts, turned to the other man and inclined her head submissively, but with her neck twisted just enough to show the most graceful, seductive line between throat and shoulder. She stopped abruptly, however, in mid-gesture and stared, for this man who she supposed was to be her new master, had bared his head and was bowing low to her, sweeping the floor with the costly plume of his flamboyant hat.

Mother Mora's hand slid forward under La China's chin and slapped upward lightly with the back of her fingers. It was not until her teeth clicked together from the force of the little blow that La China realized she had been staring open-mouthed. Nothing in all her experience or years of careful training had prepared her for such courtesy from a man, and she did not know how to respond. She merely continued to stare, tight-lipped now, and wide-eyed.

When Miguel de Sosa raised his head, he returned her gaze, steadfastly, intently. She expected his first words, but the exclamation following them confused her.

"You are very beautiful, Señorita," he said softly and slowly. "But, God's body, you are only a child!"

She turned to Father Enrique in bewilderment, feeling vaguely that the silver-haired man might help her. The priest had raised his hand in the sign of the cross, and she bowed her head quickly, as she had been taught to do. It was his turn to be surprised.

"You are Catholic, child?" he exclaimed.

She hesitated a moment before replying. She had never heard the word "Catholic" before, but it was obvious this man referred to religion. Still, she knew that this priest and the one in Manila were not the same kind of men. Vaguely she wondered if their religious faiths were also dissimilar. Her father and his court had been Fatimide Moslems, but there were other sects among the followers of the

162

Prophet. She wondered if there were different kinds of Christians, too.

"I, I am . . ." Then she remembered that she had merely submitted, and of necessity to a cursory ritual, carelessly administered by a dissolute creature surely of no true faith himself. Moreover, how could she be sure she was a Christian when no one had told her what a Christian believes, or what a Christian woman's duties might be.

"I was born . . ." Again she stopped as it occurred to her that Mohammedanism is a religion for men, and according to the tenets of that faith she was merely a creature without a soul.

"She is La China—The Chinese Lady," Mother Mora finished for her in a firm tone.

The two men glanced quickly at each other and then turned their faces away without questioning the finality of the Negress's words.

Mother Mora embraced the Princess from Cochin China and murmured the formal prayer for the mercy of death before all the horrors of slavery could be visited upon her.

"God grant that you be kind to others—as you have been to me," La China whispered in return. Mother Mora held her very tight for a moment.

Only the Englishman had overheard the women's words. After a curious glance at both, he said to the Negress in a low voice, "There is a saying in my country that the good die young. I had never thought of that as evidence of Divine Mercy, but you may be right!"

CHAPTER FOURTEEN

L A CHINA never knew her exact worth in cold cash. However, she was paid for in gold dust weighed out before her watching eyes and she knew that she cost her new master a considerable sum. When that transaction was completed, Mother Mora put a small bundle of extra clothing in her hands and pushed her toward the strangers.

"Has she no covering for her hair?" Señor de Sosa asked the Negress, who shook her head in denial.

He turned in some surprise to the Englishman, who stared back without replying. The Spaniard swept the room with his eyes, but the only cloth he saw was a heavy covering on the captain's couch and a soiled towel. He curved his lips downward in an expression of distaste but picked up the towel and started to tie it over La China's hair when the Englishman stopped him.

"I have only a handkerchief to offer The Chinese Lady. It is small, but perhaps it will do," he said, pulling a lace-edged square of linen from his sleeve.

But Mother Mora was quicker than either man. She had stripped the yellow cloth from her own naked pate and was knotting it on La China's brow in the same fashion in which she had worn it herself. Señor de Sosa's eyes twinkled at the sight of the tightly bound head and the wad of yellow cotton bunched rakishly over La China's left eye, and Father Enrique grasped his mouth and chin in one lean hand in an effort to hide his amusement. Then the three men and the Negress burst out laughing.

"Never mind," Señor de Sosa said to the girl between chuckles. "You are now decently clad so that we can take you through the streets."

164

So! thought La China silently. In Cochin China women cover their faces in public. Here they cover their hair. I must remember that!

As she climbed down a swaying Jacob's ladder into the waiting boat, the girl wondered if other customs in this new land were equally strange. Hiding one's hair under a scrap of yellow cloth might smack of the ridiculous, but who is a slave to judge! They did not walk far on shore, however, before Señor de Sosa led her into a small shop where he bought a large square of sheer black lace and a tortise-shell comb with a huge flaring, fan-shaped top.

"Take off that ridiculous yellow rag and put these on," he said to her.

But La China did not know what to do with such an unwieldy comb and attempted to twist the lace into the same knot as that in which the Negress had tied her headcloth.

"A regular heathen!" the shopkeeper exclaimed, and shouted for his wife to come and show the girl how to place the comb in her hair and drape the lace over it. Then the woman fetched her mirror and held it up before La China. The mirror was only a slab of black volcanic glass rubbed smooth enough on one side so that it reflected dimly. But when La China peered at herself in its dark depths, she caught her lower lip between her teeth in surprised delight. Little of her beauty was hidden beneath the lace, and what remained uncovered took on added charm because of the delicate web framing her face. Impulsively she lifted a corner of the mantilla and held it across the tip of her nose like a Moslem veil. Señor de Sosa laughed, but the shopkeeper turned quickly to a shelf behind him.

"A fan! A fan! The señorita must have a fan," he exclaimed.

Señor de Sosa picked three fans out of the bundle laid before them— the most beautiful and the most expensive three—and told La China to take her choice. She lifted her hands to her shoulders, palms outspread, and her eyes shone with admiration of the delicate silk and the carved ivory and sandalwood. Señor de Sosa watched her for a moment and then bought all three fans.

"I shall take my wife and my daughter-in-law each a new fan," he said to Father Enrique.

"You do not need to make excuse to me, patrón," the priest replied. "I am well acquainted with your generosity."

From the shop the three hurried to the edge of the town, where de

165

Sosa's men and animals awaited them. The merchant wanted to put as much distance between himself and the riffraff of the coastal settlement as he could before night fell.

La China had never seen a mule before. She thought it exactly what it was—a strange, misbegotten horse, probably the abode of demons. She screamed in terror when she was lifted onto one, and for the first few miles Señor de Sosa and Father Enrique had to walk beside the animal to keep her from tumbling over backward or slipping forward until the pommel of the side saddle pressed against her thigh cruelly.

As they trudged along, the two men questioned her about her former life. She did not chatter or exaggerate or withhold information, for it would not have occurred to her that she had a right to do any of these things. Instead, she answered each question obediently and with such simple honesty that each man was alternately delighted and stunned silent with embarrassment. Occasionally she was surprised at the expressions on their faces. They sometimes laughed, but more often struggled to hide their mirth while she wondered at the cause of their amusement. Other times Father Enrique's lips moved as though in silent conversations with himself, and then he would cross himself. On such occasions Señor de Sosa would exclaim in a fierce whisper, "God's body! Such barbarism!"

When she had finished speaking of her life in the Manila slave pen, Miguel de Sosa clenched one fist and hammered it into the palm of his other hand as violently as though punishing a slave. More than once he cried out, "What a beast, I am not a soldier, but I would like to have this monster at the end of a sword."

"Men without God find it easy to become bestial, my son," Father Enrique answered him. "But we are not commanded to slaughter such. Rather, we must bring them to God when that is possible."

That statement surprised La China and again she made a mental note: She must remember that Christians, unlike Moslems, apparently did not win Paradise by slaying others not of their faith. Then she found herself wondering which was the easier—to snuff out a man's life, or his religion.

She did not consciously relate her musings with the exclamation of the Acapulco shopkeeper, but something impelled her to ask, "What does it mean, the word, heathen?"

The annoyance in Señor de Sosa's voice as he exclaimed "That fool!" was unmistakable. But he explained simply, honestly and in a kindly voice, "It means someone who is not of the true faith."

One glance at the girl, and he added hastily, "Someone who is not Christian."

"Aaaah! It is the same as when a Moslem—we of the true faith—call another 'a dog of an infidel.' " La China mused, pleased that she had understood so quickly and perfectly.

The shocked look on Señor de Sosa's face, however, cut her satisfaction short. He gazed past her at the priest on the other side of her mule, and her eyes followed his. Father Enrique was smiling.

"They would mean exactly the same, daughter, were it not for one very small but also very important difference: Which is the true faith?" the priest said.

La China was silent for a moment and then asked, "The world is full of Moslems, but how many Christians are there?"

His smile widened as Father Enrique answered, "And we would say, the world is full of Christians, but how many Moslems are there?"

The girl was silent again and for a longer period than before. Both men watched her keenly as though they read her thoughts as they took shape in her mind.

Finally she asked the inevitable question, "How is one—such a one as I—to know which is the true faith? And to be certain that what we know is truth?"

"You must seek in your own mind and heart for truth, daughter," the priest answered. "And you must pray. Pray honestly, and sincerely, and humbly, and the true God, whatver name you may use for Him, will hear you. Pray especially for faith, and in His own good time, the true God will lay His hand upon your heart and you will know all that you need to know. Doubt will simply vanish like the morning mist before the sun of a perfect day."

La China swayed in her saddle as though physically drawn to the soft-voiced, kind-eyed man, saying, "I believe your words, for you do not seem to me the kind of man to deal in intrigue." She had wanted to say, "falsehood," but she was morally certain that dishonesty was as foreign to this man as true love and simple kindliness were to The Fat Devil back in Manila.

"That is the first step, belief!" Father Enrique's words of encouragement broke into her thoughts. "First faith in mankind, and then faith in God will follow. Simple faith which moves mountains!"

"Just as Mohammed commanded the mountains to come to him?" she exclaimed.

But the priest did not answer that directly. Instead he laughed and himself exclaimed, "You are quick-witted, child. I am glad there are so many days between us and Mexico City and that I shall have an opportunity to instruct you—at least somewhat before . . ." But he could not add the words, "we deliver you to your new master." He looked far away down the path and sighed heavily, and there was no longer a smile on his lips or in his eyes.

Because of the broad brim of Father Enrique's hat La China did not see the sweat on his face. And because he had laid his hand upon her mule's shoulder at the beginning of their journey, she did not realize how difficult the path was for the old man until she saw him stumble.

"Let me walk and you ride," she cried out.

"Why should we not all three ride?" Señor de Sosa asked her. "Father Enrique can hold the halter of your mule, and I can ride close enough beside you to steady you if you should start to fall, Señorita. But I do not think you will lose your seat—slip in your saddle, child— for neither one of us has had to steady you for some time now. With a little more practice, you will ride very well indeed."

Then after mounting the horse a soldier led up to him, Señor de Sosa went on, "You stand and walk straight and tall, as a young woman should. Sit your saddle the same way. You and the mule will like each other the better for it, Myrrha."

La China saw satisfaction in his eyes, and glowed at the praise she felt in his words. She liked the sound of her childhood name on his lips, too. She had also liked the subtle homage in the title, The Chinese Lady. There was at least a little of the same respect in the term as when the eunuchs and servants in her father's harem and her mother's people on the banks of the Mekong had called her "Princess." In her most secret heart she regretted the loss of her titles, no matter how perfect her outward obedience.

As they rode along Myrrha gazed upon the world about her with bright and curious eyes. The very little she had seen of Manila was ugly, filthy and malodorous. The city of her birth was low-lying, swampy and humid. The vegetation surrounding it was tropical, for the most part huge and dense. The first few miles out of Acapulco the trail wound through a tumbled confusion of boulders of all sizes from pebbles that rolled under their horses' and mules' feet, to gigantic slabs larger than houses. It was a barren land with only a straggling growth of cactus.

Then cacti and hills gave way to green valleys dotted with groves of clean-limbed trees, and cut across with creeks and rivers. The streams delighted Myrrha, for their water was clear and sparkling as the spray of a fountain. "This is all like a garden—a big—a huge—a vast garden," she said. "And the water, there is no scum or offal floating on it! It looks as though everything—the whole countryside had been trimmed and swept for the visit of a great khan or mogul."

From their smiles and their glowing eyes, Myrrha knew she had pleased them, and was glad. Glad, and then bewildered because of the sudden flood of happiness within her. Bewildered, because never before had she known women to please men without intent and studied artifice. But she had pleased these strangers, not by the submissive gift of her body or her physical beauty, but by the spontaneous sharing of a small portion of her heart. As she gave of herself there had been no thought of reward—no attempt to stave off a man's anger, no thought of the gift of a jewel or a length of silk. For a moment she had known a sort of happiness that had no place in a world where any beast of forest or field was the spiritual equal of woman. Born of impulse, the result of the gift of one's innermost being freely given—such an emotion could never live behind the locked and guarded doors of a harem.

Then Father Enrique was saying, "Child, I would like to see you educated and free. Even as you are, you little heathen, you would nestle like a jewel on a good man's heart—a man who took you in decency and honor before God!"

Myrrha only half understood the priest's words, but again that strange, fulfilling sense of happiness swept over her. She did not attempt to reply, for she realized for the first time in her life that the words to relieve an overflowing heart could only break forth in an unruly torrent—just as a pitcher that is too full cannot be poured but spills its contents.

"I would to God that that could be!" she heard Señor de Sosa say

169

to his father confessor. "I would give half of my wealth— no! More, much more than that—for such a daughter as this child."

In the short moment before the merchant spurred his horse forward, Myrrha thought she saw tears in his eyes. She could not be sure, however, for she saw nothing more of him but his broad back for the rest of that afternoon.

After a while Father Enrique pulled close beside her and questioned her in minute detail about the priest she had known in the Manila slave pen. But because her knowledge of Spanish had been imperfect at that time, because she had tried to keep herself as far away from the cassock-clad man as possible, and because his visits and instruction had been so sporadic and desultory, there was not much she could tell this very different priest about the other.

When the caravan stopped for the night Myrrha was too tired to eat, although she tried because she knew the effort would please these two kind men. The bed prepared for her—a robe of jaguar skins spread over a thick layer of leafy twigs and grass—was soft and comfortable. A second robe of tanned coney pelts, warmer and more weightless than the down of the kapok tree, covered her and protected her completely from the cold wind that sprung up every night as soon as the sun set.

That first night she was too tired for deep slumber. Father Enrique and Señor de Sosa sat beside her looking into the fire, sipping with relish a strange, dirty-looking, brown, fragrant liquid she had never heard of before that they called by its Indian name, *chocolatl.* Their low voices and their musical tongue blended with the muted crackle of the twigs beneath her into a tuneless melody as soothing as an old woman humming over a cradle. Then she was suddenly aware that they were talking about her, and she lay motionless, listening.

"Strange, is it not, that one who has been so cruelly degraded should look and seem so childlike?" Señor de Sosa murmured.

"Her degradation is the sin of others," Father Enrique answered. "She is a child, yet has such maturity of perception. She has a mind that should not be stifled, but should be free to grow. She makes me think of——"

"Of Sor María?" Señor de Sosa interrupted.

"Yes. Yet I scarcely know why. The two women are as different as two women can be different: age, looks, background, training." The priest threw up his hands as though faced with an impossible, even absurd task.

Myrrha wondered about this other woman with whom she apparently had nothing in common except the strange quality of calling the other to men's minds. She was piqued by the oddity of the circumstance, and wondered if there was some slight resemblance in their facial features that men's eyes saw but their conscious minds recorded only imperfectly. She was not permitted to dwell on the thought, for Miguel de Sosa was again speaking.

"What will the Virrey do when he learns the truth about her? God help her then."

"God help her!" Father Enrique echoed the other's words, and kissed his crucifix.

"A few stitches, however perfectly healed, will not fool such as he into thinking her virgin!" the merchant went on. "It is said that all the beauty and grace and virtue in the world are as nothing to him without virginity."

"It is only God who can help her," the priest murmured. "Pray for her, my son."

Between her long black lashes Myrrha saw the priest's lips move as though in prayer, saw him again raise his crucifix and kiss it.

"The performance of such duties as this one has always been difficult for me, father," de Sosa continued. "God did not give me and my wife a daughter, though we both prayed long and often for one, as you know. My son's wife is a fine woman, and a great comfort to us. Still, she is not flesh of our flesh. She is a good wife and mother; but as her children grow in size and strength, she herself grows frailer and weaker. It is as though their youth devoured her. We pray for her, too; but she no longer rises from her bed of mornings, and but seldom in the afternoons. We fear, my wife and I, that the day is not far distant when our son will be without a wife, his children without a mother, and we without a daughter-in-law."

He fell silent and turned to look at Myrrha. Then he put out a hand and patted her on the shoulder and smoothed the hair on her head as though she were indeed a child, but with so light a touch that she would not have roused or been aware of the caress had she been sleeping. He straightened and smoothed the robe above her before he went on.

"Many times when I have had one of these unfortunate girls in my charge, I have wished I might take her home to my wife, instead of to my lord, the Virrey. Never have I wished that more strongly than I do now, father."

But the priest could only iterate, "Pray! Pray for her, my son—and pray for yourself. Prayer is the strongest force in this world."

"I wish I might buy her from the Virrey. I would pay any sum of money he could ask for her. But I dare not suggest such a thing for it would only anger him. When the Virrey is displeased with a man, his anger spreads to cover everyone dear to that unfortunate soul."

"Pray! Pray, my son, for it is through prayer that miracles are wrought," the priest urged.

It seemed to Myrrha that the tone of his voice lacked conviction. She wondered if by this continued urge to prayer the man combated doubt within his own mind, if such personal fortification was what he had meant by faith.

"Father, is there nothing, nothing I can do?" the merchant pleaded. But the hopelessness in his voice was proof that even as he spoke he knew the futility of pleading. "How can God, the Omnipotent, condemn so rare a child to such a life of shame?" he burst out. "Why is so much power placed in the hands of so vile a creature as the——"

"Hush, my son!" the priest cried out in alarm.

Both men looked over their shoulders at the guards sleeping in small groups about their own campfires. The words had been unpremeditated and were proof of nothing but helpless, hopeless longing. Nevertheless, they were treasonous! But if any soldier had heard them, he gave no sign.

"Pray!" the priest commanded sternly. "And thank God for the privilege—and the divine blessing—of prayer. I sometimes think it is His supreme gift to His children."

Señor de Sosa looked into the fire, his face wrinkled with troubled thought. Then he turned to his confessor and said in so low a voice that Myrrha was not certain she heard him rightly. "Father have you ever wondered . . . I know this sounds blasphemous, but there is no spirit of blasphemy in my heart. Only wonder. Father, how many of the Virrey's victims have prayed, despairing creatures crying out in their agony? How many people pray and without hope even as they breathe the words?"

"My son, do you doubt the existence of grass, and trees, and rivers that you have not seen? Do you think that the moment you turn your back the grasses cease to bloom, that the trees no longer drop their leaves or put on new ones, and that the rivers no longer flow? Active life is a mantle covering the world without beginning or end. Your life is only one stitch sewing together the edges of two eternities that lie on either side of your existence. One eternity before you, one behind. Prayer can be a needle carrying the thread of your life from one side to the other. Without prayer, that stitch—that infinitely tiny stitch that is your existence here—would not be straight or firm or strong. To make your life, to make that stitch, straight and firm and strong, prayer must be the blood in your veins and the breath in your nostrils; for prayer is one of the miracles of life. You do not question your heart's beat or your breathing; they are with you even when you are least aware of them. Do not question prayer either. Prayer, pulse and breath—any one of the three is as necessary to your life as each of the others."

The voices of the men beside the fire droned on. Myrrha, lying between her snug, furred robes, listened and wondered at their words. She decided that on the morrow she would tell them that Mother Mora had forced her and her companions to pray during the sea fights and the typhoon and that they had come through these dangers unscathed. That would surely please these men of great faith.

Then she remembered that it was concern for herself that had provoked their conversation, and she stirred uneasily. Why should they worry about her life with a man who, judging by what she had overheard, was very like the other men who had dominated her? Her beauty would last a few years longer, she told herself; and after that she would surely be valuable to her lord, or to the lord of some other harem, as an accomplished musician and a teacher of his daughters.

But the thoughts these men had shared with her without their knowing, seemed to imply that there were or at least might be, in this life, other loves? Advantages? Values? She did not know what they meant, her mind groped for words which might be right. This thing which

173

meant so much to them, prayer— were the cadenced syllables she had learned really more than a verbal discipline for times of stress? Slowly, as though curiously testing the truth of a new concept, she whispered under her breath; "Hail Mary, full of grace, The Lord is with thee. Blessed art thou among women——"

CHAPTER FIFTEEN

W HEN Señor de Sosa touched Myrrha's shoulder the next morning to rouse her from sleep, the stars had not yet faded from the sky. Only the faintest gray of dawn glowed above the rims of the hills to the east; night still lay soft and dark in the valley and over the travelers' camp. Two campfires already crackled, outlining the figures of men and animals in grotesque silhouettes against the faint horizon. As the two troops of guards stumbled drowsily about the larger fire, awkwardly busy at their duties, they looked like poorly carved, clumsily jointed puppets in the hands of an unskillful puppeteer.

Beyond the second fire Myrrha saw the priest standing between her and a little bench covered with white cloth. Several small vessels of gold rested on the bench. Father Enrique was donning above his other clothing a white lace-trimmed garment that looked to her like a shift. As she rubbed the sleep from her eyes, he picked up strips of cloth, kissed them and laid them carefully about his neck and over one arm. On his head he placed a little cap much like those worn by many old men of Cochin China, not to protect themselves from sun or weather, but to hide their balding pates from the staring, scoffing eyes of coolies and women.

"Would you like to pray the Mass with Father Enrique and me?" Señor de Sosa was saying.

This is an invitation, not a command! flashed through the girl's mind. She wondered what would happen if she refused, although no real thought of doing so occurred to her. She arose, wrapped the coney blanket about her shoulders, and followed Señor de Sosa past the fire to a position before the cloth-covered, gold-decked bench. A handful of de Sosa's private guard was already there. Kneeling, Myrrha looked up into Father Enrique's face as he made the sign of the cross over her,

175

and was certain that The Fat Devil's priest had never risen at such a peasant's hour to pray.

Myrrha murmured the prayers she knew whenever she heard Señor de Sosa reciting them. She rose to her feet, knelt and crossed herself as the man beside her did these things. When the other opened his mouth for the bread and wine of communion, Myrrha did the same. But Father Enrique shook his head from side to side and interrupted the performance of his holy office to say, "There is more I must know about you, daughter, and about what happened to you in Manila, before I dare share the blood and body of Our Savior with you."

Myrrha shrank back as from a physical blow. She had known these two men less than a full day but although the time had been short, she felt she had shared a portion of their lives. Certainly her spirit had burgeoned to their regard in a way she had never experienced before. These men had respected her, not for her father's wealth or position of power, but as a human being as worthy of regard as they knew themselves to be. They had admired her beauty with frank eyes, but eyes as devoid of lust as those her father's old First Wife, or Mother Mora had ever turned upon her. Now, for the first time, and when least expected, she was excluded from something they shared, a something that the tones of their voices and every gesture of their bodies showed was very precious to them.

She remained on her knees in anguish until Señor de Sosa lifted her to her feet. Then he gave her a length of soft cloth, laid a hard lump of faintly fragrant, pale yellow soap in her hand and pointed to the nearby stream. She went to her bath obediently, wishing she might have a bit of pumice with which to smooth her skin and a spoonful of warm oil with which to soften it.

At the river's edge she slipped behind a clump of willows, hung her garments on the dense leafy branches, and stepped into the water. It was icy cold, and she gasped but did not draw back. As her body became accustomed to the frigid temperature, she waded deeper, step by slow step, until the stream swirled above her hips. But she was not hardy enough for more than a few splashes. Her legs and her body felt numb, as her spirit had been numbed when she had been denied Holy Communion.

She was conscious that two men had given her a glimpse of a way of life based at least in part upon a different attitude toward women. It had been only the briefest of glimpses, such as one catches through the crack of a door, and then that door had been slammed in her face. She wept like a child that has been punished, and does not know how it has offended.

She turned and started toward the riverbank but stopped short at the sight of a man standing between her and her garments. There was no mistaking the look on his face—the old, mesmeric gleam of lust. Previously she had always taken life for granted. It had been a verity to cling to by any subterfuge or abasement required of her. Now, suddenly, she felt that she would rather sink into the icy current and permit her life to be swept away with it than again to submit her body to such a one as this two-legged beast.

The creature on the bank beckoned to her, and when she did not move, folded his arms and waited. Because of the tears flowing from her eyes his figure seemed to shimmer like the water eddying about her. She wondered whether if she called out to Señor de Sosa and Father Enrique, either man would hear her and come.

She doubted that. She knew they could not hear her small voice because of the distance and the noise of breaking camp. Then she remembered that the word: "Pray! Pray! Pray!" was on Father Enrique's lips more often than any other. Had he not said that prayer could work miracles? What else could help her now?

Myrrha crossed herself and moved her lips in the prayer she liked best, one woman petitioning another. Surely no male creature, divine or otherwise, could understand a woman as completely as compassionately as another woman. "Hail Mary . . . Blessed . . . among women . . . pray for us sinners . . ." Then just as she had seen Father Enrique do so many times to someone standing before him, she again made the sign of the cross, but with the tips of her fingers pointed toward the man on the riverbank.

She could not be certain of the expression on his face because of her tears, but it seemed that the gloating sneer faded and that a look of abject shame took its place. In any case, he dropped briefly to one knee and she heard him mumble, "Forgive me!" Then he turned and ran, crashing through the willows like a water buffalo forcing its way through a thicket. Slowly she donned her clothing and walked back

177

to camp savoring with delight the strange calm and peace which almost seemed to lift her feet above the dust and rubble of the path.

"You were a long time at the stream, Myrrha," Miguel de Sosa said as he handed her a bowl of hominy sprinkled with piñon nuts. On the log beside her he set a thin china cup, nested in a holder of filigreed silver, full of the strange chocolatl.

She smiled happily and said to Father Enrique, "I know now, what it is, this faith of which you speak. I, too, have faith!"

Both men turned surprised and somewhat startled eyes full of anxious questioning upon her. She told them simply and frankly about the soldier in the willows and the miracle wrought by the Mother of God for one of her earthly sisters.

Myrrha expected the pleased approbation of the men and therefore was not prepared for Señor de Sosa's oaths or the priest's anger. Every man in camp was led before her and she was compelled to look at each carefully and to answer whether or not he was the one who had thought to molest her. In the end each was sent back to his duties for the best she could do was to protest, "I cannot point the man out to you, for I did not see him clearly. I shivered from the cold, and tears blurred my eyes. All I know is that he was big and strong and lusting. Then he was sorry and went away and I was spared."

"Are you sure he did not touch you?" Señor de Sosa demanded again and again.

"He did not even come near me," she protested, insisting in a voice that was a blend of eagerness and naïveté, "Do you not think it was a miracle?"

"It was indeed!" de Sosa agreed.

"Perhaps more of a miracle than either of us knows!" Father Enrique murmured. He crossed himself repeatedly, and thereafter during that day gazed at the girl with wonder and perplexity in his eyes.

In the days that followed, Myrrha was never again out of Miguel de Sosa's or Father Enrique's sight for more than a few seconds at a time. Even when the care and demands of her body necessitated privacy, the two men hid her behind blankets draped over tree limbs or held above their own heads by outstretched arms. The priest was never without a long, heavy staff which he knew how to use as a formidable weapon. Day and night, on the march or in camp, the guards hired by Señor de Sosa formed a circle around the merchant, the priest and the girl who always rode between them. Whenever one of the Virrey's men left the place assigned to him in the outer circle and succeeded by guile or brute strength in penetrating the inner guard so that he neared the girl, he was lucky if it was only the flat of the layman's sword he felt on his shoulder or across his back. Señor de Sosa left no doubt in the knave's mind that he would not hesitate to use the edge of his blade if the scoundrel did not get back into line immediately. Father Enrique's whirling staff invariably brought howls of anguish and frequently broke skin and drew blood. The bruises lasted for days, and more than one man wondered how hands and arms as frail as the priest's could deal so quick and sure and heavy a blow.

Occasionally the party met other travelers, and the two groups paused long enough to exchange news of the road. It was obvious that much that was happening in the capital city was of grave concern to Myrrha's protectors. They were even more disturbed by the messages brought them almost daily by Indian runners.

As the days passed, Myrrha became accustomed to riding her mule and to sleeping under the open sky, and she fell asleep easily and quickly now. However, she was aware that on most nights her guardians talked long and earnestly beside the fire, casting anxious glances in her direction before lying down on either side of her to guard her even while they slept. It was not unusual if she awakened in the middle of the night, to find one of them sitting up with his furred robe drawn about his shoulders staring down at her with his brow wrinkled in a troubled frown.

One morning as the party readied itself for travel and de Sosa's guard grouped themselves about the two men and the girl, Myrrha noticed that the outer circle of men seemed smaller than it had been. When she asked about the missing men, a contemptuous look spread over de Sosa's face and the frown between his eyes deepened.

"Yes, there are fewer of them every morning," he answered. "They drift away by twos and threes under the cover of darkness."

"Why do they dessert us?" she asked.

Señor de Sosa hesitated, but Father Enrique stated bluntly: "They

179

have always been bandits at heart. Now that it begins to seem likely that they will have no master to return to in the city, they choose to become outlaws in name as well."

For the next two days, almost always whenever the girl glanced at Miguel de Sosa, she found him gazing steadily at her. There was a strange light in his eyes which he made no effort to disguise or conceal. It was an expression she had never seen before on a man's face. It was a sort of hunger, but a hunger that was guiltless of all passion or greed.

Then one day two Indian runners reached them, one while they ate their noonday meal, and the second before they were well settled for their usual short siesta following. It did not seem to Myrrha that either the merchant or the priest was surprised at the first man's message although it was of the gravest importance. His Eminence, Don Juan Pérez de la Serna, Archbishop of Mexico, the first Indian said, had finally excommunicated His Lordship, Don Diego Carillo Mendoza y Pimental, Marquis de Gelves and Viceroy of New Spain.

"The representative of Our Soverign's own person!" Miguel de Sosa exclaimed.

The tones of his voice were a mingling of horror and deep respect. Then his eyes glowed with sudden, almost pathetic eagerness. The expression on his face was that of a small child as it grasps the big hand that will steady its most stumbling steps.

Father Enrique crossed himself and made the sign of the cross over his patron and the slave. Myrrha bowed her head to receive the blessing as she saw Señor de Sosa do. Then she watched both men as they stared into each other's faces as though each sought assurance from the other. Finally the grim lines on their visages relaxed.

"I cannot serve an unchurched man," Miguel de Sosa said slowly, as though reading the thoughts of his father confessor. "Now, can I?"

"No, my son," the priest agreed. "You dare not. Holy Church forbids trafficking with the damned."

"Therefore, I cannot now deliver this child into the hands of an unregenerate monster, although it was his money that purchased her."

"You may not approach the excommunicate for any purpose whatsoever," the other assured him. "You are absolved—by his own sin—

180

from any further duty to him. You now owe him no obedience, no allegiance of any nature whatsoever. In fact, if you should meet such a man face to face, you may not even speak to him, for that would be the same as greeting Satan himself."

The second Indian runner brought news that the Virrey had attempted to make good his threat of levying a tax on the Archbishop. Fellow sybarites and lackeys in his pay had swept through the city pillaging churches, seizing and carrying away the gold and jeweled altar furnishing. Even the splendid cathedral itself had not been spared. There sacred objects of no intrinsic value and others too large to be transported easily had been damaged or destroyed by the vandals. God-fearing private citizens had placed their household guards at the service of the Archbishop, and the streets of the capital city had become a battleground for the two forces.

It was rumored, the second messenger went on, that the Virrey, ever a godless man and now an excommunicate, had escaped from the palace in the confusion and, deserting his friends, had sought sanctuary in the Convent of San Francisco. This was only rumor, the Indian repeated—he could not vouch for its truth. Those men who dared venture into the streets were full of wildly conflicting tales.

Miguel de Sosa took stock of the situation thoughtfully. Then, speaking slowly and carefully, he shared his problem with his priest. "De Gelves is a bold as well as a dissolute man. He is also capable; what he wants, he has always taken. That he has raped God's altars is proof that he will let nothing stand in the way of his evil desire. This girl, now in my full charge, placed there by the will of God—she is a princess of royal blood! How many slaves are there like her? Is there anything an evil man will not do to possess her?"

He paused to give Myrrha a long searching look and then went on reflectively. "Could it not be, father, that she is really proof of the miracle of prayer? You know how my wife and I have prayed, father, for a daughter. Could she not be a divine gift to me and my wife to take the place of the daughter withheld from us in our youth? In any case, you and I must now plan carefully. When we reach Mexico City, surely we shall have to fight to keep her from the Virrey's men."

"Perhaps we shall not have to fight if we plan wisely and act accordingly," the priest interrupted. "Why should we continue on to the capital? Who is to force that route upon us?" He flung out a hand before him in a sweeping gesture.

Señor de Sosa's eyes followed the direction of the pointing arm, and his lips parted in a snort of derisive laughter. The Virrey's men had also heard the news and, realizing that an excommunicated master was worse than no master at all, were disappearing down the trail. Most of them were mounted on their erstwhile master's pack mules. Some even led animals loaded with his merchandise.

"Thieves! Stop, you bandits! Come back with my goods," the merchant shouted. But some of the absconding soldiers were already too far away to hear; others turned and laughed rudely. Some bellowed crude, insulting remarks. A few, with a mocking show of great courtesy, invited de Sosa to overtake them and claim whatever among their baggage he thought belonged to him.

Señor de Sosa grasped the hilt of his sword and started to call orders to his own guard to pick up their muskets and pursue the thieves when Father Enrique laid a restraining hand on his arm.

"While they are fleeing us they cannot follow us to rob us further," he said with a quick, meaningful glance at Myrrha. "And since they are now turned bandit, perhaps it would be wise to put as much distance between ourselves and them as we can. Bear in mind, son, that we still have valuable merchandise in hand!" Again he glanced at Myrrha as though to emphasize his words.

Señor de Sosa sheathed his sword again before it had been fully drawn. "You are right, as always," he agreed. "The value of the mules they have taken is not great. The merchandise would only be a hindrance to us, should we have to move quickly. And all of it is little enough to pay for a measure of safety and—" he glanced at Myrrha with a look of joy on his face—"and for a daughter at last."

"Where shall we go? What direction shall we take?" the priest asked, peering into the forest on either side of the trail.

The merchant was silent, but his hands seemed to pantomime one possible course of action after another and the rejection of each until he snapped his thumbs in approval.

"The scroundrels! They expect us to pursue them, and so we shall," he exclaimed. "Also we shall make a great deal of noise as though we were straining every effort to overtake them. Hearing us, they will flee as fast as they can and themselves help to lengthen the distance between us. Then we shall turn off at the first likely trail to the right and find our way across the country to Puebla."

"Will that be difficult? And how dangerous?" the priest asked. His words implied curiosity only, and no disapprobation.

"I am not familiar with the side trails," Señor de Sosa confessed. "We are now near the city of Morelia, but we need not go into the town. In fact, I think we should not do so. There have always been spies of the Virrey there, and even now they may be waiting and watching for us. This is a fertile countryside and the hacenderos here are all wealthy men who have had tax after tax laid on them by the Virrey. All of these hacenderos have heard of me. Many of them know me personally. I believe they will give me food and lend me horses and guides; and should our former evil lord send soldiers in pursuit of me, I believe they will protect me."

Señor de Sosa was right. He and his own private guard received all of the help he needed, and he would have received more had the need been greater, so profound was the respect in which all men held him. The rest of the journey he was in flight, without knowing whether or not he was pursued. He never stopped to rest or eat on the trail during the daylight hours lest he be surprised by a band of the Virrey's men, but traveled from hacienda to hacienda without pause regardless of the distances between the great estates. Thus he slept each night behind the protection of thick walls, barred gates and doors and armed household guards.

He introduced Myrrha to his kind hosts and hostesses, not as a slave but as a princess whom he hoped would take the place of a daughter in his own home.

These men and women were charmed with her great beauty of face and form, her gracious manners and her now fluent and almost flawless command of their own language. Nearly every woman exclaimed at first sight of her, "What beautiful eyes!" Their husbands, sons and brothers would add with a great show of gallantry but with the ring of simple truth in their voices, "A man could lose his soul in their depths!"

Señor de Sosa never failed to explain sooner or later, "Her own companions called her The Chinese Lady!" and almost invariably for the rest of the evening she would be La China. Myrrha liked the title as well now as the first time she had heard it, and Miguel de Sosa's face glowed with pride at the subtle homage paid her.

Every morning each family parted from her with honest regret. All of them urged Señor de Sosa to visit them again, the women repeatedly calling after Myrrha the formal: "La casa es de usted, niñita." The men accompanied the travelers a few miles on the trail and repeated their wives' invitations: "My house is always your home, Señor."

Father Enrique, the only man among them whose education had gone very far beyond simple literacy, was amazed at Myrrha's quick, keen intellect. "She must be educated!" he exclaimed over and over again. "Compared with the minds of other women, hers is like a candle beside a firefly."

He began to teach her himself without books or slate, tracing letters in the air with his fingers, or scratching them in the dust with a stick. He rode beside Myrrha constantly, on her right. So that he might be even a few inches nearer, he hooked his left leg over the pommel of the saddle. His mule pressed so close to hers that the two animals often stumbled against each other and sometimes lashed out with their hooves. So easily did the girl learn that, had script been available, she would have been reading before the journey's end.

She quickly memorized all of the commonest prayers she did not already know, in Spanish as well as in Latin, and much of the Catechism as well. Since her eyes shone with delight at the simplest story about the country and its people, Father Enrique entertained her with folk legends already growing up about the church in this new land.

Myrrha's first sight of snow was on the slopes of volcanoes they passed, Popocatepetl and Iztaccihuatl—Lord Popo and his Sleeping Lady, her companions called them. To her amazement and some fright at first, black smoke curled upward from Lord Popo's crown by day. At night the clouds above him glowed cherry red and streams of fire snaked down his sides, hissing viciously as they cut channels through his cold white blanket.

On the thirteenth of March, 1624, Señor de Sosa passed the hill, already overgrown with immense trees, which had once been a temple to strange Indian gods, skirted the village of Cholula, and paused briefly before the Church of the Forty-nine Domes. He could easily have reached Puebla and home that evening, but he did not. Instead he spent the night with yet another friend so that the girl he brought with him might be rested and bathed and clothed in fresh garments when he first presented this daughter God had given him in his old age to Doña Margareta Chaves, his wife.

CHAPTER SIXTEEN

S EÑOR de Sosa and his party were up and on their way early that last morning, but their entrance to the city of Puebla was again delayed. When they were no more than a few miles from the town. they were compelled to turn aside and make way for a party of King Philip's dragoons.

One of the merchant's men galloped after the soldiers to learn their mission. He returned to say that they were on their way to announce formally to the citizens of Puebla that because of the Marquis de Gelves' excommunication with just cause and without repentance, he had been stripped of all wealth and honors and was formally deposed as Virrey of New Spain. Also, that the Captain General and Licentiate, Pedro Gabíria had been appointed Governor and was charged with keeping due order in the provinces. Other bands of soldiers were on their way to other cities in the colony to make similar announcements.

The announcement did not take long nor make much impression on the city, since it had been expected. The dragoons were out of Puebla and already galloping down the road to Vera Cruz with their proclamation when Señor de Sosa and his companions came in sight of the roofs of Puebla above the palms and pepper trees which lined the road. They had just crossed a plain in which, Father Enrique said, there were three hundred sixty-five churches—one for every day in the year. They had been built, he added, because a group of men believed there was added merit for the Christian who worshiped in as many different churches as possible.

The plain was vast. Nevertheless, Myrrha could see many of these churches no matter what the direction she turned her head. Saw also, that man's religion fervor did not carry far beyond construction, for already many of them were badly in need of repair. A few were only tumbled heaps of stone and tile about storm-ravaged altars.

Then Myrrha looked ahead and saw the twin spires of La Cathedral de los Angeles—filigreed, fretted and gilded confections of stone gleaming alabaster white and golden in the morning sun. Charmed by the ethereal beauty of the two spires, she was so lifted out of herself that she clasped her hands together and cried out, "These are the towers that the angels built! No human arms and fingers could turn stone into lace like this!" She was so enthralled that she did not notice the group of horsemen galloping toward them until the treetops between hid the cathedral from sight.

Then the girl saw Señor de Sosa and Father Enrique sweep their hats from their heads to the ladies and lean from their saddles to clasp the hands and shoulders of many among the men. The deep, honest and unaffected regard in which his neighbors held the Pueblan merchant was so marked that Myrrha stared from woman to woman and man to man. Aside from her mother, The Pearl, she had never heard of another human being loved beyond the respect which all men pay to wealth and power.

She became aware of the fact that every one of the newcomers studied her carefully. Even as the men bowed gravely and the women pressed near enough to grasp a shoulder and lay a cheek against hers their frank admiration was tempered by a sense of wonder. There was a questioning in their eyes, queries which only time could answer.

These women were striking creatures, every one of them, not supremely beautiful by Oriental standards, but confidently handsome by any set of criteria. As she watched the women and submitted to the strange greetings with instinctive courtesy, Myrrha suddenly sensed as clearly as though she had been told, that physical beauty was not the paramount virtue in these women's lives. The thought exhilarated her with something akin to the spirit of freedom and, paradoxically, flooded her with a sense of envy. She watched the women even more keenly, wondering what it was that gave each confidence in herself as a woman greater even than an honored First Wife might assume.

Everywhere Myrrha looked she met frankly appraising eyes, for everyone in Puebla knew the nature of the errand on which the recent Virrey had sent their fellow townsman. When news of the Virrey's excommunication had reached the city, all of the inhabitants had

187

been curious as to the fate of this girl. Friends of Señor de Sosa had discussed the moral, ethical and professional problems of a man with paid-up merchandise in his possession for delivery to a man with whom he might not deal in any manner whatsoever. Later Myrrha learned that many among those now greeting her had prayed daily for her protector's safe return to his home and family—and that she herself might be delivered by some divine act from the maw of a devil incarnate.

On greeting de Sosa many among them exclaimed, "You were a brave man to travel unmapped trails and through strange forests and jungles. But traveling under God's protection you were spared the attack of *tigres* [mountain lions] by night and bandits by day!" Others alighted from their horses and, kneeling in the dust of the highway, lifted their hands and voices to heaven and thanked God that their prayers had been answered.

Myrrha acknowledged each greeting after the fashion of her own country, crossing her hands upon her breast and bowing her head until her chin touched her wrists. "How quaint, but how graceful!" "Charming!" "So beautiful! And so gently bred!" "What lovely eyes! And hands that seem to talk!" When she thanked these new friends for their welcoming in their own language, they were delighted anew and Señor de Sosa glowed with pride.

It would have been impossible for Myrrha to remember all of the new faces and strange names of those who welcomed her to her new home that day. Two among them, however, were impressed upon her mind by the especial warmth with which they and the Pueblan merchant greeted each other: El Capitán Hipólito del Castillo de Altra and his wife.

"Our home is yours, señorita," both assured her in the usual formal phrase, but the spirit behind the words came from gentle hearts eager to love.

"Since Señora de Sosa is my dearest friend, you will be a daughter to me as well as to her," the captain's wife added as she leaned far out from her saddle to throw her arms about Myrrha.

Señora Hipólito rode beside the girl the rest of the way, putting out a hand to touch her every now and then in a gesture that was half caress, half possessive. She and her husband were the last of the horsemen to turn aside before Señor de Sosa reached his own house.

188

Señor de Sosa's house was much like those of the hacenderos which had sheltered the travelers on their way up from Acapulco except that it was larger and finer. It stood on the northeastern outskirts of the city near the palace of the governor of the state of Puebla, and was surrounded by thick adobe walls which in front formed a wall of the dwelling itself. There were no openings of any kind in the wall in the first story save an immense gate through which a carriage could be driven. The second story windows in the front opened upon balconies, all iron-barred. A quick glance showed that the windows of neighboring houses, both great and small, were similarly barred.

The broad, iron-grilled gate swung open as the travelers approached, and the group rode through a covered arch into a paved courtyard surrounded by a two-storied colonnaded balcony. Aside from the fact that the arched entrance supported the windowed rooms of a dwelling rather than watch towers, archer slots and lean-to shelters for soldiers, it might have been the entrance to a lesser Oriental khan's stronghold. The courtyard, or patio as she soon learned to call it, was really a tub-rooted garden, and now it seemed full of people.

The air of the patio was heavy with the perfume from many blossoms. In the very center of the open space was a tiled fountain which at first glance seemed a tangled confusion of streams of water playing over and through big leaved vines and glossy leafed shrubs. Six chairs of rawhide straps woven together like rattan had been placed before the fountain. Three small children, a boy and two younger girls, had bounded from their chairs and rushed to the gate as it opened. Both Miguel de Sosa and Father Enrique slid from their mounts and embraced the children. Then each tot kissed the priest's hand and knelt for his blessing.

In the meantime a young man had come forward and he and Señor de Sosa threw their arms about each other and embraced and kissed as tenderly—Myrrha put the thought in terms of her experience—as tenderly as master and dearly beloved concubine. The young man, as splendidly dressed as any of the elegant horsemen they had met that morning, took the older man's hand and led him to the two women in the remaining chairs. The younger woman remained seated, and Myrrha's heart leaped with pity, for her thin face was as livid as that of any corpse. Señor de Sosa held both of her hands in his and leaned forward and kissed her on her forehead.

"Father Enrique and I have prayed for you during our absence, daughter," he said gently. His words seemed questioning, and his eyes searched her face for something he did not find there.

"I could not stand my pain, father, were I not upheld by so much love," the woman answered in a shallow, petulant voice.

Myrrha gazed at her curiously, but the first quick surge of pity died away and nothing of compassion took its place. The Oriental girl knew women, and she distrusted this one from the first sound of her hollow words. In a harem as elsewhere the blight of disease is a misfortune; but only a fool attempts to use it as a weapon in the age-old struggle between the sexes. The invalid did not raise her face but stared at Myrrha out of the corners of her eyes, and with a trace of contemptuous sneer on her lips. Myrrha met the look calmly, under level brows, her face set against betrayal of her thoughts. Still she could not help wondering if and why this woman included her, a stranger, in her seeming fear of approaching death.

Then Señor de Sosa and the older woman were standing beside Myrrha's mule. Her protector held up his arms and she slipped from the saddle to the ground with his help.

The two women looked long and carefully into each other's eyes. Myrrha was well aware of her own beauty, but as she studied the countenance of her protector's wife she thought she had never seen greater dignity or sensed more inherent charm, although youth was now only a memory for Doña Marguerita. Her eyes were as big and black as Myrrha's own, but they were framed in a network of fine wrinkles. Her iron-gray hair was streaked with bands of pure white, and her cheek muscles sagged lower than the point of her chin. When her lips parted in a smile, gaps showed between her strong, fairly large white teeth. Timidly Myrrha put out first one hand, and then the other, like one groping her way, and the two women embraced.

A little cough from the younger woman lolling languidly in her chair was followed by a fretful exclamation, and the magic of the moment was shattered. Myrrha was introduced to the family, not as a slave, or even as an inferior, but as an equal. There was Don Alfredo the son, and his son, Rosario, who was dressed exactly like his father, even to the tiny silver spurs on his small boots. Each bowed from the waist. Doña Eulalia, the invalid and Alfredo's wife, nodded slightly, but covered the necessity for words by a light spasm of coughing behind her fan. Her two daughters, Tonita and Marita, dipped their knees and at the same time swept their ankle-length skirts out behind them in the first formal curtsy Myrrha had ever seen.

Miguel de Sosa made a little speech to the Indian men and women surrounding the family, telling these servants that the newly arrived guest was a great lady, the daughter of a king. Now she was to be treated . . . He broke off briefly to glance at his wife and Myrrha's eyes followed his. Doña Marguerita was nodding her head as though she read her husband's mind and agreed with every thought before it was clothed in words. This highborn lady, Señor de Sosa ended, was to be served as though she were a daughter of the house.

Involuntarily Myrrha glanced at the daughter-in-law. Doña Eulalia's eyes had narrowed to slits; but since her face, except her eyes and brow, were hidden by her fan, Myrrha could not tell if the expression was contemptuous or furtive. The eyes were neither cold nor steady. They were hotly ablaze with the fires of disease at least, and they darted here and there, up and down, as though attempting to avoid Myrrha's and yet unable to do so. For a second time the Chinese girl's heart swelled with pity. "One is poor indeed," she thought, "to be fearful of a slave, however grandiose a new master's welcome."

Then Doña Marguerita touched Myrrha's hand and the fingers of the two women intertwined. With her family about her and her household servants following, she led Myrrha across the patio to an arched doorway under the balcony. There she paused and glanced behind her, watching while her husband and her son drew lace-fringed handkerchiefs from their sleeves and draped them over the heads of her two granddaughters.

"They are still too young to wear mantillas, and yet their heads must be covered in church," she explained. "We always say a prayer of thanksgiving in our own chapel within the hour of my husband's return from any trip. There will be a mass in the cathedral later at a suitable time."

Myrrha had never before been in a house of worship, not even a mosque. Father Enrique's instruction enroute from Acapulco to Pueblo had of necessity been largely concerned with creed and catechism. Because he was a scholar, a cultured gentleman and a dreamer whose fantasies were laced with mysticism, he had stressed the lives of the saints, history of the church and religious philosophy more than

191

ritual. The careless, bored teaching of the Manila priest had included very little of what she now saw: holy water, genuflexion, votive candles, rosaries, statuary and icons, monstrance, and the lavish use of gold leaf on carved pillars and ceiling. If there had been mention of any of these, she did not remember it.

Now, in the confusion of too much to see and understand, she recalled only a fragment of the little she did know. She walked along as close to Doña Marguerita as she could without jostling the other with her body, and tried to imitate every gesture of the older woman. She saw Doña Marguerita nodding her head with a satisfied smile on her lips as she had smiled and nodded earlier at her husband's words. Her fingers paused momentarily on her beads and she leaned closer to Myrrha listening as the girl murmured the Latin phrases of the Pater Noster.

As the group came from the chapel the elder de Sosas and their priest walked ahead. Myrrha stopped to watch Don Alfredo as he crossed himself with holy water. She started to dip her fingers into the font also, but he caught her hand in his above the basin.

"Have you been confirmed?" he asked.

The word was new to her and she answered, "No." without hesitation.

"Then I do not believe this is for you—yet," Don Alfredo told her. "We shall have to ask Father Enrique about it."

As though to soften the denial, he smiled at her gently, and she was amazed at how much the younger man resembled his father, even to the tones of his voice. He was handsome, too, and he knew it and recognized the admiration in her eyes. She turned her face away quickly, confused at memory of something Father Enrique had told her which at the time had seemed against nature and therefore foolish —that Christian men are permitted one wife only at a time and no concubines.

She could not have told why, but for the first time in her life Myrrha did not feel a sense of pride and such small power as Allah gives women with a man's admiration. She had been taught that the ability to rouse such admiration is to a woman what a weapon in hand is to a man. She was pleased that he found her beautiful, and at the same time vaguely disturbed. She wondered if, in this strange new world with customs which must be accepted whether understood or not, the weapons of a submissive chattel would be adequate. And then the thought crossed her mind: What need of weapons in a household ruled by love?

If Don Alfredo sensed the nature of her confused thoughts, he gave no sign. He tucked her hand under his elbow and holding it captive there, led her back to the patio. Seemingly his wife had not moved while the family was at prayer, not even to the extent of lowering her fan or widening her glance. "She looks very tired," Myrrha thought and stooped to pick up the handkerchief which had slid from her lap. Myrrha's skirts billowed outward on the floor and hid from all eyes but her own the quick thrust of the invalid's foot which shoved her hand aside.

"Dear 'Fredo, my handkerchief," Eulalia exclaimed. "But never mind, a servant will get it. Ah yes, the Chinese girl has retrieved it." There was no word of thanks, nor did she extend her hand to meet Myrrha's.

Myrrha had experienced so many new emotions in such a short period of time that it tired her to try to understand the satisfaction which glowed in the eyes of the invalid. Still she wondered if others had caught the innuendo. Customs and religious observances may differ with distance, ran through her mind, but women are the same. Did not this invalid realize that if one is dearly beloved the pain she suffers will cut across two hearts—the one that gives as well as the one that receives? And that if love has fled, petulance breeds impatience and then aversion?

This woman's position with her lord is in peril, Myrrha thought, and it is incredible that anyone of her age should further jeopardize that position by bad temper! Then again Myrrha remembered and with a sense of shock a further statement of Father Enrique's concerning Christian marriage; that it is dissolved only by death, regardless of the health, or age or character of the wife. This was truly a strange world into which she had been plunged, and she doubted that she would ever be able to understand laws that seemed so irrational.

Something of her perplexity must have shown in Myrrha's face, for Doña Eulalia dropped her fan and laughed. The laughter was so strangely robust that other members of the family turned to her in surprise. Slowly, and with a show of great effort, she twisted her body so that she could catch the back of her chair with both hands, and

193

started to rise. Myrrha had to step backward to make room for her outthrust hips. Two Indian women instantly appeared on each side of the invalid. The tops of their heads reached only to her chin; but they were broad, muscular women, and her weight on their shoulders was scarcely any burden to them.

The Indians brushed past Myrrha, and then stopped at a word from their mistress. " 'Fredo," she called over her shoulder, "I do not feel like sitting at table to eat. Will you not lunch with me in my room?"

"This is papa's first meal at home in a long time, 'Lala. Don't you think you could sit with us for just one cup of chocolate?" There was no impatience in his words, but the reproof was unmistakable.

The invalid let the corners of her mouth fall. The muscles of her cheek quivered like a child debating whether a prize is worth the tears necessary to obtain it. Don Alfredo sighed, lifted his daughter Marita from his knees and set her on the chair from which he arose. Unhurriedly, as though much used to the chore but with a deep frown between his brows, he murmured something in a low voice to his father, then picked his wife up in his arms, crossed the patio, ascended a beautifully arched stone stairway, and at the end of the upper balcony entered a door and closed it behind him.

CHAPTER SEVENTEEN

IFE in the de Sosa household was calm and peaceful, far more so, it seemed to Myrrha, than in a harem with its undercurrents of greed and intrigue and self-interest. There were no guards here with silken whips to compel obedience. As the days passed she could not help observing that what at first seemed the usual subservience was either a service of love freely given or, as in much of Doña Eulalia's conduct, privilege assumed as a natural right. In fact, she was seldom aware of what seemed to one of her background as restraining laws, and she responded to the unwonted spiritual and social freedom like new growth on a plant reaching for the sun. She was observant of the conduct of others and sensitive to their moods to an unusual degree, and for that reason made fewer mistakes than would have been true of any ordinary woman. But there were mistakes.

They were fewer as time went on, for she learned quickly; but in the beginning the social mores of the two widely divergent worlds inevitably clashed. There were occasions when Doña Eulalia's face registered exaggerated shock and self-righteous disapproval. At such times she gathered her two small daughters in her arms and covered their faces with the folds of her mantilla as though to shield them from contamination.

Doña Marguerita's eyes would open wide in surprise but there was more pity than rebuke in her voice when she stopped Myrrha with such words as: "The customs are different here, child."

Señor de Sosa would add if he were present: "A different land, a different religion, and a different life, daughter."

There was the time when Señor de Sosa invited a group of Indian musicians into his patio to entertain his family with an evening of music. The instruments they carried were strange to Myrrha: a marimba, two guitars and a tambourine. The music was different also.

Too loud and fast, according to Myrrha's taste; worst of all, no subtlety about it. The chords were too crudely basic and direct to challenge a delicately perceptive aesthetic sense. She wrinkled her brow in displeasure until she saw that the family enjoyed the cacaphony. When she set herself to understanding what it was that gave so much pleasure to the others, she noticed that by tapping toes or fingers, or tossing the head, each body pulsated to the dominating rhythm in some way.

"Eulalia was an accomplished dancer before her strength failed," Doña Marguerita told Myrrha. "No fiesta here in Puebla was complete until she had put the others girls to shame. It used to be said as a joke that our 'Fredo won her for his wife because he was the only man whose dancing equaled hers."

"And because 'Lala won so much money from him at cards that he had to get a portion of it back somehow," her son's father added drily.

Doña Eulalia's face was alight with pride, and Myrrha knew there had been yet a third reason for Don Alfredo's choice. Before the years, childbearing and disease had left their scars upon the woman's face and figure, Eulalia must have been a handsome, perhaps even a beautiful woman.

"Do you dance, Myrrha?" the invalid asked, and did not wait for a reply. "But of course you do. All harem women dance, do they not? Dance for us. Tell the Indians what kind of music you want and they will play—well, being Indians they will play just what they please. Indian musicians always make up their own music, whether it is what you like or not!"

Myrrha looked at the elder de Sosas. They were used to Eulalia's carping; if they noticed it now they ignored it. They nodded their heads to her.

The girl arose, slipped the mantilla from her head and held it across her shoulders and outflung arms like an Oriental scarf. Slowly, as though her body were not an angular, jointed, bony frame, but a slender, willow twig, she sank to the floor in formal obeisance to her audience. She heard the gasps of admiration and glanced briefly at Eulalia who was staring at her in surprise. As effortlessly as a puff of smoke ascending in still air she rose to her feet, postured and swung her body from knees to neck. There were many dances for her to choose from, but all harem dances had been created and perfected with one aim in view.

196

Her blood had not yet warmed to the dance when Doña Marguerita's encircling arms held her body still. "Beautiful! Beautiful! Exquisite! But we do not dance in such a manner here. Marita will show you." And she beckoned to her granddaughter.

But Eulalia's hand was pressing her little daughter's body tight to her bosom and it did not relax. Across the child's head she was glaring at her husband, whose eyes were fixed on his sombrero which lay on the pavement between his feet.

"I will teach you to dance—to dance as we do," Doña Marguerita said in nervous haste to pull her family together again. "I also danced when I was young."

"And very gracefully, too," her husband added warmly.

"Perhaps the harem girl sings or plays some musical instrument," Eulalia broke in. On the surface the words were courteous enough, but the voice was cold.

Myrrha replied that she sang but she knew no songs in the new language. She played also, she said, but the dulcimer and rebec. One of the musicians brought her his guitar to look at and examine.

"I could learn to play this," she said in simple honesty, "but I cannot learn to play and sing at the same time."

She finally sang, and the Indian, after listening attentively for a moment, began touching the strings of his guitar only a fraction of a second after each new note and so accompanied her almost as skillfully as if he were familiar with the tune. In her native tongue Myrrha sang a little song about the beauty of the ephemeral things of life: the rays of the rising sun on morning dew, the wild grasses which bloom on the dikes between the rice paddies; the pure notes of a bird which floats alike over harem walls and through the bars of the strongest prison.

When she had finished, the de Sosa family sat in wide-eyed, silent tribute—a silence broken first by the household servants who, unnoticed, had left their tasks and crept into the patio to share the music. There was a soughing sound as though many pent-up breaths were released, and then a wave of barely whispered *muy simpatico's:* Very nice!

"Ordinarily when we see or hear a good performance, we shout *Olé!* Hurrah! But such sweetness should not be followed by raucous bellows," Don Alfredo said.

197

"In your land, how do people applaud?" Doña Eulalia asked. "Men are always eager to show their appreciation of the unusual and different, you know."

"When a slave pleased my father with her music or," Myrrha paused to smile sweetly at the other, "by her dancing, he gave her a jewel. The size and value of the bauble was a measure of the pleasure he took in her service."

The girl was still smiling at the older woman when Señora de Sosa placed in her hand the broach she had just unpinned from her own bosom. "May I give it to her, Miguel?" Dona Marguerita was calling over her shoulder to her husband. "The child has no jewelry, none at all. I cannot say she needs jewels to enhace her beauty, but what gem will not seem finer worn by her!"

Before Myrrha took her eyes away from Eulalia, the girl saw the other gasp and knew that Doña Marguerita had, on impulse, given her something the other desired, and perhaps had expected to receive ultimately.

When she looked at the broach in her hand, Myrrha caught her breath with delight. The gift was no trifle! Lozenge-shaped, it was as broad across as the palm of her hand. In the center was a ruby so brilliantly red that one felt the stone should be hot from the fire within it. At each of the four corners was an uncut emerald, and the gold of the filigree holding the stones together was studded with pearls.

Señor de Sosa was nodding his head and smiling approval as he said to his wife, "Show her your jewel chest tomorrow and see that she is adorned as a daughter of this household should be." Then to Myrrha, "You like the pin? I am glad my wife thought of the gift, for your pleasure is our pleasure."

The gift was magnificent, and Myrrha wondered how one thanked the donor of such largess. She heard herself saying, "This is as beautiful as the spirit in this house. As valuable as your regard. It makes me think of this land: green for the palm trees, white for the snows on your burning mountains, and red . . ." Myrrha stopped, for red of course could mean only one thing.

"I guess one should say, red for the blood spilled by the warriors who conquered this new land," Señor de Sosa finished for her. "Mama, show her where to pin the broach on her blouse. Now these musical

198

instruments you name, I shall send to China for them immediately. You shall have the very best that money can buy." Then his face fell, "But we shall have to wait a long time. At least a year, probably much longer, before we can have them."

As he sighed, the Indian laid his guitar across Myrrha's lap and nudged her elbow gently. There was a glow in his eyes. She knew instinctively that this man had understood and appreciated the aesthetic quality of her music while the others, those of the dominant race, had merely enjoyed it. She noted that the color of this man's hair and eyes and skin and the shape of his face were all very like her own. Even if Spanish music was all he now knew, something had made him unconsciously modify the staccato rhythms with the eliding quarter tones and the undulating melodies from the Orient.

Myrrha lightly swept her fingers across the strings of the Indian's guitar, exploring the instrument, testing her ability to coax beautiful sounds from its strange strings.

Seeing her gesture, Señor de Sosa turned to his son. "Tomorrow morning, 'Fredo, find and buy the best guitar there is to be had in Puebla."

"I shall teach you to dance, and you shall teach my granddaughters to sing," Doña Marguerita said. She turned from Myrrha to Eulalia and there was no mistaking that her words were as much command to her daughter-in-law as they were promise to the Chinese girl.

"Perhaps when her songs are translated into our language, they will be like her dancing," Eulalia sneered.

Doña Marguerita turned to Myrrha with a startled look on her face. But the expression changed to respect, and she and her husband exchanged glances of gratified pride at Myrrha's answer.

"Some songs are passed from lip to lip, lady, but like much in life they lose their freshness with age. Songs are like flowers, best when newly plucked, whether from a branch or from the heart. New songs take their meaning and charm from the circumstances of the moment of their birth. I never saw very much of the land of my birth, and I am told that I have crossed more than half of this land. I have seen your deserts, plains and mountains, your streams and lakes, your planted crops and your virgin jungles, your homes and your churches gleaming in the sun. My heart has been stirred by your vast and beautiful land, and I sang of the things your land and my land have in common —the beauty of God's world."

There was a moment of silence, and then Eulalia again spoke in a brittle and somewhat grudging voice. "So you are now a poet as well as a musician and dancer!"

"Oh no," Myrrha disclaimed quickly. Then she turned to Doña Marguerita and added slowly: "As a child, I was surrounded by love and beauty. Yes, even in a harem! And I wonder if such a child does not see beauty—and love when that is possible—for the rest of her life?"

The days that followed passed swiftly for Myrrha. The rhythms, the cadences, even the chords of Western music were different from all she had known theretofore. Nevertheless, it seemed as though she mastered the guitar overnight and could draw the music of both worlds from it at will. The new dances, also, were easy for her, although it seemed strange to her at first to make so much use of her feet.

"The accomplished dancer may move about as she chooses, but she must also be able to perform the same steps in no larger space than one block of paving tile," Doña Marguerita panted as she showed Myrrha a new step. The older woman's muscles were stiff and her joints sometimes crackled like peanut shells under one's thumb, and she laughed at her own awkwardness. But Myrrha could move her body from place to place as quickly or slowly as she chose. Or she could dance with her feet fluttering above one spot like a wind whipped flower on a short stem.

Señorito Rosario, the grandson, was always tossing his hat from his head immediately upon entering the patio and, in spite of countless scoldings, leaving it where it lay. "It will get crushed some day," he was told, although there were never less than a dozen persons about, servants and family, to pick it up for him. One afternoon when the child's sombrero landed at Myrrha's feet, in a spirit of mischief she danced on the brim of the hat, moving backward and forward and circling the crown at will, never trampling the crown, never crushing the fringed, embroidered, upcurled edge of the brim. It was a feat she was called upon to perform many times for many guests of the de Sosas.

It also called attention to the size of Myrrha's feet. Her feet had never been bound, yet they were no larger than many a Chinese woman's "golden lilies." When she needed new footwear, Señora de Sosa was compelled to take her to La Calle de las Muñecas—where every shop was devoted either to the manufacture of dolls, dressing them or selling them—because the lasts of the regular shoemakers could not be used for her. Those for adults were all much too big. Those for children were too broad and were not adapted to the high heels which had only lately been imported from France, but which had immediately become extremely fashionable.

At the first public fiesta when Myrrha danced with the other young unmarried women of the village, Don Alfredo tossed his own hat at her feet in obvious challenge. He also led the thunder of *Bravuras!* and *Olés!* that greeted her performance. And so the *tapatía,* a dance that was to take a beloved place in the folkways of Mexico was born. A dance that in the decades and centuries following eventually saw many hats showered at the feet of a belle, and the hat chosen by her to dance upon indicated the direction of her interest if not affection.

Myrrha's new life in this new and in many ways incredibly strange and perplexing world, was many-faceted. It demanded a great deal more of her than music and dancing. The de Sosas were a devout couple and faithful in their religious observances. Señor de Sosa, grateful to have been God's instrument in rescuing the Chinese princess from the lecherous hands of the erstwhile Virrey and his libertine court, paid for a Mass to be said in the already famous, though still new, Cathedral of the Angels.

Myrrha remembered little of that thanksgiving mass. Perhaps it was because she was so greatly impressed by the awe-inspiring beauty of the immense, ornate church. But she was most deeply and lastingly impressed by a slight woman in the garb of a Conceptionist Sister—a flaring white headdress above a tight-fitting white coif, and a black robe caught in at the waist by a dun-colored rope such as a coolie might use for a tumpline. Myrrha knew without being told that in her youth this woman had been a great beauty. The passing years which had etched lines in her face had only heightened her charm thereby.

She was strongly drawn to the woman the moment their eyes met. It was as though an age-old bond had always existed between them, a bond of incalculable strength which could not be worn thin or severed by the friction of the years.

The woman was introduced as Sor [Sister] María de Jesús Tomelín, a Franciscan nun. Sor María was busy changing the altar linen when the de Sosa party entered the church, and she paused in her work to greet them. It was evident from that first casual meeting in the Cathedral that Sor María loved the de Sosas and that they not only held the woman in the highest respect, but loved her also like a daughter. As Myrrha learned later, in spite of the fact that the de Sosas had often disagreed with the nun's father on matters vital to the lives of both families, her parents had been, until their deaths, like brother and sister to Señor de Sosa and his wife. Moreover, Sor María's mother had shared the de Sosas' deep religious convictions.

Like the de Sosas, Sor María's parents—both now dead—had been people of great wealth, culture, and family background. Sor María, born April 9, 1579, was their first child.

From infancy María had been of extraordinary beauty—beyond even her mother. Most unusual for anyone of Spanish descent, she had green eyes of piercing brilliance, and heavy, long, curling hair as darkly red as wild mountains dahlias after the first light frost of autumn. Even as a very young child she was slender, and with the years she grew into a tall, graceful girl with an exquisite form.

Sor María's father, Don Sebastian de Tomelín, had been as proud of his daughter as he was of a perfect foal from one of his blooded Moorish mares, and he looked upon her as being much the same type of asset. Just as wealth and social position had been his primary considerations when he chose her mother, he planned that his daughter's marriage should unite him with still another of the Colony's richest and most noteworthy families.

María's mother, Doña Francesca, never forgot either her own childhood yearning for the cloistered life or her vow that her firstborn should be dedicated to the Church. From María's infancy her mother always dressed her in sober black as nearly nun-like in pattern as her father confessor would permit. When Don Sebastian bought his daughter lengths of velvets and brocades and commanded the family seamstresses to make his daughter dresses after the current elaborate fashion, Doña Francesca tried to find other tasks for those servants. Failing that, she managed to hide the fashionable gowns—and at the same time her daughter's exquisite figure—under some voluminous black cape.

María's religious instruction began almost as soon as the girl was old enough to listen and repeat by rote what was said to her, and it did not end with her mastery of the Catechism and subsequent confirmation. Fearing that her husband would forbid further education for his daughter than the merest literacy which many men of that day still considered enough for women, Doña Francesca taught the child herself at first, keeping always before her volumes of Saints' lives and the histories of the various religious orders. María learned effortlessly and soon outstripped her teacher's meager accomplishments not only in erudition but in the maturity of her grasp of theological concepts.

Doña Francesca sought the advice of her dear friends, the de Sosas, and upon their recommendation, hired a professor from the University of Puebla to instruct María in ecclesiastical subjects. Don Sebastian, like many another man of his day, surrounded his wife and family with all possible luxury except the small independence of a private purse. Doña Francesca had her reasons for not consulting him when María's teacher was hired, and he knew nothing of that project until some time after the professor refused to continue until paid for past services.

Doña Francesca paid the man with a ring from her jewel chest, a ring worth many times the sum the professor had asked. Believing he had hit upon a good thing, the impecunious scholar soon demanded more pay and received another piece of jewelry. This went on and with rapidly increasing frequency until Doña Francesca realized that her only freedom from his blackmail lay in exposing her secret to her husband and asking his help. Don Sebastian recovered his wife's jewelry, dismissed his daughter's teacher and commanded her to turn her thoughts from theology to matrimony as her mother had done before her. Like many another man whose will has been drowned in a flood of feminine tears, Don Sebastian promised his wife that María would not be compelled to wed anyone completely unacceptable to her. From that it was an easy step to extract another promise that if

María's heart were set upon anyone of sufficient social stature and wealth, he would not compel her to wed another but would bow to her choice.

María chose the Church, which at that time held title to half the land of New Spain plus rights to the persons and labor of the Indians thereon, and all minerals within those lands plus almost exclusive ownership of such manufactories as were permitted in the Colony. As a Bride of Christ, María would be allied with wealth and power beyond the comprehension of most men, including her father. Moreover, the fate of Don Sebastian's own soul throughout eternity depended unequivocally upon his obedience to the mandates of the Lord his daughter had chosen.

Trapped by his own intrigue, the man submitted with the poor grace of one accustomed to having his own way so completely that any other course of action seems irrational. So, and in spite of his anger, his daughter entered the convent of The Immaculate Conception in the city of Puebla as a novice on May 3, 1598, at the age of nineteen. An age at which, he reminded her and her mother, a dutiful daughter would already have presented him with several grandchildren!

Beaten though he was, Don Sebastian had the last word. It was the custom at that time for the wealthy father of such a novice to make a very substantial gift to her Chapter, and to remember her convent from time to time with other substantial gifts. It was expected that in return certain otherwise rigid regulations would be relaxed for the benefit of the novice, and that at the end of her novitiate, or very shortly thereafter, she would become a prioress. Don Sebastian flouted custom and disinherited his daughter who already had made something of a reputation for saintliness.

Until Miguel de Sosa and his wife came to her rescue financially, Sor María had enjoyed no greater privileges than some orphan or foundling deposited at the convent's door under the anonymous blanket of the darkest night. Even with the help of her father's friends, the de Sosas, for the rest of a long lifetime, Sor María had to be satisfied with no higher a position than Mistress of Novices—a responsibility which she fulfilled to the complete satisfaction of everyone but herself. But through it all there was never the slightest suspicion at any time that she questioned the rightness of her vocation or rebelled against the rigors of her life.

The brilliance of Sor María's mind was recognized by her superiors in the convent, and her education was continued under new teachers. When Myrrha first met Sor María in the Cathedral of the Angels, the nun was middle-aged and, although a woman, had long been recognized as one of the outstanding scholars in Mexico.

In spite of the differences in their ages and backgrounds, Sor María was as strongly attracted to the Chinese girl as the latter was to the nun—to the great delight of the de Sosas. They placed the girl under Sor María's care for further instruction in the Spanish language and culture and in history and literature, as well as religion and theology. The attraction between the two deepened constantly. Myrrha spent more and more time with her instructress at the convent, and while there shared the lay and religious duties of the sisters and was spared none of their disciplines.

Sor María recognized a kindred intellect as well as spirit in the younger woman, and while directing the girl's studies enjoyed probing her mind regarding details of her former life at another level of civilization. Myrrha bared her innermost self to the nun as she never did to another human being, and so admired the grace, the tact and the consummate wisdom of the other that her heart was soon filled with ardent desire to be as nearly like the other as possible. When in the convent she shortened her steps to the demure, straight-paced glide of the Sisters, whenever possible she hid the tips of her fingers in the folds of a shawl, and she tried to keep her eyes fixed on the floor before her, as though in meditation so deep that the world about her was shut out of her thoughts.

In the convent one day she witnessed the investiture of a young nun. Sor María had explained to Myrrha that the taking of the veil was symbolical of a wedding. That the novice, now being sure of her convictions and having proven her sincerity by her period of testing as a novitiate, had finally become the Bride of Christ and henceforth would devote her life to His service, and His service only.

The former Moslem slave watched spellbound, and marveled at the happiness on the girl's face. Myrrha had been taught the arts of pleasing men, of pandering to their carnal appetites when that would buy advantage, submission to them always, and the extreme necessity of hiding fear or aversion or shrinking from them. That a woman could approach her lord willingly and with her heart overflowing with joy was a new concept. That submission could be reckoned a great privilege and not a cruel, repugnant duty filled her mind with wonder and, eventually, her heart with longing.

She began to find it difficult to keep her gaze fixed on the path before her feet, for her eyes constantly sought and searched the faces of all the nuns she met. She found herself envying their poised calm and serenity—or wondering what might be amiss between the woman whose brow was wrinkled and her Lord. More and more often she found herself kneeling before some statue of Our Lady of Guadalupe to pray—one woman petitioning another that care might be lifted from the heart of a third.

It sometimes occurred to Myrrha during this period that she was in reality two women. For while she studied and shared the lives of the Conceptionist Sisters, she also shared the social life of her protectors. Don Miguel provided for Myrrha's wardrobe as he would have provided for a daughter of his own flesh and blood. Great lengths of the costliest silken brocades from China and the sheerest muslins from India were placed at her disposal. Since the ladies of the Colony were separated from the Court of Spain by both time and distance, the cut of their dresses depended in some degree at least upon individual taste and personal creative ability. Myrrha experimented with the hoops and bustles, gussets and flounces, laces and embroideries affected by the women of Puebla. These styles suited Doña Eulalia's tall, spare frame admirably, but the Oriental girl's tiny body was lost in the furbelows. They made her look like a child bundled up in her mother's clothes and playing at adulthood.

Alfredo's wife began speaking to her—and with increasing frequency of her to others—as though she were a child; but a stepchild, unloved and often in the way. It was only before her parents-in-law that she hid her sneers at the newcomer's appearance in Western garb.

In the end Myrrha patterned her dresses as simply as possible: full, ankle-length skirts gathered on a flat, unornamented belt, and equally simple, round-necked blouses covering a modest expanse of shoulder and forearm. Gradually and naturally she had reverted to the style of dress both she and her mother, The Pearl, had worn in Cochin China.

Once again, thanks to Senor de Sosa's generosity, she embroidered her white blouses with seed pearls, and her red, white and green skirts with gold and silver thread. The result was as beautiful and as much admired in New Spain as it had been in her father's harem. Only Eulalia made occasion to suggest that the stylized arabesques Myrrha sketched for her embroideries were nothing more than heathen symbols.

The de Sosas were honored citizens of Puebla, much sought after socially and dearly beloved by their intimates. As their ward Myrrha enjoyed an enviable position in the social life not only of Puebla but the colonial capital as well. Over and above this position, her grace and charm and her personality endeared her to her new friends, old and young alike. But at the same time something new was growing up within her, the seed of which she had surely inherited from The Pearl. A seed which had germinated and sprouted into its first feeble life when, imitating her mother, she had carried baskets of food to the fisherfolk on the banks of the Mekong. At first it was no more than a sense of pity for the helplessness of others in their misfortunes which she sometimes thought of as a weakness—until she remembered the cruelties of The Fat Devil and her own helplessness in the Manila slave pen.

Life within the de Sosa household was secure, comfortable, luxurious; but she could not hide from her eyes or shut out of her mind knowledge that beyond the iron-grilled gate of her protectors' mansion was another and different world, a world of insecurity and fear and privation.

The daughter of sybarites, there were many times when she tried to close her eyes to the misery and suffering about her, and plunged into the social life of the elite with as much avidity as she explored the world of spirit and intellect with Sor María. The fame of her beauty, her grace and charm, and her handsome although unusual costumes, spread far and wide.

It was at a state ball held in the Virrey's palace in Mexico City that envious sophisticates first nicknamed her "La China Poblana"—The Chinese Villager—although both of her foster parents always introduced her with great formality as the Princess Royal, the Señorita Myrrha Pagrís. She lived in what closely approximated royal state, and many people were impressed with the true nobility of her bearing.

But, as the years went by and she matured spiritually, meeting the frustrations of life which come to rich and poor alike with an ever broadening, deepening love for humanity, regard for her ancestry sank into the background. La China was loved, even revered by many, for the woman she herself became.

CHAPTER EIGHTEEN

I T TOOK Myrrha some time to realize that one of the chief differences between her present life and the time passed in harem and slave pen was the activity with which her days were crowded. In the old life, when her master had been born wealthy and generously inclined toward her, she had whiled away many tedious hours with thread and needle, or gambling at dice or checkers or tricktrack, and she had been an expert at the age-old shell game.

But if one's lord were not rich or generous—and she had known one such master—women sat crosslegged, often on a bare floor, and laced their idle fingers together lest a questing hand reach out as though to explore the cruel emptiness of life, and thus betray them as rebellious of their fate. As for things of the spirit, a fortunate few could sit and gaze at the floor beneath and walls surrounding them as though their prison encompassed the total of God's creation. Others achieved a sort of catharsis of their emotions through endless hours of soft weeping. And practically all inmates occasionally relieved the tedium of the void in which they lived by strident words and menacing gestures toward companions for whom they felt no real anger in their hearts.

Here in her new home, men were still lords of creation, but their domination of their women folk was of a different caliber. One was deferred to as though she were the equal of a man—spiritually and morally, his superior. It seemed to Myrrha that men's only conceits in this new land were simple and few. All of them encompassed by over-weening pride: pride in the size and strength of bone and muscle—which were easily evident; pride in the superiority of their mental abilities—which was not so evident; and pride in the gorgeous apparel they affected. As nearly as she could judge from her limited experience, it appeared that as long as a woman deferred to these vanities she might do as she pleased otherwise.

The de Sosas' attitude toward truth and simple honesty seemed strange to Myrrha, who had been nurtured in an atmosphere of callous intrigue; and it cost her some difficulty to adapt her thinking to that ideal. But once she had made the adjustment she applied it mercilessly—sometimes to the confusion of her guardians.

What she had heard of the wedding customs of New Spain intrigued her. She looked forward to the first nuptial mass to which she was invited as a guest with the keenest anticipation. Señora de Sosa, thinking of the spiritual welfare of her foster daughter, lost no opportunity to impress upon her the status of women in a Christian country, emphasizing their superior spiritual and moral qualities. Consequently, as she knelt in the Cathedral of the Angels, Myrrha was not prepared to hear a Christian woman vow to do what a Moslem knows she must without public profession: love, honor and obey.

"If women are men's superiors spiritually and morally, then that means that men are women's inferiors spiritually and morally," she remarked on the way home from the church. "Do I understand what I have been told? Is my thinking right?" she asked.

Señora de Sosa hesitated, but her husband and son spoke for her. "You are quite right, daughter," Señor de Sosa answered. "Your understanding is correct."

"Women are greatly the moral superiors of men," Don Alfredo added.

"Then isn't it ridiculous for the superior one to promise to obey the inferior?" Myrrha asked.

Señora de Sosa attempted an explanation. Her words were labored, her thinking confused by the unexpectedness of the question. She got no further than to state that there are times when superiority is inferiority and inferiority superiority, when her husband interrupted her.

"There is much in life that appears on the surface to be ridiculous, but custom which stands the test of many years is reasonable," he began, and logically enough. He went on more fluently than his wife, but it was to express his wife's paradoxical concept of the standing of woman.

Myrrha walked along quietly, listening at first to Señor de Sosa. Then it was no longer his voice in her ears, but the soft tones of the Conceptionist Sisters behind the stone wall beside her reciting the thanksgiving after communion: ". . . Thou art He that will restore my inheritance unto me. O my God and my All! may the sweet and burning power of thy love, I beseech Thee, so absorb my soul, that I may die unto the world for the love of Thee, who for the love of me . . ."

Myrrha wished she could turn, pass through the convent gate, enter the chapel and kneel beside one of the Sisters. There, life was reasonable, rational and satisfying. There was no necessity of adapting to the ridiculous. The vow each Sister had taken of love and obedience was to an unquestionable superior, One whose love and strength were unfailing.

Could such a one as I become a nun? she wondered. But she hesitated to ask her companions. For another of the ridiculous aspects of life was that these good people who worshiped at the shrine of truth could be so shocked at an honest question asked in simple sincerity.

"When are you going to shave your head and don the coif?" Eulalia asked her one day when she returned from a lesson with Sor María at the convent at a later hour than usual.

Myrrha was a long time replying in spite of the flash of anger within her, for the woman's words implied scorn of Sor María's vocation, and therefore of her dearly beloved friend as well. At first rarely, and then a dozen—a hundred—times a day she had found herself wondering if the attainment of personal serenity and abiding spiritual peace which filled the days and hearts of Sor María and her sisters in Christ could really be possible for a former harem slave.

For some reason Myrrha's memory fled backward to a square-windowed cabin under the poop deck of a brigantine and the coarse featured visage and misshapen figure of a huge Negress with a shaven head, and she heard herself saying as though it were another who spoke through her lips, "It is not hair or nose or lips that make a woman really beautiful, 'Lala."

Eulalia's eyes gleamed as though accepting a challenge and her lips parted, but something in the face of the girl before her silenced

211

further jibes. She winced visibly at Myrrha's scarcely audible, concluding words, "But a misguided tongue can rob a woman of that beauty which does not depend on features or body."

As time went on, Myrrha spoke less and less frequently of the days of her childhood and the precocious maturity forced upon her before she had reached New Spain. In the intellectual delight she experienced in the simple acquisition of knowledge under Sor María's training, events of her past slipped into dim, unimportant corners of her memory. She spent more and more time with Sor María, her mind and spirit burgeoning under the nun's intellectual and spiritual guidance, until she came to feel as much at home in the cloistered halls of the convent as in the luxurious dwelling of the Pueblan merchant.

But outside the convent and away from Sor María's influence, she threw herself into the social life of the city as though born to it. She attended the bull fights and on her return home created a dance imitating the cape work of the matador. As always, the de Sosas exhibited her to their friends who were delighted with her mimicry, even when she pantomimed the slaying of *El Toro* as she did sometimes out of sheer impishness. Her depiction of a gored matador dying in the arena, in which she used little more than the upper half of her body, was pure Oriental art, now acceptable because of the subject matter.

She was charmed by the spectacle of the *charros* who paraded in the bull ring before each fight. These young men were not bull fighters themselves, but representatives of the wealthiest families who bedecked themselves and their fine horses with incredibly ornate costumes and trappings. It was not at all unusual for the value of the silver and semi-precious stones on a saddle to equal a small fortune. The bridle was almost equally valuable. Every conceivable inch of the man's costume was embroidered with gold and silver thread of pure metal. The wealth of ornamentation on his tall-crowned, broad-brimmed hat was limited only by the weight he could bear comfortably on his head.

The charros glittered in the sun like monstrous peacocks, and with vanity equal to that of the regal birds, they preened themselves and strutted on all possible occasions. Their mounted parade around the bull ring was as much a part of the show as the duels between men and beasts to follow.

Alfredo taught Myrrha to ride his own milk-white Arabian stallion, and when his fellow charros saw her galloping across the fields and over the hills surrounding Puebla with her foster brother, as graceful and apparently as firmly seated in her sidesaddle as any of them seated astride, they elected her by popular acclaim their queen and patron. She was invited to lead them in the bull ring at the next "run of the bulls." A thunder of applause greeted her appearance, and a tumult of *Bravos!* and *Viva La Chinas!*

It was the first recorded public ovation given a woman in the Western Hemisphere. Before another year had passed, the opening event of every bull fight in Puebla consisted of the parade of the splendid charros as usual, but preceded by an even more gorgeously clad Myrrha leading a corps of the men's sisters dressed in costumes like her own.

At various times during the year the social elite of Puebla left the city. Some traveled to the higher mountains, some went to the capital, some gathered at certain resorts for several weeks of visiting and fiestas. In August the de Sosas always went to Tlalpan, south of Mexico City. The occasion was the carnival which the original fete of Saint Augustine had gradually become. There Myrrha saw all social and caste barriers relaxed except one—the Indian was still the drudge, without voice, without rights. Otherwise the highest-born ladies of New Spain in the costliest silks and velvets obtainable, their arms and fingers heavy with jewelry, sat next to beggars on cockfights, gambling, shrieking in triumph at their victories, shamming tears at their losses as a means of calling attention to themselves. A sort of legal amnesty prevailed during this carnival, and known thieves clowned and gambled with their victims—even taunted them on occasion by tempting them to try to win back at some game of chance pieces of jewelry which had just been stolen from them.

There Myrrha was introduced to monte. This was a game between two people. Its fascination seemed to be that staggering sums of money could and did change hands with equally staggering speed on the turn of a single card. The game was simplicity itself. The dealer threw three cards, previously shown, face downward upon a table and shifted them about rapidly with his hands. His opponent named one of the three cards and then tried to pick it out. If his eyes were not exceedingly quick, or if his attention could be distracted by any means, the odds were two to one against his winning. Consequently, the one who guessed was always called "the victim" whether he won or not.

213

Doña Eulalia was very clever at monte, although she would not play except as dealer. Her fingers were nimble and her tongue both quick and sharp. She knew the intimate gossip of every great family in New Spain; and, when the broadcasting of unfortunate truths did not serve her purpose of rattling her opponent, she created cruel untruths without compunction, a propensity which openly angered her husband and grieved her parents-in-law. Myrrha saw her sit day after day always with a constantly growing heap of coins before her, sweeping in a beggar's coppers with as little compunction as the gold of one of her peers.

Alfredo pressed a little bag of coins into Myrrha's hand one day and urged her to play with his wife.

"Shall I win? Or shall I lose to her?" Myrrha asked. "She enjoys winning and that will please her."

Alfredo stared in amazement. "Do you think you can win?" he exclaimed. "If you can win, please do. No one wins from 'Lala, not even I. That would be something to see! Something that would be very good for her!"

Myrrha laughed. Alfredo had no way of knowing that all harem women gambled: poor women, for a companion's portion of food; rich women, for each other's jewels. All women gambled when their masters demanded such entertainment. Then they must know how to lose; and it frequently took more wit and concentration to lose convincingly to a stupid, awkward man than to win from a hungry woman. And no one dared to win from a drunken master, for such invariably retrieved their losses when sober—with the aid of a whip if necessary.

"Say good-bye to your money, esposito," Eulalia called out gaily. "What I win is mine, you know, and I shall not give you back so much as one peseta."

"Run quickly and bring a second purse to hold my winnings," Myrrha answered, mimicking even Eulalia's tone of voice. "I am going to repay you with usury for the money advanced."

Eulalia snorted so contemptuously that her husband had to press his handkerchief upon her. Her hand trembled as she picked up the cards.

"Would you rather wait? And play another time?" Myrrha queried softly with a world of mockery in her voice. "One should never gamble except when in complete possession of one's wits—and emotions."

214

Being taunted—as she so greatly enjoyed taunting others—was a new experience for the older woman. Her face and neck reddened, and she glared at her new "victim." But she recovered quickly, controlled her hands, and retorted with a sneer on her lips, "Are your wits as sharp as your tongue? It will take gold in front of you rather than a blast of hot breath between us to convince me that your eyes are quicker than my hands, China.

"But why are you standing there?" she continued. "Sit down! Or are you afraid to play with borrowed money? Don't let that trouble you. 'Fredo can afford the loss, especially since the money will remain in the family."

Myrrha seated herself before Eulalia, stretched out her arms and laid her palms upward on the table midway between the two of them.

Eulalia stared, and when Myrrha did not move her hands, demanded, "What's this? You look as though you were begging!"

"I am!" Myrrha replied. "It is a *China's* way of saying: Nothing is risked at this table today but money. My regard for you will not be altered or diminished, no matter how much I win from you, little sister. I beg of you the same consideration."

Eulalia spilled her cards on the table, and did not honor the pretty custom by placing her palms upon those of her victim, even when instructed to do so. Myrrha withdrew her hands and folded them in her lap, smiling as though victory were already an established fact.

Eulalia flipped three cards face upward on the table with the customary, "Look well, señorita, for your next glimpse at one of them will cost you money."

After a brief glance at Eulalia's face, and an even briefer glimpse at Alfredo, Myrrha lowered her eyes to the dealer's fingers and held them there. Eulalia began chattering, making sharp, sometimes pointless, more often cruel remarks aimed at needling her opponent into anger and therefore loss of concentration. Myrrha had watched the other play and knew that she did not need to give thought to a reply, that she had only to open her lips and seem to speak, for a part of Eulalia's technique was to annoy as much as possible by deliberately and rudely interrupting her "victim."

Merrymakers began to crowd around the table, eager to note and enjoy the discomfiture of Eulalia's latest "victim" as her money melted away. But in spite of the odds in her favor, it was not Eulalia who

215

won. Since most of the onlookers had lost repeatedly to this clever dealer, they were quick and exultant in their jibes and she lost hand after hand. Other gamblers deserted their tables to join the jeering, jubilant throng.

Losing consistently was a new experience for the petulant invalid, one she did not enjoy. As the heap of coins before her dwindled, her voice shrilled. Alfredo leaned forward and asked Myrrha if he might borrow half the coins heaped in neat piles beside her left hand to replenish his wife's cash. La China did not shift her eyes for one second, but her *"Por seguro, hermano,"* was clear and distinct.

"Borrow indeed!" Eulalia sneered. "Since when does one borrow what is his already?"

There was a moment of stunned silence at this crude taunting of another with the fact of her poverty.

A muffled sound came from 'Fredo as though he cleared his voice to speak, but Myrrha's next words cut him short, "What need have I of money, 'Lala, when I am blessed with such a wealth of love?"

"Now it is the little nun speaking!" Eulalia jibed. "Did you know that the professional religious are not supposed to gamble? Or does doffing the veil when it suits your convenience come as easily as piety?"

For the first time since seating herself at the gaming table, Myrrha lifted her face. Eulalia's eyes widened and she laughed outright in exultation. One could read her thoughts with the greatest of ease. It was as though she had shouted: At last I have cracked this impregnable calm. Now she is truly my "victim!"

But there was no pique, no anger, no strain of any nature in Myrrha's voice as she answered, using the strongest ejaculation she knew to express the depth of her longing. "Ojalá! Would that I were worthy to be a nun, sister."

Slowly she stretched out her hand and laid it gently on one of Eulalia's wrists. The gesture was that of a mature woman attempting to soothe a child. Eulalia jerked her arm away irritably; but there was something on La China's face that abashed her. Sneers she could reply to, but not compassion. It was she who lowered her eyes first. Although she held her body rigidly erect, her lips twitched and her hands trembled.

The onlookers were quiet, some amused, some exultant and some uneasy at the memory of this dealer's temper. Alfredo touched his wife's shoulder and advised her to calm herself and collect her wits. Myrrha, her eyes again intent upon the cards in Eulalia's hands, was at the same time well aware of what was going on around her. She saw the trembling of Eulalia's forearms and that her fingers clenched the cards until they buckled in her hands. Her ear noted the growing stridency in her opponent's voice. She understood these physical signs well, for she had seen many another gambling woman in this same state of frustration.

Angrily Eulalia dealt three cards, face upward upon the table. "The deuce of diamonds, the nine of clubs, and the knave of hearts. Note them well, China," she chanted in the dealer's usual singsong, controlling her voice with an effort.

"The deuce of diamonds, the nine of clubs, and the knave of hearts. I see them all," Myrrha answered in the formal phrases of the victim.

Eulalia swept the cards from the table but with such nervous haste that they slithered into her lap instead of her waiting hand.

"Foul!" "Error!" "It is your right to demand a new deal, victim!" the surrounding crowd cried out.

But Myrrha shook her head. "I am satisfied," she answered. Then, looking Eulalia full in the face she went on, "This has not been a game of chance until now. Now I shall guess. And the odds will be only two to one against me. Am I not right, sister?"

Eulalia's eyes gleamed and her breath came in panting little gasps. "If you trust your luck so greatly, will you wager all you have before you against all I have before me?"

Myrrha did not reply immediately. Finally, she leaned forward and barely whispered, "Is that the way you want it, 'Lala? Think well, sister, for the stakes are high. And I who have nothing will therefore lose nothing."

"Are you afraid to trust your luck?"

"Fear is not always a bad thing, 'Lala. Would there be any, or much, virtue in the world without fear?"

The eyes of the onlookers who were crowded close upon the two women were wide with surprise and bright with curiosity. They watched and listened in almost breathless silence, while those behind them clamored for news of progress of the game.

"Did luck finally desert La China?" some demanded.

And, "Has a victim finally succeeded in breaking La de Sosa's bank?"

217

"Play!" Eulalia commanded, or leave the table and forfeit your winnings. That is a rule of the game."

Myrrha raised her head and searched Alfredo's face. He nodded for her to accept the challenge.

"I would rather not," she said. "I wish to cease playing and forfeit."

"Aaaah! Do not give up a fortune without a struggle," a woman's voice shrilled from somewhere in the crowd.

Again Myrrha leaned forward, and murmured for 'Lala's ears alone, "Have I your promise that nothing is at stake here and now but money?"

"Play!" Eulalia commanded. "Play or forfeit!"

Myrrha sighed deeply, and made as though to rise as she asked polite permission to do so, *"Con permiso,* sister." But Don Alfredo's hand on her shoulder kept her in her chair. With another heavy sigh, she nodded assent.

Again Eulalia cast three cards upon the table, this time face downward. Then to the surprise of everyone, Myrrha placed both hands, palms downward over all three cards. A faint smile hovered over her lips briefly before she asked, "Suppose that this time I name a card, but pick up the other two?"

Eulalia gasped. The blood left her flushed face, leaving it ashen and gray, but she recovered quickly. "This is not the way monte is played," she cried. "Name your card and pick it up. They were—they were—I do not remember what they were. I really do not! You took undue time making up your mind, China." She darted swift glances about as though challenging anyone to contradict her. Then she went on, "It is your business, China, to remember them, not mine."

"Yes! Yes! It is you who must remember," the onlookers agreed with the dealer.

"I remember them," Myrrha answered calmly. "The nine of clubs was one of them."

"She is right—the nine of clubs. I remember it," a score of voices shouted.

"You are the gambler, Eulalia," Myrrha went on. "How much are you willing to risk? I choose the nine of clubs! Now, may I turn up the other two? If the card I have named is neither of the two I turn up, then it would have to be the remaining card, would it not? You have

218

risked your husband's money many times before. That is all you will be risking now, is it not? Why do you hesitate, Spaniard!"

The crowd gasped, for Myrrha had mimicked the contempt in Eulalia's voice so completely that it was like a blow across the other's cheek.

Eulalia's already pallid face looked corpse-like. There was no mistaking the eager gloating in the eyes of many of her former victims.

Then clearly and distinctly came the voices of two women at the edge of the crowd, speaking as frankly and unabashedly as though they gossiped in the privacy of their own homes. "Has the Señora de Sosa lost all of her money?" one asked. "I meant to go to the fights this afternoon—they say two mastiffs were to be pitted against a bear—but I would not have missed this for the world. This is like matching a newborn calf against the most famed matador in all Spain—and then seeing the calf turn into an enormous bull before your very eyes!"

"Or an ox against a rattlesnake!" the second voice chimed in. "I wish I could see better. They say La China is in complete possession of the game. That Señora de Sosa was beaten as soon as she sat down. I wish I were half as clever as this Chinese villager. Then I could have all the jewels I want without forever having to tease my husband for them."

Doña Eulalia rose so abruptly that her chair would have tumbled over backward had it not been for the crowd. Her hips struck the gaming table, spilling the heaps of money on it across its surface and onto the ground. She turned and pressed her way through the throng. Myrrha rose and followed her. Don Alfredo turned away also, but before taking one full step swung back, picked up the three cards on the gaming table and, without exposing their faces, stuffed them into his pocket.

At his departure the carnival crowd fell upon the coins on the gaming table and the ground beneath it with shrieks of delight. The reveling fine ladies and gentlemen fought with the thieves and beggars and groveled in the dirt as though the coins meant as much to the social elite of New Spain as to the colony's social lees.

CHAPTER NINETEEN

ALTHOUGH Myrrha glided along behind Doña Eulalia and her husband with her usual outward poise and physical grace, all was turmoil within her mind and heart. For the first time in her life she had had to make a decision which involved the lives of others for good or evil. She had made that decision by exposing a cheat —therefore a liar and a thief—because the religion of her foster parents condemned dishonesty and theft as mortal sins. What she had seen of that religion put into practice, was good. Too good to be corrupted by a vain, egotistical, greedy, dishonest creature who, if she had been bórn in Myrrha's native land, would not even have been considered worthy of a soul.

Yet by exposing this woman's dishonesty Myrrha knew she had committed a violence, the results of which might possibly be shared by others who were not guilty, and from whom she had never known anything but the most loving consideration.

It was a sorry thing, ran through the girl's mind, to repay such kindness by embarrassing, and therefore inflicting pain upon, one whom they loved. Had she really been concerned only with the Christian virtue of Truth? she asked herself silently. Was it not anger? Slow, smoldering resentment kindled during her first days in Puebla by the spite of a frankly envious woman and kept constantly alive ever since by innuendo and discourtesy until it had flared out of control at the gaming table?

It was evident that Don Alfredo had shared his wife's embarrassment, which surprised Myrrha, for she had never known of an Oriental man's assuming responsibility for his wife's misconduct. But if Don Alfredo were embarrassed, might not his parents be also? And because of her anger, which was also a sin!

What could she do to spare those she loved from the results of that anger? Dumbly her mind fled to the Manila slave pen and, had it been possible, would have carried her body with it. In that beast's lair only oneself suffered as the result of one's behavior.

But the Manila slave pen was behind her. With her new life she had acquired a new religion, and with the new religion came new responsibilities. Life could no longer be accepted passively, nor could its sole aim be merely to protect oneself from the anger and violence of the spiritually petty but physically powerful. What was her duty—her Christian duty—now that, following what she believed to be the mandates of her new religion, she had exposed dishonesty?

She wished Sor María were here—Sor María, who in spite of the obvious saintliness of her life, periodically stood before her Mother Superior and accused herself of minute imperfections of conduct as though they were mortal sins. Sor María would listen to her gravely and sympathetically, she knew, and would understand her problem.

She also knew how Sor María would reply. The nun in her ever gentle way, would first make light of her problem, would gravely advise prayer and would finally send her to Father Enrique. The priest in his turn would warn against too great an emphasis on personal perfection, for that would be, he thought, an attempt at aping divinity. Then he, too, would advise prayer and possibly fasting, which tended to clear the mind and make for more rational judgment of oneself. Finally, as had always been the case in the past when Sor María had sent her to the priest with some minor problem, he would murmur sadly, "If only I might extend to you the privilege and the consolation of the confessional, but I dare not. I dare not until we hear from the Holy Father."

Myrrha knew that both the priest and the nun had been much troubled by her account of what passed for religion in the Manila slave pen. Each had petitioned the Bishop of Puebla to send an account of Myrrha's presumed confirmation there to His Holiness, Pope Gregory XV, and to ask the Holy Father if such a seemingly incredible ceremony entitled her to the full privileges and benefits of her new religion. That had been at least a full year ago, and as yet there was no reply. Nor had word been received in Puebla that the ship carrying the Bishop's letter, or one which might have brought an answer, had been lost at sea either to pirates or by act of God.

Myrrha was so deeply engrossed in her thoughts that she did not hear the greetings called out by the folk whom she, Don Alfredo and his wife passed. Consequently, she did not notice that they stared at the three of them in surprise—and in a few cases some anger—when they received no reply. Within the privacy of the wing of the inn which Señor de Sosa had reserved for the exclusive use of his family and servants, Myrrha watched Don Alfred and Doña Eulalia disappear into their own chambers. Then she entered the room she shared with their two daughters.

There she sat quietly thinking, her hands in her lap, until finally a measure of peace came to her. She was satisfied in her own mind that she had not accepted the Christian religion in Manila with adequate knowledge of the importance of the step she was taking. She had not even known the full or true nature of that step. If she had truly been confirmed there—which both Father Enrique and Sor María questioned—it had been nothing more than a Moslem woman's obedient submission to the will of her master. But it could not have been a true confirmation. For she had not made an intelligent decision based on knowledge and conviction, nor had it been an act of free will. She had not understood her so-called new faith, and so it was impossible that she should have been attracted to it. Rather, she had been repelled by the lives of those who had imposed Christianity upon her. It had made no change in her life whatsoever, neither physical nor spiritual. As a presumed Christian, she had simply become a more acceptable—and therefore more intrinsically valuable—piece of merchandise for a Christian country.

But here in New Spain her mind was challenged and her spirit uplifted by everything she learned about Christianity: the positive virtues and the guidance of one's life by their practice; the dignity it gave to woman when it elevated her to the position of equal of man—in the sight of God, at least. Suddenly she felt very very sure that had either Miguel de Sosa or his wife been faced with her choice at the gaming table that afternoon, each would have done as she had.

Then she had to smile in spite of herself at that thought, for neither of the de Sosas was a clever gambler. Moreover, being guilty of no evil in their own hearts, they would never have suspected Eulalia's dishonesty, for they thought no evil of others unless that evil were flaunted in their faces. Nor could she believe that they would hold her decision and consequent action at the gaming table against her, and she sighed with immense relief as the assurance of their understanding filled her heart.

She also became clearly aware now, as she sat staring through the balcony window at a cloudless sky, that she coveted for herself the strength inherent in the perfect practice of Christian precepts as understood by her foster parents and their priest and, most particularly, by Sor María. She would like to be such a woman as Sor María, a learned and pious nun. She must talk with Sor María—and her foster parents, of course—about the requirements of a nun's life and her fitness for it.

She was not conscious of the passage of time as she sat thinking, but presently the two de Sosa granddaughters entered the room. It seemed to her she had never seen more beautiful children. She would have liked to strum on her guitar and sing to them, do anything to make them happy.

"Grandmother says we must be very quiet, and particularly no music," Marita assured her solemnly.

"Mamá is so cross I think she is ill," Tonita volunteered with the precociously patient air of a child whose life is patterned about the capricious whims of an invalid.

So the three played at checkers for a while, and Myrrha did not let the children win easily as would once have been the case. Instead she tried to teach them how to block her moves, how to plan their own so that she would be at a disadvantage. They learned readily, but did not find the game as entertaining as when she had maneuvered a sham victory for them.

When they were too bored for further instruction, she led them out onto the balcony and they made up another game of guessing about the lives of the people passing in the street below. It was easy for the children's lively imaginations when the passersby were Spanish or Spanish colonials. But they seemed to know nothing that might fit the life of any Indian except the work of the servants in their own home.

Myrrha suddenly realized that although she had rubbed shoulders with these same Indians for many months now, she too knew as little about their lives away from the de Sosas' washtubs, cooking pots, and brooms as the children. It filled her with a vague uneasiness, as though

223

a part of herself were somehow missing—an uncomfortable feeling she could neither shrug off nor understand.

Then servants brought the granddaughters' evening meal to the room, and their brother joined them while Myrrha was called to the elder de Sosas' chamber. As she passed through the hall her eyes fell on a niche in which stood a statue of the Holy Mother of Heaven, a single votary candle flickering dimly before it. Again she remembered the peace of the Conceptionist convent with intense longing, as though it were something due but long denied her.

Without conscious thought she slowed her steps to the measured tread of the nuns, and folded her hands under her breasts as Sor María invariably carried hers when her fingers were not busy with her beads. She wished Sor María were here now, to stand beside her and give her strength—Sor María who believed that every problem in life could be lived with, if not completely solved by the help of prayer. She wondered if the nun had ever faced a problem of major proportions, if she had ever viewed life through eyes dimmed with horror and despair.

As she walked along, Myrrha wondered how beads would feel in her fingers, wished that she might at this moment kneel and receive peace. Peace from the demands of men, from the jealousies of women, from the incredible foibles of this world. But on the other side of the door which she now faced, a man and a woman awaited her—a good man and woman who had blessed her first with their protection and now with their love. She placed her hand against the latch; but after a second's hesitation withdrew it, raised her fingers to her forehead and crossed herself. The last words of the Pater Noster were still on her lips as she stepped into the room.

The faces of the three people in the room were tense and the air was charged with emotion.

"Forgive me," Myrrha said softly. Her eyes moved from Doña Marguerita's face to Señor de Sosa's, and on to his son's, and then back to Doña Marguerita. "There are so many things for me to learn here in this world where women are not the playthings of men, and forgetting is so easy. I wish it were possible for me to say that when I did what I did this afternoon, it was from the highest Christian devotion to—virtue. But I am not sure now just what the truth is. 'Lala—the sister you have given me—is not a clever gambler, only a ruthless one.

But I am as guilty as she. Yes, I accuse myself, for I treated her with as little mercy as she habitually shows others. But another's fault does not excuse fault in me, and I pray your forgiveness for giving her pain.

"When I sat down at the gaming table this afternoon I was only a harem slave in my thinking again. I shamed 'Lala, and I know I have wounded all of you who love her. I do not love her as you do. Until now, that was not a grief to me; and I know I have sinned, for Father Enrique tells me I must love all of God's creatures, even those that despitefully use me. I played to win. It seemed important then, although I do not know why. My heart is broken because I grieved you, and I shall never again knowingly hurt any of you, not even if all the wealth of the world were heaped upon a table before me."

The three de Sosas stared at Myrrha. Then Doña Marguerita rushed to the girl and threw her arms about her in a tight embrace. "No! No! Not forgiveness, but our thanks to you," she sobbed.

She continued attempting to press thanks upon the girl until her husband interrupted her. "Child, is it possible that you do not understand the true nature of the service you did my family this afternoon when you made it possible for Eulalia to leave the gaming table without exposing her hand?" He pointed to a tabouret between him and his son. Three cards lay face upward upon it; they were not the deuce of diamonds, the nine of clubs or the knave of hearts.

"I knew," Myrrha answered scarcely glancing at the cards. "Anger robbed 'Lala of even the small skill her fingers possess. It also clouded her thinking so that to win seemed everything to her—better even than truth."

"And honor!" Alfredo burst out bitterly.

Myrrha turned to him, a questioning look on her face. Until she had come in contact with this family, she believed that women gambled with other women to win. One employed every artifice to that end—tricks that would have turned Eulalia green with envy! An opponent was expected to match artifice with counterartifice; for the object of gambling was to obtain possession of what belonged to another without paying a price for it. But the standards of Christian virtue altered that attitude; the health of one's soul depended upon rooting dishonesty out of one's heart. That caste and family prestige could be adjuncts of Christian virtue had not yet crystallized in her thinking, if, indeed, the concept had entered her mind at all.

As Myrrha listened to her benefactors and disclaimed their thanks on the basis of personal unworthiness, she shrank from the confusion their protestations stirred up within her. Father Enrique had always stressed truth as a cardinal virtue, and in spite of what had prompted her at the gaming table, she had taken spiritual refuge in the thought that she had thwarted dishonesty. Now these three people whom she loved devotedly—good Christian people all—stressed family honor as though it were the cardinal virtue and, by the very vehemence of their words, seemed to infer that if honor were preserved thereby, dishonesty was something that might safely lie hidden in the dark. That sort of thinking smacked of the harem!

Myrrha knew that with her newfound freedom of action and the independence of mind which progressed hand in hand with her education, she was no longer an Oriental woman, nor could she ever again think completely like one. At the same time, it was borne in upon her that because of the discipline of her harem childhood and all that it meant in acceptance of man's domination and his primordial behavior toward underlings, whether women or other slaves, she could never be entirely of this New World. She knew with all certainty that she would not—could not—adapt completely to Western life; that the pitiless logic of the East which she had inherited with her mother's blood, would always dissect the moral code and the social ethics of the West; that the only refuge for such an ambivalent personality was to devote one's whole life to religion. Again she longed, and with a poignancy that was close to physical pain, for the peace which Sor María had found.

Early the next morning, long before anyone else in the inn or the city was astir, the de Sosa party left Tlalpan. The men, including Rosario, were on horseback, the women and the granddaughters in the family carriage. The Indian servants followed behind, perched on top of the luggage in an uncovered, two-wheeled cart. The carriage was an immense lumbering, springless affair, uncomfortable at best. It was doubly uncomfortable on the return trip for one entire side

226

had been piled high with all the cushions available, and there Doña Eulalia lay, stretched at full length, as though unable to bear the weight of her body upon her hips, unmindful of the discomfort of the other two women and the children. Her mother-in-law, her children, and La China crowded as best they could on what remained of the fore and rear seats. Eulalia kept her face turned to the side of the carriage away from the others; and when she was not demanding that her daughters plump up and rearrange her cushions, she filled the air with loud sighs and long moans.

Throughout the entire journey, Doña Marguerita ignored her daughter-in-law's seeming misery and never moved to help her in any way. When Myrrha leaned forward to do so, the older woman pushed her back into her seat while shaking her head in a vigorous "No!"

The trip to Tlalpan had taken four days; the journey homeward covered six. The de Sosa entourage turned to the right on the morning of the third day and started up the side of Popocatepetl. After a few hours' traveling they came to a toll gate, and Señor de Sosa handed over a small sum of money to the attendant. This was not for use of the road but for the privilege of breathing the air off the volcano. A few miles further on there was another toll gate, and another sum of money was paid out for the same reason. Myrrha was told that two men, each of whom owned great ranches higher up on the slopes, laid claim to the salubrious breezes which blew off the snow-clad cone of the volcano and over their lands. Each had filed claims in the colonial court against the other. Both of these men were friends of Señor de Sosa, and since he did not care to quarrel with either, he paid both, although each made free use of a road he had built through his own land.

Halfway up the slope the party came to a summer home owned by Señor de Sosa. There they left Don Alfredo and his family, explaining later to their friends in Puebla and the capital that Doña Eulalia's health required the altitude and the air. The explanation was accepted graciously for what it was—polite fiction.

Señor de Sosa and his wife and La China continued onward to Puebla. Myrrha did not see either Alfredo or his wife again until her benefactor lay upon his deathbed. She would not have recognized Eulalia then had she met her casually, for the air on Popocatepetl had been truly miracle-working. Alfredo's wife was robust, even matronly, and the mother of yet another small daughter.

When the two women met again, there was still no friendship in Eulalia's eyes. Neither was there any fear of La China. And by that time, Myrrha had learned to love, unmindful of human imperfections, and without asking that her affection be returned.

CHAPTER TWENTY

A T FIRST the mansion in Puebla was strangely quiet without the laughter and the buoyant presence of the three grandchildren, so that many of the days that followed seemed long. This was not the first time Myrrha had lived through quiet hours; but it was the first time such hours were not empty ones. She welcomed the quiet as opportunity for meditation and prayer in which she found increasing personal satisfaction.

When the carnival season again came around, the de Sosas did not return to Tlalpan. Nor did their neighbors and very dear friends, the Hipólitos go there either. Instead the two families and Father Enrique journeyed in the opposite direction, down the mountains and over the road which led to Vera Cruz, at that time almost the sole port of entry on the eastern coast of Mexico. Although that road was much traveled, the trip was still an arduous one, for the highway was as yet unpaved and the ruts in the road were either dusty or muddy pits according to the weather.

Their destination was Córdoba, a city on the coastal side of Orizaba, a volcano even more famous than either Lord Popo or his Sleeping Lady. Córdoba was a wealthy and thriving city because it had become a popular stopover for merchants who wished to rest their pack animals, or secure new ones before beginning the steep ascent to Puebla and from there to Mexico City.

While still a day's travel west of Orizaba, Father Enrique became ill of a fever and dysentery, and the party turned aside to the small village of Atzacán. They took what lodgings were to be had at the only inn in the village, a humble establishment whose guests were usually messengers on some errand for nearby landowners and their overseers. In fact, the host had never before accommodated folk of such quality as the de Sosas and the Hipólitos, and although he put his own and his family's quarters at their disposal, if it had not been for the supplies which wealthy people carried with them on extended trips in those days, the gentlefolk would have suffered.

There Myrrha learned that the religious father in such an outlying community was the shepherd of his flock in more ways than one. It was the local parish priest, Father Ignacio, who attended Father Enrique and gave him such medical care as he had. When Doña Marguerita and Myrrha had been made as comfortable as possible and shelter had been provided for his servants, and the severity of Father Enrique's illness had been checked, Señor de Sosa committed them all to the care of Captain Hipólito and continued on to Córdoba. Some overseas merchants carried their goods no further inland than that city, and he used the opportunity to inspect their wares and purchase what would be useful or profitable to himself.

Since none of the usual diversions to which the guests from Puebla were accustomed were available in Atzacán, the group was thrown in upon themselves for entertainment. The Señoras de Sosa and Hipólito embroidered countless yards of fine net into exquisite lace, prayed much and slept or gossiped the remainder of their time. Myrrha also prayed—the prayers of the sisterhood she hoped to enter and at the same hours when she knew Sor María would be on her knees. And she sat for long periods of time listening to the conversations of the two priests.

Father Ignacio had only lately been transferred to the parish of Atzacán. Previous to that he had served on a faraway peninsula to the south called Teotihuacán. Father Ignacio said quite frankly that he believed his transfer was due to his falling so deeply in love with that area and its people. He seldom stopped praising his former parish. The land was exceedingly fertile and rich in natural resources, and the native inhabitants were exceptionally intelligent. The men were all handsome, the women strikingly beautiful.

Father Ignacio sighed, for the Indians hereabout were not only a dirty, poverty-stricken lot of savages, they were liars—and therefore thieves—as well. They persisted in hiding away from him, from him their spiritual father, what little remained to them of any value after their master, the local hidalgo, had taken his rightful, lion's share. They were nothing at all like his beloved Tehuanas! Still, a priest was sworn to obedience, and somehow God's will, as revealed to him by his bishop, must be done.

The next time Myrrha stepped outside the inn, she had to pass a group of Atzacán men, and she noted with some surprise that each was dressed in spotless white trousers, starched so stiff with powdered maize that the cloth made a pleasant little crackling noise as they went by. Five minutes' walk from the inn a huge mango tree stood in an Indian's yard. Myrrha wondered if some of the luscious fruit fresh from the tree might not tempt Father Enrique's delicate appetite.

The mango tree towered a good sixty feet into the sky. The house before which it stood was surrounded by a living fence of organo cactuses. Inside the enclosure chickens scratched and a sow lay on her side nursing a litter of piglets, but the bare, sandy earth was swept clean of all debris: dung, sticks and leaves. Nor was there any sign of fallen fruit rotting on the ground. Constant vigilance and work are required to keep a pig sty and chicken run clean, Myrrha knew, and again she remembered Father Ignacio's description of the Atzancanos. She could not help wondering if he would not regard them as highly as he did his beloved Tehuanas when he came to know them as well as he did his former flock.

As Myrrha laid her hand on the wooden button which secured the gate, the sow shook her piglets loose from her dangling teats and rose grunting hoarsely. She was long-legged and razor-backed, and her tusks curled up and backward toward her eyes. Slowly she sauntered to the gate and shoved her snout and narrow head through the bars. A triangular yoke made of a forked branch and crosspiece of wood kept her body inside the yard. Myrrha drew back from the beast, and shuddered at the sight of the tusks which could have slashed a grown man's body to bloody ribbons in seconds.

A parrot, a squawking streak of brilliant green and orange color, flashed from the tree in the yard and a ripe mango plopped onto the earth and burst, splashing fragrant, sweet custard over the dust. The sow gave a last curious snuffle in Myrrha's direction, withdrew her head from the bars, trotted over to the fallen sugarplum and devoured it, seed and all.

Myrrha gazed at the house. Although she had lived in this new land for over two years, it was the first time she had ever been really close to a *jacal*, as such Indian dwellings were called. It was different in some ways from the shacks of her mother's people on the banks of the Mekong River, and very like them in others. It was a tiny, one-roomed affair, no more than a shelter for a small family. The walls were of woven twigs plastered with clay high enough to ensure privacy for those within. The roof was a thatch of untied palm leaves held down by pieces of log and stones. It was fully as poor as any shelter meant for human beings in Cochin China, but an intangible something about the jacal impressed itself upon Myrrha. This was not a hovel; it was a home.

"Hola!" she called out. "Is there someone within? May I speak with you?"

A woman came to the door. A handwoven, blue and black rebosa over her head framed her blunt-nosed, high-cheeked, broad face. There was nothing of formal beauty in that particular countenance save the great black eyes, and the lids of these were now reddened and swollen from much weeping. The woman made Myrrha think of the silk-robed, jewel-bedecked statue of the virgin in the gilded chapel of the Rosario in the church dedicated to San Tomás which she had often visited with Sor María. Two children crept up beside the woman, clutched her skirt with protection-seeking little fingers, and stared at the stranger with frightened eyes. The madonna-like illusion was stronger than ever, and Myrrha, her mission forgotten, searched for words in the face of such pervasive terror and grief.

One could not ask anything of this woman now, Myrrha knew, and she would have turned away had not a man's voice at her shoulder murmured, "With your permission, señorita, let me open the gate for you."

As Myrrha stepped into the cactus-walled yard, the sow again ambled toward her, piglets hanging from her dugs on either side. The man who had opened the gate pushed the animal aside with the sole of his bare foot on her nose. The sad-faced woman stepped back and motioned for her visitor to enter. When Myrrha's eyes became accustomed to the gloom of the windowless dwelling, she saw another woman, gray-haired and as wrinkled with age as an apple that has shriveled with dry rot on the tree.

A moan drew her eyes to a corner of the room behind the ancient crone. There a man stood leaning sideways in the angle of two walls, propping his weight against a shoulder. For a moment Myrrha did not realize that he was stark naked because chest and stomach and the tops of his thighs were a bloody mass. At his feet was a gourd full of water and a heap of freshly plucked green leaves. The old woman had been cleansing the man's lacerated torso, but now she stood aside without speaking as though waiting for something.

Myrrha stared in horror, wondering what accident could have literally flayed so much of this wretch's body while he still lived. Then slowly and painfully the man turned his face to the wall to hide the shame of his nakedness. So little strength was left to him that he propped his head against a post to keep his body upright. Myrrha clasped her hands over her mouth to keep from screaming at the sight of his back. From neck to mid-buttocks bloody strings of what had once been muscle still dripped thick, slowly congealing gouts of blood. The man had been lashed unmercifully, and to the very brink of death.

Myrrha stepped forward, wordless with pity, wanting desperately to assuage his anguish and not knowing how to do so. One step, but one step only, for the old woman was suddenly before her, her toil-warped body held painfully erect, her age-dimmed eyes once again brilliant but not with health and vigor. Rather her whole visage glowed with such venomous hatred as Myrrha had never seen before on a human countenance. Slowly her fists pushed upward, above her head, and her lips began mouthing words in a strange, Indian tongue. The girl moved backward as though pushed by a force stronger than her own will. Outside she turned and fled, scattering the chickens, stumbling over the piglets.

She had not covered more than a third of the distance back to the inn when she heard a voice calling behind her, "Please, señorita, for the love of God, wait a little here."

She turned to see the peon who had opened the gate hurrying after her. In his hand he held one of the netting baskets Indian men wore slung over their shoulders when they carried small articles. The basket was full of rosy-cheeked golden mangoes so ripely fragrant she smelled them while he was still a dozen paces away.

He dropped to his knees in the dust before her, glanced furtively over each shoulder to assure himself that his words would not be overheard, clasped his hands as though praying, and exclaimed in a piercing whisper, "In God's name, pity them, señorita. They have

233

suffered enough! Forgive the old woman's anger. Be merciful and forget what you have seen today. Forget that she raised clenched fists to you. The man is her only son—the only child left to her—and her senile lips did not know what they were saying. If there is any of God's mercy in you, I beg of you——"

Myrrha's lips opened as though under compulsion. "I—I only came to buy mangoes," she stammered. "What do you ask—for the fruit?"

Again the peon drew back as though avoiding a physical blow. Then when he saw from her face that there had been no guile behind the question aimed at tricking him into an act of theft, he answered slowly, choosing his words carefully but still unable to keep bitterness completely out of his voice.

"The mango tree, all of the trees of any kind—even we ourselves— belong to our hidalgo. We may not pick the fruit for ourselves or our children to eat. The fruit that is sound and good is for our lord only, although he may sometimes hand a mango to a very young girl. We may have the overripe fruit when it falls from the tree naturally—if we can beat the sows and chickens to it."

Myrrha glanced at the basket in the dust beside the kneeling man and saw that every mango was burst open or badly bruised.

"A man sits under the tree every night. The chickens sleep then, but the sow rouses and comes running whenever she hears anything. If it is a falling mango, sometimes we beat her to it!" There was a sly note of triumph in the Indian's voice.

"Why do you not pen the sow elsewhere when the mangoes are ripening?" Myrrha asked.

Again the man drew back frightened and searched her face with his eyes before replying. "The sow belongs to our master. He penned her there. The fruit sweetens her milk and the piglets' flesh for his table, he says. When we want meat, we can pick the white grubs that breed on the leaves of the agave plant. Roasted, they are our bacon. But hog meat, that is for our lord; and he must see the sow here whenever he rides past whatever the hour, day or night."

"The man, back there in the jacal, did he steal fruit?" Myrrha asked. "A mango is a little thing to riddle a man's back for."

The Indian did not answer her question. Instead he rose to his feet and picked up his mangoes; but when Myrrha held out her hand for the basket, he shook his head. "I must carry it for you until I give it into the hand of a servant at the inn, which I am too humble a creature to enter," he said. He stared into her face for a moment and then emboldened by the pity he saw there, went on bitterly, "My wife and my daughter must carry heaping baskets full of maize from the fields on their heads, and great faggots of wood from the forest, and drag stones from the river bed when our hidalgo wishes to build a new corral for his horses. But if I let you carry a handful of half-rotten mangoes no further than the length of my body down this street, I, too, would be dragged behind a horse through cactus barrens, and lashed."

At the doorway to the inn, the peon pulled the leather strap which rang a bell in the patio. Then he dropped the basket of fruit at Myrrha's feet and again pleaded desperately: "As you pray for God's mercy at the hour of your death, I beseech you, señorita, be merciful to us helpless ones now. Forget if you can, I pray of you, that you ever left the inn this afternoon." Then he turned and ran so quickly that he did not hear Myrrha's, "Vaya con Díos, pobrecito—wretched one."

When the servant opened the door, the peon had disappeared from sight. Myrrha never saw him again—or his gift of fruit, which was deemed unfit for the lips of gentlefolk.

The Hipólitos, Doña Marguerita and Father Ignacio were all in the patio gathered about the convalescing Father Enrique when Myrrha entered. The women exclaimed at the expression on her face and hurried to her, fearful that some misadventure might have harmed her in the street.

She threw herself into Doña Marguerita's arms sobbing, and when she could speak again poured out the story of the Indian's home. She could not speak fast enough to rid her heart of the horror she felt at the plight of the mutilated husband and father, or adequately describe their bitter but fearful neighbor. Words tumbled from her lips in such incoherent confusion they were hard to understand. Like an appalled child, she demanded over and over, "What can we do? Something must be done for this family! They eat worms while a sow eats fruit! What can we do?"

Captain Hipólito was the first to answer her. "This is not our affair and we cannot meddle in it. It is best to forget as much as you can of the suffering in this world."

Myrrha turned shocked, pleading eyes to the captain's wife and

Señora de Sosa. The former nodded agreement with her husband, and the latter asked quietly and in a low voice, "Do not these things also happen, in Cochin China? And worse in Manila? You yourself have said so. Yet what did you do when they occurred? What could you do?"

"But this is a Christian country!" Myrrha cried. "And Christianity is a religion of love! A faith for slave as well as master, is it not? One of our Holy Commandments is: Thou shalt love thy neighbor as thyself. Therefore, how can the master of this village . . ."

"Dear child, the local hidalgo can scarcely regard one of his peons as his neighbor!" Doña Marguerita interrupted in gentle reproof.

"I wonder why not!" Father Enrique exclaimed. His voice had grown reedy from age and was now weak from his illness, but it pierced the ears of those about him like a willow whistle. "Why do you think we were told the story of the good Samaritan? Did not Christ himself accept the love of a thief as the two of them died, each nailed to a cross? Is this hidalgo a better man than our Lord? Master and peon, are they not both men? One fortunate in his birth, and the other a wretch, but still men!" He looked about him as though challenging anyone to dispute his words. Lowered eyes were his only answer. Then he turned to Father Ignacio and asked more quietly, "Do you know the family?"

"Oh yes, brother," the priest replied. "Don Ernesto de Man——"

"Not the hidalgo, you fool!" Father Enrique burst out. "I knew that without asking. The Indian! What did the man do to merit being dragged behind a horse and cut to pieces with a whip?"

"I know of that family, too," Father Ignacio stammered. "They are Tlascalan Indians. They are not supposed to be moved from the soil on which they are born, but Don Ernesto made some sort of bargain— I don't know what. Anyway, they were brought here because they are all clever weavers. You should see the work they do, whether it is serapes of coarse wool to turn rain as well as wind, or rebosas for the . . ."

"What did the man do?" Father Enrique again interrupted in a stern voice. Then he added sarcastically, "Did he drop his shuttle? Or snag a thread in his own work?"

Father Ignacio was pacing back and forth across the room staring first at the ceiling and then at the floor, but avoiding everyone's eyes. Finally, "There was a girl," he said and shook his head meaningfully at the ladies. But Father Enrique once aroused would not be put off by a false pretense of modesty.

"The Indian's oldest child was a daughter, half-Spanish and very beautiful. That is often the case, you know," Father Ignacio whispered in the direction of the two men. "When the girl became a woman, her parents did not inform Don Ernesto of that fact so that he might claim his rights at his pleasure. But our hidalgo learned of it anyway. Don Ernesto demanded that the little squaw be brought to him, but the Indian spirited her away and hid her in a cave in the hills. They whipped the truth out of the father and then dragged him across cactus barrens to prove to him that he is only a clod among clods!"

"What of the girl?" Captain Hipólito asked. "What happened to her? Where is she now?"

Father Ignacio shook his head wearily, but when pressed for answer, went on in a subdued voice: "Bones in an ant hill now. I administered last rites while she still had strength to swallow the wafer and wine. Don Ernesto is a religious man! He would not send a soul to hell unshriven."

Before their eyes his tall, angular frame seemed to shrink and wither within his cassock and he pleaded for understanding like a child. "There was nothing else I could do. I couldn't help her, and if I had tried . . . Who knows? I might have shared the same ant hill with her. You know as well as I that a priest has to please his hidalgo. Oh, I know that there is nothing to that effect in canon law. But what help is law to a man buried up to his neck in sand while ants are devouring his eyes in their sockets and pouring up his nostrils and boring into his brain!"

Father Ignacio stopped speaking, stopped his pacing and scanned each face in the room, meeting each pair of eyes belligerently. When he went on, his voice was as bitter as his Indian parishioner's had been such a short time before.

"These Tlascalan Indians! They hide in their hills when they can and they've never been properly tamed. They're a rebellious, unruly lot. They say the girl refused to undress when ordered to do so, that she clawed at the hidalgo's face and bit him when he ripped her blouse from her shoulders as he had a right to do! Now my Tehuanas, they know their place, and they're . . ."

"Do you think a girl's place is in an ant hill?" Father Enrique interrupted to ask, "Do you think anyone's place is in an ant hill, regardless of race or misdeed, if you must call it that? And when a girl's sole crime has been an attempt to protect her virtue . . ." Father Enrique's voice died away without sharing the rest of his thoughts with his companions.

When he spoke again it was to say, "I am tired. Very, very tired. I must rest and pray. Forgive me, dear friends."

Father Ignacio left the room precipitately as though he sought to escape the frustrations of his position by physical flight. Captain Hipólito caught the eyes of his wife and nodded toward the door. She and Doña Marguerita beckoned to Myrrha and led her away, leaving the aged priest to rest and Captain Hipólito to serve him if there was need.

CHAPTER TWENTY-ONE

SOME days later when Father Enrique was strong enough to travel the de Sosas and the Hipólitos returned to Puebla. This time it was the priest who lay on a bed of cushions inside the carriage. To make for his greater comfort and the ease of Doña Marguerita and Señora Hipólito, Myrrha covered most of the return trip on horseback, retiring to the crowded carriage only at infrequent intervals.

The road led past the Indian home with the mango tree in its yard. Myrrha spurred ahead of the rest of the travelers, paying no attention to Father Ignacio, who called to her, pleading and then commanding her to remain with the others. She stopped at the gate which was not only latched but securely barred now. She wanted to say good-bye to these people she had seen but once and then only for a moment. She hoped they would understand that she grieved with them and regretted their misfortunes.

The door to the jacal, a mat woven of split palm leaves, had been ripped from its fastenings and was lying, torn and dirtied, across the threshhold. The sow, half in and half out of the house, stopped scratching her back against the door jamb and stared at the visitor. The chickens were gone, the piglets also, and Myrrha could see no trace of the human inhabitants. She stared at the sow and was suddenly aware of the fact that this beast was heavy with young. It was not the same animal which had been penned here to sweeten her milk —and the flesh of her offspring—on the golden fruit of the mango tree. This sow had not yet farrowed.

At the sound of hurried hoofbeats, Myrrha looked over her shoulder to see Father Ignacio galloping toward her, kicking his mule in the flanks with his bare heels. He was panting so hard from his exertions when he reached her that he could scarcely speak, but he managed to gasp, "Come along with me, señorita; and do not concern yourself with what is no concern of yours."

He leaned forward to grasp her stallion's bridle, but she turned the horse's head aside. The beast bunched its four feet together, whirled about and plunged toward the rapidly nearing carriage. She threw her weight on the bridle and the cruel Spanish bit pinched the jaws of the horse together in a barbed vice. The animal reared upright so that Myrrha, to keep her seat, seemed standing on air parallel to its body. Miguel de Sosas cried out in fright and spurred his horse toward her; but by the time he reached her, she was in complete control of the stallion again.

It was all over in ten seconds, but that was time enough to bring the former slave girl and the three Indian grooms face to face. From Señor de Sosa and those within the carriage came a babbled confusion of concern for her safety, but Myrrha did not answer at first and none of the grooms spoke at all. The girl could not take her eyes from those three men until her guardian succeeded in doing what Father Ignacio had failed at—seizing her horse's bridle and turning the animal about. Myrrha could give only half attention to those who questioned her: Yes, yes! She was all right. Unshaken. In complete control of her mount again. No, she did not want to come into the carriage. She wished to continue on horseback. She knew her companions were troubled by her short answers and again she spurred the stallion forward, this time to escape their loving though fretful concern.

She did not turn her head toward the Indian home as she galloped past it, for the faces of the three grooms were still as clear in her mind as when they had sat their mules facing her. They had not raised clenched fists above their heads, nor had they overwhelmed her with a torrent of bitter words; but only once before had she ever seen such cold, implacable hatred on a human face—and that was in the deserted jacal now behind her.

Presently she was conscious of the staccato rhythm of galloping hooves, and she pulled her horse up until Señor de Sosa could overtake her. Then the two cantered on together in silence which was broken only occasionally when one or the other voiced some triviality which touched only the surface of their minds. Finally Myrrha turned to her companion and spoke of what lay on the heart of each. "Tell me what has happened to the Indian family."

240

Miguel de Sosa started to shake his head, opened his lips to advise her once again to forget those unfortunate ones. But when he spoke it was to say, "You will not be satisfied until you have the truth, and I might as well tell you here and now."

It was a grim tale he told her, somberly, in a low voice, but without mincing words or holding anything back. The son, husband and father in the jacal had died a few hours after Myrrha had seen him. And who could name the immediate cause of his death: shock, loss of blood or sheer hopelessness? As his life slipped away, his senile mother had gone berserk and thrown herself in a frenzy upon the one thing at hand which represented the cause of her family's desolation—the hidalgo's sow. She had seized the machete with which her son had cut and trimmed firewood in the forest and had literally hacked the sow to pieces. She was pursuing the piglets, slashing at them frantically with the big blade when Don Ernesto had ridden up to check on the well-being of his swine. The slight old woman, whom grief had turned into a ravaging beast, had merely looked at her lord, and he had ridden away precipitately, spurring his horse as though he himself were possessed by devils.

When Don Ernesto's personal men-at-arms had reached the jacal, they found only chunks of pork in the yard, fragments of meat already black with flies and ribbons of entrails being dragged this way and that by turkey vultures. Inside the shelter lay the man's corpse, not yet rigid in death, two cowering women now devoid of all passion and two terrified children.

"Where are they now?" Myrrha asked. "Where did the soldiers take them?"

Again Señor de Sosa shook his head and then said, "They are dead, daughter. All dead. Let it go at that."

"I must know how they died," Myrrha prompted gently.

Miguel de Sosa looked her in the face for a long moment, and then speaking as though under a compulsion he was powerless to resist, finished the tale. The two women and two children had been taken to the edge of a thicket where two twenty-foot saplings had had their branches roughly hacked away and their tops bent over to the ground and tied there. A palisade had been built about the two trees, as though animals were to be penned therein. The old woman was spread-eagled and tied upside down to the tops of the saplings. Then

241

the ropes holding the two small trees arched over were cut and the saplings had sprung upright again, ripping the old woman's body into gory quarters. The daughter-in-law and two grandchildren were pushed into the enclosure, and the opening to the palisade securely closed. Then the soldiers had ridden away leaving no water or food behind them. Sometime during the night the mother had pressed the face of each of her children into the soft flesh of her belly until each had ceased to breathe and struggle. Then she had climbed one of the saplings, knotted her rebosa about the stub of a branch, and hanged herself. Later, no one could say just when, a puma had leaped over the palisade and feasted.

"Where is the family buried?" Myrrha asked after a long period of stunned silence.

"They are not buried. And they will never be buried," Señor de Sosa answered her. "The sow—the new sow under the mango tree—devoured the man and scattered his bones in the jacal. The palisade on the edge of the forest will remain as it is, untouched, as a warning to other peons who dare flout the will of their master."

"Two women and two children to pay for a sow," Myrrha said presently in a wondering voice. "How great the value of a sow and how little the worth of a human life!"

"Six human lives," her companion corrected her. "Do not forget the father and the half-caste daughter—the first victims of a conquering people's power. Power for which an hidalgo accounts to no one. Sometimes I think not even to God!" The merchant ended on so bitter a note that even Myrrha was surprised.

"And who has been benefited by their sacrifice?" she asked. "And in what way!"

"Who and how indeed!" Señor de Sosa exclaimed.

Again there was a long silence between them before Myrrha spoke, "Papacito, you and Father Enrique tell me to forget such things as happened to this family! To do that I would have to accept this bestiality as God's will, and I cannot. Having been taught that our Lord loves all of us, I cannot accept such inhuman cruelty as an expression of His will. There must be something I can do! Not much, perhaps, but *anything* might grow to something bigger. Tell me, is there *anything?*"

"My child, my very dear child, there are others, not many but a few,

242

who also grieve at the plight of the Indian. Good men like Father Enrique and Father Ignacio cannot find it in their hearts to believe that God ever placed an immortal soul in the body of a creature that looks like a human being but has no right to be treated like a human being. And Holy Church has commanded that the Indian be baptized and his soul be saved. These things you know as well as I. As for what anyone can do, I do not know. The hidalgo's power is unlimited on his land. He accounts to no one for such deeds as took place in Atzacán."

"Still, if these Indians are God's creatures, there must be something one can do to help them in their helplessness," Myrrha murmured.

"I can only say to you that if it is God's will that you serve these lowly creatures of His, He will show you the way in His own good time," was all the comfort Miguel de Sosa could give his ward.

It seemed to Myrrha that nothing would ever dim her memory of Atzacán or the dire fate of the luckless, transplanted Tlascalan Indians she had met so casually there. But momentous news awaited the travelers in Puebla, and the plight of the Indian peon receded into the background of her consciousness temporarily.

The Bishop of Puebla, the Illustrious Señor Alonso de la Mota y Escobar, had received an answer to his letter concerning the Chinese girl from the Holy Father in Rome. Gregory XV was well acquainted with the abuses committed in the name of Holy Church in distant parts of the world. He was also deeply and sincerely concerned not only with the spiritual welfare of the masses of his children, but of those persons whose individual plights were called to his attention. If there was malfeasance in the church in Manila, he did not consider it likely that guilty persons would admit as much in any letters they might write him. Therefore, he had sent a papal emissary to Manila who had brought back a report, common enough in a general way in those days.

The Manila slaver's self-styled priest was a man of the slaver's own ilk. He was nothing but a former seminarian who, from the very first, had shown himself unfitted for Holy Orders. He had never done well in his studies, and he had finally rebelled against the rigors imposed

243

upon an acolyte, had turned apostate and had ultimately been excommunicated. Then he had been as inferior a person in lay world as in the church. Finding the necessity of earning his daily bread even more irksome than books, prayers and fasting, he had returned to the security of Holy Orders—but without the knowledge and therefore also without the sanction of the Church.

Consequently, Myrrha was a Christian only in so far as the intensity of her longing for the religious life and the sincerity of her heart were acceptable to her Heavenly Father. No one doubted the truth of the girl's religious pretensions; nevertheless, plans were immediately set in motion for her formal confirmation and baptism.

These sacraments were administered in the spring of 1627 by the Bishop of Puebla in the great Cathedral of the Angels. The Bishop was assisted by the frail Father Enrique, who was to say on his deathbed shortly thereafter that he had felt himself as much sanctified by these rites as the girl to whom he helped administer them. The affectionate respect in which the elder de Sosas were held was so great and the fame of "La China" was so widespread that the entire social elite of the city of Puebla attended Mass that Sunday morning, and as many of the artisans and common folk and Indian servants as could do so crowded into the great plaza before the cathedral. The city of Puebla from nine to eleven by the clock on that Sunday morning was a metropolis of empty houses. No thieves took advantage of the occasion to ply their trade in the unguarded dwellings.

At the proper time, Señor de Sosa escorted Myrrha to the foot of the altar in the great church of which he was proud because his own money and faith had helped build it. He was doubly proud of the girl whom he had once, at considerable risk to himself, rescued from the devil and now led to Christ.

Exclamations at Myrrha's beauty swelled into a gentle wave of sound that rolled back and forth and from aisle to aisle. As the Bishop awaited this neophyte, he smiled in sympathetic understanding and did not rebuke his congregations' small infraction of churchly decorum.

Myrrha had made her own confirmation dress of deeply brocaded, heavy white silk, and had embroidered it with pearls. Señora de Sosa and her friend, Señora Hipólito, had netted her lace veil with their own fingers. Indian servants in the de Sosa household had shaped a wreath of white oleander blossoms for her hair. God himself filled her heart with great joy and at least a brief moment of peace, which shone out of her eyes and on her face for all to see.

Miguel de Sosa and Doña Marguerita knelt beside her at the baptismal font and took upon themselves the spiritual and earthly duties of godparents, formally assuming as a blessed privilege and not a chore, the responsibilities which they had already been discharging for the past few years. Upon the advice of the de Sosas, Myrrha was baptized Catarina de San Juan. This was the name of a nun, now dead, who had been born to Don Miguel Enrique and Doña Ana Múñoz—more dear friends of the de Sosas.

Following the services at the Cathedral, the family and a party of their closest friends accompanied Catarina de San Juan to the Convent of the Immaculate Conception. There the de Sosas gave their goddaughter into the charge of the Mother Superior as a postulant of that sisterhood. The pearls on her gown and the two diamond and emerald pins which held her veil tight to her sleek black hair, were accepted as the dowry that she, a prospective bride of Christ, brought to her divine Lord.

La China became first a postulant of the convent and then a novice, and she was greatly loved. When final vows were denied her on the basis of the freely confessed details of her life in the Manila slave pen, her grief and disappointment were shared by the entire sisterhood.

Sor María, Mistress of Novices in the Convent, had prayed long and earnestly that an exception to the Rule of her Order might be made in La China's case when the fact became known that the novice, Catarina de San Juan, was not a virgin; and very serious consideration was actually given this step. But even as she prayed, Sor María had feared that the Rule was too old, too greatly revered to be broken for anyone, no matter how spiritual or deserving.

Their Heavenly Father would direct Catarina de San Juan's life if she would submit to His will, the Mistress of Novices assured her young friend, adding that it is the spirit in which one performs one's duties rather than the outward nature of the chores themselves which

245

pleases God. Although the decision of her superiors was that she might not become a bride of Christ, it was impressed upon her that no one could deny her the privilege of continuing to serve as His hand-maiden. So La China left the Motherhouse, but her departure did not carry her far from either the convent grounds or the community life of the sisterhood.

In fact, La China accepted the decision of the Mother Superior and her Bishop more easily and with far greater humility than was pos-sible for her godfather. Señor de Sosa was a man already past middle age when he rescued the Chinese princess from the lecherous Virrey. Her expulsion from the Convent of the Immaculate Conception was a shock and a great disappointment to both him and his wife, and his health suffered as a result. He developed a malignant cough which worsened steadily in spite of the best medical care of his day.

When it became evident that his end was approaching, Señor de Sosa settled a sum of money on La China which would permit her to live out the rest of her life in the same luxury she had enjoyed in his home. This money was to be administered by his friend, Captain Hipólito, since women had no part in financial matters in New Spain. He died seconds after Father Enrique had administered last rites. He passed from this life with his family about him, one hand clasping his crucifix and the other the small palm of his beloved goddaughter.

The loss of her husband was a mortal blow to Doña Marguerita, ever a selflessly devoted wife. Her grief was so great that in spite of the advice of her father confessor to the contrary, she turned her back upon this world as completely as it is possible for anyone to do, and became a Carmelite nun. Less than a year later, she too was gone, hav-ing died in the arms of her Mother Superior.

Captain Hipólito built a small cottage at one end of his garden as a home for his friend's ward. Since his grounds paralleled the Con-vent of the Conceptionists, La China was able to share the life of the nuns almost as completely as if she had been accepted into their Order. She was also able to live under the patronage and protection of the Hipólitos.

The reverence La China felt for Sor María and the deep affection between the two women never wavered or waned, although in the last few years of the learned nun's life it would have been impossible to decide which woman taught and which learned from the other. Sor

246

María died in 1637 and was buried in a cave used for that purpose under the convent chapel. Ordinarily the bodies of the nuns rested there in niches in the earthern walls for the period of time it took nature to cleanse their bones of all corruption, or—following that time—until their graves were needed for other nuns. Then their bones were removed from the required space and neatly stacked atop the convent bone pile on a shelf in one corner of the cave. Sor María was permitted to sleep peacefully in her grave for a little better than a half century.

CHAPTER TWENTY-TWO

THE cottage built for La China by Captain Hipólito was small compared with his own and the de Sosa mansions, but it was still a luxurious abode for a woman of wealth. The sum of money left for her care by Señor de Sosa was a generous one. Her new guardians, the Hipólitos, were also wealthy, and they were childless. When La China did not share the frugal fare of the Conceptionist Sisters, she dined at the bountiful table of the Hipólitos.

At first the captain and Señora Hipólito pressed her to share their own palatial home with them, telling her that the new little cottage at the end of the garden would remain set aside for her as a study and retreat. If La China had been of a frivolous disposition, she could have reigned as a social queen of the cultured elite of Puebla under their patronage. Her new guardians assured her that if, having been denied the privilege of becoming a bride of Christ, she could at last give her heart to an earthly husband, they would provide such a dowry as would command the respect of the proudest families in New Spain.

Although La China was in her early twenties now and therefore somewhat past the age when colonial belles expected to marry, more than one caballero again sang hopefully outside her window when night had stilled the voices and clamor of daytime traffic in the streets. But although on such occasions, and regardless of the hour, Señora Hipólito always came hurrying down the garden path to do her duty as a dueña, La China would never permit a lighted candle to be placed behind the curtains of the window that faced the street.

Finally the young men of Puebla, receiving no encouragement whatsoever from this extraordinarily beautiful girl—who would also have been a juicy financial plum for any family—were forced to accept an increasingly evident truth: that although La China had been denied final vows, she was still half nun. This impression was intensified by the nun-like dress affected by her and the fact that she continued to share the life of the Conceptionist Sisters almost as fully as when she had dwelt among them. It was not uncommon to hear her spoken of as "the Hipólitos' unveiled nun."

The Mother Superior of the convent, who was as deeply under the spell of the girl's magnetic charm as the Hipólitos were and the de Sosas had been, commended her for the simple and deeply sincere piety of her life. She also stood in frank awe of the quality of her intellect. However, when the public murmurings reached her that perhaps what might have been a faulty decision did this saintly creature a grave injustice when she was denied the veil, the Mother Superior felt it wise to ask La China to leave off her black habit and to suggest that she dress like other women in the lay world. She did not have the heart to deny the girl the companionship of the Sisters or a part in the performance of their daily offices; and for the rest of her life La China spent as many hours in the convent as out of it.

La China, knowing that by birth, background, intellectual accomplishment and the yearnings of her great heart, she was different from the ordinary colonial girl, wife and mother, made no attempt to ape their costumes or life. Once again she dressed herself in white blouse and full, ankle-length, green and red skirt. She never altered that costume until the day of her death, and before the end of her long life it became well known in the streets of Puebla. As well known and as famous in its way as the ornate trappings, human and equine, of the charros, with whom she no longer paraded in the bull ring, although they continued to claim her as their patron.

When La China first moved into the garden cottage her day was patterned after the convent life which she shared. An Indian servant roused her while the eastern sky was still untinged by the first faint streaks of dawn; and before food or drink touched her lips she scurried across the street to Matins and then Holy Communion. It was on one such morning that she met a young Indian girl, her face hidden in the folds of her rebosa, but obviously crying.

"What is the matter? Can I help you?" La China asked.

But the girl brushed past her and fled down the street. She was quickly out of sight in the dark. When La China turned again to the convent gate, she stumbled against a soft bundle that immediately wailed at being disturbed.

A child without a father left with the Sisters to be reared by them was a commonplace event in the daily life of every convent in New Spain then and for many years afterward. The rearing of foundlings was only one of the small services these women who had denied themselves the joys of motherhood rendered their sisters of another race.

La China picked up the child and held it close to her bosom, crooning to it until it slept again. Later she bathed and fed the child, prolonging the chores as much as possible, for every such pathetic morsel of humanity was symbolical of her own aborted motherhood.

"Sister Catarina, we love these children, too," the Mother Superior had said to her one day. "But sometimes our love is a duty. With you that is never the case. Your affection is never forced; it is like the love of God."

She touched her beads and her lips moved in prayer lest the comparison might smack of impiety. At the door she turned, the expression on her face a study in quizzical amusement as she went on, "Many men say they believe that women should not be educated, that even the simplest literacy is destructive of feminity. They should see you with one of their bastards in your arms! And yet you are the most learned among us." The Mother Superior closed the door noiselessly behind herself, but too slowly to muffle the laughter that twisted and burbled past her usually prim lips.

The next morning La China did not assist at Matins or receive Holy Communion. Instead as soon as it was light, she mounted one of the captain's horses and circled the city of Puebla, traversing the outskirts of the town where the Indian merchants and artisans and the servants who did not live in their master's houses, all dwelt in what passed for homes. Wherever she saw people she stopped and talked with them. She longed to enter their tumble-down shelters; but although she was met with courtesy on that first visit, it was form devoid of life and cordiality. She could not have told what it was she sought in the Indian settlements, but she was conscious of a lack, a need within herself that was almost a physical, urgent necessity akin to thirst and hunger.

She could not help noting that as soon as a face turned in her direction, it became devoid of any expression that might betray the mind and heart of the creature within. The black eyes were as cold and hard as the volcanic rock mined on the slopes of Popocatepetl. Like that rock when polished into an obsidian mirror, the windows of these people's souls only reflected the life about them when a being from another world strove to intrude upon their little privacy. On every hand, one cruel truth impressed itself upon her: in spite of the fact that everywhere there was evidence of industry and frugality, there was also great need—and callous indifference to that need.

After that first morning La China, usually on horseback, became an increasingly frequent visitor in the Indian settlements on the outskirts of Puebla and in the nearby small villages. In the beginning she carried food to the poorest families; later she gave medical help according to her limited knowledge and abilities. She also raised her voice in protest against the seignioral rights enjoyed by those of pure Spanish blood, whether estate owners or not.

She could discern no difference between a Christian Indian and a Christian Spaniard, male or female. She pleaded with masters on behalf of their peons; and even the most callously indifferent listened respectfully. She reminded the Bishop of Puebla that it was the expressed will of King and Pope that the Indian be educated as well as baptized. She contended vigorously that use of the current expression —"I obey but I do not conform!"—by colonial sophisticates was not clever or witty, but a flouting of the law of the land and of the Church.

In 1673, when she was of ripe middle-age, she prevailed upon Captain Hipólito to accompany her to Mexico City so that she might discuss with the Virrey the plight of her beloved Indians. It was the first of many audiences granted her by His Grace, the Duque de Verangua, Virrey at that time. Both he and subsequent Virreys and Royal Governors were charmed with the woman and awed by her indomitable spirit; some cringed inwardly before her erudition.

Her life and her efforts sensitized many people to the injustices perpetrated upon the peons. Gradually a small group of people of influence added their voices to hers. Perhaps the most striking among these was another saintly nun, Sor Juana Ines de la Cruz. Sor Juana was one of the most cultivated women of her time and one of Mexico's greatest and best-beloved poets of any era. While La China visited, fed, clothed and cared for the sick among the Indians, Sor Juana pro-

251

tested the denial of their simple human rights by the public mortification of her body and in her eloquent, impassioned verses.

La China died on January 5, 1688, in what was probably the eightieth year of her life. With the exception of Captain Hipólito and very few others, all the friends of her youth had preceded her in death. With their passing, details of her origin had very largely been forgotten. The younger generations may simply never have known them. It is doubtful if one person in a hundred knew that the tiny, white-haired, still extraordinarily beautiful Chinese lady lying in state in the Hipólito mansion had been born Her Royal Highness, The Princess Myrrha Pagris, daughter in direct descent of the great Humayun, founder of the dynasty of Grand Moguls. The knowledge could not have raised the woman in their esteem, so great was their reverence and devotion to her.

It was the custom then as now in Mexico to inter common citizens on the day of their death. However, so many people loved La China, the fame of her virtue and exemplary life was so widespread, and her passing so greatly moved the entire city of Puebla that crowds—pushing, shoving crowds, fighting for one last glimpse of their beloved heroine's face—thronged through Captain Hipólito's home in such uncontrollable numbers that he was unable to close his doors from eight o'clock in the morning on the day of her death, until late afternoon on the following day.

Captain Hipólito, probably because of his own great age now, could not make up his mind as to where La China should be buried. He confessed that he was troubled by his knowledge of La China's "heathen birth" and the fact that she had not been permitted the final vows of a nun. He turned to the Bishop of Puebla, the Illustrious Señor Don Manuel Fernandez de la Santa Cruz, asking if interment should be in the Conceptionist Sisters' cave? In the de Sosa vault in the city cemetery? He even asked: had she right to holy ground at all?

His Grace, the Bishop, had come to know La China well and had been as greatly impressed with her character and personality as his most humble and needy parishioner. He reminded Captain Hipólito that the deceased was a confirmed Christian and, according to her Father Confessor, had died in a state of grace. He saw no reason why this saintly woman might not be buried wherever her friends chose, and in such state as their hearts dictated and their purses permitted.

Consequently, La China Poblana was laid to rest in the antisacristy of the Cathedral of the Angels in the City of Puebla.

Two years later Captain Hipólito sought permission from the church, received it, and on August 13, 1690, had Sor María's bones disinterred and placed beside those of La China so that not even in death should the two women be separated.

The End

BIBLIOGRAPHY

Alcazar. *Historia de los Dominios Españoles en Oceana: Filipinas.* Manila: 1895.

Alegría, Paula. *La Educación en México Antes y Despues de la Conquista.* Mexico City: 1936.

Bancroft, Hubert H. *History of Mexico.* San Francisco: 1883-1888. 6 vols.

Baranera. *Comprendio de la Historia de las Filipinas.* Manila: 1850.

Bravo Ugarte, José. *Historia de México.* Mexico City: 1941-1944. 3 vols.

Challomel, ed. *Les Annamites: Religions, Moeurs, Costumes.* Paris: 1906.

Compos, Rubén M. *El Folklore y la Música.* Mexico City: 1928.

Condominas, G. "L'Indochine," *Ethnologie de l'Union Français.* Edited by A. Leroi-Gourhon and Jean Poirier. Paris: 1953.

Cuevas, Mariano. *Historia de la Iglesia en México.* Mexico City: 1946-1947. 5 vols.

Delgado. *Historia General de las Islas Filipinas.* Manila: 1894.

De Vasconcellos. *As Colonias Portuguezas.* Lisbon: 1903.

García Gutiérrez, Jesús. *Apuntes Para la Historia del Regio Patronato Indiano Hasta 1857.* Mexico City: 1951.

Las Casas, Fr. Bartolomé de. *Historia de las Indias.* Edited by Fuensanta del Valle. Madrid: 1875.

Ledyard de la Lyraie. *Notes Historiques sur la Nation Annamite.* Paris: n.d.

Lumholtz, C. *Unknown Mexico.* New York: 1902. 2 vols.

Martins, Oliveira. *Historia de Portugal.* Lisbon: 1894. Fourth edition.

Moreno. *Historia de la Santa Iglesia Metropolitana de Filipinas.* Manila: 1877.

Motolinia, Toribio and de Mendieta, Jerónimo. *Historia Eclesiástica Indiana.* Mexico City: 1870.

Oviedo y Valdes. *La Historia General de las Indias.* Madrid: 1851-1854. 4 vols.

Pasquier, P. *L'Annam d'Autrefois*. Paris: 1907.

Prescott, W. H. *The Conquest of Mexico*. New York: 1922. 2 vols.

Reyes, Alfonso. *Letras de Nueva España*. Mexico City: 1948.

Romero de Terroros, Manuel. *El Arte en México Durante el Virreinato*. Mexico City: 1951.

——. *Las Artes Industriales en la Nueva España*. Mexico City: 1923.

Sahagun, Bernadino de. *Histoire Générale des Choses de la Nouvelle-Espagne*. Translated by D. Jourdanet and Remi Simeon. Paris: 1880.

Sanchez, Pedro C. *Estudio Orogénico de la Republica Mexicana*. Tacubaya, D.F., Mexico: 1936.

Schlarman, Joseph H. *Mexico: A Land of Volcanoes, From Cortés to Alemán*. Milwaukee: 1950.

Simpson, Lesley Byrd. *The Encomienda in New Spain*. Berkeley, California: 1929.

Toor, Frances. *A Treasury of Mexican Folkways*. New York: 1947.

Truonga-Vinh-Ky. *Cours d'Histoire Annamite*. Saigon: 1875.

Vásquez Santa Ana, Higinio. *Fiestas y Costumbres Mexicanas*. Mexico City: 1940.